DEATH IN VERACRUZ

A NOVEL

HÉCTOR AGUILAR CAMÍN
Translation by Chandler Thompson

schaffner
press
Tucson, Arizona

DEATH IN VERACRUZ

A NOVEL

HÉCTOR AGUILAR CAMÍN
Translation by Chandler Thompson

CONTENTS

Chapter 1
THE ROJANO FILE

What more is there to say about Rojano? It's a sob story better left untold. It consists of our two years as high school chums in Xalapa, then four as rivals at university in Mexico City where our shared obsession was Anabela Guillaumín. Rojano won. He left her, then he married her (I simply lost her.). He went in for Macazaga suits and political breakfasts at the Hilton. He joined the eternally governing PRI and became a minor functionary in the administration of López Arias in Veracruz. I went to work as a reporter on the police beat and took up the vice of journalism with all the trimmings. It was the 60s. We had come through the railroad strike and were headed towards the Tlatelolco massacre and the end of the Mexican miracle. Our lives as grownups were beginning.

After not seeing her for two years, on August 14, 1968, I ran into Anabela in the Arroyo Restaurant near the Olympic Village where she was working as a guide. She was as tall, slender and irresistible as ever with the same dazzling eyes. She owed their smoky green color and the surname of Guillaumín to the French occupiers who settled in Veracruz a century ago.

She skipped work, and we drank coffee all afternoon. She talked about Rojano, who was organizing student gangs and their leaders ("social services") at the University of Veracruz and who, in drunken pre-dawn phone calls, accused her of slighting him. For dinner we had skewers of Chihuahua beef and beans cooked peasant-style with chiles at Pepe's on *Insurgentes*. She joked infectiously about working as a guide for peace. She spoke of her father's death a year earlier–her mother died fifteen years ago—and of Rojano, his jealousy, his threats, the blow that almost tore her lip off one night, of how he had Mujica, a classmate she'd gone out with three times, beaten up. We drank vodka and danced until three in the morning at La Roca. She made fun of my qualms about being a reporter, and she talked about Rojano, the abortion he forced her to have, his demands, and his neglect. Drunk and talked out in the early morning hours, I lost her again, this time in the entrance to the Beverly Hotel, which reminded her, one more time, of Rojano.

They married two years later, the same month that Luis Echeverría rose to power and the Institutional Revolutionary Party recognized Francisco Rojano Gutiérrez as undisputed leader of the CNOP, the National Confederation of People's Organizations, for the state of Veracruz.

I moved up from the police beat to city hall, then covered the airport for a few months. In early February 1971, I was just starting out on the agriculture beat when I ran into Rojano again in the main office of what was then the Department of Agrarian Affairs and Colonization. We hadn't seen each other for four years, since Christmas 1967 when we got into a fight at the Monteblanco Bar on Monterrey Street in the Roma District.

He had sprouted a mustache that hung like a horseshoe from his lips to his chin and was dressed in a double-breasted white suit, an orange shirt, and a tie of what were then called psychedelic colors. He had a fistful of papers in his hand and was in the process of authenticating a land deed. He was talking non-stop straight into the ear of a clerk.

"You've got to understand me, *paisano*." He waved the sheaf of papers in the face of the hapless clerk and, by calling him *paisano*, appealed to the consideration one expatriate from Veracruz supposedly owed another.

As an ex-swimmer, he still had broad shoulders and a

flat torso. When he threw his arm over the clerk's shoulder, he engulfed the man in his enormous chest as if he were about to devour him. I tried not to be noticed, but Rojano caught a glimpse of me over the head of the beleaguered clerk.

"Is that you, brother?" His eyes lit up. The appeal of his vulgarity was impossible to define. He smiled and held up the papers. "I'm almost through here. Don't go away."

I got what I'd come for and left without waiting through the door of the neighboring office. He ran after me and caught up with me in the parking lot. "You don't need to run, brother. I'm not a bill collector." He grabbed my arm, gasping for breath.

He sucked air and loosened his tie. "I didn't greet you properly up there because I was working." He moistened his lips, readjusted his tie. "I was dispatching my daily lawyer. I don't have to tell you the world is full of assholes, and, if you don't knock off at least one a day, then one of them will knock you off. Where are you going to eat?"

We ate at El Hórreo, a Spanish restaurant with a lively bar that overlooks the Alameda. Rojano ordered malt whiskeys and octopus sauteed in Rioja wine. He went on and on about politics in Veracruz, an endless parade of friends, enemies, crooks and assholes. He had detailed plans for his rise to governor and then to a federal cabinet post. First he'd become a mayor, then a state cabinet secretary, then a federal legislator; from there he'd go on to governor and federal cabinet secretary. He laid out a twenty-four-year career in politics free of setbacks or delays but with variations if necessary. If becoming mayor proved impossible, then he'd settle for a job in the state executive branch that would pave the way to the federal legislature. If that didn't work out, then president of the PRI or a position in a state-owned enterprise from which, with a bit of effort, he'd become a cabinet minister. If the cabinet were out of reach, then.., and on and on.

We ordered cognac and coffee after dessert. He offered me a huge cigar from his coat pocket. On the band it said: Especially wrapped for *Francisco Rojano Gutiérrez, Atty.*

Rojano had dropped out of third-year law (I got fed up after four), so I asked him. "When did you become a lawyer?"

"When we graduated together," he replied smiling. "Don't tell me you can't remember. We did that thesis on mass politics and the Mexican state that was later plagiarized by Arnaldo Córdova. We even drew a mention from Flores Olea, don't you remember? Then you went into journalism and I took up government service. That's what got us where we are, brother, each serving the Republic in his own way. Let's toast to that, we're both doing fine."

We matched each other drink for drink all afternoon, cognac and coffee until seven when we moved on to the Impala to hear Gloria Lasso sing. I woke up in the Silver Suites on Villalongín next to a woman I neither recognized nor remembered. In the bed next to mine Rojano lay snoring atop another woman. He had one sock on and the other off and a two-strand platinum bracelet on his wrist.

I changed to a newspaper that offered me the political beat and a daily news column called "Public Life" that became self-supporting in a matter of months. I set up a file system and stocked it with the exact sources and details of things hinted at over working breakfasts or dinners, in press offices, or in the columns of colleagues. In 1973, my column drew an honorable mention in the annual competition held by the Press Club of Mexico. The following year, I won the club's national prize for timely news coverage.

I stopped seeing Rojano, but I didn't lose sight of him. He returned to his post at the University of Veracruz in Xalapa, then ran unsuccessfully for a seat in the state assembly from the district of Tuxpan. On February 4, 1972, Rojano was involved in a shootout in Juarez Park in Xalapa. The lone casualty was attributed to him, but though the victim was seriously injured (he didn't die), the charges against Rojano were thrown out in the course of a complex legal proceeding. In the year that followed, Rojano dropped out of local politics. He bought land in Chicontepec and got himself named an inspector for what was then the Rural Cooperative Credit Bank. In 1973, he resurfaced as a federal legislative hopeful in local newspaper columns and even in the column "Political Fronts" in *Excelsior*. The scheme failed although its real purpose was not to get elected but to make noise, to gain credibility within the party for achieving his real goal of becoming mayor of Chicontepec in elections to be held the following year. That didn't work out either, and he left the Rural Credit Bank in one of the anti-corruption purges the bank undergoes every couple of years. When the Veracruz state government changed hands in 1974, he returned to Xalapa as private secretary to the government secretary, a college friend who had previously been the private secretary of the incoming governor.

In 1975, I covered part of the PRI presidential campaign that every six years floods the country in a frenzy of ostentation and hope. The campaign of Treasury Secretary José López Portillo consisted, like all campaigns since Cárdenas in the 1930s, of a wide-ranging tour of the Republic, town by town, city by city with a retinue of local politicos, favorite sons, leaders, bosses, bureaucrats and orators in tow. This time the tour began in Querétaro, then moved on to the Pacific Coast. It rang in the New Year in the south with an enormous banquet at the base of the Chicoasén Dam in Chiapas (guests and food flown in by helicopter). The campaign proceeded through northern and central Mexico, then rolled through the southeast and down the Gulf Coast before winding up in my home state of Veracruz, which we entered through Agua Dulce in March 1976.

The pressroom was barely set up at the Hotel Emporio in the port city of Veracruz when Rojano came looking for me. I had trouble recognizing him. The two-strand platinum bracelet was gone along with the horseshoe mustache and the psychedelic colors. His face and waistline were beginning to fill out, the pleats of his guayabera and the creases in his pants were painstakingly precise, and his brown moccasins were freshly shined.

"Is that you?" he asked, leaning his elbows on my typewriter.

He spoke warmly without the least hint of sarcasm. Somehow it touched a chord in me. It brought back the years we hung out together in the hilly streets between his house and mine in Xalapa. Walking home from school together, we shared our dreams and ambitions to achieve, accomplish and succeed. We'd go to Mexico City, come back with degrees that would dazzle the neighbors, and ring in a new era for the politics of Veracruz. We'd stamp out bossism, rein in the cattle ranchers, beautify Poza Rica, pave the port of Veracruz, and get rid of pollution in Minatitlán. It was as if my affection for Rojano would suffice to transform the world we were about to leave and to which we would inevitably return.

"It is," I said.

He pulled up a chair, sat down next to me, and placed a mollifying hand on my thigh.

"I have something I need to talk to you about," he said.

"For more than two lines there's a fee," I replied.

"No joke, brother. This is serious. It's all about politics and the press. Something a professional like you can use."

He ran out of words, but his eyes were still lit up.

"You want to run for the legislature again?"

"No, this is personal. All I ask is an hour in private. What can that matter to you?"

"It can't, but there's a fee for more than two lines."

He gave up with a smile of submission and pulled himself together.

"If that's how it has to be, then so be it. What time do I pick you up?"

At ten that night, I climbed into the frigid air conditioning of his black Galaxy.

"Anabela wants to say hello," he said. "Do you mind if we take care of this at the house?"

"I do, but that's all right."

"What's done is done, brother."

"How's Anabela?"

"Fine. We've got a five-year-old boy and a girl, four. We live a quiet life, a boring life in the provinces. I'm in Xalapa and come home every weekend, sometimes more often. It depends. Anabela couldn't handle Xalapa. It brought back bad memories. She's right. I really screwed up, you have no idea how much. Now I'm paying the price, I've stopped drinking."

"Who are you screwing?"

"No one, brother. Like I said, I lead a simple provincial life."

"You don't even get any from your wife?"

"Watch it, *Negro*. Don't screw around with me."

"You're no family man. The disguise doesn't suit you."

"It's no disguise, brother."

"Then call it a facade. It still doesn't fit."

"If that's what you say, then it must be so. But the other stuff was killing me. Now I'm at least in limbo. It's a thousand times better, I swear."

He seemed overcome by an excess of caution, an angelic slowness. He even drove like an old man. It was both amusing and hard to believe. We went slowly around the soccer stadium and entered a recently opened subdivision with vacant lots between many of the houses. Rojano's took up two lots and had a pitched roof in the architectural fashion then popular with the provincial *nouveau riche*. The fence was a row of heavy iron bars topped with sharp white finials. The front of the house combined imitation marble walls with sliding windows of smoked glass and aluminum molding. Inside were easy chairs with woven upholstery and carved wooden arms, a plaster reproduction of the Venus de Milo, and miniature porcelain footmen in a glass showcase.

As soon as we entered, he shouted for Anabela to come down, then removed the plastic coverings that made the easy chairs awkward to sit in. He went to a corner of the room occupied by a piece of furniture meant to resemble the bar in a saloon. He looked over the bottles and again shouted at Anabela to come down. He needn't have. For several seconds she stood on the landing of the stairway, nervous yet composed, silently watching me with nothing better to do than moisten her lips and pull the sleeve of her dress down over her watch.

Eight years and two children later: Anabela de Rojano. Beneath the modest elegance of her tropical chiffon dress, her bodily perfection, the symmetry of legs and shoulders, remained intact despite the first visible bulges of a what in a few years would turn her into another kind of living statue, a matronly Venus of ample proportions.

"Is that you?" she said just as Rojano had.

It annoyed me to hear her echo him—and to realize that my adolescent jealousy still smoldered. She stepped away from the stairs and kissed me on the cheek.

"Are you going to want whiskey?" Rojano asked from the bar.

"Offer him something to eat, too," Anabela said. Turning to me, she added, "Nothing comparable to the restaurants you're used to, but the food here will remind you of home."

"I brought caviar," Rojano trumpeted from the bar.

"You see?" Anabela said ironically. "He brought caviar. And we have Oaxaca tamales made by the mother of one of *Ro's* godchildren."

She never called Rojano by his first name. She always used his surname or in more familiar moments *Ro.*

"We have deviled ham, too," Ro added from the bar. "And candied chestnuts for dessert."

He approached with a bottle of Old Parr and an ice bucket on a large tray. There was a Coca Cola for Anabela and for him soda water with no ice. He made a show of pouring it with the glass held at eye level, at my eye level actually.

In the next hour I consumed three whiskeys and twenty crackers with caviar and deviled ham while enduring a conversation about schools and the consolations of provincial life. Around eleven, using the wail of a child upstairs as an excuse, I attempted my getaway. By then I estimated that festivities would be well under way in Mocambo where the city government was throwing a party for the press.

"Don't leave," Anabela begged as she headed for the stairs and the source of the wailing. "At least wait till I come down."

"That's right, brother. Wait for her to come down," Rojano reiterated as if reading from a script.

Once Anabela had disappeared up the stairs, he reminded me, "I've still got something to show you."

As he spoke, he regarded me intensely with a stare held over from another time, then he made a nervous exit through a door in the back of the house. His demeanor confirmed my suspicion that his newfound respectability and stability were pure show, the appropriate backdrop for a proposal of whose nature I was, for the moment, unaware.

I went back to the ice bucket for a fourth whiskey and waited.

He returned from the back of the house with a package under his arm but would not let me see it in the sala. Instead, he took me into a small room, a combination pantry and office that we entered through the garage. Inside was a desk, a pair of dusty file cabinets, an empty bookcase, and several crates of mangos and oranges stacked in one corner. An enlarged photo of Anabela sat on the desk. It showed her running towards the camera with her hair blown back from her forehead by the wind and her thighs clearly defined under a black skirt with a blur of forest in the background.

He pushed the photo aside and lay the package, a bulky manila envelope marked *remittances*, on the desk.

"I've been working on this for two years," he said.

He undid the red string between the seals on the flap and the body of the envelope, then took out what looked like a leather saddlebag. It was, to be more exact, a square leather letter file with a rigid center panel and four flexible dividers that closed like an accordion over the documents between them. On each divider there was an engraving: a pasture; a factory smokestack; an oil well; and the head of an Olmec statue next to an Indian woman with long braids. Each divider bore the caption *Destroy to create* in large rustic lettering with the motto *Whoever can add can divide* in smaller letters below. Each image was framed by a border composed of intertwined pseudo-Aztec figures.

Rojano opened the leather dividers exposing three file folders, each wrapped in different-colored onion paper.

Nervously and with painstaking care—he'd begun to sweat—he opened the first packet.

It contained a set of photos of semi-nude cadavers still fresh and bleeding from wounds to their skulls and bodies as they lay on stone slabs in what had to have been a small-town morgue. Eight photos of eight bodies, among them a child of about ten, his lips pulled back by rigor mortis to expose his teeth, his small eyelids half shut. The caption in crude white lettering beneath the photos read: *Municipality of Papantla, Veracruz, July 14, 1974.* Also in the packet was a photocopy of the death certificate issued by the office of the public prosecutor, a file of some twenty pages, and the plat of a parcel of rural property with the surveyor's seals and notations in the margins.

Rojano pushed the letter file and crepe paper to one side of the desk and slapped the photos down one by one in two rows of four as if dealing a deck of cards.

"There they are," he said without looking up. His demeanor spoke volumes about hours wasted poring over this macabre game of solitaire. "What do you think?"

"What do you want me to think?"

"Don't you see something strange about them?"

"That you're collecting them so meticulously."

"I'm serious, brother. Does the date mean anything to you?"

"No."

"It's the carnival of Corpus Cristi in Papantla."

"Did they get killed at the carnival?"

"In part. They all died in the same incident."

He waited for me to ask about the incident. I asked, "What incident?"

"At the market in Papantla," he explained. "The police report said a group of armed men burst into the market screaming insults against Antonio Malerva. This guy."

He pointed to a naked man with a big belly on the top row with two punctures in his ribs. He had a large mustache and a thinning curl of pompadour.

"He was eating lunch at a food stall when they caught up with him," Rojano went on. "Witnesses said shooting broke out, and the death toll is what you're looking at. But there's a problem."

He paused, waiting for me to ask what problem.

"What problem?" I asked.

"Antonio Malerva was unarmed," Rojano said and again fell silent as if certain of the effect this revelation would have.

Granting the effect of the revelation and with due curiosity, I asked the required question. "Then who did the shooting?"

"No one knows. The fact is that none of the attackers were killed. The other fatalities were the woman who owned the food stall and her daughter."

He pointed to the photos on the right in the lower row: a woman with Indian features who had been shot in the neck; and a girl with full lips and two bullet holes in her adolescent breasts.

"The two customers eating next to Malerva were also killed," Rojano continued. "Prospero Tlamatl, a local Indian who helped at the church during carnival. He was identified by the priest." He pointed to the left end of lower row: two shots to the neck, a blood soaked dress shirt, and a jaundiced complexion that contrasted with a scruffy whitish beard.

"And this last guy's nameless. He was never identified." He now pointed to the emaciated effigy of a peasant with leathery skin and no teeth whose blazing, half-open eyes recalled the photo of the dead Che Guevara.

"What makes this guy last?" I asked. "You've got three photos to go."

From left to right next to the shot of Malerva were the

photos of a man, a woman, and the child who caught my eye first.

"That's precisely what I'm getting to." Rojano said. He placed them in the middle of the desk. "What strikes you about them?"

First of all, they were bloodier than the others. The only blood-free part of the woman's face was the tip of her nose. It was a classical face, the kind an artist might draw with a straight nose descending from a rounded forehead to flaring nostrils. Her widely spaced eyes lay deep in their sockets, and her high cheekbones all but disappeared in their final ascent to her temples from which a liquid seemed to flow, covering her lifeless features with a patina of wax.

"They belong to the same family," Rojano said. He pointed to the adults. "Raul Garabito, who was a farmer, and his wife. The child is theirs. Now look closely. There are bullet wounds in the Garabitos' bodies just like the others. The women and the child have wounds to the chest, the man's are in his abdomen and ribs." He pointed with his pen to the wounds in the photos. "But look carefully at their heads."

There followed the requisite pause.

"Do you see the problem with their heads?"

I nodded mechanically.

"I'm talking about the source of the bleeding." Rojano sounded vaguely impatient.

"From the wounds," I said.

"From the wounds to the forehead," Rojano asserted. "That's exactly the problem."

I drained what remained of my drink and once again put myself on the line. "What exactly is the problem?"

"They were all killed, but the only ones they made sure of were the ones they were after," Rojano stated with conviction.

"They weren't after Malerva?"

"They claimed they were, but the ones they made sure were dead were the Garabitos, not Malerva."

"You're saying that because of the shots to the head?" I asked.

"I say it because they were executed," Rojano replied.

Acts of bloodshed have a peculiar kind of loquacity. I'd seen it often as a police reporter. People get run over minus their socks but with their shoes still on, shots penetrate a lung but cause only minor hemorrhaging, suicides who fire a .45 at their forehead wake up at home the next morning with a new part in their hair. There was no reason for the Garabitos' head wounds not to follow the coarse logic of bullets.

"That's what happens when people get caught in a crossfire," I started to say.

"What crossfire?" Rojano insisted heatedly.

"You said there was a shootout, and these people got caught in the crossfire."

"That's what the witnesses said," Rojano noted. "What I said was that Malerva was unarmed. What's more, the Garabitos were also unarmed. So the question then becomes *which of the victims fired?* The Garabito kid? His mother? The woman with the food stall? Her daughter? Prospero Tlamatl? The unidentified guy? Tlamatl and the unidentified guy don't have twenty pesos in their pockets between them. Can you imagine them with pistols in their waistbands?"

What I needed to do was not to imagine them but to follow Rojano's logic. "So according to you, what happened?" I asked.

"The same thing that happened the following month in Altotonga," Rojano said as he reached for the second file.

He unwrapped the (purple) crepe paper and spread

the file's contents over the desktop. It was a collection of newspaper clippings that explained how a drunk had fired into the crowd in Altotonga during the festival in honor of the town's patron saint on July 22, 1974. He wounded five and killed two before fleeing, Rojano explained, growing increasingly agitated. "He'd fired at least a dozen times because he hit twelve targets," Rojano declared. "Unheard of marksmanship for a drunk."

"He fled almost four blocks, and the mounted police who supposedly gave chase couldn't catch up with him. At the very least he was a surprisingly fast drunk," Rojano surmised, "and they didn't catch him later either."

He pulled a kerchief from his pocket and dried the sweat from his lips and cheeks.

"So what happened?" I asked.

"What didn't happen. Read on."

He handed me the autopsy reports on the cadavers. Certain passages were carefully underlined in red. In stilted coroner's prose, the documents described the deaths of: Manuel Llaca, age 29, by shots from a .38 caliber pistol that struck him in the right groin area, the rib cage, and the left shoulder; and of the widow Mercedes González de Martín , age sixty-four, from wounds to the abdomen, left arm, right gluteus and left temple (the latter enclosed in a double red circle). The report went on to detail the wounds inflicted on the other five casualties.

"Count the shots," Rojano said. "Twelve shots counted one by one."

I asked about the shots.

"They show the same pattern as in Papantla," Rojano said, drying his hands with the kerchief. "Shooting breaks out, several people get killed, but only one gets the finishing shot to the head."

"The woman shot in the head?"

"The woman they made sure was dead, yes."

"What makes you think they're the same?"

"Look at the circumstances," Rojano started to say. The facade of domestic tranquility was cracking, and his habitual vehemence began to show through. "A drunk fires twelve shots from a .38 revolver, kills two, and injures five. But the .38 with a twelve-round magazine hasn't been invented. The biggest ones have eight. So..., the drunk changes magazines in the midst of the shootout or someone other than the drunk is shooting."

"Maybe he had two pistols."

"He didn't have two pistols. According to all the witnesses, he had one. But even if he had two pistols, how was he going to finish off the widow Martín? He never got that close to her."

"You're saying they were all shot in the head to make sure they were dead. So what? If you're killed by gunfire, bullets are what kill you."

"No, no, listen to what I'm saying!" Rojano leaped from his chair. "The Martín woman was already down when she was shot in the head. The shots came from in front of her. First she was shot in the abdomen, then in the left arm, and the impact flipped her over. That's why the next shot got her in the butt. But she was shot in the temple in cold blood when she was already on the ground. They took advantage of the confusion to finish her off."

His version was admirably descriptive and precise. It also betrayed many imaginative hours reconstructing what happened from a blur of forensic data.

"She could still have been hit in the shootout," I insisted.

"What shootout, brother?" Rojano began pacing about the office, wiping his collar with his kerchief. "You're looking at an execution, damn it! Don't you see?"

"I see, but I'm out of whiskey. Is the bar closed?"

"Of course not. Whatever you like."

He left the room, and I took a closer look at the files. The surveyors' plats identified properties belonging to Raul Garabito and Severiano Martín. The former consisted of 300 hectares in the municipality of Chicontepec; the latter nearly 500 wedged between the eastern spur of the Sierra Madre and the Calaboso River in the municipalities of Chicontepec, Veracruz, and Huejutla, Hidalgo.

I opened the third file and saw more photos from provincial morgues. These were from Huejutla, five bodies cut down during the town carnival (November 1974) a few months after Papantla and Altotonga.

The accompanying newspaper clip from *El Dictamen* said that gunmen (i.e. the henchmen of local political bosses) mowed down the Arrieta brothers whom it described with characteristic editorial impartiality as "leaders of smalltime communist pseudo-peasant organizations." The gunmen "achieved their objective at no risk to themselves by firing into the crowd at a cockfight killing five and wounding four. Except for the Arrietas, who were notorious communist agitators in rural Hidalgo, the remaining victims of the shooting were innocent bystanders."

A typed list of the dead summarized Rojano's very different version of events. Rather than the Arrieta brothers, he put check marks next to the names of Severiano Ruíz and Matías Puriel. I looked them up in the coroner's report. Rojano had underlined the same sentence where it was repeated in two different paragraphs: "Projectile penetration is also visible in the left parietal area with severe disruption of the encephalic mass and superficial external burns characteristic of a projectile fired from a distance no greater than thirty centimeters."

I was beginning to study the surveyors' plats when

Rojano returned with ice and mineral water which he placed on the stack of orange and mango crates next to the desk.

"The pattern is identical," he said with a nod towards the third file while opening the bottles. "The Arrietas died in the shooting, but they weren't the ones executed."

He was already into his story so I served myself and asked about the executions.

"They were half brothers," Rojano said, beginning to drink from one of the water bottles. Then, surprisingly, he added, "They were both sons of Severiano Martín, the man whose widow was executed in Altotonga."

"All from the same family?"

"Sons of Severiano Martín, a dirty old stud who knocked up every woman around and sowed the whole area with sons. He didn't give them his surname, but he gave his land to the two who got killed in Huejutla."

"In Chicontepec?"

"Exactly. You looked at the plats already?"

I nodded.

Rojano continued: "Old man Martín had 1,500 hectares of the best land in the area, and he died without a will like all the other old-time bosses. But between them Severiano Ruíz and Matías Puriel owned some 350 hectares. They killed the widow who had 500 and executed the half brothers. That makes 850 hectares in all."

"And who wound up with the land?"

"That's the thing, nobody did. The lands went unclaimed." Once again Rojano grew excited by his own words. "It turns out there are no heirs or relatives left to file valid claims to these lands. In a nutshell they can be easily acquired with a combination of money and the right political connections."

"What do you mean in a nutshell?"

"In a nutshell I mean that two whole families have been

executed in cold blood with alibis built in to divert attention at a cost of nine dead and nine more wounded."

"That's absurd. How did you manufacture this information?"

"How did I *manufacture* it?" Rojano bellowed as he leaped out of his chair. "Don't fuck around with me, brother. I didn't *manufacture* it. Ask me how I *found out*, not how I manufactured it. There's nothing slanted in what you're looking at, nothing inconsistent or made up."

"Then how did you *find* it all out?"

"Anabela was the godchild and niece of the widow Martín whose maiden name was Mercedes González Guillaumín." Rojano pulled out his kerchief as he spoke. "Aside from that, there are the letter files, the leather saddlebags the folders came in."

I picked up the folder on the desk. Rojano kept talking.

"Everyone who was executed received one of these letter files months before receiving a bullet in the head. The one you have in your hands reached the widow three weeks before the bullets in Altotongo. Here are the others."

He groped behind the orange crates and retrieved two tooled leather letter files covered with dust and pseudo-Mexican artwork. He ran his fingertips over the one he had in his hands. The quality of the leather was extraordinary, thick but smooth and malleable to the touch like cloth. *Whoever can add can divide.*

"In the leather letter files there were offers to buy the lands described in the documentation," Rojano said. "I found them in their houses afterwards. Garabito's widow had hers sewed up the sides to make a handbag. She had it with her at the market in Papantla when she was executed. Here it is."

It made a horrible handbag. There was a strap attached to the letter file with gold staples so it could be worn over the shoulder.

Rojano continued: "A servant of the widow Martín had it, a servant who was sort of a nursemaid to Anabela. There are close ties among the families with French blood. They don't say Martín, they say *Martán*, and not Guillaumín, but *Guillomé*. The nursemaid said the stepsons had received the same kind of folders. According to her, the evil eye came with them."

"But you said that what came in them were purchase offers."

"Each one was actually an ultimatum, a final offer that was the last in a series."

"How do you know that?"

"From the best possible source." Rojano rubbed his kerchief between his hands. "I was told by the buyer himself."

The whiskey had had its effect. I didn't react, but the tale with all its scaffolding struck me as quintessential Rojano: overblown and labyrinthine with an agenda shrouded in shadows. I was glad to see him return with more liquor. I set my suspicions aside and relaxed for the first time all night.

"You mean to say you know the buyer?" I asked. "You know the would-be benefactor of these ex-landowners?"

"That's not all I know, brother."

"A schoolmate?" I went on. "A childhood friend?"

"Not quite, brother. For the last two years we've been having coffee whenever he's in the city. That's where the story begins as far as you're concerned."

"You mean the man behind this massacre?"

"Yes, the brains. We have long conversations whenever he comes to town."

"To plan the future of the children of Veracruz?"

"Don't fuck around with me, brother. It's no laughing matter."

"You're the one that sits down with him, and he's the

one who collects dead people."

"To feel him out, brother. To get to know him."

"What other reason could there be?"

"Stop wising off for a minute and listen to me, *Negro*. That's not the whole story. The problem is there's almost no way I can avoid having him as a political ally."

I got up and served myself a sixth shot of the whiskey whose therapeutic effects were increasingly hard to resist. "Congratulations on your ally," I said as I sat down again.

"It's not up to me," Rojano said. "He carries a lot of weight in the municipalities in the northern part of the state."

"And what do the elections in the northern part of the state have to do with you?" I said. "You're from the south, from the coast at worst. What do you have to offer as a candidate in the north? Aside from planning the future of the children of Veracruz."

"That's what the governor wants."

"Is it what you want?"

"That doesn't matter. I'm a politician, I go where I'm needed. But if you want to know what I want, I'll tell you. Besides, you know perfectly well what I want. I want to go back to Chicontepec as mayor."

"The better to plan for the future of the children of Veracruz."

"You're jerking me around," Rojano said.

"I'm not jerking you around. Just let me guess: you want to go back to Chicontepec so you can *fight from within*."

"God damn it, *Negro*. You're jerking me around."

"To wage war on your ally from within. I mean so you can plan a better future for the children of Veracruz."

"The better to screw your mother, *Negro*."

"Of course, why else?"

"Stop playing games with me, damn it. You're just jerking me around, that's all you're doing. I'm speaking from the heart, I'm baring my soul to you, and you're just jerking me around."

He sat down in the chair behind the desk and ran his hand wearily through his hair as if his fatigue would rub off. Enervated and half asleep, he took a swallow of the highball I put on the table, then another and another until he'd emptied the glass, ice and all.

"For a man who doesn't drink, you have a taste for whiskey," I said.

"One more thing," he replied, picking up where he left off. "Anabela owns land in that same area."

I stepped to the orange crates to refill what Rojano had drunk, but the ice and the soda were gone. I poured myself straight whiskey and took a drink. It was absurd how the same old rage kept coming back, the feeling that Rojano's entanglements meant trouble for Anabela, that he was unfairly putting her at risk. "You just finished showing me a collection of photos of women and children who were killed for nothing," I told him. "And now you're telling me Anabela could be involved. What's going on? What are you getting at?"

"Anabela owns land in the same area as the Martín and Garabito families," Rojano said. "She could be part of the same scheme."

"Has she got an offer?"

"An offer? No."

"So?"

"Like I say, her land borders the widow Martín's. It's mostly hills, just a few hectares that don't amount to much at all. But they do share a boundary. And farther back, away from the river, towards the foothills leading to the Sierra Madre is El Canelo."

"What's El Canelo?"

"My farm."

"Then there's a farm?"

"You know perfectly well I bought land a few years ago, 100 hectares on the way to the mountains."

"And Anabela's 25. That makes 125."

"125."

"Of awful land I suppose. An emporium of hardscrabble caliche."

"It's excellent land," Rojano said. "But I didn't bring you here to talk about that or to have you laugh at us. Anabela inherited from her family, an old local family. I managed to buy next to hers. I did it the Mexican way. For my kids, as insurance against political unemployment. What's wrong with that?"

I served myself another small shot of whiskey and drank it, keeping an eye on Rojano over the rim of the glass. His hair was mussed as if he'd just gotten out of bed. His guayabera was soaked with sweat. His bloodshot eyes stared down at his hands and watched his thumbs rub obsessively against each other. I realized once again that I was watching a show, a display of Rojano's political will as he started down another twisted path and came to a turn that in one way or another had begun to include me. I served myself a last thimbleful of whiskey, feeling as if I were part of a bad dream in that strange office with its stacked boxes of oranges and mangos next to metal file cabinets and a desk. I swallowed, then, without the least bit of sarcasm, asked in a spirit of solidarity attributable to two doses of whiskey in quick succession,

"What do you want me to do?"

"To keep your eyes open," Rojano said anxiously. "Help me investigate this whole business. Let something drop in the national press when the time is ripe and there's something for us to gain. For the time being just keep it to yourself. We're talking about someone who's no fool. We're talking about a force that has to be stopped now before it's too late."

"What's your friend's name?" I asked.

"He's not my friend, he's my enemy."

"Your enemy and ally, your benefactor. What's his name?"

"Lázaro Pizarro."

"Where's he from?"

"The oil workers' union up north."

"Poza Rica?"

"Poza Rica."

"Can you send me copies of those files? We go back to Mexico City tomorrow."

"They'll be in your room by 10 tomorrow."

I managed another thimbleful on the way out. It was almost midnight, and Anabela was no longer in the sala. I didn't make a point of trying to see her. She'd be upstairs with her children, worn out by the maternal drudgery of rattles and diapers, just beyond the shadows where Rojano pored over files behind her back.

I returned to the Hotel Emporio, bathed, and headed for Mocambo. That night the city government was throwing a party for the national press corps at a ballroom called the *Terraza Tropicana*. The festivities were still in full swing as the new day dawned. There was music, dancing, an open bar, and girls. A young chorus girl was drinking mint juleps at the bar. She had a fine and noble nose just like Garabito's wife whose smooth and bloody countenance still floated in my head.

At noon the following day the press caravan returned to Mexico City according to plan, but neither Rojano nor his files showed up in my room. The prolonged orgy of information and money with which, every six years, the nation invents its president moved on. Nothing stops the presidential campaign. It gives the candidate seven or eight months to project and amplify his voice, his force of will, his face and his gestures. It lets him proclaim his innocence of past disasters and his patriotic determination to put things right as he marches in triumph from one town to the next. He is heard on every radio station and seen on every television screen until he becomes the great idol, the newly mythologized president of Mexico.

We were boarding the plane when news reached us of the assassination of peasant leader Galvarino Barria Pérez in northern Veracruz. He was mowed down by gunmen in an ambush near Martínez de la Torre. I recalled Rojano's files and the bloodshed typical of rural Gulf Coast politics. Then I forgot about it.

Chapter 2
ANABELA'S RETURN

On the first Sunday of July 1976, the PRI candidate, whom we in the press had helped construct, was elected president. His victory was unopposed since none of the other legal parties chose to take part in the contest. The months between the election and the inauguration were fraught with greater tension than in the previous interregnum. Senior business leaders conspired among themselves and sought to trigger a coup for the first time in the modern era. There followed the first public disclosure of a coup attempt, the first devaluation of the peso in twenty-two years, and the first ovation ever afforded such a measure in the Chamber of Deputies. Rumors abounded. The country was seemingly on the verge of Chilean-style destabilization. No one doubted that on November 20, 1976, on the 60th anniversary of the Mexican Revolution, a coup would bring the long post-revolutionary era to an end. The fated day arrived, but the army didn't occupy the Zócalo in Mexico City, and it didn't evict the civil authorities from the presidential palace. What happened instead was that Anabela de Rojano made her unexpected reappearance in my life.

By then I was living in my apartment on *Calle de las Artes*– the street that passes in front of the legendary public baths whose remains consist of a cold, comfortable rectangle of high roofs and broken pipes. The apartment was enormous, and I used only one of the three bedrooms. I turned the sala into an office next to which there was a breakfast nook that easily accommodated a table for eight. The office contained a desk, bookshelves and file cabinets plus two black leather chairs and two old-fashioned hardwood chairs with pigskin upholstery.

Doña Lila, a 50-ish Indian woman from the city of Tuxpan, kept the place clean and did the cooking. She cordially welcomed my overnight guests and picked up after them in the morning. Her one quirk was a tendency to disappear with no prior warning in pursuit of such adventures as an older woman might find. Two or three days later she'd be back, ready and willing to describe her exploits in irrefutable detail.

On the 20th of November 1976, Doña Lila was preparing a supper of tamales with stewed peaches for dessert. In my office I was dictating an update to my column for the following day over the phone. I'd written about the rumored coup and its supposed instigator, Monterrey industrialist Andres Marcelo Sada, irreverently dubbed the Marquis de Sada by the press and the political class. My back was to the door when the doorbell rang, and I took the time to finish dictating and hang up. By the time I turned around Anabela was already seated in one of the chairs smoking a cigarette with a white filter. "Did you watch the coup on television?" she asked.

Her crossed leg bounced nervously from side to side, and she smiled through the cigarette smoke. Around the white filter was a ring of bright red lipstick. Everything about her resembled the excessive brilliance of that red stain: the layer of makeup, her youthfully cropped hair in the style of Mia Farrow, the leather outfit, the long nails, the impeccably separated eyelashes, the blue eyeshadow.

By contrast, my hair was uncombed. I was dirty and sweaty with a day-old stubble, and my shirttail was sticking out the back of my pants.

"I asked if you watched the coup on television," she persisted.

I managed to ask, "What are you doing here?"

"I told you, I came to see the coup," Anabela said. The bounce of her leg from one side to the other grew more agitated. "Since there was no coup I came to see you. Tell me something. Why do they announce these things then let everyone down?"

"How did you find my place?"

"In Rojano's address book, my dear, He's got everyone in there. He even has an address for Nixon's chief aide, the one who lives in Illinois and wears bullet-proof underwear. Can you believe it? How are you doing? You look like you just ate an alligator."

"I just did."

"Then spit it out. Aren't you going to offer me anything to drink? It's six in the evening, you know. I'll take a drink instead of a coup, even if it's only a vodka on the rocks."

It was a gray afternoon, a bit on the cold side, and just as disheveled as I was. I put the Baroque Beatles on the stereo and went to the kitchen for ice.

"If you're going to have sex, I'm leaving,"Doña Lila said while keeping an eye on her tamales and peaches.

"Let me have some ice, Doña Lila."

She took some ice cubes from the refrigerator and put them in an ice bucket. "Do you want mixers too, or are you drinking it straight? That way it goes to the head faster."

"Mixers too, Doña Lila."

She pulled out the box she kept them in next to the refrigerator and dusted them off with a damp cloth. There was no dust on them, but she wanted to talk. "That's a lot of woman you have there. At least a politician's wife, maybe even a bullfighter's."

"I'd also like you to buy me some cigarettes, Doña Lila."

"You dresser's full of cigarettes, but I'll buy you some anyway. Do you want short, medium or long?"

I gave her three hundred pesos. She enjoyed going to

the Prado Floresta, and the money, which she stowed in her ample bosom, was enough for both the early and late shows.

"That's what I like about this place," she said. "The politics."

She took off her apron, turned off the burners on the stove, and left.

I returned to the office. Anabela had lit her second cigarette. She took a thirsty swallow of vodka. I served myself a whiskey and soda in a tall glassful of ice.

"Is this where you work?" Anabela asked.

"I work at the paper. This is where I keep my files."

She took another swallow.

"Are you doing well at the paper?"

"With the column, yes."

"But you're living alone?"

"Yes."

"And why do you live alone?"

She took another drink, and I did likewise with my tall whiskey. It was my first one after three hours at the typewriter working on my column. "It gives me freedom of movement," I said.

"Do you need freedom of movement?" Anabela was being playful.

"Absolute freedom of movement."

"To bring anyone you want in here?"

"Anyone who can be brought."

"And to drop them whenever you want?"

"So they can drop me whenever they want. They never last more than three days."

"That would be nights. More than three nights."

"Three days. Two nights only."

"That's all you allow?"

"More would be too much."

"That's why you live alone?"

"And why did you marry Rojano?"

She gave a quick laugh, a sound echoing the full force of her 60s' wildness. I remembered the trail of admirers that followed her through the Humanities wing at the university inspired by her body and her careless high spirits.

"But what if you had married me?"

"I'd have given one of my balls to marry you."

"I don't believe you."

"Yes, you do, but it's too late now."

"It's been less than ten years," Anabela was quick to point out. "How old are you?"

"Two years younger than Rojano and two years older than you."

"If you're two years older than I am, then you're only twenty-nine."

"Twenty-nine plus the presidency of Echeverría."

This brought another burst of sonorous laughter.

"You know politics don't interest me," she said. "I don't have a single gray hair. If you're two years older than I, then you're twenty-nine. You can't count your age by presidents."

"Alright then, twenty-nine. More vodka?"

"Make it a double so you won't have to get up again. And if you have a José Antonio Méndez record, you can play that twice, too."

I put the record on, and poured the double shot. José Antonio Méndez began crooning in the background:

> Anyone can have a blemish,
> nobody is spotless...

Anabela removed her leather jacket. Underneath she was wearing a sweater that accented the width of her shoulders and her small, perfectly formed breasts. Small rolls of flesh had begun to form just below her bra strap and across her stomach which was once as flat as a ballerina's.

"A toast to your twenty-seven years," I said as I handed

her the vodka. "May you still be twenty-seven when the new president is long gone. And may old Smiley go fuck his mother."

(Smiley was the nickname of the ex-governor of Veracruz, whose sister-in-law shot him in the face, and left him with a indelible smile that couldn't be wiped off.)

Once again Anabela smiled her smile from another time, and once again the Anabela that used to be flooded my memory. Entering the coffee shop in the Political Science faculty, she was like an apparition, her body lean and athletic, her gait full of energy as she crossed the room on long, slender legs, the curves of her arms and neck crowned by the democratic naturalness of a face with no makeup and a head of boyishly short hair.

She drained her double vodka before starting in again.

"Are you a corrupt journalist or do you just have a price?"

"I'm a journalist from Veracruz."

"Is that an obstacle or do you make it pay?"

"I follow Arteaga's rule to the letter."

"And what is Arteaga's rule?"

"If the money won't corrupt you, take it."

"And how do you know if it won't corrupt you?"

"You don't know."

"So do you take it or not?"

"Only if it doesn't corrupt you."

"And who's this genius Arteaga?"

"He's a reporter for *Excelsior*, the author of the universally applicable aphorism that 'There's no such thing as a small hangover or an idiot without a briefcase.' And you?"

"What about me?"

"Is being married an obstacle or do you make it pay? Are you a faithful wife or just a wife?"

"I've always been a dutiful wife."

"Night after night?"

"Child after child, though I have no idea why you ask. It's not as if it mattered to you. I get the impression that in the years since we've seen each other, what with politics and all, you developed other tastes. When journalists get mixed up in politics, they all end up semi-queer. At least that's what I think because politicians are all queer. They court, hug and seduce each other, and then they fight like the natives in Africa, like spurned lovers."

"I'm not a politician."

"It doesn't matter. Explain to me why you're living alone in this apartment if you're not queer. This looks to me like a place to bring your boyfriends, and when they get their claws into me, they'll tear me apart. Tell me the truth. Are you an honest bachelor or do you have a thing for boys?"

I poured a third round and put on a Pérez Prado album.

"So why don't you invite me to eat somewhere?" Anabela demanded. "You don't want to hold me hostage until the police find me here, do you?"

"Maybe I'll invite you for stuffed tortilla pockets and a bowl of soup."

"I haven't eaten that kind of peasant food since I started wearing shoes, boy. And don't tell me you got that Rolex by saving the labels from Aunt Chucha's soup cans."

"They don't give prizes for soup labels any more."

"You just told me the prizes come in envelopes from Arteaga. Take me to the Champs Elysees."

"They don't serve stuffed tortillas."

"Ask for the menu and select a white wine from France to go with the fish. White wine goes with fish, doesn't it? The waiter comes by, you snap your fingers, and you ask for a 1928 vintage. And for me Smirnoff on the rocks because as far as I'm concerned all that French piss is for queers, right?"

It was about seven when we emerged into the strangeness that holidays bring in Mexico City. Though cars were few and far between, the streets were brimming with people, large young families with children climbing up the backs and arms of their fathers and women with bodies made for having babies. The women looked prematurely worn out, their bodies fresh, new and, at the same time, devastated.

We went to the Champs Elysees, a restaurant with a terrace overlooking *Paseo de la Reforma*. The place had become a haven for politicians and dealmaking, and it featured a menu whose offerings to Mexican diners varied from the ostentatious to the refined. Anabela asked for an inside table and the imported wine list.

"Pick a white to go with the fish like we agreed." She held out the list to me when it came. "And choose the fish, too. Whatever. Just make sure it's good and dead."

I ordered trout sauteed in butter and a bottle of Chablis that went down like water.

"That's pretty good grape juice." Anabela drained the last few drops from her glass. "Tell the little queer looking after us..."–she meant the waiter–"...that he can bring another bottle."

Another bottle was uncorked and dispatched as quickly as the first. It was gone before the trout arrived. We talked about the newspaper, about politics, and Anabela's female acquaintances in Veracruz. The wife of the government secretary ordered a Mercedes Benz with purple velvet upholstery direct from Germany. The governor's secretary collected 100 peso gold pieces and had them engraved with her name. The governor's sister-in-law amassed a collection of 204 live insects, called *maqueches*, from Yucatan with emeralds encrusted in their carapaces. At a fiesta in honor of the President's wife, the chief delegate from Oaxaca was so eager to be seen that he agreed to play the part of a giant *ahuehuete* tree during a medley of Oaxacan folk dances. The mayor of the port of Veracruz was a known homosexual, and his taste for gangbangers from the district of La Huaca was duly catered to. And the number one provider of both boys and girls in the port was an old woman who enjoyed the protection of the governor. She also went through the motions of presiding over the local Red Cross and named herself godmother for life of the Veracruz Sharks, a professional soccer team renowned for its record of 14 consecutive defeats on its home field.

"When you get a close look at those limp-dicked soccer players," Anabela said as she finished off the second bottle of Chablis, "you can see they've all lost their toenails from kicking and being kicked so much. They're all bruises, scrapes and scars. From the waist down, I mean. But in case you haven't noticed, they're a bunch of queers. Why do you think they hug and pound on each other the way they do over a silly goal? They make huge pile-ups and weep for joy. I think the real reason they fall all over each other is they're queer."

The Chablis lubricated her smooth coastal accent, erasing the s's from most words and softening the d's.

"So are you going to let me disappear among all the little queers waiting on us or are we going to dance? Because what I need is a damn good rumba to clear out my fallopian tubes. And it'll be good for your kidneys."

She caught the waiter's eye with an elaborate set of gestures and, when he came, said, "I think you brought us domestic wine because it gives me an urgent need to go to the bathroom. The gentleman is very angry."

"It's Chablis from France, ma'am."

"Then why does it make me want to pee so badly? It tastes like domestic piss to me. Where's the restroom?"

At 11:00, in a climax of trombones and bongos audible from the street, we entered the Náder, a sports center in the La Merced district with a ballroom that on weekends drew huge crowds for the best dance music in the city. It was a two-story hulk with a central dance floor that could accommodate as many as 500 couples. The bands came from everywhere. There was New York *salsa*, Jorrín and his band plus the Mexican groups then reviving music from the tropics.

The Náder was rocking:

> *Your case makes me so sad*
> *So sad*
> *How sad I am*
> *your case is mental*

The group *La Libertad* was performing in a huge cage at the rear of the ballroom. A sweating mass of humanity writhed about the dance floor in its own confusion. Waiters circulated in the aisles, and groups of half-drunk teenagers imbibed and argued heatedly among themselves. *La Libertad* overflowed with sweat, chaos and insousciance as its patrons commemorated 60 peaceful years of Mexican Revolution.

For 100 pesos the waiter got us a corner table. We ordered drinks and danced, that is, Anabela danced with a precision and rhythm I had forgotten. I remembered her dancing with Rojano at a competition in Villa del Mar during a carnival that featured Lobo and Melón. I watched them move among the other dancers, circling each other, moving their feet and hips with dazzling speed and without ever missing a beat. At times they danced counter-rhythms to the music, at others they picked up on themes that were inaudible until they were expressed visually in their dancing. They didn't win, but, as I watched them holding onto each other bathed in sweat, I saw them as a couple for the first time and realized how blind I'd been to the intensity of Rojano's pursuit of Anabela.

"It's been ten years since I so much as danced in my own living room," Anabela said over the rim of her vodka. "Ten wasted years in the middle of nowhere, letting the music empty out of my body. Because music is like the muscles in your body. You either use it or lose it. It's not like women or houses that stay with you forever."

She took a drink, put her elbows on the table and leaned forward the better to look at me.

"Maybe you'll turn out queer on me after all too, just like the politicians and soccer players. But I'm going to tell you something. Do you want me to?"

"If you like, tell me."

"No, no, no. Don't come onto me with platitudes and all that queer stuff. Say you're dying for me to tell you, that waiting for me to tell you is driving you crazy."

"Tell me."

"Are you desperate for me to tell you? Or do you just want me to tell you as if I were one of your usual queers, just to humor me?"

"I'm desperate for you to tell me."

"Then I'll tell you." She raised her glass and fixed her gaze on me again. She was quite drunk, quite young. "I'm getting to like you."

"I'm getting to like you too."

"No, no, no. Don't echo me like that. When I say *I'm getting to like you*, it has to drive you mad as if the moon were rising out of your skull. You don't have to say a thing. It just has to drive you mad for it to work, that's all. Are you getting it? Because what's going on here is I'm getting to like you. And that has to be celebrated like year one of the Mexican Revolution that the queers all made. I dare don Pancho Madero to say it isn't so. He's the one they all betrayed, the bunch of lesbians."

She danced and talked until the curtain came down at

midnight and then she demanded to go somewhere else. We headed south. At one in the morning of the 66th anniversary of the Mexican Revolution, *Insurgentes* was packed with cars, and there were prostitutes on every corner. A blur of letters still streamed across the legendary marquee above La Roca: *Scooby-Doo and the band. The Fellove Trio. Dinner and dancing 10-3 a.m.* We were bound to end up here, where I'd brought Anabela during our first years in college, where I'd first seen her cling appropriately to Rojano during a slow dance, where I tried to regain her attention one night in 1968 when she kept on talking to Rojano. I dutifully brought her back to the place where we drifted apart.

She held onto my arm as we passed through an entrance lined with enforcers and bouncers. "Don't let me go."

Inside the song sung by the lead singer for *Scooby-Doo* was both timely and unfortunate:

> *Though you let me go*
> *though you let my dreams die*
> *though I know I should curse you*
> *in my dreams I smother you with blessings*

We went straight to the dance floor and continued to embrace well after the song ended. I don't recall the next song, but then they played *Don't ask me for more.*

"Now I'm going to tell you something," Anabela said as she started her next vodka. "Do you want me to tell you?"

"Absolutely."

"Don't talk dirty. If you want me to tell you, all you have to do is go mad. Do you want me to tell you?"

"I'm crazy for you to tell me."

"What I'm going to tell you comes in parts. You don't mind if I tell you in parts?"

"If you don't tell me in parts, I'm not interested."

"Then pay attention because what I'm going to tell you may be enough to shrink the Himalayas and let you catch a yeti. I mean you have to consider it in light of all the vodkas you're plying me with. I really can't imagine yetis dancing the rumba. Can you imagine a yeti dancing the rumba?"

"I can't imagine them dancing the rumba."

"Can you imagine a drunk yeti?"

"Super drunk in the heights of the Himalayas."

"You don't imagine anything. You're just leading me on, distracting me from the things I want to tell you."

"I'm distracting you, that's all."

"See? You're going to turn queer on me like the soccer players and politicians. And the Himalayan yetis. But I am going to tell you. Do you mind if I tell you in parts?"

"If you don't tell me in parts, I'm not interested."

"Then I'm going to tell you some things forbidden to queers and people like that. First, you don't snap your fingers the way you should have at the little queer in the Champs Elysees. A political columnist like you snaps his fingers to call the little queers who wait on tables in restaurants. Is that clear?"

"Very clear."

"Second, you have lead feet. They weigh you down as if you were the last of the Mohicans, the one, you know, that was killed because he couldn't run away. Third, you're mixed up with your friend Rojano in the whole Chicontepec business, right? I mean they're taking me for a country girl from Veracruz, aren't they? You're taking care of the paperwork here, and then you're going to divide my 2,500 hectares 50-50 between you while I just sway in the sunshine like the palm trees in the Agustín Lara song, right?"

She was actually quite drunk. Her vitreous gaze originated from beneath a heavy layer of mascara and a tangle of eyelashes. She had the look of a disenchanted 40-year-old, and it excited me just as much as the gymnastic transparency of her body when her unblemished adolescent features made it impossible to imagine her with bad breath. This was her other side, the version beneath the makeup where the flesh under her shadowed eyes had gone slack. She could still be playful, but she was a woman who had stopped believing in Santa Claus, who could play the hand that was dealt her without giving up anything of herself no matter how hard the game. She looked invulnerable and tough in a way I hadn't seen before, but which I always suspected might lie beneath her surface optimism and submissiveness.

"What are you talking about?" I asked.

"Don't act like you're talking to the Virgin Mary. Are you in cahoots with this Rojano guy or not? They're trying to screw me, right? You can tell me because, after all, I'm good and drunk. Tomorrow I won't remember a thing, so don't be afraid. Can't you see I've been in cahoots with you ever since high school? What kind of columnist have you turned out to be on me? And tell that bastard to shut up because the booze is making me think you got the asshole who's singing to lace my drink with yumbina. You give women yumbina, and they go for you just like that, right? *You're the love I can't resist*, and the yumbina makes them fall like flies one after the other. That's right. Why don't we go there, what do you think?"

She put her hand over her half empty glass and looked around, supporting herself with her elbows on the table. One elbow slipped. She raised it, it slipped again, and she smiled. Finally, with great effort, she said, "Let's get out of this rotten place, alright?"

The same 66th anniversary of the Mexican Revolution we stumbled back to the apartment on *Artes*. *Pitcher ready, batter up.* We made it onto the sofa where the evening had begun. I took off her shoes and began to massage her feet. She pulled my hair to make me climb on top of her, and

I obliged. We kissed very slowly at first, then in a fit of overacting, I began stroking her thighs and breasts, and she yielded to my touch. When I again tried to kiss her on the mouth, I discovered she'd fallen asleep. Her makeup had run, her lips were parted and dry, her skirt was hiked high over her knees, and one of her earrings hung loose on its open clasp. Her wrist was pulled up next to her chin as if she were resting on it. Her breathing was normal and rhythmic at once rigid and peaceful like a little girl. I watched a while, for a long while, as she slept on the sofa. Then I got a blanket and put it over her, making sure not to disturb the placement of her wrist under her chin. I made myself another drink and continued to watch her, her loose earring, her wrist, her breathing. For half an hour I wandered about the apartment full of illusions and discoveries, of loose ends to tie in the column, of possible sources. I pulled the blanket back over Anabela: she was snoring.

Daylight and Doña Lila woke me up around ten. I lay sprawled over my bed minus my shirt, dying of cold, and with a dry throbbing in my throat.

"She left early," Doña Lila said as she gathered up the sheets.

"Where is she?"

"I told you. Like a vampire she left with the dawn."

"Where did she go?"

"To a luxury cemetery, I'd say. Because that woman belonged to a bullfighter at least, not a reporter."

"She didn't leave a message?"

"No message, no tip. What do you want for breakfast? You can have the tamales from last night, fried bananas, soft tacos, lime juice with lots of ice. And your tub is full of water hot enough to boil the skin off a chicken."

I gave in to the ministrations of Doña Lila and the morning papers. I checked my notepad which contained long paragraphs of my scribbles from the previous day that I no longer understood and three intelligible sentences: "In a fight with Ro over Chicontepec / I'm being nailed / It's even possible he sent her." At one a messenger came to the door with a package from Mrs. Rojano. The bundle was held together with metal bands and had been delivered by taxi from the Hotel Reforma. I called the hotel right away, but she'd left for Veracruz on the one o'clock plane.

Doña Lila cut the strapping with pliers and handed me a cigar box. The outer label, which hadn't been removed, said: "Special selection for Atty. Francisco Rojano." Inside was a pouch identical to the ones Rojano had shown me months earlier at their house in Veracruz: *Destroying to create. He who can add can divide.* With the pseudo-Aztec border. Also in the packet were the three files Rojano had promised and an enclosure wrapped in onion paper. I tore open the enclosure and saw the photo: the small charred body and exposed teeth of a six-year-old boy totally consumed and shrunk by fire. On the back in block letters drawn by Rojano: "José Antonio Garabito, age 10, died in fire, Poza Rica, January 14, 1976. With the usual trademark." There was a small, barely visible yet obvious hole in the right temple. There were four more photos of the burnt house, the coroner's report, and a final note from Rojano. "This is the last member of the Garabito family. The others died in the market in Papantla at the hands of gunmen who were after Antonio Malerva."

I felt as if I was being manipulated by remote control from the port of Veracruz.

I went back to sleep after I ate. I dreamed I was with Anabela in the pastures along the shores of Lake Ostión. We were walking on the strips of solid, brilliantly green turf built up from the marshes along the inlets to the lagoon. Purebred Brahma cattle with their humps like hillocks of cannon balls hid among the banana palms and pawed the ground.

Suddenly, a band of cowboys on horseback burst onto the sandy shoreline. They pursued us for several meters, then lassoed Anabela. I ran after her trying to free her but sunk up to my chest in a bed of quicksand. One of the cowboys approached me and held out his saddle cinch for me to grab onto and keep from sinking. I clutched the cinch with both hands, and the cowboy pulled me towards him. He drew a pistol, shoved it in my mouth, and ground it back and forth so that my teeth left marks on the barrel. He kept twisting the pistol while muttering: "Whoever can add can divide." I woke up tangled in the bedcovers and chewing on the belt I was in the habit of draping over the headboard.

Two days later I had the same dream all over again.

Towards the end of the following week I chased down Rojano at a phone number in the state Palace of Government in Jalapa: "Lots of birds on the wire," he said to warn me his line was tapped. "What do you want me to tell you?"

"I want you to stop running my life by remote control."

"Whatsa matta, no speek inglish. What are you talking about?" Rojano said.

"I'm telling you to stop pestering me about Pizarro. And if you have something to tell me about him, why do you have to say it through Anabela?"

"Whatsa matta, who's Pizarro? No speek inglish," Rojano insisted. Before I could answer he hastened to add: "I really don't know how to thank you, brother. Anabela told me all about Mexico City."

He sounded ambiguous, and he paused for what to me felt like an eternity. Then he added, "I'm really grateful for the way you looked after her. You know how I have Anabela shut in looking after kids and keeping house all day. Thanks for taking her to the opera. And she loved the Museum of Modern Art."

It was my turn to be caught short. Finally I managed to

say, "She liked the paintings, but that's not what I called you about. I already told you why I called."

"You didn't beat around the bush, brother. Say no more."

"I'm going to look into the way land is distributed in Chicontepec."

"Perfect," Rojano replied.

"And if it's not the way you say it is, I'll make you pay for it in the column. Agreed?"

"Signed, sealed and delivered, brother. You can't imagine what you're going to find."

It was nine in the morning, and the apartment reeked of stale drinks from a party the night before. There were cigarette butts in the ashtrays and glasses on the table. The unopened curtains that kept the heavy odor of tobacco from dissipating now evoked the aura of Anabela and the tale she told Rojano about our revolutionary evening.

The government was on the verge of change. Pundits and soothsayers gossiped obsessively about who would get what cabinet post when the new administration took over on December 1st. Among their incantations: "The political class is through," "Echeverría's the new strongman," and "López Portillo's a puppy on the technocracy's leash." In the midst of all the dire predictions and murky conjecture, I began to look more favorably on the Pizarro matter. It gave me an excuse to see my contact in the Government Security Ministry and avoid getting off on false leads.

This, like so many others, was a contact I made through René Arteaga, the reporter for *Excelsior*. When I met René Arteaga in 1969, the wounds of the Tlatelolco massacre were still fresh, and I was even fresher at the outset of my career as a police reporter. I was 23 and Arteaga almost 40. He was drinking watery *Cuba libres* (so-called *mahogany Cuba libres* due to their color, which bore a curious resemblance to dark rum) at the La Mundial Bar. He let me sit next to him at the bar.

"So you run copy?" he said before draining half his first drink of the day in a single swallow.

Running copy was the entry-level job in the newspaper business. You shuttled stories between the reporters' typewriters and the copy desk and from the copy desk to the press room.

"No, sir," I replied with the pride that came from having insinuated myself into such distinguished company. "I'm a police reporter."

"Then you're the remains of a copy boy," Arteaga said. "You've been blooded."

He drained the second half of his drink with his second swallow. "It's how we all begin. In the morgue. And it's the best way to start. After that nothing scares you. But I'll tell you the rule. The morgue is a training ground, a stage. Don't get caught there for more than three years. Don't pay too much attention to anyone who's spent a lot of years around blood and corpses if you're serious about becoming a reporter. Keep your distance. If you stay down there too long, you get jaded. Good reporters can't be too sensitive, but they have to numb their nerves and control them, not kill them."

He added a small splash of Coca Cola to his next *Cuba libre*.

"So it's a great beat. It's spawned lots of great reporters, and the public loves it, but there's one thing you always have to keep in mind."

"Yes, sir."

"Don't call me sir, damn it. I'm not your boss. I'm your colleague even though I'm older than you and have probably forgotten things about the job that you haven't learned yet." In two swallows he drained a quarter of his watery drink.

"Do you know the Jesuit definition of education?"

"No, sir."

"Then *Sir* is going to tell you. Education is what's left over after you've forgotten everything else. Don't you agree?"

I wrote it down.

"Don't take notes," Arteaga said. "You can find that in any collection of quotable quotes from *The Readers' Digest*. What you need to take down in your head, not your notebook, is what I'm going to tell you about cops. First, they're all the same. Second, there never has been or ever will be a human society that doesn't need them. Third, history is full of revolutions the police have outlived. They wind up as the underpinnings of the new regime. Fourth, it follows that if you want to know what makes a society tick, what stays the same no matter what, then you have to do time on the police beat. Wouldn't you agree?"

"Yes, sir."

"I told you I'm not your boss. My name is René, and quit acting as if I were your boss."

The bartender served him two more watery *Cubas*. Arteaga ordered them in twos, two very tall drink glasses filled to the rim with ice and with dark rum trickling down to within two fingers' width of the top of each glass.

"I'm about to quit drinking," he said. "I'm going to get so damn wasted that for the next month if anyone so much as mentions the word alcohol in my presence, I'll curse his mother. Do you get what I told you about cops?"

"Yes, sir."

"Then just imagine what the political police must be like. You haven't a clue about them yet. What are you drinking?"

About eight months later, on a day when I'd finished writing, I stopped by the bar at Les Ambassadeurs Restaurant to see who was there. I wound up at the bar with Miguel Reyes Razo, who was just beginning to show signs of the brilliant reporter he'd later become. We talked and chatted. A half hour later the waiter approached with an air of deference that would have done justice to General Obregón inviting nuns to the Sonora-Sinaloa casino.

"Sir, I've been asked...," he said, speaking to me, "... would you be so kind as to step into Mr. René Arteaga's private dining room? He'd like to offer you a cognac."

Arteaga was holding forth in one of the Ambassadeur's private dining rooms with a group of *Excelsior* reporters. Seated to his left was a man with a slight wave in his graying, neatly groomed hair and an impeccable trace of mustache above lips so thin they were barely visible. He was the director of federal security in the Internal Affairs Ministry, the chief of Mexico's political police.

"You're both from Veracruz, you're *paisanos*," Arteaga said by way of introduction. "And painful as it may be, you always will be."

The after-dinner drinks continued to flow for nearly half an hour. The guest got up to leave around seven.

"Come see me, *paisano*," he said affably. "I'm at your service in our offices on Bucareli."

"Be sure you look him up." Arteaga sat between us as we talked. "Some day you'll show that bastard there's no such thing as an insignificant friend."

"Thanks, René," my *paisano* said with a smile. "You people always teach me something."

A week later at Arteaga's instigation, I went to see him, and we chatted briefly. He asked if there was anything I needed, if I was earning enough, if there was anything he could do for me. All I asked was what Arteaga told me to ask: that he answer the phone when I called. Nothing more.

Our relations remained distant but cordial, punctuated

by meals and phone calls that grew notably more frequent in 1974 upon the launch of my column, "Public Life." From then on I had in my fellow Veracruzan an unbeatable source. The information he provided was slanted and never complete, and it always served the interests, however obscure, of his superiors. Our cautiously professional relationship existed in the strange limbo of mutual usefulness well known to journalists and Mexican politicians.

(In the words of my *paisano*, "Newspapers are the government's seismograph, and columnists are the seismographers.")

I can now admit that through him I learned the details of stories and political developments that appeared first in "Public Life:" the column about the CIA and its Mexican agents in February 1975; Mexico's involvement with the Chilean fascist group *Patria y Libertad* in July of the same year; the Chipinque conspiracy, named for the park where senior Monterrey business leaders plotted to overthrow the government, a scheme that was later unmasked in a speech by then presidential chief of staff Ignacio Ovalle.

Throughout the presidential campaign of José López Portillo, from September 1975 to May 1976, I received an uninterrupted flow of information about grassroots groups, interests, deals and maneuvers thanks to my Veracruz contact on Bucareli Street. The information arrived with a regularity surpassed only by the cinematic discretion of its provider. It came in the form of calls from his observers, subordinates, friends and agents. Anything I could use from his network I took, and, one way or another, I compared it to what I got from other sources. Almost without exception, the information turned out to be first class. Though very rarely inaccurate or padded, it invariably served the interests of the sitting president rather than the candidate soon to replace him. I compensated for any bias by seeking information on my own and following my own leads while always keeping an open channel to Bucareli. He never complained about what I left out of my column or what I included, even when it conflicted with the interests he served. He came out ahead simply by being where he was and playing the game fairly, cleanly, and with unflagging consistency. Each month I tallied the results of our long distance game as if it were a chess match played through the mail. I struggled for balance and considered my sources. I asked all the questions and dug for all the details that elementary prudence demanded. But, invariably, he succeeded in imposing his line on about half my columns.

I recount all this to explain why, in late November 1976, amidst all the political speculation brought on by a change of administration, my guide on the campaign trail seemed to be the one light that might show me the way to a reasonably accurate assessment of Pizarro and the charges made against him by Rojano.

He listened to my account of the Pizarro case without interruption, holding a pencil in front of his face and rolling it over and over between his fingers. When I finished, he rang a bell beneath his desk. "What did you say the man's name is, *paisano*?"

"Lázaro Pizarro."

"I mean your informant."

I hesitated before giving his name, then remembered I'd mentioned it already.

"Francisco Rojano Gutiérrez," I replied.

"Rojano. It sounds familiar."

He kept a long silence. "Wasn't he with the CNOP?"

"That's right."

"And the Rural Cooperative Bank before that?"

"Yes."

"He got involved in a scandal of some sort, didn't he?

Corruption. Or a shootout somewhere or other. I vaguely remember."

"Both," I said. His memory astonished me. He hid it behind the small eyes of a 40s' movie idol. They were guileless and bright as if eternally searching for a woman who would understand him. He rang the bell again, this time with a touch of impatience. The man who stumbled in was huge and wore a brown jacket and yellow tie over his enormous paunch.

"Bring me whatever you can find about this guy," he said, holding out a card he had written on. "Do it yesterday."

"Yes, chief."

"I have nothing on Pizarro," he told me. "That is, nothing regarding the issue you raise. But he has a reputation to be reckoned with. Pizarro Tejeda, known as *Lacho*. He's the leader of the oil workers' in the area around Potrero del Llano, a mid-level union boss. He's been mayor of a town in the district, very much a populist and advocate of so-called 'petroleum Maoism'. As well as every other form of extremism you might think of."

In contrast to his usual fluency, he was speaking slowly, measuring every word.

"He's a man much loved by the workers he leads," he went on. "He has lots of followers and lots of appeal. He's founded regional *union orchards* in the area he controls, and the fruits and vegetables they raise sell for half-price in union stores. A hundred per cent cheaper than in regular markets. Rumor has it he's a descendant of Adalberto Tejeda, the left-wing governor in the twenties. Don't underestimate Pizarro, my friend. You ought to meet him."

"The photos I have show a different side of him. They're quite impressive."

"Blood is always impressive."

"And shots to finish off the victims execution style?"

"Don't make a movie of it, my friend. Shots to the head in any case."

The subordinate returned with two sets of cards that he placed on the desk before his boss. He studied them closely one by one, beginning with Rojano's.

"Here's where you come in," he said, handing me a card.

It documented my meeting with Rojano during the campaign stop in Veracruz the day he began showing me Pizarro's miracles.

"I have trouble understanding your friend," my *paisano* said upon completing his review. "He has political ambitions in Pizarro's sphere of influence, and he's attacking him. Or he's beginning to attack him. He also owns land around Chicontepec, where the victims are from."

"A 100 hectares between him and his wife."

"Rather more, my friend."

"How much more?"

"Twice that and then some."

"400 hectares?"

"About that. Don't you think your friend wants more?"

He began going through the other set of cards, the ones about Lázaro Pizarro. Also one by one and in detail. He furrowed his brow and was lost in concentration, his eyes ablaze with the intensity of his scrutiny. Then he looked out the window, distracted as if he'd forgotten I was there.

"What more would you like?" he said.

"Whatever you have on Pizarro."

"There's nothing on Pizarro."

"Nothing on the cards?"

"They're routine. None of the bodies you're talking about. Anything else?"

"A hint."

"Nothing."

He stood up to indicate the interview was over. "What

I can do is find a way for you to meet *Lacho*. Are you interested?"

"I am."

"It can be done," he said, escorting me to the door. "I'll let you know."

On my way past his aide's desk in the hall, I heard his bell's insistent ring. It sounded almost hysterical coming from the desk of my acquaintance from Veracruz.

Chapter 3
PIZARRO'S WORLD

We got a new president, and his economic stabilization program had unexpected teeth. It featured salary caps and the first *public* disclosure that Mexico's finances were in thrall to the dictates of the International Monetary Fund. We played the chess game that comes with each new administration as the press and the government sound each other out.

In late February 1977, I received a hand delivered envelope marked confidential with a message advising me of the possibility of an interview with Lázaro Pizarro during the first week of March. On the back of the card I wrote: "With the sole condition that I may write about whatever I see and hear." The following day the same messenger returned with another card: "March 6 in Poza Rica. The interested party should be at the Hotel Robert Prince."

I wrote a detailed report on the whole affair (protocols, sources, contacts, conditions for conducting the interview). I sent the original to the editor of my newspaper along with the files from Rojano. I also made sure my friend on Bucareli Street got a copy. Then I planned my trip. Doña Lila was on a month-long vacation to her home in Tuxpan, a few kilometers from Poza Rica. I phoned and asked her to reserve me a hotel room. On the morning of March 1, I took the seven o'clock flight to Tampico, rented a car at the airport, and completed the two-hour drive along the road that follows the sparkling Tuxpan River as it winds its way to the sea. Shipyards lined the right bank, and on the left stood the eponymous Tuxpan de Rodríguez Cano, so named in honor of the politician regarded as the city's most illustrious native son. From Tuxpan it was less than an hour's drive to my final destination in Poza Rica.

Doña Lila was waiting in the lobby of the Hotel del Parque, immediately in front of the park itself, eating a guava.

"You came alone in all this heat?"

From the window in my room you could see the sandbar at the mouth of the river and in the distance–at once vast, dirty, and brilliant–the iron gray of the Gulf.

"Do me a favor, Doña Lila."

"You name it."

"Find out where Lázaro Pizarro has his office in Poza Rica."

"And what have you got to do with Lázaro Pizarro?" Doña Lila said. For a moment she ceased gnawing her guava.

"Do you know who that man is?"

"You know him?"

"Around here everybody either knows or knows of Lacho Pizarro."

"Can you find out where his office is?"

"I don't have to find out. His office is in the Quinta Bermúdez in Poza. Anyone in Poza Rica can take you there. Why are you going to see Lacho, if I may ask?"

"I'm going to interview him."

The following day, March 2, I left Tuxpan very early. Four hours before the appointed time I was on my way to the Quinta Bermúdez. Just as Doña Lila said, everybody in Poza Rica knew where it was. It was the hulk of an old mill dating from the time of Porfirio Díaz. It had a high mansard roof perfectly painted cinnamon brown. A white stripe along the upper slope led the eye around the building as a whole. Rather than a mill, it was now a huge warehouse bursting with perishable produce such as citrus, vegetables, and fruits as well as grain and bales of hay. Half the structure was taken up by docks for unloading the produce. When I arrived at seven in the morning, the day's activities were already on the wane, but trucks continued to pull in, rolling over the moist green droppings from prior deliveries and crushing them. Behind the loading docks and storage facilities were the mill's living quarters. The large, rough-hewn wooden door in the front was held shut by thick bolts and wrought iron hinges. A detail of armed guards kept watch over the entry, walkie-talkies in hand.

As previously agreed, I showed them the business card of my *paisano* on Bucareli Street. That got me admitted to what at first glance looked like a garden where another guard detail stood watch. A second look made it out to be rather more than a garden. A dense grove of India laurel trees filled much of the space. Their shiny roots snaked in and out of the ground like the tentacles of an octopus, and their fronds kept the fierce sun of Veracruz at bay. There were also clumps of bamboo and oleander bushes spilling torrents of red down the walls. A system of paths led over a reinforced cement bridge. In one corner of the garden was a small kiosk with wooden grillwork and the pinkest honeysuckle imaginable wherever it managed to take hold. One of the guards went to request instructions. I waited with the others, hypnotized by the honeysuckle.

A quarter hour later I was let into another small patio, an enclosed orchard flanked by the rooms that made up the house's interior. We followed the corridors–all painted cinnamon brown with white striping–that led past the rooms to an even smaller patio that in times past must have been the stable. A handful of people waited there. Next to the wash tubs an enormous oleander bush arched over one wall so lush and red that I at first failed to notice the small doorway through which I was led by the guard.

I entered the penumbra of a large room with an opening at the back leading to a kitchen and another brightly lit patio. In the room was a small parlor set plus a dining area with two glass china cabinets. The room was separated from the two rooms to its right solely by a pair of curtains that revealed, as they waved in the breeze, an old box-spring bed with a brass headboard and a studio with wicker rocking chairs and a large desk where two men were conversing.

What was most distinctive and in a way most disconcerting about the place was the lack of decoration. The dining table expressed even greater austerity than the whitewashed walls. All the chairs had been pushed back against the walls except for the one at the head of the table where there was a plate, on top of which was a lone jar of yogurt or whey. A spoon, a salt shaker, and a sugar bowl were deployed around the plate along with a slender water glass and a honeysuckle bloom from the kiosk.

A man emerged hurriedly from the studio, his pace so rapid he seemed to float. He was wearing a tee shirt and sandals, and his hair was wet from recent bathing. He looked about fifty, his skin leathery from long exposure to the sun. He was short and very dark, his posture decidedly erect. He glanced at me as if I were a piece of furniture and proceeded to the lone chair at the table.

"Have a seat," he said without looking at me. He took the place at the head of the table.

It was Lázaro Pizarro. Three men followed him into the room. One pulled up a chair for me; one gripped my arm, directing me to sit; and the third took his place behind the seat of the man in the tee shirt. I seated myself as I'd been told and began to observe him. He had a low forehead, and his hair had gone white at the temples. The narrowness of the space between his slightly hooded eyes added to the intensity of his stare which was magnified through his bifocal glasses. "Have you had breakfast?" He sounded stern and still refused to look at me. He stared into his jar of yogurt, or perhaps whey.

"No."

"Give him some breakfast."

One of the men went to the kitchen. Pizarro reached for the sugar bowl and made a precision task of carefully removing the lid. As I watched him jiggle the spoon in his right hand, I saw that half his little finger and a phalange of his index finger were missing. It was an extraordinarily strong hand, a strange instrument of calluses and hard curved nails. There was a malarial whiteness to the skin of its palm, and its sun-cured back was lined with nerves, wrinkles and tendons. His arms and neck matched the hand as did his collarbone and face, especially the forehead. He had the look of someone long acquainted with effort and adversity. They had left their mark on a body that seemed both dignified and mutilated by much hard work.

He put the first spoonful of sugar into the jar and stirred.

"Yogurt or whey?" I asked.

I listened to the echo of my own voice which failed to affect Pizarro's concentration.

"Fresh cream," he replied. His voice was thin but resonant, his words clipped. "Cream fresh from the barn. Do you want to try some?" Once again the stern question. He sounded cordial though very much accustomed to giving orders.

"Give him some fresh cream," he commanded, still without looking at me.

The crackling sound of hot oil and the smell of lit burners wafted from the kitchen where two women and a boy with bare feet were hard at work.

"You weren't supposed to come until next week,"

Pizarro said, poking at his cream.

"That's right," I said. "But I was on vacation in Tuxpan. It was nearby, so I decided to come sooner."

"Once I went to a celebration of the saint's day of a *paisano* named Manuel Talamás," Pizarro said. He continued to work at his cream and had yet to look up from his plate. "He was a very dear friend, and we agreed that I would arrange a serenade to begin after midnight. But it was raining, so I decided to start early. I changed the time to Wednesday, June 10, 1971, at 10:30, and he didn't hear us arrive. Manuel lived outside of town where there were no street lights and no sidewalks. We got there around 10:20. We began setting up, and people started to gather for the serenade. But that's not what it sounded like to him. He thought a fight was brewing because he didn't expect us until later, and he'd had problems in the neighborhood that day. Somebody was after him, or that's what he thought. The point is he heard us and got confused. He started firing his carbine out the window to defend himself against the mob he thought was coming to lynch him."

"The woman who keeps house for me is from Tuxpan," I said. "She came to spend a few days with her family, and I came to see if we could do the interview ahead of time."

Pizarro's aide brought a large bowl of heavy cream from the kitchen and put it next to me. "Serve yourself, sir."

Behind him the barefoot boy brought me white bread rolls—toasted and sliced in half—on one plate and my own sugar bowl, not the one already on the table for Pizarro, but a different one. I praised the fresh cream and served myself generously.

"Juice and fruit." Pizarro's order sounded purposely frugal as if he disapproved of my portion of cream. "The climate of Poza Rica is ideal for work," he said, starting in on his carefully doctored cream. "The gas flares and the natural heat put people in a bad mood so they work harder."

"In the heat you tire faster," I said.

"You don't need to worry about getting tired. Around here nobody's working so they can live longer. They work because they have to. Being in need is humiliating, and humiliation turns to rage. When you're angry, you have more energy and you work better. The heat helps sustain the anger. When did you get to Tuxpan?"

"Yesterday"

"You got tired of Tuxpan in a hurry."

His people brought in an enormous dish of fresh tropical fruit, mangos, pomegranates, melons, bananas, small sapotes, guanábanas, and a plate with cubes of papaya, watermelon disks, sliced lemons. And a glass of orange juice. It was all laid out to my left well away from where my right arm brushed the space occupied by the sugar bowl, the plate, the flower, and Pizarro's conversation.

"Did you stay at a hotel in Tuxpan?" Pizarro said in the stern voice that made questions sound like statements.

"The Robert Prince, yes."

"That's in Poza Rica," Pizarro said.

"The Hotel del Parque. Excuse me."

"It's on the river," Pizarro remarked as if testing me and requiring an answer.

"Overlooking the shipyard."

I took some papaya cubes. Before I could finish, the boy in the kitchen was back with a plate of small Veracruzan meat pies oozing with lard, sauce and cheese plus a beaker of *atole* made from beans.

"Are you from Veracruz?"

"From around Córdoba."

"But not from Córdoba itself."

"Not exactly."

"Then from where?"

"Near Huatusco."

"Near Huatusco has a name."

"I was born in Coscomatepec."

"Then you're Veracruzan to the bone. Small towns are the real Veracruz. I'm from Chicontepec."

He pushed his dish of cream aside, and one of the men immediately removed it from the table. He also picked up the napkin Pizarro had just used to wipe his mouth and the sugar bowl from which he served himself. He was then served carrot juice on a new plate with a fresh napkin. I in turn was served fried eggs swimming in a red sauce laced with an herb called *epazote*. The boy who brought them placed the fruit dishes a comfortable distance to my left alongside the platter of eggs and a basket of fresh tortillas wrapped in a white cloth. One of the women from the kitchen also appeared and set next to the basket a new plate of very small, perfectly arranged stuffed chiles. Before I could react to the abundant spread before me on the table, the boy brought a steaming mug of *atole* and another of coffee. The combined aroma brought back memories of my childhood full force.

"Who are your relatives in Tuxpan?" Pizarro said upon taking a first sip of his juice. He continued to ask questions in a tone of voice that made them sound like statements, and he still wouldn't look at me.

"A family by the name of Ceballos," I replied. It was the surname of Doña Lila's family.

"Your relatives or your servants?" Pizarro said after a second sip.

"Relatives of a woman who works for me in Mexico City."

"It's an old Tuxpan family. There's an old lieutenant colonel named Ceballos who fought with Pelaez in the mountains," Pizarro said, gazing at the sprig of honeysuckle in its fragile vase. "She must be related to those Ceballos."

"I wouldn't know."

"She must be. There aren't that many Ceballos to chose from around here. Do you live in Mexico City?"

"For the last fifteen years."

I was served a new basket of warm tortillas though I'd barely nibbled at one in the first basket, which was promptly taken away.

"Fifteen is a lot of years," Pizarro said, then resorted once again to his odd way of asking questions. "Don't you like your breakfast or did you lose your appetite?"

He took another sip of his juice and dried his lips with his napkin. One of the men quickly removed the glass, the dish, and the napkin. I understood that breakfast was over. What remained in front of him were the things that were there when he came in, the corolla of honeysuckle in its solitary vase.

"You must be a good journalist," Pizarro said. He slowly looked me over, facing me for the first time. His black eyes were small and set close together. They seemed extraordinarily alive and at the same time ice cold, twice distorted by his bifocal lenses. "And we're going to let you into our small world. We'll do it despite your attempt to catch us off guard by showing up early. But I have nothing to hide so long as you're a man of good will. All I ask is that you try to understand rather than catch us off guard. And you will understand if you try. Otherwise, we'll just put up with you, but you won't surprise us again. Eat your eggs while I put my shirt on. People start coming in at eight."

He got up and left. Alone at the table, I suddenly realized I was totally surrounded by trays laden with fruit, eggs in chile sauce, atole, beans, bite-size meat pies, tortillas and mugs of assorted liquids. It was the exact opposite of the place where Pizarro's sat. The space he left at the table looked frugal and untouched. It was utterly empty now because, upon getting up, he had also taken with him the vase with the honeysuckle.

I ate some of the eggs in chile sauce and drank some of the *atole* before Pizarro's aide approached and told me to follow him. I entered the room with the wicker chairs and the desk. The desk was huge, fit for a pharaoh, though it consisted solely of one broad plank. It was thick and unvarnished but very well polished. Its legs were similarly thick. There were no papers, no drawers, no decoration except a wedge of opaque glass nameplate. Against its red background was lettering the color of aluminum. In lieu of a name it read: *Don't criticize. Work.*

Pizarro was seated behind the desk reading newspapers when I entered. He'd put on a white guayabera. Next to him was a man I hadn't seen before. The man had a clipboard with a ballpoint dangling off it, and whenever Pizarro finished with a newspaper the man set it on a small table against the wall.

"This is from the governor. Someone needs to talk to his pal," Pizarro said, pointing to a story with a red check mark next to it. All the papers were checkmarked in red or blue. "You can handle the guy from *Diario de Xalapa*. Don't let him stay too long. Don't let him think we're being defensive. Come in," he said to me before turning back to his aide. "This is a reporter from Coscomatepec. He's based in Mexico City. This is my friend and secretary Genaro Roibal."

The man named Roibal extended his hand without saying a word. He looked about forty. He was white and impeccably shaved with a quasi-military haircut. Though no taller than Pizarro, his muscular physique attested to a serious commitment to the martial arts.

"He'll be with us," Pizarro explained, "the same as you, the same as everybody else. Let him see and hear everything.

So if he's willing to understand, he can."

"Whatever you say, Lacho," Roibal said as he recovered the last newspaper from the desk. Then, in movements that brooked no nonsense, he gestured for me to sit in the wicker chair beside the desk to the right of Lacho Pizarro. An armed man stood at my side, and there were two more in the doorway to the diningroom. There were no windows, just the intense glare of two neon tubes in the middle of the ceiling. On the white wall behind Pizarro was a heavily retouched portrait of Lázaro Cárdenas with the presidential sash across his chest. He looked very young, his eyes sweetly melancholy as if lost in post-coital contemplation. Beside him was another portrait which, though also large, was considerably smaller and whose subject was José López Portillo, then President of the Republic. To the sides, above and below these two objects of devotion, were far smaller portraits depicting the presidential succession from Ávila Camacho to Echeverría. A purple rag covered the face of Miguel Alemán from the nose down, endowing the former president with a comical resemblance to a bank robber in a western movie.

"What have we got?" Pizarro said.

"*El Negro* Acosta is back. He came very early," Roibal replied.

"Money?"

"No," said Roibal. "The usual."

"Send him in," Pizarro said. He pulled a rubber band from the pocket of his guayabera and began fidgeting with it.

El Negro Acosta came in, a huge, dark-skinned Veracruzan with African features and curled eyelashes. He hadn't shaved in days, and his eyes were bloodshot. He wiped the sweat–and possibly some tears–from his face with a handkerchief that darted in and out of sight between his hands.

He stood before the desk (enormous back, enormous gut, enormous buttocks) trembling like a child. The handkerchief shuttled from one side of his face to the other as he gasped for breath. Finally, he collapsed sobbing into the chair in front of Pizarro.

"What's the trouble, *Negro*?" Pizarro said.

"You already know, Lacho. I don't have to tell you."

El Negro Acosta dabbed his eyes with his handkerchief. He seemed horribly ashamed and out of control at the same time.

"I want you to tell me," Pizarro said. "Tell me exactly what the trouble is."

"My wife Antonia, Lacho, the day before yesterday she slit her wrists. She did it in front of the children, and now she's in the hospital."

"Where are the children?"

"With their grandparents."

"You mean Antonia's parents?"

"Antonia's, Lacho."

"And why did your wife slit her wrists?"

The spasm of grief that overcame *el Negro* Acosta made him bounce up and down in his chair.

"You know why, Lacho, you know already."

"I know, but I want you to tell me," Pizarro said. He ran the palm of his left hand across the top of the desk. "Now quit crying. You're not even crying for real. You're crying for a drink because you're hung over, and I want to talk to you, not your hangover. So talk to me, tell me the whole story."

El Negro Acosta sat up straight in his chair, smoothed his handkerchief, and wiped his face one last time. "Right, Lacho. I'll tell you just like you want me to."

He launched into the sordid tale of a prolonged bender. He drank with friends for two days non-stop, then went home for more money. He was after the savings for his daughter's *quinceañera.* He beat up his wife, Antonia, to get it, then left. But the next day he returned with a friend to continue drinking at home. His wife wasn't around, but his daughter was. He forced her to sit down and drink with them, and then he offered his daughter to the friend as a gift. The girl ran out of the house. This frightened his two small boys, and when they began to cry, *el Negro* Acosta beat them. Thinking that her daughter, who wouldn't stop crying, had been raped, his wife stormed back into the house. She grabbed a kitchen knife and accosted the two men who were still drinking. She tried to attack *el Negro* with the knife, but when he threw her on the floor, she began to slit her wrists. The two boys raced out of the house shouting that their mother was dying, and that brought the neighbors out. They took the wife to the hospital and the children to their grandparents. That was the day before yesterday. Yesterday *el Negro* Acosta stopped drinking, and today he'd come to see Pizarro. It was the fourth time this sort of thing had happened in the past year.

"If there were any justice in the world," Pizarro said very slowly in his thin precise voice, "you'd have been castrated before you ever had a daughter, *Negro*. But there is no justice in this world, so there you sit, sorry for what you did and humbly begging for help. You make it hard to remember that you're a brother of ours."

"I want you to help me get Antonia back," *el Negro* Acosta said. "I want my kids back. What am I going to do without Antonia and my kids, Lacho?" Once again he was overcome with sobbing, his suffering so intense it couldn't be ignored.

"I'm going to ask your wife to go back," Pizarro said after several twists of his rubber band, shaping it into one form after another between his fingers. "I'll have a talk with her and the children."

"Yes, Lacho."

"And they're going to go back."

"Thank you, Lacho." *El Negro* got to his feet and stepped towards Pizarro to shake his hand. Roibal stopped him with a single move that ended in a knuckle jab to the sternum.

"I'm going to tell them they can go back because you're never going to take another drink," Pizarro continued as if Roibal hadn't lifted a finger, his gaze fixed on the rubber band stretched between his hands.

"I won't have another drink the rest of my life, Lacho. I promise you. I swear by my children."

"That's right, Negro. But this time you're quitting for real," Pizarro said. "And you know why? Because the last time I lied to your wife for you was the last time you got drunk."

"Yes, Lacho."

"This time I'm telling her the truth. You're never going to have another drink as long as you live because we're going to make sure that you don't. Because nobody in Poza Rica is ever going to serve you another drink, and if anyone anywhere ever does, somebody's going to be right there to keep you from drinking it. And every time we hear about you ordering a drink that we keep you from drinking, you're going to get beat up at least as badly as you beat up Antonia in each of your last four drunks. And if you do manage to get a drink down before we can stop you, just one drink, it will be your last one because we'll make sure it is."

El Negro Acosta was still on his feet, staring down in horror and exhaustion at the little man in the guayabera who never raised his voice. His eyes remained fixed on the rubber band he wove between his fingers as with no further ado he sentenced the man standing over him to sobriety or death.

"Lacho," *el Negro* blubbered. "You're like a brother to me, aren't you?"

"Like a brother, Negro," Pizarro said. "And we're going

to cure our brother who's been terribly sick. We're going to drag him out of the hell where he's been living and where he's left his wife and kids. And the hell he's put us through, too. Because we suffer with him and with his wife and children. We're going to cure you."

"Yes, Lacho."

"There's nothing for you to worry about because you're in our hands now," Pizarro said. "Any time you're thinking about having a beer, just think about what you heard here where we love you. And don't give it another thought. Just make sure you behave yourself. We're going to get you out of the hell you're in now."

As if hypnotized, *el Negro* nodded. Pizarro continued:

"Go home and wait. I'll go by the hospital to see your wife today. And to your in-laws' house to see about the kids."

"Yes, Lacho."

"Take a bath, shave, and put on some clean clothes. Get someone to clean the house for you, and be sure there are flowers in the diningroom. Your family will be home this evening or tomorrow at the latest."

"Yes, Lacho."

"So get going."

Demolished, *El Negro* staggered off. Pizarro turned to Roibal, who promptly approached him.

"Go tell Antonia we had a talk with *el Negro*. Tell her to go home, that this is the last time I'll ask her. And if she won't go today, then tomorrow. Pay the hospital, and keep an eye on *el Negro* all afternoon. He's going to get nervous waiting, and he's going to want a drink. If he tries to get one, work him over. Work him over so he won't be able to get out of bed tomorrow or the day after. And then put the word out on the street that *el Negro* Acosta doesn't get a drop to drink in Poza Rica. And if he leaves town, I want to know about it.

And I want to know where he's headed."

"Yes, Lacho."

"And for every month that he's sober send him thirty thousand pesos from me, a thousand for every day he stays dry."

Roibal made an entry in his notebook.

"Who's next?"

"Your friend Echeguren and your godchild, his oldest son. They've been waiting for more than an hour."

"Send them in."

"Echeguren wants to come in by himself first, to explain."

Echeguren, Pizarro's friend and the father of his godson, entered in a redolent cloud of lavender water. He had a large bracelet on his right wrist and a gold watch on the left. There were large rings on his fingers. His chest and forearms bristled with hair, and more hair sprouted from his ears and nostrils. He wasted no time extending his hand to Pizarro, who shook it without getting up.

"What can I do for you, my friend?" Pizarro said.

"It's my bonehead kid, brother." Echeguren spoke without sitting down. He stood gesticulating in the middle of the room, then began pacing from one side to the other, visibly discomfited by my presence. "He's thinking with his prick, Lacho, and I can't control him. He's been out of his mind for two or three months. He wants to marry his girlfriend, and he wants to do it by law, in church, and with the blessings of both families."

"What's wrong with that?" Pizarro said.

"The punk is barely sixteen years old," Echeguren said with all the emphasis he could muster, "and the girlfriend's fifteen. They're nothing but a pair of brats who don't even have full crops of pubic hair."

"They have to start sometime."

"I know that, friend, but they can't live on illusions."

Echeguren looked me slowly up and down. "He's a great kid, you know that, but he hasn't even finished high school. He wants to drop out, find a job, and get married. I keep telling him, screw your little darling on the sly so you can both feel what it's like and then take it easy. Take the time to grow up. I'll tell you how to do it without getting her pregnant and so her parents won't find out. I tried to tell him one day, and he chewed my ass out. He's thinking with his prick, and he's out of his mind, but he's so damn pious and self-righteous, the little punk. You know what I mean."

Once again Echeguren turned to look at me, disturbed by my presence and his own vehemence.

"And what do you want me to do?" Pizarro said.

"I want you to convince him I'm right."

"And are you right?" said Pizarro.

"Suppose I'm not," Echeguren said, looking back at me. "Suppose the little prick's right. Fine, I'm asking you as a friend to do me the favor of convincing him he's wrong. I've already tried everything. All it's done is make him more determined to be stupid. The reason we're here now is because, according to him, you're the only one who can get him a job. As far as he's concerned, we came to ask you to get him a job. So tell me I'm not screwed."

"So what do you want me to tell your kid? I'm not a marriage counselor. I'm not his confidant."

"You're Lacho Pizarro," Echeguran said, hands flailing. "Tell him whatever crosses your mind, whatever sounds good to you. Otherwise, he can go to hell. But you're my last resort."

Pizarro smiled. "Tell your kid to come in. I'll have a talk with him, but you stay outside."

"I'll stay wherever you tell me to, but you tell it like it is to that little creep," said the father of Pizarro's godson. He gave me one more look and fled from the room. Young

Echeguren came in, a strapping adolescent in a tight red shirt without an ounce of fat underneath it. He had blue eyes and the kind of youthful shyness that made it hard for him to do such simple things as walk without stumbling or shake hands or say good morning.

"Sit down," Pizarro said while getting to his feet and beginning to pace about the room. He made a point of moving in and out of the boy's line of vision.

"I want to congratulate you," he said from behind Echeguren's back. "According to your father, you're a person who knows what he wants."

"Thank you, sir."

"Don't thank me. I mean what I say. Some assholes spend their whole lives screwing around without ever deciding what they want. People in their eighties, seventies and forties who go through life like a piece of seaweed floating with the waves wherever the tide takes them. You're just sixteen, and your father tells me you've made up your mind. You know what you want."

Praise made the youngster blush. Pizarro continued. "The world is full of small-minded people who never own up to what they want because trying to get it would be risky and they refuse to take risks."

Young Echeguren buried his chin in his chest and stared at the floor.

"Above all," Pizarro went on in the same tone of voice, moving placidly about the room as if strolling though a large garden, "you've convinced your father you want to marry and in order to marry you want to work and in order to work you have to drop out of school. What's your girlfriend's name?"

"Raquel," young Echeguren said in a hollow, dry-throated voice.

"Raquel," Roibal hastened to add by way of reinforcement.

"Who's her father?" Pizarro said.

"Raquel Mandujano," young Echeguren said upon getting his voice back.

"Chito Mandujano's girl?"

"Yes," said the boy.

"You've got good taste," Pizarro said. "And so does the girl."

"Thanks." The boy's voice rang hollow once again.

"It just so happens that your father talked me into doing things your way, and that's what's going to happen. You're going to get a job, and then you're going to marry Raquel Mandujano. What do you want to do?"

"Nothing," the boy said. "I want to get on with PEMEX and begin at the bottom. Be a grunt, whatever. Just to get started."

"That's what I thought," Pizarro said. "That's how it has to be and how it's going to be. But there's one thing I need to tell you first. Can I tell you?"

"Yes, sir," the boy said.

Pizarro stopped pacing. He stepped towards the desk and set himself directly in front of the youngster.

"If you're going to work for PEMEX and start from the bottom, there's one thing you ought to know," he said, fixing him with his stare. "You don't need to live the lesson in order to learn it, and plenty of others learned it before you. It's as true as the earth is round. Even though experience tells us it's flat as a witch's ass."

The kid gave a nervous, involuntary laugh. Pizarro sized up the laughter before sharing in it.

"And for flat asses, cocks at the upright," he went on, evoking from the kid another nervous laugh. "It'll have to be like a drill to get where you want to put it." Pizarro persisted, sensing he'd found a weakness. "Do you know about Japanese cunts?" Young Echeguren squirmed and let out another laugh. "Do you or don't you?"

The kid shook his head, still staring at the floor.

"Well, they're sideways," Pizarro said with a comic flourish and a horizontal slash of his hand.

Echeguran held his head up for the first time. He had a beautifully radiant smile and perfectly straight white teeth.

"What are they like?" Pizarro said in a commanding voice but without turning to Roibal, looking straight at the kid.

"They're sideways," said Roibal.

"And if you stare at them sideways, you know what happens?"

"No." Echeguren scratched at one of his nipples.

"They wink." Pizarro made a wink-like gesture with his fingers.

Young Echeguren relaxed in his chair and burst into open uninhibited laughter. Pizarro stepped closer to him and put a hand on his shoulder as if to congratulate him while also setting him up for some serious advice.

"You're a good wholesome kid," he said with a pat. "You're the new blood that will wash us all away one day. It's the world's best cleanser. But there's something else I was going to tell you about the job. Are you ready to listen?"

"Yes, sir," young Echeguren replied.

"Here's the deal," said Pizarro. He stood with a hand on the boy's shoulder and looked him in the eye. "Around here work is hell. It's dirty, it's sweaty, and people get hurt. They burn out. They lose their energy, and then they lose hands and legs. They squander their lives in the muck. They have accidents, and they're underpaid. In the Second World War, it's said that a leader offered the English blood, sweat and tears. Here it's like that on the job. Except this is a war without great speeches. It's an everyday war of workers against their work, against gears, shafts and grease. The daily grind. You're still getting over one day when the next day comes and you've got to get up and do it all over again whether you want to or not. Even though you're bored and don't have enough to eat, you go back for another shift that lasts all day and sometimes into the night. You just keep going. So there you are working like a fool, drenched in sweat and dreaming of a clean shirt or a Japanese girl with a sideways snatch. And suddenly, wham!" Pizarro took his hand off the kid's shoulder and waved his mutilated fingers in the boy's face. "Wham! The drill shaft got you. Wham! It went right through your leg. Wham! You get blown into the air, and when you land, you bust your ass on a rusted pile of castoff machinery."

Once again he started walking back and forth. He paced the floor behind, around and next to the boy, holding his attention in a clipped voice meant to impress him and also me. "Then on the night of your day off, you leap on your old lady with a shout of glee, then you wake up crying because the fucking horn hasn't gone off to end your shift. You wait and wait for it to go off. But you're not in the factory, you're at home enjoying your day off. You're resting in bed next to your old lady. The trouble is you can't even rest there. You sleep in fits and starts. You cuddle up to the little Japanese girl with the sideways snatch, you put your hand in the groove, and all of a sudden the groove is between the gear teeth on the drill shaft where your hand got caught. You're not dreaming now, you're on the job, and you just lost two fingers. That's the war of the workplace wherever you are. And like any war, you only fight it out of need. You know who the smart ones are?"

"No," the Echeguren kid said. He'd sunk back in his chair and was staring at the floor.

"The deserters," Pizarro said. "The ones who don't go in the first place, the ones that take off running the minute they can and who refuse to get stuck in hell. And that's what I want you to understand if you're able to. And this as well. The sweat, blood and tears from this war are what the world is made of, what you see in the street, what you eat, what you wear, the things you buy in stores, the special panties Japanese girls wear. And the fucking job is the only goddamn thing on earth worth respecting. The only thing."

He planted himself in front of the boy one more time and glared at him with his cold inimitable stare. "If you want to volunteer for that, all right. You can have the whole fucking thing, don't worry. It's your blood, your dirt, your nightmares. You're going to plead for titty and beg to get out of there like all the others. And like all the others you'll have a houseful of kids and a wife with a big belly and a loose twat by the age of eighteen. I married my girl, and she died in childbirth. Did you know that?"

"No, sir," the Echeguren boy said.

"The baby died, too. You know why?"

"No, sir."

"Because I didn't have enough money to take her to Mexico City where they could have saved her life. Because I was just a temporary day worker with no hospital benefits and no money to pay the fee. You'll have your share of that. Sooner or later everybody does. They get their share because there's no way out of it. No one chooses this shit. It hits them, and they can't get out of the way. I didn't choose to have my wife die from being poor. She died from being poor because that's what we were. But if I'd been able to, I'd have sent her to get better not in Mexico City but New York. You want to volunteer for hell and take your wife with you. That's not love. We have another name for it around here. But if that's what you want, that's what you'll get."

He began pacing the floor again, rubbing his hands together as if purged by the outpourings of his own sermon.

He pressed his hands to his temples and pushed the heavy shock of hair that had fallen over his forehead back into place. He massaged his eyes like someone suffering from conjunctivitis or prolonged sleeplessness. I had the feeling I was looking at an insomniac, a man who slept little and badly. It added unexpected meaning to his repeated descriptions of hellish nightmares and dreams in his talk with young Echeguren.

"I don't intend to die of hunger," the boy said, breaking a long silence. "How did you get out of that hell?"

"By shafting whoever got in my way, son." His words sounded melancholy and paternal. "Stomping on other people, making them pay for my wife's death as if everyone I screwed over was guilty of killing her. So I gave them the shaft, I got back at them, but to this day it hasn't helped. It didn't get her back because what matters most in the world is what you let go of and don't have any more."

"Then I'll stomp too, sir," young Echeguren said, summoning the courage to stand up to Pizarro.

The reply took Pizarro by surprise. He looked pleased and at the same time disconcerted. He paused for a moment.

"You may have the balls for it," Pizarro said. "Being hungry helps just like it does for bullfighters, but it's not everything. You just may have the balls to do it."

"I want to prove that I do," young Echeguren said.

"Then you'll have your chance," Pizarro said. He returned to his chair behind the desk and resumed fidgeting with the rubber band. "Give me two weeks to tell you where and how," he added in a tone that made it clear the interview was over.

The encounter ended with a handshake. Young Echeguren left, and Roibal stood at attention before Pizarro awaiting further instructions.

"Let's find out what this young stud is made of," Pizarro

said, sounding mildly sympathetic.

"Yes, Lacho."

"Get Imelda after him, and once she's got him milked out, make sure they hear about it at Chito Mandujano's house. Have a talk with him. Tell him my godson's father came to see me, tell him about Imelda, and, if he'll listen, get him to understand."

"Yes, Lacho."

"Then, after he breaks up with Chito's daughter, find him something to do. He may be mean enough to be useful. Who's next?"

The brother of a woman whose son Pizarro had baptized came in to ask for a temporary job in the oil fields then opening up near Villahermosa, where his wife was from.

"Write a letter to the local in Villahermosa," Pizarro told Roibal. "Have them give him a temporary job. I'll sign it tonight, and they can pick it up tomorrow. Who's next?"

A woman brought in tamales, as she did every week, because Pizarro had pulled strings to get her son a scholarship for the Polytechnic Institute in Mexico City.

"I hear you were by last week and didn't come to see me," Pizarro complained. "Tell him I don't care about him, just his grades. When he gets them, I want to see them. Next."

Two farmworkers from the El Álamo cooperative came in to see if Pizarro could help with a heretofore impossible tangle of red tape in the Veracruz governor's office in Xalapa. "Have them see Idiáquez. Tell him to get it all straightened out and put it on the local's bill. Have him get back to you right away. Who's next?"

A woman from the red light district came in to complain that the mayor's office wasn't letting her work due to the whim of a councilman who wanted her all to himself. She asked Pizarro to do something about this obstacle. "Call the distinguished councilman and tell him the young lady's working for us from now on. Tell him the right to work is inalienable. Who's next?"

A PRI youth leader sought help in buying ten sewing machines and ten typewriters to raffle to his constituents. He got them. A mother of three children whose husband worked in the oilfields and had abandoned her asked Pizarro to guarantee payment of her food allowance. The union was resorting to legal maneuvers to deny her benefits, she said. Pizarro gave her a memo to give the union. A group of striking workers asked for help because their strike fund had run out, and management was sowing dissension with handouts of cash. They got 300,000 pesos.

By ten o'clock the heat in the office was unbearable.

"How many more?" Pizarro asked as if about to shut up shop.

"Ten or twelve."

Pizarro headed for the door and signaled me to follow him. The guards in the entrance stepped out in front of us. In the blinding light and heat of the orchard, beneath the jagged shadow of the huge oleander and the row of banana palms behind it, was Lázaro Pizarro's waiting room. Two Indian women from Zongolica rushed to kiss his hand as if he were a priest. A widow clung to the arm of her adolescent son. Also among the waiting were a group of temporary PEMEX workers, two representatives of the local Red Cross, a municipal police officer, and a circle of peasants. They held their hats to their chests, and their hair either stuck up from their heads in sweaty spikes or lay plastered to their foreheads by the heat. Pizarro greeted them one by one and explained they could either leave their requests in writing with Roibal or come back tomorrow. "You can go to union headquarters," he told the temporary workers. "And you'll get your full pension, don't worry," he said to the widow.

He lowered his voice to address the Indian women from

Zongolica. "You don't have to kiss anybody's hand."

Minutes later we were in the main patio. Ahead of us were some four, six or eight men who served as his escorts in the vehicles Pizarro used to get around in. His car waited at the entrance to the main house. Pizarro and I climbed in back, and Roibal got in front.

"Dinner party at *Mostrador*," he told the driver over the intercom. "L-1 on Zero. Expect fifteen casings at *Mostrador*. All on the way, in 4."

A vanload of armed men pulled out in front of us, and two Galaxies fell in behind.

"Leave me at union headquarters, and go back to take care of those people," Pizarro told Roibal. "I'm taking our journalist to La Mesopotamia, and we'll be back to eat this evening. That's all. When we get back we'll have dinner with *Cielito* and our journalist if he's willing to dine with us. One more thing. Find out if the piece in the paper came from the governor or from his asshole security chief.

Rojano worked for state security in Xalapa. I got the message without blinking an eyelash.

Chapter 4
AROUND THE PYRAMID

Pizarro's escort blocked off the street in front of the union headquarters before he got out of the car. Roibal opened the rear door for us, and I walked towards the entrance at Pizarro's side. His bodyguards closed ranks around us as we stepped indoors. As if setting up guard rails for an oncoming vehicle, they deployed in pairs before each doorway in his path. The instant barrier set off a magnetic stir. He attracted greetings and pledges of loyalty from every office he passed. Secretaries stood on tiptoes. Lowly staffers looked on respectfully while others eagerly extended hands to be shaken as he made his way toward a thick glass door of the sort most often used on public restrooms. The wood paneling in the entry to Pizarro's office was painted battleship gray. On the glass in peeling letters was the inevitable admonition: *Whoever can add can divide.*

Pizarro's office was on the fourth floor at the center of a large rectangle. A wide hallway set it apart from the other offices all of which had clear glass in the doors, making it easy to see inside. By contrast, Pizarro's office had cement walls from floor to ceiling and artificial climate controls that blew mechanically cleaned air in and sucked stale air out. In front of the door were banks of chairs like the ones for waiting travelers in a bus station. Here visitors sat under the watchful gaze of aides who wrote their names on cards noting the reasons for their presence.

Like his house, his union office was furnished with a rustic table—no drawers, no papers—that served as his desk. Behind him was another photo montage: Pizarro

flecked with confetti in an auditorium; Pizarro in a throng of petroleum workers embracing their maximum leader, Joaquín Hernández Galicia, *La Quina*; Pizarro atop a tractor holding an enormous papaya over his head; Pizarro greeting President Echeverría at the foot of a speakers' platform; Pizarro holding aloft the arm of presidential candidate López Portillo as if he were a victorious prizefighter; Pizarro escorting a frail and decrepit ex-President Adolfo Ruíz Cortines; Pizarro in the midst of a group around ex-President Cárdenas.

And an enlarged photo of a youthful Cárdenas in full dress uniform (gloves, cape and sword) gazing into infinity with the languid expression Pizarro seemed so taken with. In the blanks and white spaces of the photo a hand that hadn't fully mastered the art of penmanship had written:

For Lázaro Pizarro, last spawn
of the Mexican Revolution
L. Cárdenas
November, 1958

In the office, a male secretary minded a red telephone which rang constantly. Pizarro again had me sit next to him, and I witnessed a second session of Lacho's court of miracles. The procession of supplicants included an injured worker who needed special surgery to avoid loss of mobility in his right thumb, a soon-to-be-married couple who wanted the union band to play at their wedding, a widow who demanded a lot in a union subdivision about to open on the outskirts of Poza Rica.

Most of the supplicants asked for money. Roibal placed slips of yellow paper on the desk for Pizarro's scribbled signature authorizing loans and advances to the workers. Pizarro controlled and kept tabs of these vouchers himself, account by account. He put one, two, or three check marks on each slip before signing it at the bottom. One check meant:

Tell him to watch out. He's already had one loan. Two meant: *This person hasn't made any payments. This is the last loan he gets.* Three meant: *Make sure he pays in person because he's spending too much and falling behind.*

Around 12:30, a leader of the teachers' union came to ask for Pizarro's support in his bid to become mayor of Altamira, a municipality two hundred kilometers north of Poza Rica in the state of Tamaulipas.

"That's too far away," Lacho said. "It's out of my territory."

This was true. It was the domain of the maximum leader, Joaquín Hernández Galicia, *La Quina.*

"I have lots of support in the municipality," the teachers' union leader, one Raúl Miranda, insisted.

"I'm telling you it's too far away, and it's not my territory. You know the saying: 'In heaven God, but in Tamaulipas, *La Quina* '. What's more, it's been agreed that Altamira belongs to a district controlled by the workers' sector of the PRI. You get your support from the CNOP. So even if it were my territory, I'd be disloyal to my own sector if I backed you."

"That's all been taken care of, Lacho," Miranda went on. "The people are behind me, I can't lose. You're more important than *La Quina.* That's what everybody says in Tamaulipas, as well as here."

"Stop bullshitting, brother. It's important not to shoot your mouth off," Pizarro said as he got to his feet. "What I'm telling you is this. You know what your chances are if you run, but, remember, no one backs a loser. In other words, play politics the right way, and forget about settling personal scores. Don't break party ranks. Help your people get ahead. I've said time and again that you don't just win by winning. Especially if you're plotting against Joaquín. Loyalty is what comes first in life. Didn't they teach you that?"

"But everyone's behind me, Lacho."

"I've told you what I know. Now. it's up to you to learn what's good for you. If you don't, then just carry on, and at the end of the day we'll see who's right. Meanwhile, this show is over, and it's time to hit the road."

As soon as he spoke, he bolted for the door. Roibal yanked my arm and lodged me squarely back into the scrum near Pizarro. His bodyguards piloted him through the gauntlet of instant barriers and walky-talkies, hallway by hallway to the elevator and the street.

Instead of Pizarro's car, we now climbed into a large van. Its interior was outfitted with chairs upholstered in burgundy velvet and a table where Roibal placed a report with blue covers for Pizarro. He spoke to the driver in their odd code: "L-1 in zero. Leaving for G-23 in two casings."

L-1 was code for Pizarro, zero referred to the vehicle we were in, G-23 was for our destination, in this instance the union's farming operation. Casing meant minute.

"Let him know R-1 is staying at Dinner Party," the driver went on "until L-1 arrives at 05. And everyone on 4. Over."

R-1 was Roibal, Dinner Party was Pizarro's house, 05 meant 5 p.m., and 4 meant all points bulletin. It was a complicated and ridiculous code that changed every three or four months. At the time, 61 meant "wait", 53 was "be advised"; 57 was "affirmative" and 75, "negative". 58 meant "outsiders listening in", 34 meant on assignment. Hummingbird 007 meant "danger: prepare to fire".

"To La Mesopotamia," Pizarro said when we had settled in.

Another guard climbed in the front. From under the seat he pulled out a submachine gun and a pistol whose holster he left on the seat. A black Maverick pulled out in front of us with three guards inside, and a Galaxy fell in behind us with two more.

We made our way through the streets of Poza Rica towards the road north to Tuxpan. The noonday sun seemed to melt the asphalt beneath the tires of tanker trucks, trailer trucks, and dump trucks parked at the corners. Passenger buses unable to negotiate the narrow streets lurched to a halt, spewing out plumes of black smoke from poorly refined diesel fuel. In the distance, a homely array of squat buildings crept along the horizon in an astonishing display of money and bad taste topped by a clear blue sky riddled at intervals by smoke from the gas flares surrounding the city. Flames from the stacks made the air around them shimmer and punctuated the skyline with small dashes of soot. We crawled past imported eighteen-wheelers, pickups, and cranes, symbols of a kinetic petro-civilization, its machinery, and its debris. A bulky accumulation of wealth had grown up with no traditions or culture of its own. The city was full of junkyards piled with drills, pulleys, and the rusting hulks of cast-off vehicles and the high-priced vulgarity of first class hotels with polarized windows set in gold frames. Broad thoroughfares were puddled with oil stains, clogged with junk cars, and lined with upscale restaurants with fried food stands in the doorway. The same streets served as a stage for fire-eaters displaying their prowess among the passersby. On the way out of Tuxpan a pair of young girls stood by the side of the road in short white skirts with burst zippers. They were sun-burnt the color of cinnamon and as thin and taut as two pieces of wire. They sucked on wedges of oranges and threw the rinds into a ditch filled with beer cans and garbage next to the sidewalk.

"Twenty years ago there were explosions around here every couple of months," Pizarro said. "When there was a gas leak, the whole town would run because you never knew where something was about to blow up. You didn't have to worry about that where you come from."

"No. All we had to worry about was malaria and polio."

"And decent land, my friend, which is the worst disease of all." Pizarro sounded distracted as if he were reciting a lesson learned by rote. "That's been the main cause of death in Veracruz throughout its history."

"Before oil?"

"Before and after oil, my friend. People come here from the farm every day with the same old story. A guy got killed for refusing to rent. Another guy got killed for refusing to sell, and still another for planting a crop on someone else's land. And then there's the guy killed because his cattle got into somebody's cornfield. The death toll is beyond counting."

"Which is why you travel in an armored van?"

"The van is armored to protect you," Pizarro replied ironically. "My people look out for me, the ones behind us and the ones in front. But nobody's looking out for you, and nobody's going to."

The question annoyed him. He sat up straight in his seat and began shuffling the papers Roibal had given him, underlining them with an emphasis that made it clear he was ignoring me. Through the window I saw eroded fields, flaring smokestacks, the footprint of the oil industry on the outskirts of Poza Rica, and several kilometers of factories, oil spills, machine shops and open space buried under a proliferation of metallic trash. I took out a notepad and passed the time writing in it. When I looked up, I found myself gazing into the cold stare of Pizarro, his eyes implacable and lifeless, sizing me up before re-immersing himself in Roibal's report. Forty minutes later, on the far side of El Álamo, we turned down a dirt road. An afternoon wind blew in from the north, bringing with it a blanket of clouds and a blast of heat and humidity left over from the rain that had turned the road to mud the night before.

Five kilometers ahead we pulled up at the gate to La

Mesopotamia. It was an enormous, 5,000 hectare agro-industrial complex, surrounded by wire fencing and *ocote* pines that first hove into view at the beginning of the dirt road. We entered along a robust stand of mangroves that gave way to a corral some 500 meters wide. The guardrails of its whitewashed fences stretched out of sight from east to west, and the center-pivot irrigation system watered some areas while leaving others dry. From the corrals, our dirt road led past housing units, warehouses and the maintenance shops that kept La Mesopotamia humming. We came to a stop before a row of prefab offices with huge red letters on their sides: Mesopotamia. *An achievement of worker power for the people. Don't criticize, work. Oil Workers' Union.*

A noisy group of women awaited us. Its leader was a bleached blonde with rolls of flesh overflowing her tight pants. "A cheer for Lacho," she shouted as Pizarro emerged. The women unleashed a cacophonous full-throated cheer for Pizarro. "You didn't think we'd make it, did you?" The blonde spoke in a style that was part stump speech and part whorehouse. "Well, we're here for Lacho, like it or not. We're here to complain to you about the bastards that wouldn't let us in. Those assholes really know how to treat women."

It sounded as if their complaints stemmed from recent grievances. Several guards smiled and so did Pizarro.

"Who's the leader of the oil workers' union with the biggest balls?" shouted the blonde without missing a beat.

"Lázaro Pizarro," was the dissonant response.

"And the biggest stud?" shouted the blonde.

"Lázaro Pizarro," they all shouted back.

"And the best looking?" shouted a young girl from the rear.

"Lázaro Pizarro," shouted the others.

"Thank you," Pizarro said with amusement, "but I can't praise you for your good taste."

"You're as good as it gets, boss," the blonde said. She emphasized her words by slapping her hips with the palm of her hand.

Altogether there were about thirty women, some young and some not so young. They clustered about Pizarro. They reached out their hands to touch him and took turns posing for photos with him.

"Thank you," Pizarro said, "but I'm busy right now. Have a look around the farm. Take them to the pyramid so they can sightsee. We'll get together at dinnertime."

"We traveled all night to see you, Don Lázaro," one of them said.

"And we haven't had a bit of sleep," added another.

"The bridge was out, and the ferry sank," said a third one.

"Do what I tell you," Pizarro said. "If you need to sleep, the sheds are over there, and we'll meet later on. Where's the journalist?"

A dozen arms thrust me towards Pizarro from whom I had been separated by the enthusiasm of the cheering squad.

"Shall I drive, Lázaro?" an aide inquired.

"No, not you. You come, Loya," he told another aide. "And my journalist friend too. We need to talk."

A young girl cut in front of him. "Don't you remember me?"

"Of course I do, girl. How's Lupe, your mom?"

"She's well, sir."

"Give her my best. What can I do for you?"

"I'd like you to give me a recommendation, Don Lázaro."

Pizarro took out a small notepad, tore off a sheet and drew an elaborate green L on it. "Go see Genaro Roibal at union headquarters in Poza Rica. Tell him I sent you, and ask him for whatever you need. And be sure to give my best to your mom, Lupe. It's going on eight years since I saw her.

Tell her to remember me, there's no such thing as a greeting that goes to waste. And give me a kiss."

She kissed him on the cheek, and we walked towards the van. A guard handed Pizarro a bag of figs. His bad mood had completely vanished.

"Don't you want a fig?" he asked me. "There's nothing like figs and fruits. Aside from Veracruz, nothing in the world compares to natural foods. That's what I eat. I also do yoga, lift some weights, and bathe in cold water. Have a fig. Have as many as you like, my journalist friend."

We boarded a jeep with oversized tires for a spin around La Mesopotamia with Loya driving and Pizarro next to him in front. I sat in back with a guard.

"Loya's going to be mayor of Poza Rica next year," Pizarro announced while sucking on a fig. "I'm going to raise ten million pesos for you to pave streets with in the first quarter, Loya. How does that sound? The streets are in shameful condition, wouldn't you say so?"

"Yes, Lacho," Loya replied.

"Yes, what?" Pizarro was suddenly abrupt.

"The streets," said Loya. "They're a disgrace."

"But I'm telling you you're going to get ten million pesos to fix them. Didn't you hear me? Ten million. I'm not asking you to thank me, Loya." Pizarro spoke without looking at him. "All I want is your loyalty. Hear me well. Your loyalty because without it you don't get anything else. You can be ungrateful, but you can't be disloyal. Because then you're worthless, you forget who you are and what your place is in life, you understand?"

"I understand, Lacho." Pizarro's insinuations appeared to annoy him. "I told you I'm grateful, and I am. What more do you want me to do? You want me to drop my trousers?"

"Don't be so sensitive, Loya," Pizarro said with amusement. "You sound like a girl. You know perfectly well that all I ask from you is loyalty. I got you the mayor's office, and now I'm going to get you ten million pesos. Good deeds speak for themselves, and that's what I want yours to do. Is that perfectly clear or isn't it?"

"Perfectly clear, Lacho."

We emerged from the mangroves en route to a cluster of buildings surrounded by an impeccably weeded grove planted with oranges and squash. An army of pickers were gathering oranges. They wore khaki union overalls with the inevitable motto on the back: *Destroy to create. Whoever can add can divide.*"

"They're volunteer workers from the union," Pizarro explained. "We all do volunteer work here once a week. A few hours' work never hurt anybody. Those women haven't even been here two hours. They'll get a break, and then they'll eat here at the complex." He pointed to the buildings that still lay ahead of us. "They eat better than they ever do during the week, luxury fare. Then our buses take them home. Others are coming tomorrow. No one gets hurt, it's like a party. And little by little they create this abundance. Take a good look, my journalist friend. Take a look and then tell what you saw. Don't be sensational, just tell the truth. I don't like to do the talking. That's up to the celebrities, it's their job. Here I just organize and work with my people, that's all."

Every hundred meters along the roadway was a sign reiterating one of the ideals that guided Pizarro's workers' revolution: "Work will make you free." "This is where the Revolution of the Oil Workers' Union grows." "He who chirps and sings all night wakes up poor." "Don't criticize. Work." Suddenly, I was overcome by the sensation of having entered a meticulously ordered world apart, a world torn meter by meter from jungles and swamps regardless of the cost in isolation and disease. It catered to the genuine but empty zeal of its builders whose deeds were summarized in its mottoes.

"Let me tell you, *paisano*," Pizarro continued, "as one Veracruzan to another, loyalty is the key. Without it we're lost. You need to be loyal to the nation, the country, your homeland, your ideology, your friend. That's what brings you here, isn't it, *paisano*? And it's why I agreed to let you come. You're being loyal to your friend Rojano, right? Of course you are! But I have nothing to hide, and out of my loyalty to those who work with me and their loyalty to me, I don't mind showing you everything we're doing. That's how we fend off the attacks and insults of our enemies. Loyalty gives us the strength to fight back when others are paid to attack us and to win over the indifferent. Loyalty is what lets us make believers of the workers, the people, and the government too. My kind of loyalty gets results, loyalty on behalf of everyone and in plain sight. La Mesopotamia is one of those results. Take a good look, *paisano*. You can't deny what you see with your own eyes."

What was visible beyond the orange grove was a complex of buildings, sheds for laying hens, and corrals of tall grass awaiting the cattle that had grazed out neighboring corrals. What this indicated was a system of grazing rotation among the feedlots.

"No English grasses here," Pizarro said. I was bemused by what I saw, and Pizarro knew it. "We sow only native grasses. Just look, it's amazing. We spend next to nothing on seed because we did the work necessary to adapt and improve grasses that grow here naturally. Come see the rest of the complex."

The complex consisted of a large quadrangle of buildings interspersed with storehouses for the bounty of La Mesopotamia. There were facilities to box eggs, polish and package rice, and pasteurize milk. There was a refrigerated slaughterhouse where the carcasses were butchered and dressed out on an automated production line. There was a carpentry shop, a machine shop with its own parts department, an electric power generation plant, an agricultural laboratory with a half-hectare experimental plot, and a railroad spur.

"We built the rail spur from here to El Álamo to cut down on shipping costs," Pizarro said. "Shipping over dirt roads is expensive. We fill two boxcars every three days, and they're ready to go to Poza Rica, Ciudad Madero, and Veracruz. All the railroads in Mexico belong to the government except this one that belongs to the oil workers, the people who built it. There are twenty kilometers of track. We did it with our own engineers and our own hands. Because here the revolution of the workers and the people is on the march. We're making a socialist revolution because we're going to take over the factories, the capital, and the means of production. And we're doing it peacefully. In time, the workers will peacefully dislodge foreigners and private enterprise through honest competition. The oil workers' union is standing up for all the people who have been marginalized in this country. And those are not just empty words and demagogy, my journalist friend. They're facts, the ones you see right here. Come see our maintenance and repair shop."

He didn't sweat. In the smothering heat and humidity of a cloudy day at La Mesopotamia, Pizarro didn't sweat a drop. He spoke and gave orders with the natural imperiousness of a tribal chieftain. Though he was the sun and everything orbited around him, there was nothing dazzling about him. He could easily be confused with the aides, workers and supervisors who came out to greet him. They gave him information, awaited his bidding, and fell in with us like metal filings attracted by the magnetism of a demanding but unshining sun. As he proceeded about the complex, the throng around him grew into a small crowd. At its center Pizarro continued speaking to me non-stop, his eyes ablaze, his manner genial and relaxed though alert to my every reaction. Beneath the intoxication of showing off La Mesopotamia, he remained as cold and calculating as ever.

The parts department amounted to a gigantic hardware store and the machine shop to a canopy over rows of Gringo tractors and German mowers.

"This parts department serves the whole region," Pizarro explained. "There's nothing like it from Brownsville in the north to São Paulo in the south. We repair and sell parts for less than anyone. We make them too. We buy from outside once, but as soon a part comes in here, we start figuring out how to make it ourselves. And our only area of weakness so far has been electronics where our failure rate is twenty percent. Anything else goes out of here defect-free. So long as we find a supplier for any special steel that's needed, we can ship it. How much are we selling?" he asked the man behind the long parts counter. The man hesitated.

"How long have you been here?" Pizarro demanded.

"Barely two weeks."

"Then how come they put you out front so soon? That's not right, that's not how our cooperative is supposed to work. We need to learn from private enterprise. They all know how to add two and two, they're not like you. Come on, my *paisano* journalist, let's have a look at the shops and see if we can find someone who knows what's going on. We do jobs for PEMEX here too. We designed a pulley for drill rigs that saved millions of dollars. We've got a patent on it, and the Venezuelans and the Arabs are using it. And though we charged PEMEX plenty, it was less than a third of the price anywhere else. And not even a fifth of what contractors in this country would have charged. All they ever do is buy abroad and resell here. They're parasites, middlemen. But we're not. We have properties worth billions, not because we're hungry for money but because, as long as we live in a capitalist society, it's the only way for workers to be autonomous. When you run with wolves, you learn to use your teeth, my friend. That's what I always say, no matter where I go."

He stopped and so did the small crowd of followers. He wiped away the saliva that had accumulated at the corners of his mouth. He looked down at the floor and then at me. Once again he turned cold and dry without a trace of the triumphant air and the vanity he'd displayed only minutes before. "I talked about this with your friend Rojano the last time I saw him in Veracruz. Didn't he say anything to you?"

He moved briskly on without waiting for an answer. "Who dumped oil on the grass? You can't do that. You can't blame the grass for what we do."

Our tour ended back at the parts counter. "How much are we making on replacement parts?" Pizarro asked the man behind the counter.

"Six million a month, Lacho."

"Good, but that's a mark you have to exceed. You have the experience now, and you've got plenty of support."

"Yes, Lacho."

"Anyway, tell our journalist friend here how many customers you have here in your shop."

"Well, everybody around here, Lacho."

"Otherwise, they'd have to go to Brownsville," Pizarro went on. "It costs half as much to come here. And the same applies to everything else. The food we produce here is sold in our stores in Poza Rica. We make a good profit and still sell for less than half the price in private stores. Our union shops make clothes for two thirds less. We build schools and offer no interest loans because we're not loan sharks. Come on, let's go to the pyramid. This land even came with a pyramid. From there you can see the rest of our operation."

We climbed into the jeep with Loya at the wheel. We drove towards the sheds for the laying hens before heading into the foothills, beyond which the green wall of the Western Sierra Madre rose into the clouds. This way lay Chicontepec and the towns where Rojano's blood-drenched photos were taken. After passing several more corrals and a hog nursery, we were back in tropical jungle twilight amidst tangled vines and the shrieks of spider monkeys squabbling in the treetops. Though the heat and humidity made Lacho's glasses fog over, he never sweat a drop. His skin never appeared oily or showed any other trace of uncontrolled secretions. Even his glands seemed on notice not to dampen the image of monastic, quasi-religious dryness projected by the formidable rival Rojano was determined to challenge. We got out of the jeep and walked some 500 meters with two guards in front of us and Loya behind. Suddenly, we were shrouded in darkness and overcome by the dense odor of rotting jungle vegetation. I was gripped by the thought that our real destination might be someplace other than a pyramid. I felt as if I were being smothered. This didn't escape Pizarro, who came to an abrupt stop and peered at me over his fogged glasses. "You don't like the jungle?" he asked in the voice that made his questions sound like statements, a smooth violence-laden voice. "More than one journey has ended here. There's malaria, vermin, and wild animals. But look. Here's a gift from La Mesopotamia that you'll never forget."

He pointed to an impenetrable curtain of vines and, barely touching my shoulder with his hand, pushed me towards them. I had the clear impression I was being made part of a ritual that would end with my execution, but I walked where Pizarro told me to. I parted the wall of vines with my hands and stepped forward. As I did, I heard the guards lock and load their weapons followed by the crack of the report echoing up to the sierra one, two, three times, then thundering down against the back of my neck. I ran forward into the wall of vines that anointed my body with stinging saps, scratched me with thorns, and sliced me with leaves that cut like razors. I was not alone in my flight of frenzy. An insane circus of monkeys stampeded from branch to branch, thrashing about the dense canopy above me and letting in the only slivers of light to penetrate the exuberant green trap.

Before I could take stock of my predicament, the jungle gave way and I saw the spectacle Pizarro had prepared for me. I had flailed my way into a huge bubble of air and light with the pyramid of La Mesopotamia at its center. The ruin stood a good fifteen meters high, encrusted in the lime and vegetation that rounded the edges of its steps and corners. The sight of it in the midst of the jungle was overpowering. So were the howls and screeches of the stampeding monkeys with their childlike faces and twitching tails as they stormed madly about the pyramid. It was like a revelation. I felt as if I'd stumbled into a time utterly alien to the squareness imposed by technology on the world beyond this jungle island.

Behind me a smiling Pizarro stepped through the wall of vegetation followed by Loya and the guards.

"The effect wouldn't be the same without the gunshots. You can appreciate that now." Pizarro pointed to the monkeys swarming the pyramid. "I hope you don't take this the wrong way. We don't belong in an insane asylum. We say what we have to say very clearly. And what we have to do we do without dithering. Come here. There's a path you can climb."

We walked around the pyramid and climbed the side outfitted with a recently poured cement stairway and a handrail. Pizarro and I went up it by ourselves. For the first time since my surprise arrival at his house in the morning there was no one else near him. We stood at a height from which the boundary between the surrounding jungle and La Mesopotamia with its complex of corrals, buildings, and mangroves was clearly discernible. The jungle ringing the pyramid turned out to be a band no more than a hundred meters wide that had the contrived look of a moat. Naturally, there was a road cut uncluttered by weeds and vines that led to the pyramid, but that was not the route Pizarro had chosen for me. He squatted by the pyramid's guardrail and took a long look down at the civilized domain snatched from the wilderness. "This is La Mesopotamia," Pizarro said without looking at me. "Three years ago it was all wilderness, but the building plans were already on the drawing boards. Look over there towards the fork in the river. Do you see where I mean?"

There were, in effect, two rivers—two threads of sluggish red water—bordering La Mesopotamia. "From time immemorial these lands were meant to be shaped by human hands and were fit to be called La Mesopotamia. Civilization is said to have begun in Mesopotamia, right? It lay between two rivers, the Tigris and the Euphrates. I doubt those two rivers have anything these two don't have. The soil here is as good as any in the world. Come on, I'm taking you to the dam we're stocking with carp and trout. That's another thing they didn't know how to do in Mesopotamia on the Tigris. But fame is like that, *paisano*. And history's the same way. If something is meant to happen, there's nothing humans can do to stop it."

He descended the stairway with the agility of a teenager. I understood the pride he took in the pyramid. From its peak he could overlook his domain in its entirety and let its name resonate in his ear with an echo reaching him from the dawn of civilization. He seemed to see his own destiny embodied in a name marking the beginning of history. We visited the dams and went back to the complex. In the dining room he said goodbye to the women waiting for him. He drew Loya aside for a talk, then took leave from him before getting into the van. It was four in the afternoon.

"L-1 on zero bound for Dinner Party as planned," the driver said in code. It meant Pizarro was in the vehicle and we were leaving La Mesopotamia on the way to the Quinta Bermúdez in Poza Rica.

"Have a fig, my *paisano* journalist, to keep your hunger at bay," Pizarro said. "And don't worry. There's a banquet waiting for you in Poza Rica."

I ate one fig, then another. My mouth was dry. So were my tongue and throat.

"If you'd like a beer, there's one under the seat," Pizarro said while looking out the window and sounding as if he were giving orders to a subordinate. The plastic beer cooler was where he said it was. I eagerly fished for a beer and then for an opener. First, I looked in the cooler, then I felt through my clothes until I came up with the small one on my key chain. Little by little I succeeded in opening the bottle. Pizarro glowered back at me from the front seat. In his hand was a bottle opener he'd been holding out to me for several seconds. I could feel his disdain and his ironic assessment of my faltering composure. It made me realize that his dealings with others were rarely more than a series of tests of strength in the form of veiled competitions and secret traps and triumphs accumulated to prove his own importance, his superiority.

We got to Quinta Bermúdez shortly before 5:00. Crossing

through the garden of India laurels, and then the other patio, we entered Pizarro's inner sanctum where a group of supplicants as large as the one in the morning awaited him. Roibal was seated at the table where we'd had breakfast along with a pale, heavily mascaraed woman of about thirty. She rushed to greet Pizarro with open arms and called him "my love." To my surprise, Pizarro responded in kind. Throughout the meal he addressed her as "little darling." He embellished this with such endearments as "my little darling," "my little girl," and "my love" whenever he spoke to her. Just as they had for breakfast, the cooks loaded the table for dinner. The spread included mugs for a variety of beers, toasted tortillas with assorted toppings, spiced *mole* stews, a marinated ham, and fresh tortillas. Yet Pizarro's place at the head of the table remained pristine except for two servings of yogurt and a plate of tomatoes and lettuce. No one spoke except Pizarro, his little darling, and Roibal when issuing instructions to the cooks. We hadn't gotten to the *mole* when Pizarro announced he had business to take care of and withdrew to his office. Roibal went after him. Little Darling and I served each other toasted tortillas and kept on eating for another half hour.

"I used to be a singer in Tampico," Little Darling suddenly announced. "Do you know the bar at the Hotel Inglaterra?"

"I do," I said.

"Well, that's where I used to sing with the *Jaibo Tecla Trio*. Do you know it?"

"No," I said.

"It's the most famous trio in Tamaulipas. Their *requinto* guitar played with Los Panchos, *el Güero Higuera*. It was one success after another, night after night until Lacho locked me up."

"Where did he lock you up?"

Little Darling picked up a bit of toasted tortilla with her

fingernails and put it in her mouth. "In his arms," she said melodramatically. "Lacho's arms are my halter as the song from Yucatán says. Do you know it?"

She began to hum and stayed right on tune:

I told myself your eyes are my destiny
and your brown arms are my halter.

"Now do you remember?"

"It's called *Premonition*," I said.

"We've been happy. There's not a happier couple in Poza Rica. Are you from Poza Rica?"

"From Coscomatepec."

"Lacho is the man most loved in Poza Rica. And I'm his woman. I quit singing and gave up my career for him. I'm living in sin for him, because we haven't married. It's a common law arrangement as they say. Our love doesn't need any blessings here on earth. What did you come to ask Lacho for?"

"I came to interview him."

"Lacho likes to be asked because giving is his whole life. He'll give anything. He gave one of my nephews life. He sent him for a cure in Houston when he was dying, and he was saved. His love has given me happiness."

For dessert there were peaches in syrup and caramels from Guanajuato. Little Darling had small bags under her bulging eyes, but they were the same color as Anabela's.

"And he's also given me peace. He rescued me from alcohol and from darkness." She spoke humbly and with emotion as if praying.

I heard footsteps behind me and saw Little Darling stare at the floor as if we hadn't been speaking. It was Roibal. "Lacho wants you to come in," he said. He held the chair for me as I got up.

Pizarro was waiting for me with his elbows planted on his desk, fidgeting once again with a rubber band between his fingers. There was a chair placed directly in front of him. He glanced at Roibal, and the guards left the room with Roibal himself in the lead. Without further ado, Pizarro began speaking.

"Your friend Rojano is going to get his mayor's job. Just tell him I said to calm down. Tell him to get over his first-time jitters. And not because he might hurt me, as you're now well aware, but because he might hurt himself and his family."

He paused to let what he said sink in. I looked at the figure he'd shaped between his hands with the rubber band.

"I'm talking about political damage," he explained. "Damage to his political career, nothing else."

"That's what I understood." For the first time I attempted to play Pizarro's game of innuendo.

He smiled.

"You were born in Coscomatepec de Bravo, but you're a Mexico City columnist," he said. "There are several things I ought to tell you. First, never get into a fight you don't care about winning. Second, never fight on strangers' turf. Third, you've been told I had people around Chicontepec killed to get their lands. Don't let that bother you. Civilization has killed more people than you and I could ever mourn. In my opinion, two lives are worth more than one, and three are worth more than two. That's historical arithmetic and what equality is really all about."

He began to pace around the room.

"I myself have witnessed it. We turned a swamp into a garden. We have yields of fruit, grain and other food crops from land that used to be wilderness. This wealth is the work of thousands of hands, and it's bettered the lives of thousands of people. There's nothing personal about who dies and who lives. If at a given moment you had to choose between the development of penicillin and the death of everyone in Poza Rica, including yourself, which would you choose? I'd opt for penicillin because that's what progress is all about. You always have to choose the many over the few. That's what's happening in Chicontepec. There are two killings a day in that area, and you know why?"

"Land disputes," I said.

My reply irritated him. As he turned towards me, his speech grew smoother and more measured than ever.

"Try to understand," he said in a voice that was barely audible. "Listen to what I'm telling you. People there are dying at the rate of two a day just from drinking mezcal. Have you ever been in one of those jails? I was in the one in Chicontepec last week. One of the inmates had killed his mother. Another a friend he was out drinking with. Another raped his daughter and almost beat her to death. None of them remembered what they'd done. All that death and suffering was pointless. It bore no fruit. Nothing blossomed or contributed to the wellbeing of others. These are the deaths that must be stopped, the barren ones driven by mezcal and ignorance. There are always going to be violent deaths, that's the law of history. It 's up to us to make sure they're fertile and creative, that's all."

He stood contemplating the picture of Cárdenas on the wall, his near adolescent features, the big ears, the languid gaze. "How many people had to die for that man to become president?" he said. "Do the numbers, my *paisano* columnist, don't be squeamish."

He returned to the chair behind his desk and faced me directly.

"You people, your friend Rojano and you, are amateurs. Like so many others who claim to know and practice politics, you're just amateurs. You're people who've been given everything or at least enough so you never have to learn the real truth about life."

He let the rubber band fall on the desk and fixed me

with his unbearable glare. "You don't know what it is to be powerless, to be forced to put all your eggs in one basket every day, every hour of the day, and every minute of every hour because with each move you make you either win or you die. You can't let yourself be screwed over because, if you give a single millimeter, it's all over. They'll forget you ever lived. The pressure's on all the time. It keeps on coming all day every day in every way you can think of. And you always have to be the first one through the door because otherwise you don't get in. And everybody else is shut out too, the losers, the scum, the shit, the people. We can't have manners. We are what we are, the unwashed masses, the ones the nation shits on. And we're on the lookout for revenge every day because winning is not enough. We must win twice to win at all. We need victory, and we need revenge, period."

There were no more questions.

"Come anytime you like," Pizarro said. "You're at home here even if you sneak in."

I got back to Tuxpan at midnight. On my bed was a carved and polished wooden box. It contained a .45 caliber pistol with a mother of pearl handle and an envelope with 50,000 pesos. Inside the envelope was a card with Pizarro's inimitable L and his handwritten motto: *Destroy to create. Whoever can add can divide.*

Chapter 5
CHICONTEPEC

In May 1977, the national desks at newspapers began receiving lists of possible candidates for mayoral elections around the country, including the 207 in Vera Cruz. Rojano's name didn't show up, but I took the liberty of calling him a shoo-in for mayor of Chicontepec. The following day I underlined his name and sent the clip to Pizarro with a note saying, "He wasn't on any of the lists. I put him in on the basis of our conversation. Is that right or has there been a change?" Days later, on a Friday, a messenger showed up with the answer, "It will be Rojano, as we said. Almost all the rest of your list is wrong." There followed a city-by-city line-up of PRI candidates in the northern part of the state. In closing, Pizarro wrote, "It doesn't matter how you sound. What counts is what you do. It's like a horse race, there's no such thing as a bad start if you're ahead at the finish."

I looked for Rojano in Xalapa, but he was out of town. I found him in Vera Cruz.

"You're confirmed by your godfather in Poza Rica," I said. "Just like we said in March."

"You called him?" Rojano's voice was full of excitement.

"I have it in writing."

"Then it's a done deal?"

"It's a written promise. But if you want my opinion, I hope it gets broken."

"It's our only chance," Rojano insisted heatedly.

I had the impression he wasn't exactly talking about his feud with Pizarro.

"You're the one who discovered Pizarro, remember?" I said.

"Exactly, brother. That's what I mean. It's our only chance to stop him."

"How are your kids?" I changed the subject on purpose. My question wasn't exactly about his kids either.

"Fine," Rojano said. "Anabela left for Mexico City this afternoon. She has a bunch of people to see. Check with her for the latest details. She's staying at the Hotel Regis. Tell her the news, and see if you can arrange to be here for the candidates' coming out. If you can swing it, take her to the Museum of Modern Art like you did the last time. She loved the Toledo iguanas." I understood that the purpose of Anabela's trip was to make sure my agreement with Rojano stayed on track. Could there have been any other reason for her previous visit? The idea that Rojano and Anabela might be working as a team cast her in a different light, an unpleasant and entirely new one in my eyes. Still, it wasn't that much of a change. Simply put, she remained his stalwart supporter, his messenger, and his public relations agent. Or, to be simpler still and even more blunt, his partner.

I didn't call the hotel. I waited for her to come to me. Despite what Rojano said, I was certain that I was the only reason for her trip, the one contact in a position to serve their purposes in Mexico City. She neither called nor came to see me that Friday, but on Saturday she made her presence felt via a taxi driver who delivered a blue envelope with the first message from Anabela. "If you know I'm here, why are you being so stubborn and refusing to come?" I paid the taxi driver to go back and tell her there was no one home. That night another blue message arrived. "If the mountain won't go to Mohamed, then Mohamed's going to the Champs-Elysées tomorrow, Sunday, at three. Then we'll go where you want."

She really did go to the Champs-Elysées at three, but the restaurant didn't open Sundays. She was forced to wait nearly an hour. First she stood on the corner, then she strolled up and down the tree-lined sidewalk on Reforma. Later she took a seat on a bench near the restaurant, keeping constant watch on the entrance. I observed her from the car for nearly the whole hour. She was less than at ease in the city, and I liked watching her grapple with uncertainty. She was tall, lithe, and a sight to see as she negotiated the red tiles of the sun-dappled sidewalk. She still wore her hair short, like Mia Farrow, as she had at university. She was wearing dark stockings and high heels. A jumble of necklaces cascaded down her chest. At certain points along the sidewalk the sun shone through her light dress and thin shawl revealing the fullness of her legs and the upright silhouette of her breasts. When she looked about to leave, I drew nearer by a half block and, while staying in my car, sounded the horn. She trotted happily towards the car, her hips and shoulders swinging with childlike enthusiasm. She was a couple of kilos lighter. Her face had thinned out, and her features, though sharper, showed no sign of fatigue. She looked as if she'd slept peacefully for days, as if long rest had cleared and even refreshed her complexion.

"You owe me one, *Negro*," she said as she got in the car. "I should have known those French queers don't work Sundays. That's why they came to Indian country, right? To goof off, as they say on the street. So let's see where you take me now because I'm dying of hunger. And you owe me one. You could've told me, you creep. Couldn't you? What are you laughing at?"

"I'm taking you to a place called the Virgins' Hideaway."

"God help us, why?"

"Because that's where they all lose it."

"So how many rooms do they have?"

"How many virgins are there?"

"You mean they don't have any rooms? You're just dragging me into the woods? Don't laugh. What are you laughing at?"

I went up to the Palo Alto Motel on the road to Toluca where I requested a suite, a meal, and two cold bottles of French Chablis. However, their only Chablis was from Hidalgo, not France. We had a drink at the bar, then went to the suite. We had fresh asparagus, hearts of palm, and shrimp sautéed in garlic butter. We drank all of one bottle and half of the other before making love or something, based on the pats and gestures, quite similar, once around 5 pm and after about 5:30. We fell asleep briefly, then left the place at 7:00. Night had already fallen, and the highway was choked with a long line of cars returning to the city. We fell silent, and Anabela turned on the radio. At 8:00 I parked the car in front of the Hotel Regis. "Where do you have the information?" I asked.

I'd have liked it if the question surprised her. It would have been nice not to be so blatant about her role as a messenger, but she replied with utter nonchalance.

"Here in my bag."

Then she added, "The bar here is quite pleasant. Why don't you come in for a drink?"

"I've got to go to the paper."

"After the paper then."

"It depends on the time, but I doubt it."

"All right. Marc Antonio and Cleopatra saw even less of each other."

She handed me a wad of papers. Folded in half, they had all but filled her woven Huichol handbag.

I gave her photocopies of my column, my message to Pizarro, and his reply. We kissed, she got out, and I went to my apartment on Artes to read the papers she'd given me. They turned out to be a lengthy memo from the PEMEX

Office of Projects and Engineering to the Office of the Director General. It outlined an immense federally subsidized project to be centered around a prehistoric waterway near Chicontepec called the *paleocanal*. According to the memo, the area's potential oil reserves equaled the sum of all prior discoveries in the country put together. Under the planned project, Chicontepec would within four years become the biggest oil and petrochemical complex in the Americas and one of the biggest in the world. It would be surpassed only by Kuwait's facilities on the Persian Gulf and the ones then becoming operational in the North Sea. The project called for phase one investments totalling 1.5 billion pesos beginning in 1978; 5 billion in stage two from 1979 to 1981; then 12 billion in phase three after 1981. Pumping an expected 10 billion barrels of light crude would require the building of a complete system of primary and secondary petrochemical refineries and processing plants. Four instant cities of 80,000 each would spring up, and local farming and cattle-raising capabilities would undergo major expansion in order to feed this new demographic. All that. And right on time to make Francisco Rojano Gutiérrez's craziest dreams of riding the crest of the wave to wealth and power come true.

Doña Lila came in at ten and proceeded to fix herself a late-night snack. Looking pale with her hair somewhat uncombed, she sized up her current state by muttering to herself. "You look like a rooftop cat. You're never satisfied till you're scratched bare."

She made me sandwiches, and I turned on the television to watch the Channel 13 news, then anchored by Verónica Rascón. About 11:00 someone knocked. "I want to sleep with you," Anabela said when I opened the door.

I gave her a vodka and tonic and one of the sandwiches Doña Lila made, and we finished watching the news. She removed her makeup, donned a transparent nightgown, and clipped a toenail. We carried on a conversation with the television still on just like a married couple. Later we made love until very late as if we hadn't seen each other for a long time. In the early morning, half asleep with our arms intertwined, I wondered if this was her way of celebrating the victory my photocopies confirmed for Rojano.

Doña Lila woke us up by opening the curtains and shouting that the whole apartment smelled like sin. "This is going to take papal absolution," she said as she approached the bed with a tray of orange juice and coffee. "It looks like every jot and tittle of the sixth commandment has been broken here."

She stopped to watch Anabela sip her coffee. Though still sleepy, she looked fresh and relaxed. Doña Lila paused in the doorway on her way back to the kitchen. "Blessed child," she said. "You can tell me later what disgrace brought you to this den of iniquity because this is the first time I've seen the man you're in bed with wake up next to a woman who wears shoes."

We bathed, drank the juice, and then ate the breakfast Doña Lila prepared for us. I'd already gotten to the coffee when I looked up from the newspapers I was going over and found Anabela looking at me over the rim of her cup. She was sitting perfectly straight with her elbows on the table. She'd put on a long-sleeved blouse with frills at the wrists and neckline and small pearl earrings. A very thin film of makeup redefined her eyebrows and lashes. She'd dusted shadows onto her eyelids as wide as her mocking eyes. She blew on the coffee before drinking it, holding the cup at the height of her lips.

"So how many hectares did you inherit in Chicontepec?" I asked.

She sipped her coffee and waited a moment before answering.

"A hundred and fifty."

"From the widow Martín?"

"From my grandaunt, yes."

"And that makes how many hectares that you own in Chicontepec?"

"I told you everything I inherited."

"But how many do you have?"

"Maybe another fifty."

"According to my sources, you have around *two-hundred-fifty more*."

She took another sip.

"About that, three hundred or so in all."

"Four hundred in all."

"Yes, more or less."

"And how many does Rojano have?"

"So far as I know, the farm at El Canelo, about a hundred hectares,"

"And that you don't know about?"

She finished her coffee and poured herself more.

"I don't know. Probably another sixty."

"Another *three hundred,* according to my sources."

"That could be," Anabela said. "Why the interrogation?"

"For information purposes only."

"Well, I feel like Mata Hari in the clutches of the Gestapo."

"Don't feel that way. Does El Canelo share a boundary with your lands?"

"Partly."

"Which part?"

"All of it except a twenty-eight-hectare wedge that belonged to my Uncle Arvizu, the one who was shot in Huejutla."

"Executed by Pizarro, according to Rojano."

"Yes."

"Who owns that land now?"

"It's in litigation."

"With whom?"

"With Local 35 of the oil workers' union."

"The local headquartered in Poza Rica?"

"Yes."

"Then with Pizarro?"

"Well, yes."

"So why do you want those other twenty-five hectares if you already have *eight hundred*?

"I know nothing about that, *Negro*, so stop pestering me. Get Rojano to explain it to you."

"I'm asking you. You're the one who interests me, not Rojano."

She stood up and began walking in circles as she spoke.

"There's a spring on those twenty-five hectares. It's the main source of the Calaboso River."

"And?"

"I'm telling you I don't really understand. But having that spring is the difference between irrigating those lands or not. Otherwise, watering them would cost a fortune."

"But you two are supposed to be getting another fortune."

"Don't play games, *Negro*. You're making me very nervous. Feel how cold my hands are."

She lay a hand on my neck. It really was cold, but no colder than they'd been one night ten years before, because Anabela was a woman with cold hands.

"You're going to rule the municipality that gets the most federal money during this administration."

"That's enough, *Negro*. You don't know the area. It's an inferno without a single passable road. Going there is a punishment, not a reward. But it's all Ro was able to get. Don't you understand that?"

"Which is why you're so critical of him?"

"All I want to do is live in peace and preserve my children's inheritance."

"And you look down on Rojano because he failed as a politician?"

She was in the sala when she spun around towards me, clearly a bit out of sorts. Though furious, she maintained her self-control.

"Rojano's just beginning, *Negro*. Don't talk about failure. You know about politics, about the ups and downs. It's like a wheel of fortune. Who was José López Portillo six years ago? He was an out-of-work loser who played his cards wrong. And now he's president of the republic. What's political failure? It's an excuse for small-minded people. A real politician never fails. He's always in the game. It's a wheel of fortune, and the most important thing is never to let go. Sometimes you're up, sometimes down. But that's not what's important. The important thing is to keep spinning the wheel, to hang on and not let go, damn it. Not let go."

She was standing in the middle of the apartment's huge sala with her clenched fists pressed to her body. "And not let go," she repeated with fierce conviction.

I thought I understood where the motor was that drove Rojano.

The following week, PEMEX director Jorge Díaz Serrano attended the regular Wednesday lunch meeting of the *Ateneo de Angangueo*, one of the most popular political discussion groups during the López Portillo years. Every Wednesday a senior government official—on several occasions the President himself—showed up for these sessions to talk about current events with columnists and writers. Since a regular member of the group was going to be absent, I was invited to the luncheon with Díaz Serrano on June 17, 1977, in the gray months preceding what would become the Mexican oil boom. All the talk in political circles—among reporters, government officials, business and labor leaders—was glum, focusing on austerity and crisis, the country's disastrous financial situation, the breakdown in productivity, lagging investments, waning confidence, etcetera.

The first surprise was that everything Jorge Díaz Serrano had to say was just the opposite of glum. He spoke of an end to poverty in Mexico, the dawn of an historic new opportunity for the country to confront its incredible backwardness with regards to basic necessities, income distribution, and the general welfare. Oil, Díaz Serrano said, had the potential to reverse once and for all the low rate of domestic investment that was the number one determinant of our underdevelopment.

Mexico, whose colonial rulers squandered its mining wealth in the 17th and 18th centuries, was getting a second chance. In the austere and melancholy 1970s, Mexico could look forward to the possibility of controlling its own destiny, thanks to resources to be extracted directly and indisputably from beneath its own territory. These resources belonged to the Mexican people, according to the country's noblest political tradition, national control of the oil industry.

Diaz Serrano was a man of limited eloquence, tall, lean, and healthy looking despite going gray. His heated insistence that Mexicans lived atop riches as yet to be explored was contagious. By the year 2000, he said, this resource of mythic proportions would bring economic development and justice to Mexico. There was something touching about the simplicity and ingenuousness of his optimism. Instead of our traditional resignation to the idea of an unproductive Mexico doomed to failure, mediocrity, and exploitation by foreigners, Díaz Serrano spoke of a country on which nature was about to bestow a brilliant future. It was a speech that sought unabashedly to convert, to be both profoundly and superficially flattering to all of us by putting a charge of positive energy into the idea of national pride. It offered real hope that we could overcome the kind of defensive nationalism born of resentment and jealousy. It evoked visions of collective euphoria and an achievable utopia; of a rich, sovereign and desirable Mexico no longer crippled by the brutal deformities of its past; a new, noble, and generous country like the one we'd always believed in and longed for; a great country worthy of our nationalism and hitherto unrequited love.

I took advantage of the occasion to ask about plans to invest in Chicontepec, and Díaz Serrano confirmed that there were such plans. I followed up immediately by asking if he knew Lázaro Pizarro. He nodded. I then asked about his corps of escorts and bodyguards and his strong-arm approach to leadership.

"He's a solid, longtime oil worker," Díaz Serrano replied. "He started at the bottom with PEMEX when he was a kid. He's a master welder who will be entitled to a generous pension when he retires. He's a born organizer and leader. Go to Poza Rica and take a good close look at him. I challenge you to show me a single enemy of Lacho Pizarro's anywhere in his area."

"I've been in his area," I said. "Everybody loves him, and everybody's afraid of him."

"That may be. But we don't work with saints or devils, we work with flesh and blood human beings. We didn't elect them. They were there when we arrived. And I can tell you that, whatever their defects, Mexico's oil workers are an even greater source of wealth than the oil itself."

"They say the machinery is very expensive to lubricate," Manuel Buendía broke in. He was Mexico's most widely read columnist until he was shot from behind and killed on May

30, 1984. His remark alluded to the fact that the union was notoriously corrupt. "Petróleos Mexicanos reputedly spends millions of pesos to keep those gears well oiled. How much do those exemplary leaders cost you, sir?"

Though somewhat annoyed, Díaz Serrano answered with a smile.

"That may be so, Manuel. I don't deny that there may be something to what you say. But I came here to talk about the good news from PEMEX, about its greatness, which is what matters to me, and not the deficiencies that are never in short supply anywhere. What you're unlikely to find elsewhere in this or in many other countries is what oil can give Mexico, a doorway to enter the 21st century as a strong country, as a major player on the world stage."

In mid August, Rojano was named the PRI candidate for mayor of Chicontepec. He took the candidate's oath in an auditorium in the port of Veracruz. He appeared the following day on the front page of *El Dictamen* with his hand raised and with an ascetic pair of glasses he didn't need. He looked very focused and stern. My telegram read, "Congratulations. Excellent step towards greatness and disaster."

That night he was on the phone to me. "Brother, you have to come. You can't leave me alone now."

"How are the kids?" I asked.

"Anabela's pleased," Rojano answered. "She wants you to come. We want you here. The governor didn't know we were friends. He wants to speak with you too."

"And what does your godfather say?"

"Pizarro was at the ceremony. He's very supportive."

"I'm pleased for the children of Veracruz. But don't forget you're a bantamweight, and your godfather's a heavyweight."

"In politics weight is relative, brother. What counts is being able to seize the moment, the opportunity." Rojano sounded triumphant and sure of his future. "Just a minute. Anabela wants to speak to you."

There was a moment of silence broken by the voice of Anabela. "*Negro?*"

"How's the land baroness?"

"Very happy, *Negro*. Are you coming to celebrate?"

I did not go celebrate. Rojano won the election unopposed ("electoral legitimacy is basic, brother"). Thanks to the local Indian population, which abstained, not a single vote was cast against him. The swearing-in took place in mid-September. There was no paved highway to Chicontepec, which lay a hundred kilometers from Poza Rica over a dirt road that was not always passable. It turned to mud in the rain and was susceptible to washout where rivers and streams crossed the right of way. Lázaro Pizarro organized a small convoy of three vans, a bus with four-wheel drive, and portable winches. The logos of the PRI and the oil workers unions adorned the doors of each vehicle and all the tents. A jeepload of Pizarro's guards headed the convoy, followed by the van with Rojano and members of the PRI. Then came a second van with a group of Chicontepec notables who had traveled to Poza Rica in order to accompany Rojano to his swearing in. Anabela, Pizarro's Little Darling, his aide Roibal, Pizarro, two bodyguards, and I climbed into the third van. Behind the vans a special bus carried 50 male and female oil workers who were along to enliven the political ceremony with cowbells and cheers. Bringing up the rear was another jeep with four more guards. The campaign tents were folded and stowed in two of the vans and the bus.

On September 18, 1977, this outlandish safari set out from Poza Rica as if for a trip to the moon. Pizarro sat in front with Little Darling between him and the driver. Anabela and I occupied the middle bench with Roibal and the bodyguards in back. We made good time until we passed the pyramids and left the pavement on the dirt road to Álamo, the same route I'd taken with Pizarro in March to visit La Mesopotamia. It had rained torrents the day before, and the road was largely mud except for the long stretches of flooding that had to be negotiated at a crawl. The Vinazco River, whose tributaries bordered La Mesopotamia, was on the rise. A fleet of tractors and dredges was hard at work trying to open a drainage channel. We followed the river, then started towards the northeast foothills as they climbed towards the Sierra Madre. The jagged mountaintops rose through blue haze and clouds in the distance. The volcanic accidents that built them had also produced the fertile tablelands and valleys where rivers flowed and springs bubbled incessantly out of the ground.

"The peaks you see over there are the seven peaks of Chicontepec," Pizarro said without turning around. "Around here the Indians speak of the will of the seven peaks. For them seven is a sign of bad things to come. It's the dark side, as they say, because cold winds blow down from those heights bringing storms and lightning."

"I like thunder," said Little Darling.

"The Indians say the seven hills of Chicontepec unite heaven and earth," Pizarro went on expressionlessly, "and that the forces of evil pour down those rock columns." He laughed. "It's a land full of superstitions. There are ghosts and the evil eye and practicing witch doctors."

"My grandaunt used to talk about these things," Anabela said, channeling her memory of the widow executed in Altotonga.

"Your grandaunt Martín?" Pizarro said, countering the allusion. "I'm willing to bet she didn't know the story of the light of the plain."

"She knew all the stories," Anabela stated. "She grew up learning these things, and the poor old lady believed what she heard."

"Extra poor if she died unloved," said Little Darling.

"Did your grandmother tell you about the light of the plain?" Pizarro insisted.

"According to my grandmother and her sister, the light of the plain foretold the death of my grandaunt's husband."

"All I heard was that it told fortunes," Pizarro said.

"Well, my grandmother told the story about her sister," Anabela continued. "Her husband was killed in a land dispute here in Altotonga. And it was the light of the plain that gave her the news. It came spinning and whistling into the corral, and when it left, a colt lay dead. A bat was clinging to the back of its neck, and it was bleeding from the ribs. There was also blood coming from the print left by its shoe. It was her husband's favorite colt, so she said 'they killed Juan Gilberto'. And the following day, she learned it was true. The light had appeared just at the moment he was shot."

"From then on she must have lived without love," Little Darling said, embracing Pizarro.

"The light of the plain only discovers treasure," said Roibal, who rarely said anything.

"Your grandmother didn't tell you the tale of the giants, did she?" Pizarro said.

"No, she didn't," Anabela said.

"They got what was coming to them," Pizarro said ominously. "The Indians say giants once lived around here, and they discovered fire. They decided to dispense with the sun and tried to light up the moon instead by hurling balls of fire at it. The spots you see on the moon when the sky is clear are from the impacts. The gods retaliated with a lightning bolt that incinerated everything. The giants' burnt blood became the oil and tar deposits you see all over these parts. The whole region seethes with the anger of the vanquished giants, especially in Chicontepec from where it is said the giants could reach the sky."

A flock of *chachalacas* flew up from a marsh, then we passed a tar pit where ten men were tugging on ropes. They were trying to free a pinto cow that had sunk up to its belly in the black muck. It was submerged head and all in the swamp with only the curves of its dappled haunches sticking up. Pizarro took advantage of the scene to remark, "If horseflies and hoof infections don't get them, then the tar pit does. One minute they're grazing, the next they're mired in the swamp with no idea how they got stuck. As they struggle to climb out, they put their heads in the oil and start to swallow it. They thrash desperately about until finally they're upside down. And all because they got into something they should have stayed out of. Sing us something, *Cielito*."

On command, Little Darling broke into song.

> *Praise God for letting me have you in life*
> *so I don't need to go to heaven, my love.*
> *All the glory I need is you.*

She proceeded to run through a repertory of border *corridos* and forlorn love songs that lasted nearly the rest of the way.

We arrived around three following two stops to haul the bus out of the mud with the help of the portable winches and the traction of the vans. Chicontepec barely passed for a town. It was more a jumble of rock-walled barrios. The paths snaking through them were lined with huts made of reeds and palm fronds for roofs. Each hut had its own ragged orchard and a small patch of corn to feed its occupants.

Tattered PRI party banners were draped over the rock walls along with some freshly printed posters with Rojano's picture on them. A misspelled cardboard sign read: *Wellcum Mayor Rojano Gutiérres*. Clusters of onlookers—kids with bright eyes and bare feet, women with market baskets—watched the convoy go by. We wound past the huts for another half kilometer before coming to a wide cobblestone lane where the stone houses had corrugated zinc and tile roofs. Here the music and civic jubilation began. Everyone in the small crowd that greeted us had a placard or hand flag to wave to the frenetic beat of a string band playing out of tune. A small man with a loudspeaker orchestrated the cheers and gave uninhibited voice to the emotion stirring the citizens of Chicontepec de Tejeda on this banner day.

As we got out, we fell in with the contingents pouring from the bus to add their numbers to the welcome. They also added the clang of cowbells, the howl of a siren, and enough extra cheering and shouting to drown out the violins in the bands. Behind them came townspeople, awed men and timid women who smiled and excused themselves for getting in others' way as they scurried from their barrios towards the stone street.

Flanked by the bands, Rojano and the PRI party members advanced towards the two blocks of the town with pavement and street lighting. Here the large, single-story houses had high roofs. Their walls were covered with faded pink, green, and blue paint, and the large doors in their entries displayed battered photos of Rojano. Whatever wealth Chicontepec had was concentrated on these two rustic streets, which ended at a wide plaza. Its gardens and walks were perfectly manicured and maintained, and at each corner there was a gigantic poinciana. The trees were in bloom, and their wide red crests overpowered the prevailing brown of the modest plaza. Around it there clustered a church with a single bell tower, a town hall that had seen better days, a string of shops selling groceries and household goods, and the police headquarters. "I put those in." Pizarro was at my side. "I brought the grafts from La Mesopotamia."

A speakers' platform decked in red, white, and green had been set up on one side of the plaza. From it an announcer sang the praises of Rojano and, as members of his retinue mounted the platform, called out their names. Pizarro's oil workers stepped up the beat of their chants, alternating cheers for Rojano and, in the very next breath, Pizarro. At the foot of the platform, the sandwiches and drinks that came in the bus were handed out, and the meeting got under way.

Young Echeguren, the teenager I'd first seen during his March audience with Pizarro, was at Rojano's side as the two climbed the steps to the platform. He had a kerchief around his neck and was wearing a cowboy jacket with a visible bulge of pistol underneath. He cleaved to Rojano, opening a path for him and issuing orders through one of the bodyguards, while also shoving his platinum bracelet to a more comfortable spot on his muscular arm. I drew close to Roibal in the Platform's second row.

"That's the Echeguren who wanted work so he could marry?" I posed the question in the form of a statement the way Pizarro did.

"He's working," Roibal answered.

"As Rojano's bodyguard?"

"He's the security detail for His Honor the mayor," Roibal said.

"And who taught him to use a pistol?" I persisted.

"Real men learn to use pistols when they have to," Roibal asserted.

There was pride in his answer, and he watched young Echeguren with obvious satisfaction.

"Did the woman you got after him do her job?" I continued.

Roibal looked pleased by my impertinence. With a facial gesture he directed my gaze to the foot of the platform where the sandwiches and drinks were passed out by a very young and dynamic looking mulatta woman whose red dress was impossible to overlook. With her shoulder-length hair and prominent breasts, she stood out from the crowd. She regarded her surroundings with a look of disdain and, at the same time, fulfillment.

Rojano read a speech about the new era in Chicontepec. Anabela sat next to him, unblinking and solemn as stone as if at attention for the playing of the national anthem. The oil workers' siren and cowbells punctuated the speech, which lasted half an hour. The final paragraph brought forth an especially vigorous response with a musical exclamation point from the bands.

Then, from one moment to the next, the sky went dark. Thunderclaps rolled down from the sierra. The wind swept dust and fruit rinds through the streets. The poincianas shuddered, and large drops of rain slapped down, stinging before they wet. They landed randomly at first, hitting the ground one by one. Then they came in torrents. People scattered to shelter in the narrow doorways while young Echeguren and two other guards herded the notables off the platform towards a large discolored house on one corner of the plaza. It had double doors in the entry and three windows with grillwork that reached to the roof. Inside there was an orchard of orange and guanábana trees surrounded by large clay planters with hydrangeas, camellias, and dwarf banana palms. The floors were red brick and the whitewashed walls slightly uneven. We proceeded to a large room with heavy wooden furniture where two portraits hung. The larger one was of a man with a white mustache dressed in the garb of a nineteenth-century *guerrillero*. His pose afforded the painter a three-quarter view of his face, and the look in his clear eyes seemed both arrogant and humorous. It was old Severiano Martín, Anabela's grandfather. With a shiver of recognition I grasped that we were in the house of the widow killed in Altotonga. It was Anabela's legacy and Rojano's headquarters in Chicontepec.

Bottles of cider were opened for the toast followed by a chest stocked with other forms of liquid refreshment. Young Echeguren set up the bar together with two guards and women from the household staff. Along with the drinks came trays laden with toasted tortilla disks with assorted toppings, crisped pork rinds, stuffed chiles, and steaming cups of lamb consommé.

The gathering consisted of some twelve people, the outgoing mayor and town council, PRI and state government notables, the platform announcer. Pizarro took up a position in one corner of the dining room. To his left he had Rojano and the state government representative. Little Darling was at his side, and Roibal was behind him. People circled in from the sala seeking to join the conversation, but Pizarro said nothing. He raised his glass of thin yogurt to others' toasts and, instead of consommé, ate figs and *chicozapotes*. Liquor continued to flow and barbecue was served, but the occasion's center of gravity never wavered from its single magnetic pole. Outside, the rain pounded down with an intensity I've encountered nowhere else. It was about six in the evening when Pizarro spoke in a voice that filled the room.

"We have celebrated the well deserved victory of our friend, attorney Rojano Gutiérrez. Those returning to Poza Rica will be unable to do so today. They must wait until tomorrow due to darkness and because the road will be impassable after the rainstorm. We will thank the gentlemen of the town council for offering us their hospitality."

The town council members left with the party notables who were to be their overnight guests. Pizarro didn't budge. When they had gone, he spoke to Anabela. "Now, ma'am, if you would kindly offer us a glass of cognac, we'd be grateful. We're family now."

A small circle gathered about Little Darling and Pizarro. Rojano, by now somewhat drunk, remained at Pizarro's side with Anabela and me facing them. Roibal disappeared along with Echeguren. Pizarro handed his glass to Little Darling and began to speak.

"People around here say we all have doubles in the animal world. The ones who never give up are tigers, the cowards are rabbits, the strong are lions, the gullible are colts, and the peaceful are deer. I want to tell each of you what I think you are because it's a way to tell you what I expect from all this."

He pretended to take a sip of the cognac Little Darling was holding. Though he feigned a swallow, he only wet his lips.

"The Guillaumín girl is a part tiger and part deer," Pizarro declared, looking past me as if I didn't exist. "I'm not saying she's wants war, but she's no peacemaker either. His Honor the mayor of Chicontepec is a mix of tiger and chameleon, which means exactly what it seems to mean. Don't interrupt me," he said when Rojano tried to defend himself (he didn't sip the cognac, he drank it). "Our journalist friend," Pizarro went on, "is what's called a *wa' yá* in Totonaca, a hawk or vulture. He glides along looking for a meal, then soars back into the sky. Cielito here is a *maquech*."

"I'm your *maquech*," Little Darling said, clinging to his hand.

Pizarro explained that the *maquech* was a species of cricket or scarab found in Yucatán. People decorated the living insect with stitching or precious stones three or four times its own weight. Thus burdened, the *maquech* remained so strong and well trained that it would perch on shoulders and necklines, serving as a brooch on a woman's blouse or bosom without releasing a drop of its poison.

Once again Pizarro feigned a drink, then continued his lecture. "This town of Chicontepec will be, or ought to be, like Noah's arc."

"At least it's raining enough," Rojano said in alcoholic jest.

"My point is we must learn to live together without hurting each other," Pizarro paid no attention to Rojano. "Like any ship, this one must be kept upright and there has to be someone at the helm who knows where the ship's headed. Together we'll bring Chicontepec back to life and rescue it from backwardness and injustice. Even if others don't care, we'll do the caring for them. That's our goal."

"That's right, my love," Little Darling blurted sweetly.

"Fate is an arc," Pizarro said. "Think about it. The animals we know about are the ones who got off Noah's arc, not the ones who got on. Because on board, someone had to get rid of the ones who rocked the boat. Someone put an end to that animal world to make way for the one we have now. And no one knows how many of the animals that got on the arc never got off. But we all know the job was done right, and nobody misses the ones that wouldn't help keep the ship upright and on course. They tried to make trouble and weren't around to tell the tale when the storm cleared. They didn't get off. As the saying goes both here and elsewhere, whoever can add can divide. Which is another way of saying that whoever is going to unite must know how to weed out anything that disunites."

He spoke in the flickering yellow light of the oil lamps. The poorly hung doors let in drafts of damp outside air that wafted through the big house, chilling its interior. We began to sweat as a stifling brew of humidity and embarrassment permeated the atmosphere. While speaking, Pizarro's eyes had remained focused on Anabela. Then his gaze turned to me and, finally, to Rojano who managed to station himself where Pizarro could barely see him out the corner of his eye. "That's what I wanted to explain to you," Pizarro said while again pretending to sip the cognac." Rather than drink it, Little Darling discreetly, though in plain sight, poured the liquor onto the floor. "And I ask you to understand my comparisons."

When his speech ended, I asked Pizarro which animal was his double. He paid no attention. I heard Roibal open the door behind me at almost the same moment that Pizarro got up and began to leave. He let Little Darling go ahead of him while saying a ceremonious goodbye to Rojano and Anabela. Upon shaking my hand, he ventured a smile that ended just below the cold sparkle of his eyes in the semi-darkness. "I don't play this game," he said. "I, my journalist friend, am the dealer."

They left, and Rojano served himself another cognac before letting himself collapse triumphant and relaxed onto the rustic sofa. "Pizarro is the hyena," he said before taking yet another long drink. "A political hyena."

"I need to get your rooms ready," Anabela said as if avoiding a disagreeable subject. Her face was suddenly overcome with fatigue. Her mascara had smudged, the bags beneath her eyes had swollen, and her high cheeks had paled.

She picked up one of the oil lamps and made a solitary retreat into the depths of the big house.

Chapter 6
THE SACRIFICIAL DOE

In November 1977, the daily *uno*más*uno* made its debut with René Arteaga as its economics correspondent, a post he held to the day he died. We gathered in the early morning hours to toast the first edition, and everyone got drunk on liquor and incredulity. We drank until noon with a group of reporters. Arteaga and I kept at it until nightfall, then he pressed on by himself until dawn of the following morning. I found this out that same day when he showed up at my apartment on *Artes* with bloodshot eyes and the shakes. He hadn't shaved or changed his clothes, and he couldn't remember where he'd left his glasses. I served him a Bloody Mary in the bathroom where he spent more than half an hour under a steaming shower. An hour later he appeared before my work table poached, freshly shaven, fragrant, and clean. He demurely asked for another Bloody Mary. I got up to make it, but we'd run out of tomato juice. Doña Lila wasn't around, so I went down to the Rosas Moreno store for more. When I got back I heard the typewriter going full blast. I prepared the Bloody Mary and took it to Arteaga who was just about to finish his three-page news story.

It was a gem of a piece, a scoop of the agreement the government had signed with the International Monetary Fund the previous year. It went on to sum up in two dry and succinct paragraphs how the discovery of oil and its earlier than stipulated sale on the world market violated key clauses in the agreement. The energy sector alone had borrowed more than the three billion dollars approved by the IMF. Up until then, no one knew the exact nature of the agreement with the IMF though it was known that some sort of agreement had been reached. Nor did anyone know until then that in the two preceding months PEMEX on its own had borrowed more than the whole Mexican government in all of the preceding year. It was, as the years would come to show, the first journalistic foray into the inner workings of the López Portillo administration. It laid bare the machinations and expectations that would come to characterize the new government over the next six years. Where, I asked, did this come from.

"The Negresco Bar," Arteaga answered with no hesitation. He finished his report and recounted its history. He'd run into a former treasury official at the Negresco. The man was as drunk as Arteaga himself but was far more distraught. The ruin and disaster awaiting Mexico had brought him to tears.

"He had a copy of the IMF pact in his jacket pocket," Arteaga said. "He was carrying it around like a Dear John letter from his girlfriend. He left it behind for me to read while he was taking a leak. He's still looking for me."

"And the bit about PEMEX?"

"I've had that since last week. All I needed was something to confirm it. The IMF stuff isn't exactly relevant, but it will do. It's as good as an admission from Díaz Serrano."

"I don't understand," I said.

"If you don't understand that, you'll never make it as a reporter," he said.

Tremulously, he held out his glass. It was empty again, and he wanted another Bloody Mary. "I'll trade you for the document," he said, and I took the deal.

That afternoon the first fissure in the López Portillo administration came with the resignation of Carlos Tello and the firing of Rodolfo Moctezuma, respectively ministers of planning and finance and among those closest to the president. For the first time in many years, a genuinely political resignation letter reached the news desks of the dailies. Tello offered a tart explanation of his differences with the López Portillo regime. Only *unomásuno* ran it in an exclusive that, fortunately for me, blunted the impact of the piece Arteaga composed in my apartment while I plied him with Bloody Marys. I underlined the document he'd given me and that evening began a gloss of it for my own column. A sensation came over me as if I were entering a different world, one where you could see with absolute clarity what had happened to the country and its people during those months. An agreement signed almost a year ago had gone unreported in the Mexican press until the previous day when Arteaga disclosed and expanded upon it in copy he cranked out on my typewriter. Beyond transcribing the agreement, I did little more than interlineate a few sarcastic remarks to avenge the feeling of powerlessness that overcame me as I wrote. For at least twelve months, according to this evidence, the country had been ruled by deceit, its future in hock to an accord which had never been made public but which nonetheless dictated the rules the new administration was bound to follow. It was to our obsessive observation, praise, and deciphering of this regime that we, as Mexican columnists, journalists and reporters, owed our spurious slice of glory. ("The stuffed envelope, a higher state of commentary," Arteaga said, parodying Lenin. It was his way of referring to columnists and to the bribing of journalists as practiced in the days before moral renovation—after moral renovation the practice continued but under a different name.)

My disconsolate summary ran to three columns. I sealed it in one of the envelopes I used to send columns to the paper and had Doña Lila deliver it by taxi. A half hour later Doña Lila returned, but she wasn't alone. Francisco Rojano walked in behind her. His big mustache was back, and his hair was long and loose. Having also dispensed with his glasses, he looked as ostentatious and overbearing as ever. He had two bottles of aguardiente and a sackful of cheeses slung over his shoulder and a blindingly white Panama hat on his head. Folded over his arms were a garish *huipil* blouse and a muslin shirt with the colors of the flag embroidered on the front. He also had a wicker basket with pre-Hispanic statuettes from the Olmec region. He placed these presents on the floor with a theatrical flair worthy of Marco Polo and with due ceremony announced, "Brother, let's get shitfaced."

He was wearing an extravagant linen outfit and a cowboy-style shirt with pink stripes and yoke. A perfectly knotted and triangulated silk tie filled the gap between the collar points. As he hugged me, I caught the sharp yet delicate scent of the old Jean Marie Farina lotion we regarded as the quintessence of elegance and good taste during our university years.

He extracted from his pants a wallet bulging with bills and from his jacket inside pocket a billfold from which he released a torrent of credit cards. "Tools of the trade, brother. I've come to work with you because big things are happening beneath the skies of Chicontepec."

"Especially to your bank account."

"Especially when it comes to righting historic wrongs, brother. But I've got things to tell you. May I invite you to eat?"

He insisted we dine at the Passy in the *Zona Rosa* and that we be given a table in the middle of the restaurant. We sat facing the lobby with our backs to the windows and started in on the whiskeys. Before we'd ordered a second round, half the major players in Mexican politics and journalism had passed through that lobby. We were on our fourth round when the director of PEMEX appeared with four top figures from the energy sector, among them Pizarro and *La Quina*, in tow.

"Did you see them? Did you see them?" Rojano asked eagerly. "They're all there, aren't they? Only Cárdenas is missing, damn it. Do you know Díaz Serrano?"

"We met at a journalists' lunch."

"If you approach him, will he recognize you?"

"I'm not approaching him."

"But if you did approach him, would he recognize you?"

"I don't think so."

"But, brother, you're right in the thick of things. There can't be more than a couple of thousand guys that are in as deep as you, that make things sizzle as President López Portillo likes to say. If you approach Díaz Serrano and tell him who you are, there's no way he can blow you off, damn it. You're one of the top half dozen columnists in the country for Christ's sake. Who doesn't recognize you, brother?"

"Díaz Serrano doesn't know me."

"So, I mean, what harm can it do? I need a meeting with Díaz Serrano. Because of my job, brother. Couldn't you give me a bit of help? For you it's no big deal, for my town it could be a matter of life or death. Put it in perspective."

"The fish is excellent here, and so are the Mexican dishes. The imported wines are also first class."

"Don't jerk me around, brother. Get some perspective."

I ordered another drink and the menu from the waiter.

"How are things in your Totonacan fiefdom?" I asked. "Ready for the leap to petro-modernity?"

"Ready for the plunge into isolation and misery, brother. It's something you can't even imagine. It's like a colony except the Spanish empire's been gone for four hundred years. It's a fossilized remnant from the nation's past."

"That's nothing to worry about. The whole country's a fossilized remnant from world history."

"No, brother. Just think what it means to be in a place where babies are weaned on pulque. Aspirin is unknown beyond the three blocks at the center of town. Once you get past Tejeda's fruit and vegetable shop, hardly anyone knows much about either Spanish or aspirin. We're about to put in a water system, and guess what?"

"I don't guess."

"The first families to get running water refused to use it. The fact is they're not using it. They say they don't know where it comes from, that there must be something wrong with it if it has to be pumped underground where no one can see it."

"So you see, they're not that dumb."

"Wrong, brother. They hardly know their ass from their elbow. They think women get pregnant according to the phases of the moon."

"Maybe they only screw by moonlight."

"They screw anything any time. Day or night. Chickens, sheep, calves or women, they're all fair game. And they don't do it in private either. They do it openly to show how macho they are. By the way, I need to make a phone call. Excuse me a minute."

They brought my snails and Rojano's salmon along with a bottle of red wine that Rojano ordered and the highball I ordered. It was then that I saw Roibal enter the lobby. He was impeccably dressed in a very new suit and shoes shined to a high gloss.

"Mr. Díaz Serrano noticed you were eating here," Roibal said, "and he asked me to see if you'd like to have coffee with his party when you're through with your dinner commitment or, if you'd like, you could join them right away for an aperitif. They haven't eaten yet."

"Which is better?"

"Sooner is always better," Roibal said. "If you want, I'll make excuses for you with the mayor."

"Then I'd rather drop by for coffee," I said, just to be

difficult, and busied myself with my snail fork.

"As you wish," Roibal murmured. He took two steps backwards and withdrew.

"Your friend invited me for coffee in their private diningroom," I told Rojano when he returned.

"With Díaz Serrano?" he said, feigning surprise.

"With your colleague from Chicontepec," I said, "and the rest of the colleagues."

"Everything that goes down must come up, brother. Do you think I'm doing this for myself? If I'm going to get anything for the poor devils back home, I've got to come and make contacts, spend money, rub elbows. All I get from being holed up in Chicontepec is being holed up in Chicontepec. I can't solve the problems of Chicontepec by staying home. I have to solve them here, brother. That's the way our system works." He took a drink, looked around, then turned back to me.

"What are you going to tell him?"

"Tell whom?"

"Díaz Serrano."

"I'll tell him you and I are are sitting here drinking cognac and solving the problems of Chicontepec."

"Seriously, brother, what are you going to say to him?"

We ate. Rojano had his trout and I had my sirloin. We ordered our first cognac around five, and Francisco Rojano, Atty., broke out his cigars. We had yet to light up when Roibal appeared to remind me of my pending invitation. I proceeded to the private dining room where the senior leadership of the Gulf petro-industrial sector was gathered. I received a cordial greeting from Díaz Serrano himself, and the director of PEMEX made a point of personally introducing me to those present. When he got to Pizarro, he said, "I understand you two already know each other."

"We're almost neighbors," Pizarro replied obsequiously.

His manner couldn't have clashed more with how the imperturbable and remote Pizarro conducted himself in Poza Rica. He turned to *La Quina* and in the same tone of voice said, "Joaquín, this good journalist is the childhood friend of our friend Francisco Rojano, the mayor of Chicontepec. In fact," he said, turning to me, "you're having dinner with Mayor Rojano right here in this restaurant, aren't you?"

"That's right," I said.

"Then invite him in for coffee and cognac, too," Díaz Serrano said to Roibal, who was waiting in the doorway through which he'd escorted me.

Before I could come up with a way to thwart this maneuver, Pizarro changed the subject. "What does the free press have to say for itself, *paisano*?"

For the second time that day, I had the clear impression that I was being manipulated according to someone else's intentions. Rojano appeared, and the conversation degenerated into platitudes. Finally, as the evening was about to end, he got close enough to Díaz Serrano to beg for a meeting. He got his wish in the form of an appointment the following day thanks to his insinuated links to my column and to Pizarro. When we left the private dining room, two girls were sitting at our table drinking our cognac and smoking mentholated cigarettes. I don't remember their names. It was November 17, 1977.

By 6:30 the Passy was emptying of its evening diners. An hour later its nighttime clientele began to arrive. We stayed on with an open tab courtesy of PEMEX (as we were advised by the maitre d') drinking cognac with Rojano's invitees. We went from there to the suite Rojano had rented in the Hotel Genoa. There was iced champagne in the sala and a rolling mini-bar with more cognac, whiskey, and imported liquors. Rojano's guests smoked marijuana. They wore silk panties and bras, had partially shaved pubic hair, and preferred anal intercourse. At 10:00 they were still prancing about the suite and making a show of arousing each other. At 11:00 they clocked out. They wrapped themselves in their maxi-skirts and left. After long restorative baths, Rojano and I went back to the *Zona Rosa* with its chaos of bars and hustlers. We had a drink at the Sapphire Bar in the Hotel Presidente where Cuco Sánchez played to a full house nightly. From there it was on to the then fashionable Lion's Bar on Brazil Street, and thereafter to a giant dance hall on Palma where about 1,000 women danced and tendered sex for hire. Most were castoffs from other dance halls with an admixture of young girls recently imported from provincial brothels or migrant girls on their way from the rural poverty to urban prostitution. They served rum when you ordered whiskey and aguardiente if you asked for rum. There was watery beer, cider relabeled as French champagne, and diluted brandy from the flea markets of Tepito. It was all displayed on this darkened dance floor for clients who were themselves the dregs from the better bars and nightspots that shut down at dawn. We ordered a bottle of *Anís de la Cadena*, of which Rojano declared himself a connoisseur, and shared it with a young girl whom Rojano discovered among the shadows. I woke up in blinding sunlight beside the two of them in an ice cold bed on the third floor of the Hotel León de Brazil. The girl was breathing on my neck. She had wide bands of smudged mascara on her eyelids and cheeks, two skeins of tangled hair, and thick, partially open lips. Minus her nocturnal accessories, she was just another country girl, unwashed and a bit coarse. I nudged Rojano, who was sleeping like a log. He awakened red-eyed, still drunk, and humming a Juan Gabriel song it was impossible not to hear three times a day in Mexico City ("...*which is why I am where I always was, in the same place with the same people*"). He gave a start upon discovering his acquisition from the night before and began to slap her cheek with his penis to wake her up. I went into the bathroom where I found to my surprise there was hot water. I was drying off when I heard Rojano groan and the girl whimper from beyond the door. When I looked out, I saw Rojano jumping up and down in the middle of the room. The girls legs were forked around his waist, and he was holding her up by her buttocks, penetrating her with every jump in a grotesque kind of dance punctuated by his gasps and her whimpers. She was a slender woman and not very tall, fragile and bony with the physique of an adolescent. She began to laugh and, finally, to show some small signs of pleasure. I wondered if he did that with Anabela. By my estimate at the time, he wouldn't be able to suspend her like that. By my later estimates, he probably could.

We checked out around one. With her damp, disheveled hair and evening wear, the girl looked ridiculous amidst the midday commotion of food stalls and professional letter writers doing business from their desks on the sidewalks of Brazil Street. At that moment, she was the saddest semblance of a woman to be found in all of Mexico. Rojano kissed her on the mouth in the doorway of the hotel. He pushed his tongue between her uneven teeth and held her to him in a prolonged embrace that to my eyes mimicked the anti-erotic simplicity of what he'd done to her the night before. He finished kissing her and ran his hands over her buttocks at the height of midday in the middle of Brazil Street. He dispatched her with 1,000 peso bill which he placed between her drooping breasts.

"Take a taxi," he told her as if issuing an order to a sister or wife. "And don't forget me. I'll go see your mom at the Social Security clinic where she's having her baby, just like I said. I'll have you meet with a friend of mine there. And take care of that ass as if it were your own."

With a pat on the bottom he sent her into the streaming sunlight of the street. She went unsteadily on her way on frail legs and high heels, her damp hair bleached partially blond, swinging her pocketbook.

"That's what happens when they drop out of school," Rojano said, slowly scratching his crotch. His tie was loosely knotted, and he had a day's growth of stubble. He threw an arm over my shoulder, and we started walking. "Provided I don't come down with a case of Vietnamese clap, I consider myself well served." He continued scratching. "I say that not just for myself but for my community, too. Imagine what it would be like for me to show up in Chicontepec with an inflamed cock. The witch doctor couldn't cure me so the whole town would be wiped off the map within a year by an army of spiral bacteria, an epidemic of venereal disease that Dr. Pasteur himself couldn't stop. Because there's no holding back the onslaught."

"What onslaught."

"I've never seen a raunchier town, brother. The priest has three wives, and he's limited by professional restriction. I can't get through a week there without some kind of incident. I even did it with a doe one day. Is there a bar around here?"

We were two blocks from La Puerta del Sol on Palma Street, so we headed in that direction.

"If I tell you what happened, you'll think I'm making it up," Rojano went on. "I mean a group of elders from one of the barrios showed up one day and invited me to a ceremony. It seemed the barrio of San Felipe wanted me to have their staff of leadership, and this involved a ritual for men only. So one afternoon we gathered in the house of the local headman. It was all very formal and hush-hush. First, we sat down to talk, then the bastards opened a jug of mescal to break the ice. Alright, so how about a second jug? Sure. And a puff of marijuana? A joint makes the rounds with the third jug. It's getting dark, and it turns out they have a special gift for the honorable chief municipal authority, for me that is. But the mayor will need to take a short walk in the forest in order to receive his gift, which he must accept before taking the staff of leadership. So we walk out of town and into the forest, and they tell my aide Echeguren, a great kid you're going to meet..."

"I already know him."

"Alright, then. These bastards tell him, 'You can't come into the forest. This is strictly between the honorable chief municipal authority and the elders of Barrio San Felipe.' Now I'm thinking, 'What the hell do these bastards have in store for me once we're alone in the woods?' Still, I tell Echeguren, 'Okay, it's all right if you wait here for me,' and I say to myself, 'But if I'm not back in an hour, burn the fucking town down.' They light their torches, and we march into the woods for some fifteen minutes along paths that only they can follow. We come to a clearing where three or four other bastards are waiting with torches, all smiles and ceremony like a bunch of Chinamen. So they all gather around me, and the barrio headman repeats that the gift is very special and it is being given to the chief municipal authority as a sign of special appreciation. Once they finish buttering me up, another bastard appears out of the woods leading a doe by a rope, a really beautiful animal, not too tall, not yet fully grown, and quite calm for a deer. They tie her to a stake, step aside, and gesture for me to approach her. So I go ahead and approach her. I pet her muzzle and flanks and express my gratitude to the distinguished headman and elders of San Felipe. And as I'm saying this, I realize they look annoyed at me, and the headman keeps gesturing to me to get going. This continues until one of the headman's aides comes up and whispers in my ear that, if I don't show my appreciation for what they're giving me, then they'll give me something I will like. And like an idiot, I say, 'No, the doe is enchanting.' And more thank yous and more dirty looks, and the bastards are getting restive, then one a bit smarter than the others comes up to me and whispers, 'With all due respect, honorable chief municipal authority, this animal is being given to you to see if you acknowledge her as female and get from her the same pleasure as we do'. And that's when it dawned on me. These bastards wanted me to fuck the doe.

And, what's more, they wanted me to do it right there in front of them. I remember that bastard Pizarro comparing Anabela to a deer, so what they're offering me is my wife in animal form, her double, you understand? I mean Pizarro's word is law in that town, and if he says Anabela's double in animal form is a deer, then she's a deer. So here I am deep in the woods with these bastards standing around feeling snubbed and immersed in an I-don't-know-what symbolic universe with the doe in front of me. God damn it, what do you do then?"

"What did you do?"

"What do you mean what did I do? I took a taste of doe. And you want me to tell you the truth?"

"Yes."

"Those bastards were right. It was a superb gift. It made me understand why the Greek gods liked to fuck while disguised as animals."

"Don't make excuses."

"I mean it. The next time you come to Chicontepec, I'll make you the gift of a doe."

I took what he said as an allusion to Anabela. We went into Puerta del Sol, ordered beer, and went to town on the hors d' oeuvres.

"Then we went back to the headman's house," Rojano went on. "You know why?"

"No."

"So the headman could offer me his daughters. The oldest was fifteen, the youngest about eight."

"Didn't he have a one-year-old?"

"No, that's not how it is. He wanted me to see them so he could save them for me, if you know what I mean. Only the fifteen-year-old was available right away."

We ordered shrimp broth, breaded cutlets, and a bottle of cold white wine.

"After all," Rojano said philosophically, "everything should be like screwing. You get hot, you come, you relax, then you get hot again. All the other stuff is pure shit. Leave my wife alone, don't touch your sister, stay away from little boys. And screw animals? How degenerate! So much bullshit. I mean why wouldn't you share your best lay with your best friend. It's only natural, I don't know why it's such a big deal."

I was glad he kept bringing up Anabela. We ordered another bottle of wine, and he started to hand me the check. "Aside from the does," he said, "we need to talk. I didn't really come to see the director of PEMEX. I came to put you on notice."

He took a drink of wine, wiped his mouth, put his elbows on the table, and hunched forward to speak to me in confidence. After looking around to make sure no one was listening in, he said in a low, flat voice, "The war has begun, brother."

He hadn't shaved. His hair was uncombed, his lips were cracked and dry, and his eyes were bloodshot. In his current state, he looked a bit ridiculous as if he were overacting.

"The war of the whores," I replied.

"I mean it, you bastard." Rojano grabbed my wrist and hung onto it. He ran a hand through his hair and finished his glass of wine in two gulps. "Don't be fooled by my tranquilizers, brother. Whores and good wine are facts of life. In Chicontepec it's the law of the jungle. And the one has nothing to do with the other. Don't be fooled."

"What's new with Pizarro?"

He took two photocopies each folded four ways from the back pocket of his pants and slapped them on the table. The first was a brief from the oil workers' union to the Chicontepec town council demanding 2,000 hectares of municipal property for the union's social services activities. The second was Rojano's denial of this request. They bore the dates of September 19 and 24, 1977.

"These are two months old. Why show them to me now?"

"Because last week we got a personal notice from Pizarro. The tooled leather."

"*Who* got personal notice?"

"We got a purchase offer for the lands Anabela inherited in Chicontepec."

"What has Anabela got to do with this fight? It's the municipality's fight."

"It's a fight, brother. It's more than a fight, it's a war. It's our war, and it's started in Chicontepec. I came to tell you and anyone else who would listen. If I can, to tell the director of PEMEX this afternoon. But I've already learned from experience. The whole thing's so crazy that nobody believes me. It's so outlandish that sometimes I don't believe it myself."

The bags had swollen more under his eyes. Their bloodshot whites were now a sign, not of confusion, but of desperation.

His appointment with the director of PEMEX was canceled, and Rojano left town without seeing him. He didn't see me either, though he was quite persistent in his efforts to reach me by phone. The columns about the International Monetary Fund that Arteaga traded for Bloody Marys triggered almost 50 editorials in the days that followed along with a call from the President of the Republic, who invited me to breakfast with three of the country's leading columnists on January 16, 1978. By media standards, this meant I had ceased to be just a columnist and was now something else— "a national opinionmaker" as the director of my paper liked to say. Perhaps it was the autonomy that came with this change that made me write the column in which I tried to win the war in Chicontepec for Rojano and Anabela. Due to my bad timing and miscalculation, I succeeded only in casting them into a fray in which they were defenseless.

The headiness and novelty of that breakfast had yet to dissipate when Anabela called from the Hotel Roma on January 25. We had dinner at the hotel and spent the evening in bed. She had become splendidly slender. Her legs had regained the harmony of bone and muscle they had when we first met. She was beautiful in the boyishly carefree way I remembered, a beauty that was only enhanced by the stretch marks from her pregnancies. Her thinness, however, had nothing to do with being young again. When she started to talk, almost five hours after we met, her iron self-control was on full display, and it was impossible not to see how completely she'd cast her lot with Rojano.

Her version of events was a litany of bad news. They had received a second leather pouch from Pizarro with a plat including the lands that belonged to Anabela and Rojano. The union of municipal workers was demanding a total of more than two thousand hectares (all of which were predictably contiguous). The prior week, on the exact day when I was having breakfast with the President, a small disturbance had broken out in one of the town's barrios. A child had died, and someone blamed it on the drinking water system that had come on line a few days before. Pizarro had posted a permanent detachment of his guards in one of the larger houses on one side of the plaza. In a bar fight Echeguren had injured a guard who was hurling insults at Rojano. The incident struck me as strange because, so far as I knew, Echeguren was unconditionally loyal to Roibal and Pizarro.

"Echeguren is unconditionally loyal to me," Anabela shot back. She looked me straight in the eye in yet another show of her self-assurance and power.

"The point is, the time is quickly coming when we're going to need your help. Things are starting to happen, *Negro*, and we're not ready."

"What kind of help do you want?"

"The kind you can give. Press coverage and public relations. Do you have any contacts in Internal Security?"

"I'd have to check."

"It's important for Internal Security to hear about this from an inside source because it's beyond belief. It's so outlandish and crazy that sometimes I don't even believe it myself."

Her words were identical to Rojano's at the Puerta del Sol. I wondered who was echoing whom and if I were now hearing them from their source.

"And who's your contact in PEMEX?"

"I don't have a contact in PEMEX."

"In the Defense Ministry?"

"Maybe."

"It's important that you memorize this, *Negro*." Anabela was coldly analytical as she laid out the logistics of her situation. "The war has begun. Everything you can do for us helps. Every columnist you know, every newspaper that carries you, every political opening, every conversation, every step towards the fall of Pizarro is fundamental. Every printed line, every doubt planted in the minds of people with the power to take action counts. You know better than I how to do it, you know the ropes. Of course, if something were to reach the ears of the President, that's excellent. Right now we have to get the children out of Chicontepec and down to my sister Alma's in the port. All our friends in state government are on notice, and I do mean all of them. It actually comes to quite a crowd. They're are only two of them that are trustworthy. And you, *Negro*. You more than anyone. You're our bridge to the outside world, our lifeline."

She kissed me as if what she'd just finished saying had aroused her. We made love and fell asleep in each other's arms. At dawn I woke up to go to the bathroom, and she wasn't in the bed. She was sitting naked on the sofa, sleepless and deep in her own thoughts, looking down at the city spread out below the window of our fifth-floor room in the Hotel Reforma.

She left two days later, and in the two days following her departure, I felt an unaccustomed urgency to see her again soon. I was anxious for her to come back. My column for January 29 was a projection of that anxiety in the form of a long think piece about Lázaro Pizarro, more an outgrowth of depression and longing than the tension that makes for good journalism. I wrote:

"In the less visible outposts of his empire, disciples of *La Quina*—oil workers union boss Joaquín Hernández Galicia—have begun to hatch, and they show every indication of surpassing the exploits of their master. They surpass him in ambition, audacity, and initiative. And also, according to detailed reports that reached "Public Life" first, in cruelty and bloodshed. "So far the biggest egg the serpent has hatched is the emerging lord of lives and lands who rules the oil workers union in Poza Rica and is now extending his blood-stained grasp to the remote and fertile realm of Chicontepec in northeastern Veracruz.

"There the up and coming leader of the heroic Oil Workers Union of the Republic of Mexico is taking to extremes *La Quina's* recent infatuation with *union farms* as a means of reducing members' living expenses. He has begun to purge allegedly 'spurious' property owners of some of the best land in the municipality of Chicontepec in the floodplain of the Calaboso River as it flows down from the Sierra.

"The purge has been nothing less than radical. Land owners who decline to sell their holdings on the buyer's terms have simply been wiped off the face of the earth. And the buyer leaves a calling card: a bullet to the temple of his true targets in the midst of shooting sprees or horrible accidents that claim the lives of many more persons than those the oil workers' benefactor aims to get rid of. To date the following incidents have come to light..."

The column summarized the cases contained in Rojano's files. It cited dates, names, and circumstances while holding back on some issues and documents that could be used as ammunition against detractors once the column had its effects.

"The new benefactor in the oil workers' world, the perpetrator of these radical expropriations, is, like *La Quina*, a revered and determined capo, an enthusiastic practitioner of what has come to be called *petro-Maoism*. This is a disciple who is certain to surpass—or who has already far surpassed, at least in shots fired—his mentor.

"Engrave the name of this disciple and successor on your memory because you'll hear it often in coming years. His name is Lázaro Pizarro, the terrible *Lacho*, the new family benefactor of the oil workers of Vera Cruz."

The Internal Security Ministry acknowledged my efforts. By this, I mean a colleague called and invited me to dinner at a restaurant he liked in Colonia Roma. We were to eat at La Lorraine and nowhere else. The owner, a widow from Marseille, had turned the place into a cooperative and bequeathed it to her workers, who all belonged to the Revolutionary Workers and Peasants Confederation. Everything remained as it always had been. The waiters wore black tuxedoes, the patés were made on the premises, and the cheeses were nearly worm-eaten with age. We had barely stepped between the planters in the entryway when we were confronted by my contact on Bucareli Street, who was dining with a friend. He sent us a bottle of Chateneuf-du Pape during our meal and had the waiter who served us dessert invite us to his table for cognac. Predictably, when we went for the cognac, his friend had left, and the issuer of the invitation was alone smoking an acrid *Te Amo* cigar from Tuxtla. As he smoked, he rolled the cigar between his lips , which were noticeably red and moist beneath his pencil moustache. The look in his partially open eyes was perfectly placid. On the pretext of needing to make an urgent phone call, my colleague left, and the appointment began.

"You got it wrong," my contact said. I glanced at his hands and shirt cuffs. He exuded a faint but perceptible aroma of lotion and tobacco that clung to him almost as if it were his sweat. There was a long silence.

"I am speaking about your column today," he went on. "What you say isn't exactly accurate."

"I have proof for what I wrote," I replied.

"I know about your proof. That's why I can tell you things are not the way you described them today."

"Then how are they?"

"They're more complicated," my contact said with a smile. "As they always are."

He took an envelope out of his coat pocket and placed it on the table. Inside were the photos of the killings in Papantla of Antonio Malerva and his family. They had been retouched in several places with a very fine red marker.

"The photos aren't originals." He puffed delicately on his cigar. "They're photomontages. The red lines show where two photos were superimposed. The lines were drawn by the expert who did the analysis."

I picked up the afternoon paper he'd left on the table, the edition for February 2, 1978. With my pen I traced the front-page image of Jimmy Carter greeting an astronaut.

"This is also the work of an expert," I told him.

"No, sir, it isn't," my contact replied with a touch of irritation. "I mean what I say."

He reached his hand into the other side of his coat, brought out an envelope identical to the first one, and laid it on the table. I opened it and got my first look at its incredible contents. It was the most unexpected photo I could ever have imagined, a photo of my own cadaver laid out naked on the slab of a morgue, full frontal and taken from above the body. It showed major hemorrhaging from a bullet wound to the forehead plus several more wounds to the torso, and, what's more, I appeared to have died young. The ruined countenance was my face as it was 20 years ago. I had the body of an adolescent, almost of a child. Underneath, in the inimitable and spidery lettering of a small town official with limited schooling, was a caption that read: *Papantla, Ver., February 17, 1978* (two weeks later than our February 2 conversation).

"Laboratory prophecy," said my contact. "The photo's from your military registration card. The body is real but obviously not yours. The blood, the bullet wounds, the shadings of gray, the montage are also ours. The magic of an expert I should say."

"What did Rojano's expert add?"

"You can tell by the red lines," my contact explained. "He didn't add much, just the shots to the temple, but it was done systematically. An execution-style shot to the temple was added to each photo. The rest—the photos and the corpses and the dates—that's all real. But, as I understand it, that's the crucial detail."

It was.

"There are coroners' statements documenting those shots," I said.

"There are, but they're not decisive. They could also have been arranged. My point is, minus the shots to the temple, what's left? What's left is the piece of the truth that's in your column. And what is that truth? What it amounts to is this. Several property owners around Chicontepec died violent and bloody deaths. Their holdings were contiguous, and they owned the best land in a region of good lands. It cannot be said that this is normal for the area, but it wouldn't frighten anybody in the foothills of Veracruz."

"And who bought these lands?"

"The oil workers' union did. So did Lacho Pizarro. But what does that prove?"

"It indicates that those deaths had a sole beneficiary."

"Sole, no," said my contact. "There were two other buyers. Do you know who they are?"

"That you'll have to prove to me," I said, anticipating the answer.

"I have proof." He removed a third envelope from his coat as if laying a final card on the table. "Francisco Rojano Gutiérrez and Anabela Guillaumín de Rojano are the other beneficiaries."

In the envelope were photocopies of records from the land registry in Tuxpan documenting up to three land purchases by Anabela and Rojano. Between the two of them they bought a total of nearly a 1,000 hectares.

"These are in addition to the 800 I first told you about," my contact said. "Pizarro and the union made similar purchases. But Pizarro didn't doctor any photos to incriminate his friends. Do I make myself clear?"

I understood all too well. My stomach churned uncontrollably. I'd been taken advantage of. It made me angry, but as usual it was too late to do anything about it.

Some two weeks later, Anabela returned to Mexico City and sent word that once again she was at the Hotel Reforma. I stayed away. I didn't go to her room, and I didn't answer the phone that rang incessantly in my apartment for the next two days. Finally, she spent all of an afternoon and evening waiting for me in the newsroom of my paper, which is where we ran into each other at nine o'clock on February 20.

"I spent two days going mad looking for you," she said once we were in my car. "What's the problem?"

"What news are you bringing?"

"I've been looking for you for two whole days. I came to Mexico City to see you. I've spent two days shut up in a furnished room waiting for you to call me, wanting to be with you. You make me feel like a character in some awful soap opera. What's going on?"

"Lots of work, that's what's going on. Didn't you go the Museum of Modern Art?"

"Listen, you bastard." Anabela was livid. "I'm not your typewriter that you can bang whenever you damn well feel like it, and I'm not your bitch either. You don't get to feel hurt and offended on my account. What the hell do I owe you, anyhow?"

"You refer to the column?"

"No." Anabela's eyes welled up with tears. "I mean your use of my ass, creep."

She got out of the car and slammed the door. For a moment I watched her in the rear view mirror. She walked as fast as she could down the sidewalk past a brightly lit shop window. She wiped her eyes. I watched the stride of her long firm legs moving precariously atop her high heels. I activated my door locks and pulled away.

The next day a messenger brought a letter and package from Anabela. The letter said:

"It's possible you know who I am, but you don't know what I feel. I missed you those nights just as I've missed you other nights when you're not around. In Chicontepec, that is. I don't know what's happening, I don't know what's the matter with you. I know you hurt me. I hated you for it, then I again began needing you at night. I have fresh news for you. The situation is critical. Your column stirred up the hornet's nest. The wasps are on the loose and ready to sting. This is all important as you'll see. But, I repeat, I missed you, and you weren't there."

The package documented a new case, the death of a Chicontepec notable in a bar fight in El Álamo. According to Rojano, "Negotiations with Lacho over the use of some community lands had broken down. The package included a crude map of the disputed lands, practically the whole east side of the municipality, a total of some five thousand hectares. In his impeccable block lettering in red ink, Rojano commented, "He told his loyal followers that he now has his Mesopotamia, and this is where he wants his Babylon."

Lázaro Pizarro, leader of the people, founder of civilizations. I picked up the new file together with the others that I had on my desk and threw them in a drawer in a closet I never used.

Chapter 7
DEATH BY WATER

On March 18, 1978, I attended the festivities marking the anniversary of the expropriation of the oil industry in Ciudad Madero. Lázaro Pizarro sat on the reviewing stand next to *La Quina,* but in a clearly subordinate position. Roibal sought me out halfway through the proceedings. Characteristically, I didn't notice as he slipped up behind me and poked me in the rib. His finger might as well have been a pistol.

"The boss wants to know if you'd like to have a word with him." There was an edge of sarcasm in his voice.

"Wherever he'd like," I answered before Roibal could say more.

"Wherever you say."

"At the bar in the Hotel Inglaterra," I said without hesitation. It was the most centrally located hotel in Tampico.

"Are you spending the night in Tampico?" Roibal asked.

"I'm flying out at seven this evening, on the President's plane," I stressed.

"Then in the bar at the Inglaterra. At four?"

"At five," I said. "After the dinner."

"At five then," Roibal agreed.

The meal for 300 people was served at union headquarters. I drank giant Cuba libres over ice from glasses made from the bottom half of Bacardi rum bottles, and acquired through a friend in the presidential entourage. They held nearly half a liter of liquid. We drank three of these as pre-meal refreshment and three more while dining on a profusion of crustaceans, fish, ribs, shrimp and tripe on taco shells, corn and flour tortillas, and a variety of sauces and marinades. Shortly after 5:00 I requested a car from the chief of the press office and a driver from the presidential entourage.

I told the driver whom I was going to see and asked him to leave me at the back of the hotel, then go around to the front and enter the bar like a normal customer. That way he could keep an eye on our meeting. When I entered the bar at exactly 5:30, or half an hour late, the driver was already there nursing a beer. Pizarro was alone at a corner of the bar. He was seated with his back to the wall and a bottle of iced mineral water on the table. Roibal was waiting for me by the street entrance, and two guards stood in the doorway to the hotel. Pizarro remained absolutely motionless as he watched me approach as if I weren't there, or as if he just hadn't noticed me. I'd brought my glass from the dinner with me and was just beginning to feel an alcoholic buzz, "euphoric and ecumenical" as René Arteaga would say. I asked the waiter to refresh my drink over a large dose of ice. On my way to Pizarro's table, I changed my mind and went straight to the bar to have my glass refilled with rum, ice and Coca Cola. Only then did I go to the table where Pizarro had been waiting for half an hour.

"How've you been, chief?" As I spoke, I spun a chair around and sat down spread-eagled on the seat in front of him.

"Waiting for you, my journalist friend," Pizarro said in a nasal monotone that resonated with anger.

"We were delayed by the President," I said after a swallow of my drink. "How are you?"

"I've been slandered, offended, and plotted against, my journalist friend." He spoke in a low voice, nearly a whisper. "The national press says I covet the job of Joaquín Hernández Galicia. They even say I've overshadowed him, that the disciple surpassed the master. Have you read anything like that in the national press, my journalist friend?"

It was hard not to admire his style and his irony. He was indirect and at the same time precise in the way he got to the heart of our dispute without so much as alluding to it. His tone of voice, because it was so flat and impersonal, made any criticism seem doubly hurtful and unfair.

"I've read things like that, chief."

"And what do you think of these accounts?"

"They've been proven false for the most part, chief."

"But there hasn't been any retraction, any effort to repair the damage in the court of public opinion, my journalist friend."

"There has been where it counts. The President was informed as soon as he inquired."

"It's a relief to hear you say that, my journalist friend," Pizarro said. "I worry about your failure to understand, your impudence. Did I mistreat you in Poza Rica? Didn't you like what you saw? Did your brief visit displease you? So why haven't you come back? The door was open for you. Or were you just distracted by visions of doe flesh?"

"That was probably it," I said, then took a long drink.

"If that's the case, it's understood. All you have to do is look at her," Pizarro said. "But you worry me, friend, because I don't think you listened to what I told you. Either that, or the most important part didn't get through to you. You listened to the tales told by your friends instead, the ones they're still telling you. And to what's passed on to you between the sheets. But here's the truth. None of you know what you're getting into, you least of all. You don't know the size of the battle or the size of the force needed to fight it and not lose. Your friends are trying to start a fight they have no business getting into. I told you this before, but you didn't listen. Where these things are concerned, they're amateurs. They think they know what they're doing, but they don't.

They think they see what they're looking at, but they don't. They think they can, but they can't. They hear the sound of the river, but they have no idea how much water it carries, and they know nothing of the streams that form the river. I do know, friend, because I dug the trench that made the river. I know exactly why I did it and what I want the river to irrigate. You people come along with a thimble and think you can change the course of the river by the thimbleful. Just because it's in front of your nose, you want to own it. But you don't know what it took to get the water to where it is and to irrigate what it irrigates. You don't know how much work it took to build that river drop by drop, providing help as needed and getting obstacles out of the way. It takes years of work, my friend. Every month of every year, every day of every month, every hour of every day. And then you people come along and want to take over. You become one of the obstacles that get in the way. And you know why? Simply because you're a bunch of amateurs. You think it's there for the taking by whoever sees it first and decides to grab it. That's not how it is, my friend. There's no such thing as an asset nobody owns or has any claim to. Whoever wants it has to push the prior owner aside and usurp that claim. And that's what I've spent my life doing. It's what I've lived for, it's my profession. What I've learned is simply this. What makes the difference in this game isn't who wins or who gets to keep the assets. The issue, my friend, is who survives because this game is about survival. First, you take care of your enemies, then you look out for yourself. This second form of survival is what really matters, and you can only achieve it by what you build, by what you leave behind for others. Now do you understand?"

"I was bewitched by my diet of doe meat," I said.

"Stings like these last longer than the pain," he said. Once again Pizarro withdrew into himself as if anger had drawn him out of his cave and now, having returned fire, he was staging a cautious return. "Don't declare victory."

He got to his feet, and Roibal was immediately at his side. "I told you what I needed to tell you," Pizarro said. He took leave of me without shaking hands. "I just don't know how long it will take for it to sink in."

He stared at me long enough to make me feel ridiculous, a drunk holding a huge, half empty glass of Cuba libre. "You owe me one, *paisano*." He touched the palm of one hand with the index finger of the other. "I'm making a note of it right here."

He left, and I stayed behind, fixated by his river metaphor. As a snapshot of the way Lázaro Pizarro viewed his earthly mission, it was unequaled. The certainty that buttressed his will had reached the extreme of making him see himself as a kind of god who brought streams together and turned them into a river of his own creation. He was right about that, but what did it have to do with his aspirations as a puppeteer? How many of the strings that moved the plot really were in his hands? He controlled the region with an iron fist. He had Rojano elected mayor, had prior knowledge of what PEMEX was up to, and was in a position to exploit the company's plans for his own ends. In Chicontepec, where he was born, his word was the unwritten law. He'd found jobs for half the youths who left the town, and in it he'd stationed machine-gun-toting guards to watch every move Rojano made. Was he wrong to consider himself a sort of supreme architect, the man in charge of the world around him?

In mid May 1978, on Tuesday the sixteenth, President López Portillo began his trip to the Soviet Union and Bulgaria. His ample entourage included a press plane for reporters from all the media plus a handful of "leading columnists" as *The New York Times* correspondent, an unbearable flatterer, put it in his dispatch for the day. We flew to Gander, a military stopover in Newfoundland, and then to Hamburg where we spent nine hours on the ground before flying on to Moscow. I wrote, "Riding the coattails of President López Portillo were the four airplanes for his entourage of some seven hundred people. These included the presidential family, ministers and directors of decentralized state-owned enterprises, journalists, technical support crews for radio and television, organizational staff, singers and actors, the corps of the Mexican folk ballet, museum directors, and the anthropologists charged with setting up their exhibits. We watched the sun rise over Glasgow and saw the moist and renovated city of Hamburg come into view below us, precisely spread out amidst an astonishing number of trees and green zones. A red-eyed press corps succeeded in finding a place to eat pozole in the Rothembaumhaus. In the lobby of the Hamburg Plaza Hotel, Fidel Velázquez, the ageless head of the Mexican Workers Confederation, chatted with his relatives in monosyllables. He was not part of the official entourage, but when Mexico travels, so do its traditions."

The night of Wednesday, May 17, we landed at Vnukovo 2, the airport on the southwest outskirts of Moscow. Two kilometers of parked commercial aircraft flanked the taxiways. The tour of the Soviet Union lasted a week. We visited the Kremlin, bought nesting dolls and amber necklaces, and spent a white night in Leningrad. We saw where Lenin printed *Iskra* in Bakú on the Caspian Sea, and at night we heard the eerie sound of the wind crying through the narrow trenches miners dug into coal seams around the city. We went to Novosibirsk and the city of science, Academgorodok, the campus home of 30,000 scientists.

Then we went to Bulgaria. We spent hours walking the tree-flooded streets of Sofia and won 5,000 dollars at the casino in Varna where the trip ended. Reyes Razo and I broke away from the entourage to celebrate our luck at the casino with a side trip to Athens. We imposed on the hospitality of Ambassador Cabrera Maciá and spent two days with a pair of Cypriot sisters who taught us the Greek words *lestá* (money) and *thalasa* (sea). From Athens we flew to Paris where we strolled our way through museums and cafes. We had sumptuous meals at La Coupole and Fouquet's where Reyes Razo turned down two already opened bottles of a world famous vintage because he considered the wine slightly thin. We visited Cortázar and the dives of Montmartre. We drank champagne, chatted up chorus girls, and hired our own company for four days of partying after which we still had 3,000 dollars left over. We spent half of that in London and the other half in New York. On June 12, I wired my newspaper for two plane tickets back to Mexico City. Reyes Razo put the 300 dollars we owed the hotel on his credit card.

On June 15, 1978, we landed at the international airport in Mexico City. A reporter from my paper was waiting for us. The look on his face was not good, and he didn't hesitate to say why. A week earlier, in the early hours of June 9, the town of Chicontepec had gone up in flames. There had been an attack on the city government building, and Mayor Francisco Rojano Gutiérrez had been lynched.

Doña Lila had taken a tidal wave of phone calls and messages. A good many of them were from Anabela, long distance calls from Veracruz and Tuxpan and two from Chicontepec the day after it burned. "The woman's gone crazy. She's called you two and even three times a day every day," Doña Lila said. "Like a lost soul in Purgatory."

I called Veracruz to check in with Anabela's sister, but Anabela wasn't there. I got my first account of what happened from her sister. The town hall was surrounded on the night of June 8 in mourning for two children who died of dysentery. The demonstrators accused the municipal authorities of poisoning them with drinking water from the pipes laid the month before. The attack came around midnight after someone fired at the grieving relatives. The crowd charged the government building, and more shots were fired, wounding two of the protesters, one of whom subsequently died. Then the building was torched. They got Rojano out and dragged him around the plaza. A town leader entered the Guillaumín house with his sons. They held Anabela captive all night and refused to let her leave, thus saving her life.

I hung up and went to look for my contact in the Ministry of Internal Security. I was trembling, bitten by the irrational conviction that there was a causal link between my absence from Mexico and Rojano's death. I went over and over my own activities during the crucial day. Eighth of June, lunch at El Plaza, *Deep Throat* at a porno movie theater, the evening performance of *Oh Calcutta* on Broadway followed by martinis at Dino's on Sixth Avenue and listening to Brenda McGuire sing *"killing me softly with your fingers"* while Rojano was being surrounded in the government headquarters of a non-existent town in western Veracruz.

No one answered at Internal Security. I checked the newsroom file at the paper. All I found was a terse account filed two days after the fact from our correspondent in Veracruz. "Chicontepec Mayor Francisco Rojano Gutiérrez was killed yesterday during a popular uprising that claimed the lives of at least two others. At last reports, the incident also left five injured, two of them seriously. The disturbance on the night of June 8 was sparked by townspeople protesting the deaths of two children. Rioters blamed the deaths on contamination of the water system installed in the town a month ago.

"Eyewitnesses interviewed by phone said the mayor

and his staff were dragged from their offices and lynched, and the town hall was burned down. The mob apparently became violent when shots were fired from the building where the mayor and his aides were holed up."

I reached our correspondent in the newsroom at *El Dictamen* in Veracruz. By phone he added more details. To begin, he gave me the name of the source who spoke to him directly from Chicontepec: Genaro Roibal. The information for the one published report of the affair had come from Roibal. In later inquiries the reporter had pieced together a more complete approximation of what happened.

On June 8, 1978, the bells of Chicontepec rang in mourning. The whole town knew they rang for Miguel Yacomán, leader of the Barrio San Antonio. He had been gravely ill and his condition had deteriorated in the past week due to the water. This marked the third death attributable to water problems, specifically to the pipelines laid early that year to supply two thirds of the town (which had previously depended on wells, ditches and rainfall runoff) with drinking water. The two prior deaths, also the result of serious stomach infection, were in the barrio of San Felipe, also served by the new system. Residents began to blame these deaths—preceded by the bouts of vomiting and bloody diarrhea quite common in the area—on water from the pipelines. Yacomán's funeral procession followed the traditional route from one side of town to the other, but as it passed the town hall, the marchers pointed to the coffin and shouted in Totonaca, *Here's your water, honorable authority.* That same day there was another unrelated death, and the townspeople, who were already in a dark mood, took it as proof that the evil eye was at work. It happened in Yucuman's own barrio when a young Indian boy attempted to mount a yoked ox. The animal threw the youngster against a fence and broke his neck. His small coffin was added to the procession, compounding the community's grief. By 6:00 in the evening the funeral had become a demonstration. The coffins were placed before the town hall, and the ensuing wake quickly became an orgy of protest and blame. It was about 6:00 when prayers began, minus the priest, who refused to officiate outdoors. Torches were lit, and the mescal started to flow. The mayor made an appearance and, standing before the crowd, spoke at length with its leaders. Some of the demonstrators even went inside the town hall and stayed there for over an hour. Around 11:00 the town council ordered the serving of two barrels of atole at public expense. At midnight the women began a long lamentation in Totonaca. In the midst of this commotion the first two shots rang out. One came from a corner of the plaza, the next two from its opposite side. Then machine-gun fire pelted the plaza from all sides like a thunder and lightning storm. The panicked crowd clustered about the dead. After one of the leaders spoke, old carbines, pistols and scythes appeared. More rounds of machine-gun fire raked the plaza from all sides, and the angry crowd shouted threats at the town hall. There was one shot and then another. Two of the mourners were downed. Others broke through the door of the town hall and set it on fire. Burning torches were hurled through the windows. Shortly afterwards, the crowd surged into the inner patio where there was more shooting and more casualties as protesters dragged out the mayor and his aides, some seven or eight persons in all. When they got to Rojano, an aide stepped forward and tried to intervene. He had a pistol and threatened to shoot whoever came near. No one was deterred by the threat of young Echeguren. The youth got off a single shot before being bludgeoned and hacked to death by machetes. Protesters hauled the captives into the plaza, bleeding, beaten, and with their hands tied. Another round of machine-gun fire further infuriated the crowd, and they vented their wrath on Rojano. The morning sun rose over his body on the paving stones in front of the town hall. He was half naked, and his hands were tied behind his back. He lay in the middle of a pile of stones, rigid and bloated beyond recognition.

"Who fired the machine guns?"

"Rojano's people," the correspondent said.

"What people?"

"The people Roibal was leading."

"But those weren't Rojano's people?"

"They weren't townspeople either. They were there to look out for the interests of the mayor and Lacho Pizarro."

"Then why didn't they intervene?"

"Intervene? If you don't mind me saying so, intervening would have been idiotic," the correspondent said. "Who would dare get a crowd like that even more riled up?"

"The people barricaded in the town hall might dare."

"You mean you agree with me that it would have been idiotic?"

"I agree it's something they might have considered."

"Are you going to write about this? I can get you more information. The widow's here in the port, and it's under investigation by the state government."

"Never mind the widow," I said. "Help me with the official investigation."

"Whatever you say."

"That's what I say."

"All right. How do I get back to you?"

I gave him my phone numbers and re-dialed Veracruz looking for Anabela. I found her this time, or I almost did. She'd returned home, but it sounded as if she were somewhere else. Her voice was cold and her reflexes slow and subdued as if they'd been buried under a landslide of obstacles and barriers.

"I want to go to Mexico City with my children," she said at last. "I'm thinking of taking a plane tomorrow. Can you pick me up?"

Naturally, I said yes. I hung up and again tried to reach Internal Security. One of my contact's aides answered. He wanted to know exactly where I was, how long would I be there, and if I could stay put for an hour. The hour was nearly up when Doña Lila answered the door. The aide was outside with my contact standing behind him.

"I'm about to receive another set of doctored photos from Chicontepec," I told him before he could sit down.

"A terrible occurrence," he said expressionlessly. He unbuttoned his jacket and made himself comfortable on the sofa. "There's one fact about all this that makes us extremely uneasy."

"I warned you about this more than a year ago, sir. I warned you when it had just begun."

"With skewered information, *paisano*."

"It was true."

"No, it wasn't." my contact said. He took out the gold cigarette case where he kept his aromatic, dazzlingly white Dunhills. "*It came to be true*, but it wasn't at the time."

"How many deaths do you need to make something true?"

"None, *paisano*. What I'm saying is that your case turned out to be true in light of the fact we find deeply troubling."

As was his custom, he reached for an envelope in his coat pocket and handed it to me. In it were photos of Rojano's body lying in the cobblestone streets of Chicontepec before the town government building. His nose was broken, his forehead looked out of line, and there was blood on his exposed teeth. One eye was open. The other was swollen into a welt resembling a pear sitting on a chopping block formed by his eyelid. The skin had peeled off on parts of his head, his collarbone had been broken on one side, and the arm connected to it was sectioned into three pieces.

"This could have been avoided if your people had acted in time," I said, dizzied by the sight of the ruined remains on the stone street.

My contact observed a brief silence.

"Do you see the detail? I'm referring to the hole in the mayor's left temple from the final bullet."

I looked again, and there it was. Part of the impression created by the smashed face in the photos was attributable to an impact that deformed the forehead and left side of the skull.

"That must be a photo doctored by his wife to trick you into blaming Pizarro." A knot formed in my throat. I was nauseous from looking at the mutilated corpse.

"It's a shot from a .357 Magnum, a collector's item. Nobody in Mexico has one. It's hard to see how anybody could own one in Chicontepec."

"Then you already have a report with the facts?"

"We have a report with the facts."

"And what does your report conclude?"

"Our conclusion could be exactly what I'm telling you. The things your photos lied about came true in these. The mayor of Chicontepec was finished off by a shot in the head, and he was shot in the head without the least need to do so. That final shot is a kind of signature, the work of people that had nothing at all to do with the lynch mob, people in a position to own such oddities as a .357 Magnum."

"I want a copy of the report," I said.

"Fine. I'll just need to review it."

"Go ahead and review it, but my war in the paper begins this afternoon, and I don't care where it leads."

He lit the cigarette he'd taken out and held it between his manicured fingers. There was something soothing about the symmetrical flame from his gold lighter. He inhaled and exhaled while leaning back in order to return the lighter to his pocket. Then he leaned forward again.

"In my eyes," he said, "you and I are friends. Professionally and politically I respect you. And I personally admire the way you handle yourself politically, and professionally. And your human qualities. So don't misunderstand what I'm going to tell you. Consider it the opinion of a friend who wants the friendship to continue and grow in the future. What I want to tell you is this. Your wars in the newspaper have a way of becoming shooting wars in real life. I'm not saying that was the only reason, but your column about Pizarro contributed to the lynching of your friend the mayor of Chicontepec. A saying that applies equally to politics and war is that the ground in hell is paved with good intentions."

"But what makes this country a living hell are the things the government overlooks," I said. "So you're right. The rest of us only pave the way."

I picked her up at the airport, and Doña Lila went with me. She appeared on the stairway to the baggage claim area wearing gold-rimmed glasses and lipstick as bright and pink as a bougainvillea. She had outfitted herself in a tailored orange suit set off by a scarf that fluttered about her collar as she walked. Her children trotted along behind the scarf, spurred on by Anabela, who strode purposely forward on a minimal pair of flesh-colored shoes.

"She's making no secret of her grief," Doña Lila murmured over my shoulder while we waited for them to reclaim their checked luggage which consisted of an enormous old-fashioned trunk, three sets of suitcases, and four cardboard boxes.

Francisco Rojano Guillaumín, nicknamed Tonchis, was

eight, and bore a disconcerting resemblance to his father. He had the same long straight eyelashes that had the effect of making him look cross-eyed and slightly drunk, the same thick, very black hair that combed without a drop of oil, the same slightly protruding chin, and ears without lobes as if they were simply extensions of his jaw. His torso was a bit longer than his legs, and there was a magnetic sparkle in his bright eyes. They seemed alert and insatiable as if nothing in his surroundings escaped them. While awaiting their bags, he talked to his sister Mercedes, making her laugh, and held Anabela's arm as if he were escorting her, the mildly comedic gesture of support yet another reminder of Rojano.

At seven, his sister Mercedes was a child whose sculpted features suggested the beauty to come. She wore a cyan blue dress, and there was not a single bulge of baby fat on her face or body, which already showed signs of replicating, upon reaching adolescence, the appearance of her mother. Doña Lila greeted Anabela, planted a kiss on Francisco, and drew close to Mercedes, playfully instructing her about how young ladies ought to behave. Everyone coming and going in the wide airport passageways, she said, kept an eye on young ladies arriving from Veracruz, especially the ones in blue dresses.

"I'd rather not go to a hotel," Anabela said as we started on our way to the parking area with a parade of porters behind us.

"We can look for a furnished apartment," I said.

"We can set up the rooms you're not using on *Artes*," she told me.

There were, in fact, two rooms on *Artes* where I had nothing but file cabinets, books and junk. Doña Lila kept them clean and turned one into a sewing room with a Singer, a dress dummy, a cutting table, and an ironing board.

"I need to be someplace safe," Anabela said. "A known

place. I can't be alone with the children in a hotel. Just thinking about that is out of the question. Do you understand?"

"I do."

"And do you want to?"

"I understand, and I want to. I'm in mourning too."

"I'm not in mourning, *Negro*," Anabela said. She increased her pace to catch up with Mercedes, who was holding onto Doña Lila's arm. She put a curl that had escaped the little girl's ponytail back in its place. This left Tonchis on his own by my side. He quickly closed the gap between us and took hold of my arm.

"My mom's been crying for four whole days," he said without being asked. "Her eyes were like this: look. She wouldn't come out of her room. She kept it dark the whole time, and she wouldn't even watch television."

It was 11:00 in the morning. We left the trunks and boxes at *Artes* and went shopping for things to put in the vacant rooms. The rattan furniture Anabela wanted was very expensive. She bought two small beds for the children, a chest of drawers, two chairs, and a bed for herself. She paid with a sizable check which nonetheless left a substantial balance in her account.

I got back from the newspaper about 10:00 that night. The house smelled of chocolate and toast. My papers had been organized to where you could see the desktop beneath them. The furniture was rearranged to make the sala look larger, and pictures and photos previously strewn about the vacant rooms now hung on the walls. Lamps and sofas had been moved, and a set of individual place mats adorned the diningroom table. The children had gone to bed, and Doña Lila and Anabela were cutting the baggage tags off the last of the cardboard boxes.

"All I've done was follow orders," Doña Lila said by way of explaining the renovations.

Two pages with lutes emerged from the box along with the rest of our newly acquired population of porcelain figurines.

Doña Lila got ice and served two vodkas with quinine water. "If you don't need anything else, I'll take my own bottle to the attic and see you in the morning," she said on her way to the door.

Anabela set her porcelains aside, embraced her, and thanked her. They walked down the hallway to the door with their arms about each other exchanging words that culminated in another longer embrace.

Anabela went to the bedroom and returned in sandals. She had wrapped herself in a blue eiderdown robe with big shoulder pads and a high collar. She took a long drink of vodka, settled into the sofa with her knees under her chin, and regarded me with round, exhausted eyes.

"Thanks," she said.

Though her deep-set eyes grew moist, she shed no tears.

"Mercedes is gorgeous." I said.

"Yes."

"And your son really looks out for you."

Again she said yes, and broke into tears.

"They didn't see or hear anything," she said. "They just know their dad died. The don't know any of the details."

"It's better that way."

"There's no such thing as better, *Negro*. It's horrifying."

"It is. I spent yesterday investigating it. It doesn't end here. At least not as far as I'm concerned."

She wiped her eyes and smiled before finishing the rest of her vodka. "Give me another."

I made her another drink and refilled the vodka and ice in my own half empty glass.

"Where were you?" she asked. "I heard you called in from New York, but nothing else."

"I got my share of the oil windfall," I said.

"How many New York girls?"

"No New York girls."

"How many New York boys, then?"

"Boys, yes. Around seventeen."

"I knew there was something the matter with you," she said smiling. "After all, why let them go to waste? Right? Have you heard the latest revelation from the historians of the Mexican Revolution?"

"No."

"They proved Pancho Villa was a lesbian. That's why he was so fond of women."

She laughed softly with a naturalness born of fatigue. She drank more vodka, this time just a normal sip. She tilted her head to one side on her knees and slowly, mechanically began rubbing her shin through the fabric.

"What is it that you investigated?" she asked, massaging herself.

"The death of the headman Yacomán, the death of the boy with the ox, the crowd in the plaza."

"What else?"

"That a deal had gone down. They'd gone into the town hall, they'd negotiated, the atole had been served."

"That's right."

"And then someone fired."

"Yes."

"It was Roibal and his people. They fired into the air, round after round to get the crowd worked up and angry all over again."

"Yes," Anabela said. "But they didn't just fire in the air. They shot at the people too."

"From where? Where were they located?"

"All over the place, on the roofs. But the only ones who shot at people were the ones on the roof of the town hall."

She spoke in a low hoarse voice as if she'd been drugged. "That's why the crowd attacked the building?"

"Yes."

"I was told you were kidnapped by one of the headmen and his sons."

"That's what happened. They were actually saving my life, but I didn't realize that until later. During all the hours I was shut in and the momentary outburst of violence, I was certain they were going to take care of me the way the crowd took care of Ro. I also wondered if they'd hand me over to Roibal's people. I wasn't scared. It made me angry but not scared. Powerless and angry."

She took another drink. She re-accommodated herself with her thighs drawn up next to her body, her long thighs.

"They told me about Ro and what happened to Arturo Echeguren when he tried to defend him. Do you remember Echeguren? He turned against Roibal and Pizarro. He was on our side now. They hung him naked from a tree."

The image of the poincianas came flooding back to me like an orange wave from the day of Rojano's swearing in.

"We could hear the mob from the house." Anabela's voice was slow and measured. "The lit torches passed by the window, but they wouldn't let me look out. They had me tied to a sofa, and only the headman—Sebastián—and his sons watched through the window. Two of them minded the door. We heard the machine-gun fire and people screaming. They all screamed in Totonaca, but it might as well have been Swedish. I didn't understand a thing except that they were shouting and screaming."

Once again the tears welled up. She simply and involuntarily cried without sobbing, with no lump in her throat. The tears flowed from her eyes and down her cheeks in thin bright streams.

"The army came in the morning. By then, there was

nothing left to be done. The town was deserted. The monkeys in the mountains were noisier than ever. So were the cicadas and the crackle from the burning remains of the town hall. The soldiers came to my house, a Captain Lerma. He was wearing camouflage fatigues. You know the kind, mottled green to blend in with the jungle. Sebastián's sons went to get them. They handed me over to them and left. I must have been in really bad shape because, you know what the captain did first?"

"No."

"He asked if I wanted him to get the priest. He'd already been told who I was. I asked him if he'd found Ro. He said yes, and I said I wanted to see him. It wasn't a pleasant sight, he told me. I'm not asking your advice, I said. I'm telling you to let me see my husband's body. So he took me to see it."

"I have photos," I said. Or tried to say since I'd lost my voice.

"They were so awful," Anabela said, also losing her voice.

"I saw photos," I repeated, this time audibly.

"He was tied up face down in front of the building," Anabela went on. "They were taking pictures when I got there. Two soldiers carried him into the house and laid him out on the big table, remember? My great grandfather brought that table from New Orleans the year Porfirio Díaz took power in the revolt at Tuxtepec. That's where they put him. I put water on to boil. I did it myself because all the women on the household staff had left the night before along with the rest of the town. The priest actually did come by, but I forbid him to do anything. I cleaned up Ro's body myself, washing away the blood, dissolving the clots in his hair, the dirt, and the injuries. I stood vigil by bathing him. He had a day's growth of stubble, his beard was very thick. I'll tell you something that's going to sound crazy to you, but it's true. By the time I finished bathing him and wrapping him in his white *huipil*, two hours had gone by. But by the end of those two hours, I swear he had more stubble. It grew, *Negro*. And that was more than I could take. The sense that he was alive, that under that cadaverous pallor, he was still alive. I fainted."

She closed her eyes, her legs still folded against her upper body. Then she was still. She barely breathed for several long minutes. "Come on," she said at last, inviting me to sit next to her where she was on the sofa. "It's been a very long day. I can't thank you enough for everything you did today."

She leaned back onto my chest so I could put my arm over her shoulders. Her hands as always were cold, but her whole body trembled like a rabbit when you hold it in your arms. We spent an hour in silence, united by her trembling.

Chapter 8
THE EMISSARY

The day after Anabela arrived in Mexico City, June 17, 1978, I wrote up the Chicontepec story and the lynching of Rojano using all the information I'd been able to gather including my off the record interviews with my *paisano* at Internal Security. It took up five columns—nearly thirty pages in all—and ran on successive days from Monday to Friday, June 19 to June 23. It was my first ever act of unfettered free expression, no self-censorship, no weighing of interests and sources. All the cards went on the table face up.

Inevitably, there was a furor, a barrage of phone calls, alarms and explanations. Fists were pounded on tables in government offices in Veracruz. There were debates in the state legislature and calls for a political investigation from the opposition. Incidents from the violent past of the oil workers' union were exhumed amidst a welter of threats and disclaimers. A cyclone of words and paper riled the atmosphere for three weeks, after which Rojano was still dead, the investigation of his death plodded on, and the state legislature named as interim mayor of Chicontepec a Pizarro loyalist. Now more than ever I was a national opinion maker, and Anabela continued to sleep alone in her rattan bed in a room of my apartment on Artes Street.

On July 29, 1978, I got another call from my contact on Bucareli. We ate from a stand that sold tamales and pozole on Alvaro Obregón. He asked me to interview Pizarro. Pizarro himself wanted me to, he said, and from that night on he served as an unofficial intermediary. The public backlash from the Chicontepec case was on its way to becoming an affair of state, he said. Provided there was no interference with the ongoing investigation, it was in the government's interest for the opposing parties to negotiate.

"I have nothing to negotiate with Pizarro," I said.

"There's always something to negotiate, *paisano*," my contact answered characteristically. "And in this case more than ever. I've investigated Pizarro, and I can tell you he stops at nothing. He'll go after you as readily as he'll go after the widow. Or the widow's children."

"Threatening me is part of being an intermediary?" I said.

"Part of my friendship is to tell you the truth and to protect you as best I can," my contact said. "I understand you're providing Mrs. Rojano and her children with a place to stay."

"That's right."

"Don't be upset. Those kids have been touched by tragedy, but their parents have enormous holdings in Chicontepec, holdings that don't do the children a bit of good where they are. They might as well be heirs to buried treasure. With all due respect, let me suggest that's something else that could be negotiated with Pizarro."

I got to my feet and marched off from the food stand without another word. I'd agreed to meet the director of my paper at the grill in the Hotel del Prado where our after-dinner conversation lasted past midnight. I got back to the apartment around one. Everyone was asleep in the penumbra. I got out the paperwork on a proposed nuclear energy bill and reviewed it with a nightcap of whiskey in my hand. I read the bill, underlined it, and began to review its history and implications as outlined in the support materials. At one point I looked up to see Anabela standing in the doorway, deigning to visit my room for the first time since Rojano's death.

It was nearly dawn when I told her of the encounter with my contact the night before. She waited in silence for my indignation to subside.

"Your friend's right," she said at last. "We have to negotiate with Pizarro."

"What is it you want to negotiate?" I asked, or shouted rather.

"My life and the life of my children."

"Are you afraid he'll kill the three of you?"

"I'm not afraid of anything, *Negro*. After what happened to Rojano, I'm less afraid than ever. But I need time."

"Time for what?"

"To get back at him, *Negro*. To get back at him, that's all."

I made it known that we would negotiate provided the talks took place in Mexico City under the aegis of Internal Security. The conditions were accepted provided that I— and not Anabela—attend the meeting. We gathered on the morning of August 9, 1978, in a small conference room at the Hotel Reforma. My contact came for me at eight thirty, and shortly after 9:00 Roibal escorted us to the table where Pizarro was already waiting. He was alone with only a glass of mineral water in the no-man's-land he always created between himself and the food and eating utensils elsewhere on the table.

"I'll witness the negotiation," my contact announced. "Let me just remind those present that to negotiate means to yield on some points in order to gain on others. The President will be briefed on the outcome of this conversation."

"My thanks to you, sir, and to the President," Pizarro said, slowly rotating his glass of mineral water. "Tell me what I can do for you, my journalist friend."

Without further ceremony, I laid out Anabela's

conditions: indemnification for Rojano's death, payment at market value for all family properties in the municipality of Chicontepec (some three thousand hectares with grazing herds and four houses), clearing Rojano's name on the public record, and an end to harassment of the family, Anabela, and her children.

"The things it's in my power to give are granted forthwith," Pizarro said. "Let Internal Security and the state government determine the market value of family properties within the municipality, and the union will promise to purchase them at the best prices. The indemnification you request for the mayor's death is not in my power to grant because I'm not an insurance company. Nor am I in a position to clear anybody's public record. Concerning harassment of the family, I haven't harassed them. I have no reason to harass them. What I can offer, with help from Internal Security, is to look into who's responsible for this harassment and to let you know so you can negotiate with the responsible party."

In reply I spoke directly to my contact. "I want an explicit commitment from the leader of the oil workers not to make any attempt on the lives of the Rojano Guillaumín family."

"There's no need to ask for that," Pizarro hastened to add. "It's a given."

I'd touched a nerve, and I pressed the demand. Pizarro refused to give in. "He's claiming the oil workers resort to such tactics, and that's a charge we cannot accept."

"Absent an explicit commitment from the leader of the oil workers," I responded, "I request that the President be advised that I hold the oil workers' leader responsible for everything that has happened or may happen in the future affecting the physical wellbeing of the Rojano Guillaumín family, and that includes the murder of the mayor of Chicontepec."

"What you're saying is unfair, my journalist friend."

Pizarro sounded deflated, and there was no mistaking the anger in his voice. "And so is what you've written. I had my differences with your friend, political and historic differences that I described to you with the example of a river. Fundamental differences. But you need to accept reality. I didn't kill your friend. Your friend was killed by the people of Chicontepec, the people who lived with him, the people he governed. Those are the facts, friend. The rest is anecdote, circumstantial. You're asking me to take responsibility for a death brought on by the anger of the people. All right, I'll accept that responsibility. I accept responsibility for that death along with each and every one of the inhabitants of Chicontepec who lynched your friend. I'll even go so far as to agree in the name of the people of Chicontepec and the union of oil workers to indemnify the widow for her terrible misfortune in marrying a man who was executed at the hands of his own people. But as an oil worker I cannot acknowledge any responsibility for the harassment you say the family has suffered or the catastrophe that was your friend's own doing. I have no interest in other people's wives." Pizarro's allusion to my situation with Anabela was crystal clear. "For better or for worse."

My contact hastened to intervene. "We now have agreement on two of the issues under negotiation. The purchase of family property within the municipality at a fair market price and indemnification for the death of the mayor. Correct?"

Pizarro agreed.

"All right, then," my contact continued, "I now ask that the family take off the table its demand to have the name of Rojano Gutiérrez cleared on the public record. There's nothing the oil workers' can do about that, anyway. The state government has to take care of that, not the union."

His words amounted to an unspoken promise that

the question of Rojano's record would be pursued in other channels. I accepted.

"And I also ask," my contact went on, "that the family rephrase its references to the harassment it's suffered in a less confrontational way. If you agree, Lacho, the compromise could be that you and your group *will be vigilant* in seeing that no further harm comes to the relatives of the tragically deceased mayor of Chicontepec."

"Especially the children," Pizarro said.

"I consider the distinction inappropriate," my contact said, sensing Pizarro's reticence with regard to Anabela.

"It's appropriate," Pizarro said, "because children are the country's future, and we must give them priority since the rest of us belong to the past."

"That's not the case," my contact said.

"Sir, it is precisely the case," Pizarro said.

"If Anabela's not part of the deal, then there is no deal," I said.

"I already told you, my journalist friend, I have no interest in other people's wives. For better or for worse."

"Does she remain part of our agreement?" my contact inquired.

"As far as I'm concerned, she's always been part of it," Pizarro stated ambiguously. He fixed his eyes on the glass of mineral water from which he'd yet to drink. "So, Mr. Undersecretary," he told my contact, "if you would be so kind, I'd ask you to inform the President that we have buried our differences since I only agreed to this negotiation in order to serve him."

"So be it, Lacho."

"And, my journalist friend, the door to my humble house in Poza Rica remains open, and you're welcome to visit whenever you like."

We shook hands. Roibal stepped up to escort him.

Attentive and withdrawn, Roibal ignored me as if we'd never so much as crossed glances in the past. "Give my regards to your man Echeguren," I said as they filed through the hotel lobby, but they gave no sign whatsoever of recognition.

"Are we going to sign the minutes?" I asked my contact.

"As soon as there's an assessment and the contracts are drawn up."

"When?"

"Three months at most. Are you worried?"

"On two counts. The first is that the sale price be adjusted upwards in light of PEMEX's planned investments in the Chicontepec paleocanal."

"And the second?"

"That there be no distinction between Anabela and the children in the clause that binds the union to be *vigilant* in seeing to it that no further harm comes to the family."

"Agreed."

"And if anything does happen to the family, your people will again be responsible."

"Calm down, *paisano*. Pizarro put his standing with the President on the line here. If he violates this agreement, he loses everything. It would be suicidal."

"All Lázaro Pizarro cares about is his standing with Lázaro Pizarro."

Three months later, on November 6, 1978, we traveled to Xalapa to sign off on the sale of Rojano's and Anabela's holdings in Chicontepec for 30 million pesos, or slightly less than 1.5 million dollars according to the exchange rate at the time.

The attorney for Local 35 of the oil workers union made the lump sum payment under an agreement that also required the union to cover all transfer fees and taxes. By this time I had rented an office on Hamburg Street where

I wrote, kept my files, and handled all other aspects of my job at the newspaper. An accumulation of furniture, planters, hangings, and porcelain statuary had converted my apartment on *Artes* into a rough approximation of Anabela's and Rojano's house in Veracruz. Tonchis and Mercedes called me uncle. With every passing week, Anabela slept more nights with me,though we made a point of waking up in our respective beds every morning. Doña Lila was surprisingly maternal in the way she looked after the children, especially Mercedes. Anabela went to the gym mornings after dropping her children at school and ran the household with the condescending yet cordial support of Doña Lila. She signed up for classes to improve her French, and in September she unexpectedly returned to the Faculty of Political Sciences to complete the semester and a half she'd needed to graduate upon dropping out in the 60s.

We ate out frequently, going one by one through the restaurants along *Insurgentes* and *Reforma* and in the small world of the *Zona Rosa*. Then, we'd lock ourselves up in a motel, almost always the Palo Alto (first encounter), though there were other times when we took an upscale suite in a stylish hotel just because we could afford it.

We did and we didn't live together. I often traveled to cover political events outside the capital, and then, after six months of staying put, in late 1978, Anabela made her first trip to Veracruz. A month later, she went back to arrange the transfer of Rojano's body to a crypt she bought especially for him in the French Cemetery. In mid January 1979, we collected the coffin at the airport and took it by hearse to its destination in a bower of tall eucalyptus trees. Anabela, the children, Doña Lila, and I attended the burial by ourselves. We threw a dozen red flowers and two modest wreaths in the grave. "He's better off close by," Anabela said as gravediggers finished their task. Her deep-set eyes filled with tears.

Life went on–or appeared to go on–undisturbed. Anabela began organizing dinner parties and get-togethers on *Artes*. The guests were friends and acquaintances: politicians, columnists, reporters, press officers, and staff from my paper. Once or twice a week part of the crowd would show up on *Artes*, and, unfailingly, Anabela would make some sinister reference to Pizarro or tell some dark tale touching on her experiences with him. This seemed only natural given what she'd recently been through and the recurring impact it was bound to have on her state of mind. I quickly understood, however, that neither sentimental weakness nor any psychological difficulty accounted for her refusal to stop thinking about the hell Pizarro put her through. Anabela was conducting a disciplined assessment of the means at her disposal for vengeance. For the time being, that meant filling the heads of those who sat down at her table with information about the world of Pizarro, especially the heads of those in a position to disseminate—or take action on—what she told them.

She had, in fact, built a thick dossier on the man, a meticulous accumulation of news stories, photos and official reports on Pizarro and his workers' revolution (manifestos, flyers etc.). Our correspondent in Veracruz contributed a substantial collection of interviews, state government documents, family history, union history, and crimes and abuses he was found or alleged to have committed. Between Anabela's arrival in Mexico City with her children in June 1978 and the day the land sale was completed in Xalapa, her file on Pizarro grew from two to twelve organized boxes. It included a small bibliography of books and articles about the region of Chicontepec, the oil industry, the union, agrarian issues, violence, indigenous groups, area bosses, and life in the municipality.

During those months, the city was undergoing a frenzy of street widening, and *Artes* was among the thoroughfares targeted for modernization. On the morning of November 18, 1978, the entrance to the building was blocked when a rear-end loader dumped a mound of dirt and gravel in the doorway. I wrote a column about the horrors of the urban renewal to which the city was imperiously subjected by its tycoon mayor, Carlos Hank González, but it was well after noon before I could get out. I used the downtime to review Anabela's files, including one I paid particular attention to. It contained detailed information about the union's social service activities around Poza Rica over the past ten years, the years of Pizarro's leadership. Nothing was left out. There were clinics and child care centers, schools, discount stores, scholarship programs, interest-free lending agencies. Plus the famous union gardens.

Aside from "La Mesopotamia," the union had fostered within Pizarro's sphere of influence two more agricultural operations. "Egypt" was located near the Tuxtlas and grew tobacco and coffee. "Tenochtitlán" was near Rinconada on the road to Veracruz. A variety of crops grew on other farms whose state-of-the-art practices and equipment dramatized the potential productivity of rural Veracruz. A strange and incredible economic system was emerging, a closed circuit unaffected by any market and governed solely by its own rules of cost, price, and supply. Prices stayed unchanged within this circuit of self-sufficiency even as they skyrocketed in the rest of the country. The cost of credit remained zero at a time when bank interest rates were prohibitive. The economic rules of the outside world had simply been abolished in an odd system that walled itself off from the forces controlling trade and productivity everywhere else. It struck me that its self-sustaining character perfectly matched Pizarro's determination to depend on no one other than himself, and to make his own rules. It also seemed clear to me that his iron will was not his alone. It was a force that came from the world he ruled and from which he arose. It was as if Pizarro, disturbed psychology and all, was the personification of a collective will—just as the agricultural complexes were a precise expression of his will, his inner rigidity, and his delusions of autonomy. Nothing in that fertile and abundant world evoked the dark side of Pizarro, the deaths in Chicontepec, the mutilation and the death that his rage burnt into Anabela and her children and into her relationship with me. This world of order and harmony harbored a community rescued from the abuse, speculation, and collapse that afflicted consumers and producers throughout the rest of the country. The file on these farms documented the creation of something like a utopia. It explained and justified the loyalty of its beneficiaries as well as their fervent support and even veneration of Pizarro as their leader.

Prior to that morning, I'd passed through Pizarro's idyllic domain but I hadn't seen the whole picture. I hadn't understood how the civilizing impulse and the dealings of its founder and leader might seem justified by the threats confronting his people. They lived in a reality that was being hacked out of the jungle little by little in defiance of the corruption and brutality of the world surrounding them. A modest, fiercely defended City of God had grown up in the marshes of northern Veracruz, in its rain forests and in the chaos of its awful cities, despite segregation, cutthroat competition, red light districts, and the law of the gun. What could Rojano offer instead? What good could he and Anabela have done for Chicontepec, once the sinister influence of Pizarro had been eliminated? A new dynasty of obscenely rich Veracruzan land barons with an endless parade of heirs educated in New York?

At 5:00 in the afternoon the dirt pile was removed from

the doorway (Anabela didn't come home to eat), but I didn't go out. My review of the boxes and reports that made up the Pizarro file continued through the evening and into the night. It ended at dawn the following day when, for the first time, I was able to see Pizarro whole. I saw him as he was: in the miserable barracks of Poza Rica's first oilfield, a nine-year-old orphan in a red light district rampant with venereal disease, malaria, pityriasis, chiggers, and explosions in abandoned oil pipelines; I saw him climbing on a crate to reach the bar in the saloon where he hawked newspapers as a youngster afflicted with a host of allergies—to powders, chocolate, mangos, seafood, pollen, leather—that isolated him from normality and explained his aversion to physical contact and the circle of fear within which he lived his life; I saw him join the oil workers union as an adolescent peon and lose two fingers, a wife, the two children she bore him, and his best friend in one of the many union meetings that ended in gunfire; and, on March 27, 1952, as a first-time delegate from Local 35, I saw him rise in protest at yet another bloody union gathering after a deranged gunman in a nearby saloon opened fire on the rival candidate.

During elections four years later another fanatic tried to kill him with a bullet that passed cleanly through the middle of his chest with no damage to vital organs. In 1961, he was fired on again, but this time the three attackers were mowed down on the spot by his embryonic corps of bodyguards. In 1962, the first Lázaro Herón Pizarro primary school opened in what had been the city's red light district after its transformation by the union into a green residential zone. In 1966, he was elected general secretary of Local 35 for the first time. A year later the first agricultural complex, *Egipto de los Tuxtlas*, was founded followed by the 1968 founding near *Rinconada de Tenochtitlán*. During the Echeverría presidency, there were three attempts on Pizarro's life, the last of which occurred in May 1973.

From 1966 to 1976, under Pizarro's leadership, the budget of Local 35 increased a hundredfold (from seven million to seven hundred million pesos). It developed two more residential districts, 35 union stores with prices 40 per cent below the market, seven movie theaters, 17 schools, eight packing plants, and the two agricultural complexes. The deaths of four political rivals (an auto accident, a bar fight, a plane crash, and a drowning in Veracruz) were never fully explained. But during those years, not a single political campaign turned bloody in Poza Rica. There were no pitched battles in the streets and no meetings whose outcomes were determined by pistols or submachine guns.

Pizarro first won recognition as Poza Rica's favorite son, and then he became the favorite son of the whole state of Veracruz. His name adorned the entrances of two more public schools in the state, and, in 1975, his birthplace, the hamlet of Pueblo Viejo near Chicontepec, was officially renamed Pueblo Viejo de Pizarro. That was the year he began the creation of his third agricultural complex, "La Mesopotamia." A year later, upon the election of Rojano as mayor of Chicontepec, he'd begun to develop his fourth complex, "Babilonia," to whose construction we were on the way to becoming a bloody footnote.

In October 1978, René Arteaga died from overindulgence and substandard medical care in the ward of a Social Security hospital. We went to his burial in a new cemetery behind the heights of Tecamachalco along with his dumbstruck children and his devastated wife whom he'd left with no resource except her own tears. The paper he worked for covered the funeral expenses and in black on gold letters named its newsroom for him.

In January of the following year, Anabela used money

from the Chicontepec settlement to buy a house above Cuernavaca. It sat on a lane lined with bougainvillea across from the military encampment and near the access ramp to the Mexico City expressway. It was called The Hideaway, and it had three bedrooms, a red tile roof, an unusable fireplace, and a small orchard of rubber and avocado trees. On a terrace above the house, surrounded by carob trees and jacarandas, were 600 meters of unkempt garden with an abandoned, empty and dirty swimming pool in the middle.

She had the garden spruced up, painted, and filled the pool, turned the adjacent cabana into a studio, and converted the central sala into a kind of terrace. Light flooded in from all sides, and there was a long carved wooden bar, and a rectangular table of varnished planks. Both Mercedes and Tonchis had their own rooms. Anabela and I had the other. Honeysuckle and azaleas poured through a large window with a panorama of blue sky. Sometimes, on a clear day, you could see the volcanoes in the distance.

The house drew Anabela, and Anabela drew me. This led to a routine of leaving for Cuernavaca at noon Fridays with the children's friends, and on Sundays with our friends for meals and barbecues.

"I'm moving here," Anabela announced one day. She was wearing the gardening gloves she used when pruning and weeding the dwarf banana trees in the planters.

This would have been in March 1979. The hearings on political reform were in full swing, and the greatness of Mexico as a petroleum power was the topic of the day. She started to look for a school for Tonchis and Mercedes. In Cuernavaca she found the most expensive one in Mexico, the summer program of a Swiss school whose curriculum included a yearly term in Geneva. It was trilingual, with a riding program, courses in computer science and set theory, and tuition of a 100,000 pesos (the exchange rate at the time was 24 to the dollar) plus 40,000 for what was termed *menage* (supposedly uniforms but in reality a wardrobe).

She put the children in school and bought herself a Chrysler van with a wooden dash, adjustable steering wheel, power windows and locks, and cruise control. You could go 80 mph on the highway and still not feel as if you were going very fast.

In early June, she began moving out of the apartment on *Artes* and into The Hideaway. Every Friday she filled the back of the station wagon with small mountains of clothes (her staggering accumulation of clothing over the past two months). She also transferred her jewelry to safety deposit boxes in a Cuernavaca bank. One Saturday they extended her the courtesy of opening the vault so she could check her belongings (at the time banks weren't opening Saturdays), and I accompanied her and the manager who handed her the keys and left. Anabela opened the first box and began verifying its contents against a typed checklist, a task that clearly delighted her. She furrowed her brow as she touched each piece, rubbing it like a lucky charm.

I left and, while I waited, read newspapers in the cafe across the street. Later, we had a pre-dinner drink at Casino de la Selva.

"King Solomon's mines," I said over the first martini.

She had now acquired the habit of drinking martinis made from imported gin.

"You can't lose with jewelry," she said, oblivious to the joke.

"Especially if they reproduce themselves the way yours do. They're more prolific than Mexicans."

That struck her funny.

"You were playing the reporter, right *Negro*? You think I'm rich, don't you?"

"And your tastes are expensive."

"Do you consider yourself to my taste?"

"I'm from the press. It's above class, perfectly objective."

"How much do you have in the bank, *Negro*?"

"You are as close as I've come to having something in the bank."

"Seriously," Anabela persisted. "How much?"

"Maybe twenty thousand in my checking account. Of course I haven't gotten my commission for the Chicontepec deal yet."

She laughed again. Heartily. It was our first joke about Chicontepec since Rojano's death.

By late July the apartment on *Artes* was finally all mine, unoccupied and twice as empty as before.

"It should serve as your office in Mexico City," Anabela contended. "Make Cuernavaca your de facto residence. You can live at The Hideaway and work here weekdays. When you have to stay late or have dinner commitments, you can spend the night here. When nothing's pending, you can go to The Hideaway. You can have an office there, too, with a phone and peace and quiet."

"If you agree," she went on, "Doña Lila can come and go from Cuernavaca as you wish."

"And as I wish," Doña Lila said. She took part in the deliberations with Mercedes in her lap. "I can't let this little tramp grow up like a wild flower. Right, little tramp? And it's time to start keeping an eye on Tonchis too or the little shrimp will be putting his tool where it doesn't belong."

In the end, Doña Lila didn't go. At least not permanently, just weekends. And the apartment on *Artes* almost reverted to what it had been before. I gave up the office on Hamburg Street and relocated my files and desk back to the space Anabela had made into a diningroom. I put a photo of René Arteaga where Anabela had a photomural of San Juan de

Ulúa. On August 19, 1979, a beginning reporter from the cultural desk at *El Sol de México* spent the night at *Artes*. Come the second week of September 1979, we were duly surprised upon finding ourselves separated by the move, by routine, and by mutual abandonment. One Sunday night Anabela phoned from Cuernavaca.

"Let me remind you my door is open," she said. "It's been three weeks since you stopped in."

"Too much work, ma'am."

"That's pretty lame, *Negro*. I'm not calling to criticize you, but I'm not your suffering wife, remember?"

"I remember."

"That's exactly what I want you to remember. Even cars need to be serviced. How many girls have you taken to *Artes*?"

"It's all news all the time."

"Just little lady reporters. Isn't that right, you bastard?"

"I told you nothing but news."

"Oh, *Negro*, I wish you were here."

"Get a grip, ma'am. This line is tapped."

"Your cock's been tapped, *Negro*. Tonchis says hello. They're teaching him show jumping. When are you coming?"

"Next week."

"Not next week, *Negro*, because next week *I'm* going to Mexico City. I'm warning you now to set aside five days for me. I have travel plans and things to tell you."

She did indeed show up the following week. She arrived at the apartment around 8:00 Friday evening in a black silk pant suit that was open in back, revealing an expanse of tanned skin all the way down to her buttocks. She'd had her hair cut short again, and her face was as toasted as her back, intensifying the brilliance of her eyes. She was also wearing gold earrings and a matching necklace engraved with pre-Hispanic motifs, red lipstick, and a beauty spot on her left cheek.

"You owe me this night and five days, as we agreed," she said.

She went straight to the bedroom. She turned on the shower, then selected, and laid out on the bed a suit and tie, a shirt, and socks and shoes. Half an hour later we climbed into her Chrysler van, and by 9:00 we were at the Champs Elysées. The night was cool and clear, and by 9:00 we were seated on the terrace overlooking Reforma. We ordered fish and shrimp, and from the wine list a vintage dry Chablis. We went through the first bottle in a hurry just as we had in the past, then we ordered the second.

"This dinner's on me," Anabela said. "You know why?"

"Because you're the rich widow."

"You don't have to be a widow to be rich. You invited me to dinner here once, and you're still the bachelor outcast."

"But you're the Queen of Sheba now."

"And now you're a maker of national opinion who doesn't understand a damn thing. You know why I invited you to dinner?"

"I already said I did."

"And I said you didn't. I'm inviting because you put my life in order. That is, you straightened out all the problems one person can solve for another. It's a given that the rest is nothing but booze and Chicontepec. Agreed?"

The wine was beginning to have its affect, making her tongue careless and loose as it always did.

"Agreed."

"There's no way out, right?"

"Right."

"And remembrances aren't worth much. Vengeance may help, but it doesn't bring back the past, does it?"

"No, it doesn't"

The trout came garnished with almonds as requested, and Anabela ordered a third Chablis.

"You're the one who introduced me to these European delicacies, *Negro*. Before I was just a Little Red Riding Hood from Veracruz. How was I to know about European wines and first class restaurants? I want to ask you something."

"Ask me something?"

"And I want you to answer as if you really were a national opinion-maker. Not as the fag you actually are. Understand?"

"What's the question?"

"Just one, *Negro*, here and now between the two of us, looking each other in the eye."

We looked each other in the eye.

"I want to know if you like the way I am," she said with her gaze fixed on me.

She was very tan from the sun. Her eyes were brilliant and clear, and the elongated oval of her face glowed from the wine that reddened her cheeks and dilated her eyes. Her lipstick was smudged from eating, and the meal left a film of grease on her lips.

"You've seen better times."

"No, no, no," Anabela said, beginning to crack up over her own joke. "What I mean is would you let your cock be cut off just to get a smile out of me? Would you hock the fucking newspaper that made you a national opinion-maker if I asked you for money? Would you die for me or are you just screwing around with me? That's what I want to know."

"I'd give up the column."

"All right," Anabela said. "What else?"

"There is nothing else."

"No, no, no, that's just the beginning," Anabela said. "You've got to keep going. You need to trade the newspaper for my earlobe, your apartment for my used underwear, your birth certificate for a piece of my tail. Something romantic, *Negro*. Because I'd give anything. Believe me. No, you don't believe me, but I would. That's what I came to tell you tonight, and now I've said it."

We drank the rest of the wine. Unburdened and relaxed, Anabela dug into the desserts and liqueurs with a relish born, she said, of the four months of diet and exercise that turned her into a tanned and rejuvenated jet-setter as slender and robust as a beach bunny.

We went to hear Manzanero at Villa Florencia and rented a suite at the Fiesta Palace at 3:00 in the morning. At seven we sipped the last of the cogñac we'd brought with us, and I felt Anabela fall asleep with her head resting on my legs.

She woke me up at noon, freshly bathed and in full voice. "Let's go, *Negro*."

She had two tickets on the afternoon flight to Cancún. In the suite's sala a breakfast with cold beer and *huevos rancheros* awaited us, luxuriously served under a silver cover.

She refused to go by the apartment on *Artes* for clothes, preferring that we buy beachwear, sandals, and a pair of travel bags at the store in the hotel. We were in the airport waiting area long enough for two drinks apiece, and we had another two along with the in-flight meal. We landed as night fell on Cancún. We checked into the Hotel Presidente and went for a nighttime swim on its blissfully quiet beach where we remained until our legs were shivering. We ate a candlelight dinner at Casablanca in the Hotel Krystal, a dive stuffed with Bogart memorabilia and assorted pieces of the usual Hollywood kitsch. Anabela ordered a bottle of champagne.

"Love me, *Negro*, and don't forget me," she said by way of a toast, "because after me they broke the mold."

I toasted the mold.

"I'm going to show you my refuge, *Negro*. And once you've been to my refuge, you'll know everything there is to know about me."

Very early the next day we set out for the refuge in an automatic min-van driven by a man with a small mustache. His name was Julio Pot, and he treated Anabela with the curious and attentive familiarity of a driver and secretary.

"Did you say we were coming?" Anabela asked after we boarded the min-van.

"I went yesterday to see for myself that everything was in order," Julio Pot said. "All that was needed was gas for the generator and more of the insecticide that was used up and never replaced. How long has it been since you last came?"

"A year and five months, Julio."

"You left in January of last year."

"January of last year," Anabela admitted.

We headed towards Tulum on the road that also goes through Carrillo Puerto, formerly Chan Santa Cruz. In the 19th century, this was the center of the Maya rebellion known as the Yucatán Caste War. We drove for an hour next to a curtain of jungle through which an endless array of foxes, iguanas, and armadillos broke out onto the highway.

At the Tulum-Pueblo crossroads, on the far side of Akumal and Playa del Carmen, Julio Pot turned into a corridor that stretched down the middle of a long tongue of land separated from the mainland by a lagoon called Boca Paila and from the open ocean by a reef that fended off the tempests of the Caribbean.

Coconut trees lined the beaches on either side, tall slender palms bent inland by the prevailing sea winds. They created a landscape punctuated only by patches of mangroves along the lagoon and an abundance of wild almond trees. It was a spur of land occupied by copra farms and waterside fishing villages under gradual invasion by *fishing resorts*, meaning bungalows with no electricity and the other rustic charms that attract tourists seeking a way back to nature.

Julio Pot maneuvered the mini-van onto one of the

side roads. We stepped out into a weeded clearing planted with perfectly aligned palm trees forming a lush walkway that led to a cluster of small dwellings topped by thatched roofs. They were built to look like *palapas*–the simple shelters characteristic of the region since time immemorial. A slender white woman stood in the middle of one of the paths drying her hands on her apron. Her broad smile revealed a pair of gold incisors.

Anabela kissed her.

"Are you coming to la Punta?" the woman said.

"Yes, *Güera*," Anabela said.

"Have Julio let me know when so I can make you a meal."

"We want to go to Punta Pájaros," Anabela said. "And Cayo Culebras. How is your brother?"

"You know, either hungover or drunk. There's no middle ground with him. But when it comes to fishing, he can't be beat. I'll tell him to get you some snails and lobster for tomorrow. He's sure to get us something."

Julio Pot went to the back of the largest palapa and started a generator. He unloaded the luggage and several boxes of groceries from the mini-van.

Behind the large palapa was a long strip of beach edged with snail shells. A ribbon of white sand curled southward for some two kilometers, ending at a rocky point with waves breaking over it. In the shallows the water was emerald green. Farther out it turned turquoise, then purple some three hundred meters offshore where it washed over the ragged barrier of the reefs.

There were three palapas with stone and masonry walls and thatched roofs supported from within by beams whose lower ends came together in an inverted cone. The two smaller palapas were rooms with baths. The third and largest included a diningroom with a bar, an empty bookcase, and wicker sofas. A mounted sailfish hung on the wall. Next to the bar were a kitchen and a room housing the generator that provided electricity and a shadow box in which the acrylic paint was peeling off a boat named the Mercedes. Salt-caked green lettering identified the spot where the craft was beached as Paradise.

Julio Pot placed a dish of abalone with Havana chile and a pair of Tom Collinses on our table. Shadows of palm trees swaying in the breeze moved back and forth across its surface.

"This is my refuge, *Negro*," Anabela told me. "We bought it five years ago."

"With funds from the Veracruz CNOP?" I asked.

At the time Rojano headed the state chapter of the National Confederation of People's Organizations.

"Funds from the Guillaumín family. They sold seventeen hectares of copra here for three million pesos. For four hundred thousand I was able to get the five least profitable, the beachfront that was of no interest to the buyers. Later we built the palapas. We built the big one first, and we used to sleep here one on top of the other. Then we built the other two."

It was not yet noon. The day was a bit overcast, but the sun beat down hard. We walked a kilometer towards the tip of the reefs. There were pelicans and heron, a thick anchor rope washed up by the sea, and blindingly white sand as far as the eye could see. Anabela picked up the plastic thigh of a doll, cleaned the seaweed off it, and put it in the pocket of her *huipil*. The beach took an unexpected turn and curved inland in a semicircle.

"This is the refuge of my refuge," Anabela said, pointing to a small green inlet, a sort of natural swimming pool. "Come."

She dropped her huipil on the sand and entered the water naked.

When we returned to the palapa, Julio Pot had prepared a ceviche of snail and mullet. There was also a bottle of cold Chablis.

"I got my taste for this from you," Anabela said by way of a toast.

We made love one more time in the palapa before the siesta and again upon awakening as the sun began to set. We did it with an intensity that came not from ourselves but from the place, from a need of nearly adolescent urgency.

We stayed three days. On the last one we went to the point with la *Güera* for the excursion to Cayo Culebras in the middle of Bahía de Ascensión. It was an irregular agglomeration of islands on the way to becoming overgrown with mangroves, a huge natural snake nursery. Clouds of frigatebirds with inflatable red throat pouches wheeled overhead, and those in flight were a small fraction of the thousands perched nervously on the canopies and branches of the mangroves. In places clusters of birds blotted out the green foliage with their white breasts and black flanks.

"They're suicide birds," Anabela said. "When they can't find food, they nosedive into the trees and break their own necks by getting them snagged in the forks of the branches."

"Like politicians out of a job," I said.

La *Güera* laughed.

"Like widows abandoned by the leaders of national opinion," Anabela said.

In her house la *Güera* prepared a Belize dish called fish *cerec* (fish broth with coconut milk), and we had drinks with her brother, who by that hour of the day had already downed half a bottle of Viejo Vergel rum. We returned to the palapas at nightfall in the mini-van. Shadows stretched seaward as the sun set over the lagoon. A stiff breeze came up, rippling the water with waves and rustling the palms. Anabela put on a blue turban, and the lotion on her face glistened. Her green eyes seemed larger and brighter than ever.

We drank without speaking.

"Did you come here with Rojano?"

"Is that the best question you can come up with in a place like this?"

We fell placidly, refreshingly silent once again.

"Who was I going to come with if not Rojano?" Anabela said after several minutes. "With Rojano and the children. We came to fish. You can go deep sea fishing or fish in the lagoon. Rojano preferred the lagoon. He went crazy over bonefish. You know what a bonefish is?"

"No."

"It's a flat fish with the face of a piranha. It's harder to catch than a sailfish. You have to get very close and drop the hook right in front of it. But if you get too close, it swims away, and if you keep too far away, you lose it. You have to do all that just so they'll bite. Once they bite, nine out of ten get away because they're very strong and it can take a whole hour to land one. You break the line if you pull too hard. You have to use a very small hook to keep from injuring them, which is why they can fight so long. That was the fish Rojano liked to catch."

The kind of fish that cost him his life in Chicontepec.

"And you?" I asked.

"Deep sea fishing for sailfish. I caught the one mounted on the wall of the palapa in 1975. I got it in January, two months before you showed up in the port with the López Portillo campaign."

She closed her eyes as if she were about to fall asleep, then, keeping them closed, she began to speak shortly afterwards.

"There's something I want you to know." Her voice remained smooth and relaxed as it had throughout the conversation. "It's something you ought to know, and I'm going to tell you."

"What?"

"I just want you to know, that's all. In case anything happens. I'm not asking for anything. I just want you to know."

There was a long pause. Her eyes still closed, she began to trace the profile of her nose with her finger.

"I'm going to have him killed," she said in a rasp as if her throat had gone dry.

"Kill whom?" I said slowly, deliberately ignoring the obvious.

"Kill Pizarro," Anabela answered in the same tone of voice.

"What are you talking about?" I said. "We're in Quintana Roo in southeast Mexico. You're gazing out over the Caribbean. What's the matter with you?"

"It's taken me a year to find the right person," Anabela said.

"In the want ads of *El Universal*?"

"I'm serious, *Negro*." Anabela opened her eyes and turned to look at me.

"I'm serious, too," I said. "Anyone who tells you he can kill Lázaro Pizarro is a second-rate con artist."

"This one's a professional," Anabela said.

"Who's a professional?" I sat up straight, jerked upright by the news that she had a candidate.

"The name doesn't matter," Anabela said. "He came to see me at the house in Cuernavaca so I could tell him about Chicontepec."

"How did he get to Cuernavaca?"

"Through a friend in the government of Veracruz."

"A shithead."

"A friend."

"A shithead," I repeated angrily. "What made you and this shithead think you could get to Pizarro?"

"You start by wanting to do it," Anabela said reproachfully.

"Wanting, my ass," I said, getting to my feet. "Drop it, Ana. Forget about it. Just forget it, damn it. Let the dead bury the dead."

"In my world, the dead are alive, Negro. They let me make fun of them, but they don't let me live."

"No, that's not so. It's crazy. You can't kill Lázaro Pizarro. How many times do you want him to get the better of you?"

"Always or never." Anabela withdrew once again into herself. "Not any more."

I slept badly and woke up several times during the night. At 5:00 in the morning, I'd chain-smoked one cigarette after another for 20 minutes while staring at the ceiling. Anabela slept without twists or turns. She lay tanned and moist on the sheet, glistening with sweat. Her perfect ears, the oval of her face, and her smooth straight jaw shone under a film of perspiration. It shook me to imagine her unbridled rage, the bloody memories that were still alive despite her relaxed face and body. Her maturity and composure made her look more beautiful than ever.

We didn't speak over breakfast.

"I want to ask you to rethink that crazy idea," I finally said.

"The emissary is on the way," Anabela replied. "There's no way to stop him now."

Chapter 9
IN THE FLOW

We returned to Mexico City two days before November 20, 1979. We thought about spending the 20th together in Quintana Roo to celebrate the renewal of our acquaintance on that date three years earlier. It was the same memorable day a coup was supposed to have solved the crisis at the end of the Echeverría government and brought to a close the long era of civilian rule following the Mexican Revolution. Three years later, Rojano had been killed, more crises was brewing, and Anabela and I had been together, then separated. Now we were back in the dark playing a new game whose unreality made it all the more unnerving. Like the country, we were burning up in mid-air, set ablaze by the speed with which things were happening. Anabela's inner turmoil and chronic fever were becoming apparent in her face and gestures, unmasking the rage she'd been able to contain up to now. In retrospect, it seemed as if the whole Rojano affair were simply the tragic outgrowth of her cold and unyielding will that was rivaled only by the fury seething beneath Pizarro's equally impassive exterior.

I couldn't get her to name the emissary, but I did piece together the history of his alleged triumph over Pizarro eight years earlier. It all began in March 1971 with the union elections at the Atzapotzalco refinery in Mexico City. It was the first time Lázaro Pizarro fell prey to temptation and ventured beyond his natural sphere of influence in Poza Rica. He cast his lot with a slate of Veracruzan immigrants that he supported with money, organization, and his by then notorious clout with the union's national executive committee. He circulated confidential information about the corrupt doings of the rival slate and offered PEMEX a sweetheart contract with the Poza Rica local in exchange for supporting his candidates at the refinery. He also activated a so-called "security detail" which accomplished its pre-election mission by threatening key workers (departmental delegates whose influence and prestige could swing the election). Certain members of the rival slate were roughed up in bar fights or on account of supposed romantic rivalries. Shooting broke out at a meeting of the rival slate, and the gathering turned into a pitched battle. Several of those present suffered bullet wounds and one man, the brother of the candidate for secretary general, was stabbed to death.

The brawl on May 15, 1971, drastically altered the tone and strategies of the pending election. The dead man's family was sufficiently extended to include a group of secret service agents who, thanks to the sacking of a police chief and the ensuing moral renovation campaign, had been fired. Driven by the affront to family honor and the promise of soft union jobs in the event of victory, the out-of-work cops sided with the slate being harassed by Pizarro. Before the week was out, news reached Poza Rica of the death in a bar fight of the leader of the security detail Pizarro had dispatched to the plant, and the disappearance of two subordinates following a night of carousing. The tale was credible except for the fact that the deceased, like each and every one of the bodyguards hired by Lázaro Pizarro, didn't drink.

Pizarro swore to avenge these deaths with others and to restore union autonomy to the refinery by eradicating the non-union violence besetting it. The commando related to the opposing slate didn't wait in Mexico City for Pizarro to take the offensive. They correctly surmised that recent losses and the dispatching of additional security to the capital would leave Pizarro lightly protected in Poza Rica. They hit the road at nightfall and by dawn, with help from another foursome of fired cops, proceeded to occupy Quinta Bermúdez. They caught the guards on the loading docks and the ones dozing in a van near the main entrance by surprise and tied them up. They climbed over the walls and subdued the guards inside who also were asleep. At 6:00 in the morning, they broke into Pizarro's own office just as he and Roibal were meeting to plan their day. They beat, bound, and blindfolded Roibal and sat Pizarro in the chair behind his desk. The leader of the assailants sat down in front of him, put one submachine gun on the desk within Pizarro's reach and another within his own reach. Then he slowly lowered his hands until they rested on his legs.

"I know you ordered me killed," he told Pizarro. "Here I am so you can kill me."

Pizarro didn't move.

"This is between you and me," the commando leader said. "No outside interference."

Pizarro didn't flinch. The scene lasted half an hour with the submachine at his fingertips on the desk while his rival waited for him to make the first move. Finally Pizarro said, "What do you want in return?" Under the arrangement that followed he capitulated. The opposing slate gained control of the refinery local in a peaceful election, and the union's national leadership, having feared division and unseemly violence, breathed a sigh of relief .

The chief of the commando who had challenged and subdued Pizarro was Anabela's emissary.

"Is that the emissary's version?" I asked shortly before our plane landed in Mexico City.

"It's my friend in Xalapa's," she replied.

"He's not your friend," I said. "He's an idiot. He's your enemy."

"I go by what he does," Anabela said. "I'm not afraid of

what might happen, the worst has come and gone already."

"You and your children are left," I said, purposely excluding myself from the survivors' list.

"My children aren't in this fight," Anabela said. "I'm the one left, and it's going to cost him."

She wanted to go straight from the airport to Cuernavaca upon landing, but I wouldn't let her. I had the children brought from The Hideaway to the apartment on *Artes* and then called Internal Security. My contact was out of town, so I spent the afternoon tracking him down and finally caught up with him by phone in Ciudad Victoria, Tamaulipas, where a noisy split in the state chapter of the ruling PRI was heating up. The affair would later trigger riots and an electoral triumph for the very moribund Authentic Party of the Mexican Revolution.

"Delighted to hear from you," my contact said. "Is it something urgent or can it wait for me to get back to Mexico City tomorrow?"

"It's urgent for me."

"What's up?"

"More of the same."

"Our friend in Poza Rica?"

"He's broken his agreement with the widow," I said.

"Broken it, how? Has something happened?"

"It has."

"I'd rather not talk about it on the phone," my contact said.

"Just answer my questions, yes or no. Has anyone been hurt?"

"Not yet."

"Answer me—yes or no," he demanded. "Are you together in Mexico City?"

"Yes."

"At your place of residence?"

"Yes."

"Is the place of residence where you are under pressure or surveillance?"

"No."

"I'm sending a protective detail to stand guard until tomorrow when you can explain the situation to me in person."

Comandante José Luis Cuevas came with two of his men. He checked the apartment and the accesses to the roof, explained that the entrance would be under constant watch, and left a walkie-talkie with which we could reach him at any time.

"What's going on?" Anabela asked when the commandante and his men had left.

"An Internal security detail."

"You called Internal Security?"

"I did."

"Why did you call them?"

"As a basic precaution," I said.

"What kind of precaution, *Negro*? What did you tell them?"

"That's what we need to talk about."

"There's nothing to talk about. Everything's been taken care of. Don't get in the way. There's something else you ought to know. I didn't send the emissary. He came to make me an offer on his own, and told me what he was going to do. He was going to do it anyway."

I nodded towards the table in my office where Tonchis was listening intently to our conversation while pretending to skim an issue of *National Geographic*. Anabela took him to the bedroom where she and Doña Lila had improvised cots for him and Mercedes. She got him into his pajamas and turned on the television, then resumed her complaint.

"We can't stay too long in this apartment. We seem like

gypsies. Our house is in Cuernavaca. We have nothing to do here."

"You're not leaving here until security has been arranged for you and the kids," I said, refusing to drop the subject.

"What are you talking about, *Negro*? Under the circumstances the worst thing I can do is seem concerned."

"The worst thing you can do is try to look smart. Who do you think you're dealing with?"

"I'm not afraid, *Negro*. I already told you I didn't do anything."

"This is a battle I don't want to fight. I want to stop it."

"You want to stop it? That's why you called Internal Security?"

"No."

"What did you tell them then?"

"That Pizarro was breaking the agreement to leave you alone."

"Did you tell them about the emissary?"

"I told them you were in danger, but tomorrow we're going to discuss it face to face."

"And you're going to tell them about the emissary?"

"Maybe."

"You can't do that, *Negro*. I told you that because I love you."

"I have no idea why you told me."

"What does that mean?"

"Just what I said. I don't know what your reasons were for telling me. What did you expect from me?"

"I expected your complicity," Anabela crossed her arms. "Your support."

She sat down on the sofa next to me. She lowered her head and hunched her shoulders as if trying to ward off the cold.

"That's exactly what you're getting," I told her.

"What are you talking about? You're making me nervous. My hands are freezing. Feel them."

She lay a cold hand on my neck, reminding me that I'd been through this scene before and was in no mood for a rerun.

"You're going to be protected while the emissary does his job." I said.

"Don't talk to me like that." She got up from the sofa. Her arms remained crossed as if she sought shelter in the safety of her own embrace. "Don't lie to me. I haven't done anything."

"Then give me the name of the emissary."

"No way."

"With his priors it would be easy to get."

"Only if you tell them what I told you. Are you going to tell Internal Security?" She sat back down on the sofa.

"Did you plan on Internal Security's finding out?"

"What plan, *Negro*?" she said, leaning back.

"The plan you set in motion on the assumption that I'd get you protection while your emissary did his job," I repeated. "And if the emissary fails, we at least have the beginnings of a defense in place. If he succeeds, then everything's taken care of."

"You're crazy. What are you talking about? Don't lie to me." She leaned over me and made a very convincing show of embracing me.

"The question is, do I tell them about the emissary or not?" I said.

"Don't tell them," Anabela said, holding onto me now, adjusting the rhythm of her breathing to mine.

"If I tell them, he could be stopped."

"The emissary could be," Anabela said. She nuzzled my neck, and her nose was also cold. "But who's going to stop Pizarro?"

"That's not the point."

"That is the point, my love," Anabela said. "The point has always been, who's going to stop Pizarro?"

At 2:00 the following afternoon my contact arrived at Sep's Restaurant on Insurgentes Centro. We were a block and a half from my apartment and three blocks from where the Federal Security Directorate had its offices on the Plaza de la República in front of the Monument to the Revolution. In those days Sep's had tables overlooking the street, but I sought an inside corner protected from the sun. My contact entered behind me as if he'd been awaiting my arrival from somewhere nearby.

"I can't eat with you," he said. He took his seat and removed his glasses. They were slightly tinted to protect his light-sensitive eyes, and they served as an apt symbol for the shadowy nature of his work. "But I didn't want to let your call go unanswered either. I was very worried when you phoned me yesterday because I assumed everything had been taken care of. Tell me what happened."

He'd come to Sep's with no clear idea of what I was going to tell him. Driven by a sense of obligation, he seemed more than certain about how to proceed. When it was my turn to speak, I listened to myself as if I were listening to another person.

"We got two phone calls threatening Anabela."

"Meaning the widow of the mayor of Chicontepec?" My contact avoided the familiarity that the use of her first name would have implied.

"The widow, yes."

"What did the calls say?"

"They were death threats to her and her children. Both said what happened to the mayor would happen to them, that they hadn't been forgotten."

"When were the calls?"

"November 2nd and November 3rd," I heard myself say.

"Today's November 19th," my contact replied. "You let two weeks go by without telling me. Why was it so urgent yesterday?"

"Because the widow didn't tell me until yesterday. She had a panic attack."

"She's not the kind of woman who has panic attacks. She must be very worried."

"She wasn't. We even went on vacation," I said, knowing he could easily find out. "But yesterday there was an incident with her son in Cuernavaca."

"What kind of incident?"

"He disappeared for three hours. He went to a friend's house without letting anybody know and came back three hours later. It was all quite normal, but that's not what the widow thought."

"What did she think?"

"That the threats were for real. We were just back from our trip and were here in the city," I said, continuing to elaborate. "When she heard from Cuernavaca that her son hadn't come home, she told me about the threats. That's why I didn't call you until yesterday."

"Is there anything to indicate the calls came from our friend in Poza Rica?" my contact said.

"The phone call repeated Pizarro's motto."

"What motto?"

"Destroy to create. Whoever can add can divide."

"Anyone who's read your column knows those mottoes," my contact said.

"Before you try convincing me there's no problem," I said, "let me remind you how this all started and how it ended."

"I remember perfectly well." He took a cigarette from his case and lit it with his habitual fastidiousness. I watched his small eyes through the smoke. Irritated from lack of sleep or from the smoke itself, they were fixed on me in a suspicious stare. "What can we do to avoid risks?"

"Leave the surveillance up for a while," I requested.

"Agreed, but that's a temporary solution."

"It'll suffice for the time-being. The widow's planning to get out of Mexico. She's probably going to live in Los Angeles."

"When is she thinking of leaving?"

"In two or three months."

"That's too long in a situation like this, *paisano*." Smoke from his cigarette curled about my contact as his inner calculator went to work. "We also need to negotiate with Pizarro."

"We already negotiated with Pizarro."

"Then we'll do it again," he said with mild irritation. "I'm surprised that he'd continue this fight on his own."

"I'm talking about facts," I said, raising my voice. "You can believe them or not, but don't forget how this began and how it's played out."

"Do I have your permission to sound out Pizarro?" my contact asked, ignoring my flareup.

"He'll deny everything," I predicted, discrediting once and for all what Pizarro would say by way of discrediting me.

"I know. But do I have your permission?"

Since he was going to do it anyway, I simply repeated that it didn't make sense and agreed.

"Tell the widow she'll have all the protection she needs while she makes her travel plans." By his tone of voice my contact brought the interview to a close. "Here or in Cuernavaca as she likes. In Cuernavaca it would be even easier. And I'll find out if what you and she are thinking has any basis in fact."

He put out his cigarette without crushing it, simply scraping away the burning tip.

"I have to go." Once again he gave me a hard look. "Do you have anything else to tell me?"

I said no.

"Then we'll be in touch. And don't worry about the security."

"Let me know what you find out," I said.

"And you be sure to tell me all you know," he said meaningfully. "I wouldn't want to be operating on false premises."

Nothing happened on *Artes* in the days that followed except for the stowing of the cots and the children's boredom. We spent our impossible anniversary, the 20th of November, disgruntled and immobilized, avoiding discussion, leafing through newspapers and magazines, and watching television. Comandante Cuevas checked regularly to see that all was well, and it became apparent to the children that an odd silence went along with their confinement. Mercedes passed the days making a Christmas manger out of papier maché attended by cows, mules and goats in unheard-of numbers. Tonchis memorized every photo in the collection of *National Geographics* in my office. Anabela acted as if she'd been shut in against her will, and slept with the children the whole time.

In early December 1979, I took part in a one-day presidential tour of the port of Salina Cruz, Oaxaca. The place showed signs of developing into the major deep-water industrial port that would mark the beginning of a new era for Mexico as a 21st century power in the Pacific Basin. We toured the naval base, visited a model warship, and dined in the warehouses on a meal served by the dockworkers. From there, I went looking for an aide in the press center that had been set up in the customs office some 800 meters from the dinner. I had an urgent call from Anabela, but by the time I got to a phone, it had been cut off. I called my number on *Artes* and got an immediate answer. (When reporters were with the president, whether in Salina Cruz or Moscow, they always had an open line that could reach any phone in Mexico City, simply by dialing a few extra numbers.) She asked if I'd seen the inside pages of *La Prensa*. I hadn't. She asked me to look at them and call her back.

I found a set of daily papers in the press center, and recovered a copy of *La Prensa* from the sailors on guard at the entrance to the wharf. It was the most widely read paper in Mexico City, a tabloid that leaned heavily to police stories, natural disasters, major accidents, and especially brutal crimes with banner headlines on the outside and lots of details inside. I redialed my phone on *Artes*.

"It's on the back page," Anabela said. "Have you read it?"

On the back page I read that a pearl-colored LTD sedan had crashed and exploded on the road between Tulancingo and Poza Rica. Its four occupants—two of whom were ex-members of the secret police—had burned to death.

"I already read it," I told Anabela. "What about it?"

"I'll tell you what about it," Anabela said. "The second name on the list was the emissary."

I found the rest of the story on the inner pages. The second name on the list was: Edilberto Chanes Corona, age 45, former member of the secret police, a smalltime crook all his life who fancied himself a contract killer. His obituary followed.

"It could have been an accident," I said.

"He had no business being in Tulancingo," Anabela

replied. "He said he was taking the plane to Veracruz."

"He could have been returning overland via Tulancingo."

"No," Anabela said. "If that were so, we'd have gotten other news as well. When are you coming back?"

"Tonight. Possibly tomorrow."

"I'm asking one thing of you." Anabela's voice on the phone sounded crestfallen, not angry but exhausted. "I don't want you doing anything. Don't ask any questions, don't go looking for anybody. Don't do anything until we talk."

"Right."

"I'm very unhappy, Negro."

We returned that same night very late. It was almost dawn by the time I got to the apartment on *Artes*. Anabela was awake and sitting on the sofa, her eyes bloodshot from prolonged crying. She was pouring vodka straight from the bottle into her glass. She seethed with frustration and rage that flared out of her like flames from a window at night. Her eyes were red. The tendons in her neck and the veins of her arms were bulging. Her cheeks were puffed, and her lips were swollen. I tried to get near her, but she wouldn't let me. She gulped the vodka and threw the glass down on the sofa.

"It can't be. I'd have to see Pizarro alive to believe it." Her voice was hoarse and broken, as misshapen as her face.

"It was an insane idea," I said.

"All right," she continued, paying no attention to what I said. "Suppose he's alive. I'll only believe it if I see him, but suppose he's alive. Then the question is what to do, where to look. That was my only card, but there have to be more. Where are they?" She paced back and forth across the sala. "In what cave should I look? Because there has to be one. Somewhere in the cellars, in the slime there has to be someone able to make Pizarro another notch on his gun. Where is he? The imbecile screwed up, it says so in *La Prensa*. So all right. Suppose for a moment that Pizarro's alive."

"Pizarro is alive," I said irritatedly.

"No, *Negro,*" Anabela contradicted me, and her fury grew a degree hotter. "He *appears* to be alive. But he's been dead for quite a while." She rubbed her arms and started to tremble. "He's very, very dead though he may not know it and you may not know it. *Perfectly dead* ever since that night in Chicontepec."

"He beat you again," I said drily. "You have to get out of the country."

"I'm not leaving. I'm not going to run."

"You're not in this alone. Tonchis and Mercedes are also involved."

She spun around and glared at me again, out of control. She lunged towards me, turning into a scrawny, suddenly strange being, a woman I didn't know. Her hair had gone dank and curly, her hands were wrinkled, her neck was a knot of bulging veins and taut tendons.

"I have no fear, *Negro.* I had none before, and I don't have any now. This fight has nothing to do with Tonchis and Mercedes. But they're in thrall to the fight. And so is Little Darling and anyone else who happens to care for Pizarro. They became orphans in this fight, and I may very well lose them in this fight. But that's the way it is, and God help anyone who thinks they can get away. You listen to me, whoever gives in is doubly fucked. They can kill my children, they can tear me to pieces, but they'll never make me the least bit afraid of anything. Because the minute they think I'm horrified by what could happen to my children, they'll tear them apart on the spot. Do you understand? This isn't about Tonchis or Mercedes, *Negro.* It's about where there's a man up to killing Pizarro. That's the only question. Because Pizarro's dead. Good and dead ever since that night in Chicontepec."

She poured herself another shot of vodka and drank it in

a single gulp. She went to my desk and sat down behind it with her hands in her hair and her elbows on my typewriter. She sobbed convulsively and groaned with rage. "Imbecile. Imbecile. Imbecile."

She slept in the room with the children, and I slept alone in my own room. Early the following morning, I was awakened by the commotion echoing through the apartment. I heard Anabela's voice issuing orders to Tonchis and the babble of Mercedes coming and going in the hallway. As I looked out, Anabela scurried past with a suitcase on her way to the sala. She had on what looked like tailored overalls and had tied her hair in a bandanna. She came and went, kissed me on the cheek, and left a perfumed fragrance in her wake. I caught up with her in the room where she was tying a bundle and got her into my room.

"What's going on?"

"We're going back to Cuernavaca," she said with a smile as fresh as her perfume.

"You can't go back to Cuernavaca," I said.

"Yes, I can."

"You've got Pizarro on your tail," I reminded her.

"When you get right down to it, the only one who's ever been on my tail is you," she joked.

"I mean what I say."

"And your breath smells awful."

"You can't go back to Cuernavaca. Staying in Mexico City is bad enough."

"I'm going to Cuernavaca with my children and without your goons. I have nothing to fear, and I fear nothing. How do you think it looks for me to be cooped up in your apartment surrounded by your goons?"

"It's not a question of appearances. Pizarro is not an appearance."

"I have no memory of Pizarro. Have you forgotten that I'm the merry widow?"

"Last night you were just a widow, period."

"I wasn't myself last night. Erase last night from your memory."

"You can't go, Ana."

"I'm going, *Negro*. It's for the best, it's safer. Do you really think those three idiots outside with their walkie-talkies can stop Pizarro?"

"They can make it difficult for him."

"It's not a matter of difficulty. Is he out to get us or not? That's the question. Once his mind is made up, you can put every officer in the Federal Security Directorate outside, and he won't care. He'll find a way."

"The difference is making him have to find it."

"The difference is I'm not afraid. That's all you have to understand. And love me."

She got to her feet, took my face in her cold hands, and looked at me for a long time. Her eyes were clear and unclouded without a trace of last night's fever and devastation. "And love me," she repeated.

I couldn't stop her. I asked Comandante Cuevas to guard her in Cuernavaca, and two hours later, around ten in the morning, I went to the offices of my contact in Plaza de la República.

"I want to apologize for what I'm about to tell you," I said.

I proceeded to recite in every detail the saga of the emissary. He wasn't annoyed. He slowly took a white card and his gold pen from his jacket pocket. He wrote a few lines on the card and rang the bell hidden beneath his desk drawer. His gigantic aide appeared with the aplomb of a ballerina.

"For Raul," my contact said as he handed him the card.

"Have him dispatch a detail today."

He took out another card and wrote on it. "Whatever there is in the files on this." He passed the card to the aide. "And get me the office in Veracruz right away."

He swiveled his chair so he was sideways to me and stared out the windows that looked down on the Plaza de la República.

"I don't like hearing about things after the fact," he said, twirling his pen between his fingers. "I don't like your attitude or how far this has gone. What do you want from us?"

"Friendship and understanding, *paisano*."

It was the first time I'd appealed to our shared origins in Veracruz since the days when I was doing favors for Rojano. My contact took it in with a grimace that bordered on a smile.

"I hope you understand the seriousness of the situation," he said. "Tools are like magnets, *paisano*. They attract users. This being the case, we can assume that the response from Poza Rica is on its way."

"It could be."

"We have very little time, and I don't know if we'll succeed," he said, turning his chair back towards me. "What I want you to understand is this. You and the widow have gone beyond my range of operation. We'll certainly keep the guard detail in place, we'll even reinforce it. What I have to tell you, though, is if the train has left the station, the guard detail won't be enough to stop it."

"I know."

"I hope you keep it in mind. We'll investigate exactly what happened and try to negotiate with Pizarro. But it's now up to him and not us to decide. Everything depends on them now. Stay in touch with the guard detail throughout the day. Make sure they always know where you are so that I'll know. And check with me every afternoon to find out what we've got."

He escorted me to the door and put me out of his office without saying goodbye. By going beyond his range of operation, I'd come under his authority.

I went from there to the newspaper. I needed urgently to track down our correspondent in Veracruz. It took three phone calls to catch up with him at the mayor's office in Xalapa.

"I want you to run a check on Lázaro Pizarro in Poza Rica," I told him.

"Right away. Are you after anything special?"

"Just find out if he's in Poza Rica. See if there have been any recent incidents, if everything's in order, if there have been any rumors of something out of the ordinary. All you need to do is run a check."

"Right," the correspondent said. "If you give me a number where I can reach you, I'll get back to you in an hour."

I gave him the phone number of the bar in Les Ambassadeurs Restaurant on Reforma and had him give me his number. Though it was 11:30 in the morning, I headed for the bar. It was empty at that hour, recently swept and redolent of air freshener. I ordered a whiskey on the rocks and let the sensation of being caught in a countdown sink in. I imagined for the thousandth time the emissary's confession in front of Pizarro after his capture, and how Pizarro might go about sending a return message. On what number of the countdown were the emissaries with the return message? Internal Security's investigation got under way that same morning, but the fact remained that it was starting late. I also couldn't discount the possibility that the emissary had been taken out early on, well before he could talk. Pizarro may have considered the whole affair nothing more than the settling of an old score, in which case all the morning had accomplished was to tie me to Anabela once and for all in the black hole of Internal Security's confidential files.

Two whiskeys later, my imagination remained stalled on the same track, obsessively recycling the same sets of variations until the call came from the correspondent in Xalapa.

"Everything seems to be in order," he said, "but Lacho's not in Poza Rica."

"Where is he?"

"No one knows. I asked for his aide Roibal, but no one could find him for me."

"Find out where he is."

"From here in Xalapa, that's hard to do, sir."

"Then go to Poza Rica."

"That's what I was going to tell you. The union local is giving a dinner for state government officials today in Poza Rica. The secretary of internal security for the state is going and he's taking a helicopter from here in Xalapa in half an hour. If you tell me to, I'll sign on and be in Poza Rica in half an hour."

"Get on the helicopter. I'll talk to your editor."

"I was going to ask if you would."

"I'll tell him."

"And where do I call you from Poza Rica?"

"Right here. I'm not going anywhere."

I called the newspaper and explained to the editor what I needed from his correspondent. He wasn't fond of done deeds either, but he agreed. I got to my fourth whiskey before checking with Anabela in Cuernavaca. It was nearly one, and she and the children had arrived two hours earlier without incident.

"Your goons have already taken over the yard and the entrance," she said, pretending to be more annoyed than she really was. "And reinforcements arrived just a few minutes ago. Did you tell the other side something?"

"Not a thing," I said. "I'm checking on Pizarro in Poza Rica."

"Very good," Anabela said, "because if he's in Poza Rica, we can send him flowers. Are you going to keep me abreast of your investigation or do I have to resort to feminine intuition?"

I gave her the bar's phone number so she could give it to the guards.

"Don't worry," Anabela said. "If I get killed, you'll find out anyway."

"That's not the point."

"Of course not. But do you realize how long it's been since we've screwed? I've just been thinking that if Pizarro's on the rampage, he better not catch us with any sexual accounts pending."

"Yes."

"So then what's the mystery, what's to investigate? Send Pizarro some flowers, and come here where it's warm."

The Ambassadeurs bar seemed warmer for the moment. It showed early promise as a place to run to, and served as an undercover center of operations.

Around 2:00 in the afternoon a couple of radio reporters and Miguel Reyes Razo, who at the time worked for a major Mexico City daily, showed up at Ambassadors. Though they'd come to eat, they joined me at the bar for an aperitif, which naturally led to my ordering a fifth whiskey. Half an hour later the next call from Poza Rica came in.

The dinner had gone off without Lacho Pizarro, the correspondent said. Loya, who was by then mayor, had attended as his representative. Loya made the appropriate excuses but said nothing to explain the absence. His silence triggered rumors and speculation, but neither the union or Pizarro's own people knew anything.

"The rumor is that he made an emergency trip to Houston for a checkup," the correspondent said.

"An emergency checkup?" I said. "What about Roibal?"

"He's not here either, sir. They left together."

"Is there a way to verify the Houston trip?"

"No, because, as I said, no one's talking. I got it in an aside from one of the guards."

"Offer that guard money and get him to tell you what he knows," I said.

"Yes, sir."

"And call me right here as soon as you have something. I'm not going anywhere."

Reyes Razo and his friends invited me to eat. We took a table in the rear next to a Cuban piano player whose nightly repertoire was a mix of Agustín Lara and Cole Porter. They ordered steak and wine. I had a shrimp cocktail and my next dose of whiskey.

"You're drinking quite heavily, esteemed master," Reyes Razo said.

"Fellow travelers are welcome, good sir."

"You have me at a great disadvantage, esteemed master, but I will allow myself to journey with you a ways."

He called for the head waiter. "Don Lorenzo, my esteemed master here has been drinking alone for many a half hour. Does such self-absorption seem fair to you, such disregard for basic solidarity?"

"By no means, Don Miguel. It's absolutely unfair."

"What suggestion have you to remedy this situation? Because the situation is intolerable."

"I suggest that you drink with him, Don Miguel."

"Then you agree that a situation of this sort must not be tolerated?"

"Under no circumstances, sir."

"Then bring me a double whiskey over lots of rocks."

We drank in solidarity with one another during the meal at a ratio of two whiskeys to one, Reyes Razo's doubles to my singles. We'd reached the dessert when another call came in.

"He's at Methodist Hospital in Houston," the correspondent said. "He apparently got sick and fainted."

"When?"

"Early this week."

It was Friday. The car Chanes and his henchmen were traveling in crashed early Wednesday morning. The assassination attempt must have been Monday or Tuesday. Had they gotten to him?

"What else did the guard tell you?"

"Nothing else. There was no need for money. That's all he knew."

I thought I recalled a stringer in Houston who occasionally sent stories to my newspaper. I tried to look him up, but two months previously he'd moved to Los Angeles. I returned to the table with a fresh whiskey provided straight from the bar where the phone was. Its tranquilizing effect was giving way to a bout of active euphoria followed by an insatiable and unquenchable thirst.

"Has your reverence's paper a correspondent in Houston?" I asked Reyes Razo.

"Only in Falfurrias, Texas, your reverence."

"Seriously, have you got someone?"

Reyes Razo laughed.

"It's all they can do to hold onto me. Do you need a connection in Houston?"

"Urgently."

"Then ask, esteemed master. Say, 'I need a connection in Houston.' What would my paper be doing with a stringer in Houston? It's all they can do to remember where Toluca is. You know how our correspondent in Durango datelined his first story? Seriously, you know what he put? He put 'Durango, Dur., such and such a date.' Durango, Dur! Do you think we'd get someone in Houston just so he could put *Houston, Hous.*?"

"Seriously, your reverence."

"Seriously, your reverence. The other day for purposes of publicity and my own information, I asked the front office what our circulation was, and I got an answer from the director himself. He acted insulted and annoyed as if I'd called his mother a bad name. 'And what difference does our circulation make to you, Reyes Razo? Are you our advertising agent or are you going to place an ad to sell your fleabag hound, your used wife, or your defunct Packard? Circulation figures are a state secret at this paper, Reyes Razo. You don't play around with them, they're sacred.' So it turns out that circulation is sacred. Damn, I start back to the newsroom and on my way past the presses I run into *El Ulalume*, the chief pressman Don Pedro Flores Díaz. *El Ulalume* is jet black, an ex-alcoholic who never stops preaching. 'I've now gone ten years eight months and twenty-five days without a drink, Miguelito. I'm a new man, I swear I'm a new man' and the next day, 'You know how long I've gone without a drop of the poison, Miguelito?' 'Well, yes,' I tell him, 'you've gone ten years eight months and *twenty-six* days, Don Pedro.' 'That's right, Miguelito. I see you keep track for me.' I got him a watch so he could count the hours too. I really did. So I'm going from the front office to the newsroom and on my way by the presses I run into *El Ulalume*, and I say, 'What was last night's press run, Pedro?' And he says, 'Well, last night 30,000 complete copies came off the presses, Miguelito, 3,603 to be exact plus 312 for the night watchmen to sell on their way home. So that comes to 3,365 copies of your paper, Miguelito.

But if the information is for advertisers or the general public, I have the latest memo from the front office right here. It's dated May 31, 1979. It says weekday circulation 152,300; Sundays 224,150.' Just think," Reyes Razo went on, "that was the paper's state secret. And if I were to ask *El Ulalume* for a copy, he'd keep the copy and give me the original. So, your reverence, what makes you think such a paper would have a stringer in Houston, Hous.? If what you need is a connection, say so, and get it over with. Do you want a connection?"

"Once you finish slandering your paper, good sir."

"Over and done with, dear colleague. But description's not slander. Do you want a connection in Houston, or not? You want one? All right. Here you go." He got out his address book and paged through it. "Come eight, come nine, as my mother used to say. Let's see. Mendoza, Mexueiro, Miller. Marjorie Miller, your reverence."

"Marjorie what?"

"Your connection, dear colleague, Marjorie Miller. She runs *The Los Angeles Times* bureau in Houston, Texas. Or, as they say, she's *based out of* Houston, Texas. She's the author of the most in-depth piece on the Mexican oil boom yet published in the United States."

He proceeded to describe with numerous digressions how, early that year, he'd served as Marjorie Miller's guide during her month-long trip to Mexico City and Tabasco to cover the oil story. "A first-class journalist, good sir. She went to the jungle and visited the off-shore rigs where even our Mexican men won't go. She came down with a case of dysentery so bad I thought I'd have to send her home with a coroner's report. Do you want her address and phone number?"

He retrieved his address book once again, took off his glasses, and poked through it with his nose so close to the pages he seemed to be sniffing them. "Technical difficulty," he said, still flipping the pages. "It's not in here. Partake of another whiskey, your reverence, while this grievous oversight is remedied."

"He brought the dictionary to eat with us," one of our tablemates said.

"By oversight I mean error, mistake, foolishness, ignorance, or outrage," Reyes Razo said. Turning to me, he went on, "I beg your forbearance, your reverence, while I enlighten these ignoramuses. But I leave it to you to explain that ignoramus has nothing to do with ignition or igniting."

He got Miller's phone number from his house following a series of heated altercations with his maid and returned exactly one whiskey later with the reply in hand. Marjorie Miller answered the phone.

We exchanged jokes about her contact in Mexico, then I asked her to check for any Mexican nationals admitted to Methodist Hospital in the past five days with specific reference to the surnames of Pizarro and Roibal and with the reason for admission if possible.

She agreed and asked us to call her back at 7:00.

"That's 8:00 our time, esteemed master," Reyes Razo said. "There's an hour's difference. We are delayed, as they say, by the imponderables of the profession."

I thanked him for his willingness to keep me company. He had just completed a long and successful series on the dark side of the musicians' and tourist haunts in and around the Plaza Garibaldi, and was taking time off to prepare his next project. When our table mates from the world of radio left, we took care of the bill between us and retired to the bar to lubricate our forced sojourn. It was 7:00 in the evening. When Marjorie Miller called back at 8:00 all systems were well lubricated.

"No Pizarro," Marjorie Miller said from Houston. "But

there is a Roibal."

"When was he admitted?"

"Patient G. Roibal entered Tuesday at two *en el noche*," Marjorie Miller said in broken Spanish.

"What kind of sickness?"

"The list doesn't show sickness. That's confidential at Methodist."

"Can you find out, Miss Miller?"

"I can try."

"And there's no Pizarro on the list?"

"No Pizarro. There's a Pintado, a Pérez-Rosbach, and Pereyra. That all the P's."

"Yes."

"Then there's a Rodriguez, then a Tejeda and so on."

"A Tejeda?"

"L.P. Tejeda."

"L.P. Tejeda. That's the one."

"Be discrete, your reverence," Reyes Razo said at my side. "You're audible all the way to Bucareli."

It was true. My shouting had caught the attention of the other bar patrons. I turned to face the wall and hunched forward over the phone. "When was Tejeda admitted?"

"Tuesday, two at night."

"With what sickness?"

"The sickness is not on the list. It's confidential at Methodist," Miller repeated.

"But can you try to find out why they were admitted?"

"I can try," she reiterated. "Is it urgent?"

"Very urgent."

"Can it wait until tomorrow?"

"We must know today, Miss Miller."

"Today is difficult."

"Today."

"I can try. Call me at nine. Same number."

"Nine on the dot."

I hung up, and Reyes Razo asked, "Pizarro en Houston?"

"Get it out of your head, your reverence. This is a deal between Mrs. Miller and me. How old is Miller?"

"Twenty-seven."

"Good reporter?"

"First rate."

"The next call's at ten. Another whiskey?"

"Only until I start seeing pygmies, your reverence."

I lost count of the whiskeys, doubles on the rocks for Reyes Razo and singles with soda for me.

"You have something good on Pizarro in Houston, your reverence?" Reyes Razo asked.

"You wouldn't believe it."

"Heavy duty?"

"Heavy as a tombstone, your reverence. And quiet as a cemetery."

"That's a dress parade of metaphors, dear colleague. Your allusion to cemeteries rules out the murmur of the trees, I suppose."

"And the howls from the tombs. But this whiskey is much too pale."

When I redialed Marjorie Miller, my speech was slurred. "The people you look for left Methodist Hospital this noon," Miller said. "They gave the Hyatt Regency in this city for an address, but I checked the Regency, and those people are not there. About sicknesses, I got nothing specific. Patient Tejeda was admitted to traumatology. Patient Roibal to surgery."

"Roibal to surgery? He was injured too?"

"Injured? I don't know. It's the report I got from Methodist Hospital. More information requires more time."

"Tomorrow?"

"I can try tomorrow."

"I'll call tomorrow, Miss Miller. You're saving my life."

"My pleasure. *But get some sleep. I can smell your booze through the line.*"

"*Whatsamara, mis Miller, nou spic inglish?*"

"Get a little sleep. The phone line smells of alcohol."

"When I go to Houston, I'll give you the whole story straight out."

"Just say when."

We ate, then kept drinking until nearly one in the morning, becoming more dogmatic and repetitious as the night wore on. An icy wind blew down Reforma as we left, and I insisted to the point of blackmail that Reyes Razo go somewhere else with me. He refused. He was a lot less drunk than I and was not in the habit of exceeding his limit. I wouldn't let him help me into a taxi. He paid the fare anyway and made the driver promise to look after me. I could barely keep my balance, but I knew exactly and urgently where I needed to go.

At 1:30 in the morning the dance hall on Palma where I'd last gone with Rojano still looked half empty and lifeless. I ordered Anís de la Cadena as we had then and, face by face, outfit by outfit, set out to find the woman he picked up. I found her waiting in line to use the restroom, and paid the fee to take her out for the night. Stumblingly, I led her to the Hotel del León where we'd slept with Rojano the last time. We took a room, and she began to undress. Before she could finish I tried to hoist her onto my hips and penetrate her the way Rojano had. But she wasn't the slender woman with crooked teeth and peroxided hair that she was the last time. She was a well-padded mulatta who wasn't about to let herself be pushed around. She pushed back and staggered out of the room, leaving the door open behind her. I could neither stop her nor go after her. I could barely move. A cold draft wafted between the door and a window that hadn't been closed. I lay slumped next to the bed with my mouth open, listlessly drooling down the left side of my body onto the floor. With the cold came the unshakable illusion that I was lying, not in a draft on the floor of a hotel room on Brazil Street in Mexico City, but at night on the cobblestones of the plaza in Chicontepec like Rojano beneath the darkened poinciana, all energy gone, awaiting like Rojano the stones, the blows, the torches, the ropes, the flaying, the smothering, the bullet in the temple from Roibal.

Chapter 10
THE UPSHOT

I awakened with the weight of the world on top of me—lying where I fell—on December 9, 1979. I spent half an hour in a steaming shower followed by two Bloody Marys, an injection at a pharmacy, and two high potency Valiums. By 11:00, unsteady but revived, I called Marjorie Miller in Houston. Pizarro and Roibal had vanished without leaving any trace in Houston's top ten hotels. The inquiry into the reasons for their hospitalization hadn't progressed much either because Methodist kept such information confidential and Marjorie's contacts had come up dry. So I called the correspondent in Veracruz and had him check to see if Pizarro had shown up in Poza Rica.

"He and Roibal probably had operations," I told him.

"Operations for what?" the correspondent said.

"Bullets most likely."

"Pizarro? Bullets?"

His surprise told me I was being imprudent.

"I don't know for what," I said. "That's exactly what I want you to find out."

"Yes, sir."

"If necessary, rent a helicopter and get there today."

I gave him the phone numbers for my house and The Hideaway in Cuernavaca.

Then I lay down for a moment on the bed—11:30 in the morning—overwhelmed by the memory of my own hallucinated image of the night before. The drafts in the hotel seemed to have lifted me out of my body and brought Rojano back to the place of our final encounter. I woke up choking and bathed in a cold sweat. My heart beat unevenly.

I felt as if swarms of ants were crawling up my back. My arm was swollen, and drops of perspiration ran down my neck. I was going to turn 40 the following August, but by noon I'd be dead—alone in my apartment on *Artes*, short of my 40th birthday—from heart failure and a hangover. And fright.

I went to the kitchen for a glass, dropped ice in it, and poured myself four fingers of vodka, which I downed in two gulps. Then I gagged. My chest caught fire, my hands broke into a sweat, my stomach knotted shut. Fits of coughing wracked my body as it rejected the liquor, stinging my nose as in an allergic reaction. Little by little the throbbing diminished in my temples, my chest relaxed, and a feeling of mild euphoria brought up the image of Anabela naked and tanned against a backdrop of water the color of amethyst and blindingly white sand.

Before 2:00 in the afternoon, I was on my way up the path of bougainvilleas to The Hideaway in Cuernavaca, my lust for Anabela renewed and consumed by the urge to celebrate. Tonchis and Mercedes weren't back from school yet—they got out at 6:00—and Anabela was pruning bamboo shoots in shorts and red gardening gloves. Amused but without great enthusiasm, she let herself be guided to the bedroom where we lay with the window open, proceeding slowly at first and then with abandon. She was having her period.

"Do I pay the fee for service to Mr. Wyborowa?" she said upon finishing. She seemed relaxed and playful while attempting to tease the stained sheet from under her body.

"Mr. Johnny Walker and the fabulous producers of Anís de la Cadena come first."

"My thanks to them all." She couldn't get the sheet out from under her. "This matter of the failed emissary even left my hormones out of kilter."

She chose to get to her feet and remove all the bedclothes

completely. The cover over the box spring had also been stained.

"Not that much of a failure." I found a bathrobe and made my way towards Mr. Wyborowa. Mr. Wodka Wyborowa, that is.

"Did you hear something?" she asked anxiously, holding the sheets in her arms.

"Something got to Pizarro."

"You see? You see, *Negro*? It was the way to go."

"He was a poor devil. And didn't we agree that you didn't put him up to it?"

"Tell me what happened, *Negro*. Don't preach."

"They went to a hospital in Houston. Apparently they were wounded."

"You see?"

"But they've already left the hospital."

"What do you mean?"

She put the sheets in a wicker basket.

"I mean you have to get out of the country."

"Oh, no."

"For a while."

"I'm not running."

"You've got to run."

"We've said enough about that. I don't want any more arguments."

She reached her hands into the linen closet and irritatedly yanked out a fresh set of sheets. They came loose along with two more sets after which one of Pizarro's original leather pouches tumbled out. I picked it off the floor and looked it over just as I'd once done with those I'd taken from the hands of Rojano. It was the same smooth leather I'd been shown before with the same pseudo-Aztec border and death threat.

"Give me that," Anabela said, snatching the pouch.

"When did it come?"

"What difference does it make to you? It's none of your business."

"When did it come?"

"Don't argue with me. Get out of here. You came to fuck, and you've fucked. So stop pestering me. Let me live my life in peace any way I want to."

I got hold of her arm and again asked when had it come.

"Yesterday," Anabela said. "You're hurting me."

"How did it come?" I persisted without letting her go.

"Your goons found it in the yard."

"You should have told me. How did it get here?"

"You're hurting me, *Negro*. You're hurting me a lot."

"How did it get here? Who brought this pouch?"

She began to cry and fell back onto the bare mattress.

"Tonchis," she sobbed, rubbing her arm.

"It was delivered at school?"

She nodded her head between sobs. He'd gotten it yesterday.

Once again I was dizzy, breathless and overcome by tachycardia, confirming that now as before, alive or dead, I was tied inextricably to Rojano's mate. I was her accomplice and her victim. Everyone else—Tonchis, Mercedes, and me included—was secondary. As usual, I'd underestimated Rojano's hold on Anabela, the degree to which, ever since Chicontepec, the one force that kept her going was the urge to regain what had been ripped away from her that night. Her children were simply an extension of herself, and I was just another resource to draw on in her quest for vengeance. Or for something more specific and real than vengeance: self-destruction in a new and chilling bid to share the fate of her beloved spouse.

I called Mexico City in search of my contact. He claimed to have spent the whole day trying to find me.

"I'm in your custody in Cuernavaca," I said.

"Hidden in plain sight," he replied. "May I expect you in my office this evening?"

"Please don't make me leave here," I answered. "There's been a new development."

"Have you new information to support your charges?"

"Information, yes," I said. "Charges no."

"That's more realistic, *paisano*. I'll see you there this evening."

I got bread, cheese, ham, and paté from the refrigerator, poured refills of vodka, and took the whole lot to the bedroom. I dialed Marjorie Miller in Houston, but no one answered. I checked my calls at the newspaper in Mexico City. There were messages from my *paisano* and two from the correspondent in Veracruz, which I immediately returned.

"They're not in Poza Rica," he said, sounding upset. "There's no sign of them. The prior source had nothing to add. I went to the Quinta Bermúdez and got all the way to Pizarro's office, but he's not here. I tried talking to his girlfriend, but she's gone too. The mayor refused to see me and just sent word that Pizarro had gone to Houston for a routine checkup."

"Then where is he?" I said impatiently.

"Not in Poza Rica," the correspondent said. "He could have gone to Mexico City."

"Why Mexico City?"

"The Valle del Bravo local has a rest house with a heliport."

"Can you check that out?"

"I can ask around here and see what comes up."

I called the paper again and asked for the reporter who covered the airport. I asked him to check the passenger lists of flights from Houston the night before as well as the non-commercial hangars—especially PEMEX's—for flights to

Houston in the past 48 hours.

Tonchis and Mercedes got home shortly after 6:00. Anabela had put on a white caftan with gold piping. She'd put a Virginia ham basted with pineapple, cloves, and cinnamon in the oven.

"*Negro*, why haven't you been around?" Tonchis said.

"Because I've been preparing a trip for you."

"Ah, damn. Hot damn," Tonchis said.

"Mom, Tonchis sad a bad word," Mercedes tattled.

"A great big trip to Los Angeles to your Aunt Alma's," I said.

Anabela's only sister, Alma Rosa Guillaumín, bought a condominium in Los Angeles two months after Rojano's death. She'd moved there with her husband, a Tamaulipan from Brownsville who was in the real estate business.

"Is that where Disneyland is, Uncle?" Mercedes asked with her perfect diction.

"And that s.o.b. EJMog," Tonchis added with an exaggerated Veracruz accent. He was nine by the calendar but years older according to the glint in his eyes and his muscular body.

"That's where Disneyland is," I told Mercedes.

"And when are we going?" she asked.

"I'm getting tickets for next Monday," I said with a sideways glance at Anabela as she set the supper table.

There was no reaction, not the slightest wince.

"But, Uncle, on Monday school won't be out yet." Mercedes sounded worried.

"We'll let the school know."

We ate the Virginia ham at 8:30, and Tonchis went to watch television after we finished. Anabela and I stayed behind in the sala, and Mercedes curled up next to me. She had a finely shaped oval face. Her childlike features bore a strange resemblance to those of a grownup woman. She had a very wide forehead, high cheekbones, and sharply defined chin and mouth. Her eyes looked out at the world from behind lashes so long and black they seemed false.

I began to play with her, pretending to nip at her arms and cheeks.

"You're not going to grow up to be like your mother, are you?" I said.

"Like my mother?" Mercedes said, clearly articulating each word in her child's voice.

"Your mother's crazy, and she lies," I told her.

"My mother does not lie," Mercedes said, "and you smell of liquor. You're drunk."

"When you grow up, you're going to be like *el Negro*," I said.

"Like you?"

"Like me. Drunk and with no place to hide."

"No place to hide?"

"No place to hide one thing while saying another."

I nipped at her cheek and then her buttocks.

"I'm biting you to make sure you grow up like *el Negro*. Except for one thing."

"What's that?"

"The one way you're going to be like your mother."

"What way is that?"

"You'll fall in love with a total jerk."

"With you?"

"With me, no. With the jerk who will be your one and only love."

"With you, *Negro*."

"No, not with me."

By 9:00 the children were asleep, and Anabela began turning off all the lights in the house.

"Not so fast," I said. "There's company coming."

"More goons?"

"One more."

"The one making our travel plans?"

"Your children's life insurance."

"They don't need life insurance."

I took her hand and sat her down on one of the wicker sofas. It had a high back that resembled a crown. I sat on the footstool in front of her and held her cold hands in mine. She was unbearably beautiful and remote, striking more sharply than ever the key she'd always struck in me.

"I don't get it," I said, "but let's suppose I do. You want to go all the way to the bitter end, and for you the end is letting Rojano drag you down with him. First, he beat you up, then he had you under house arrest with his kids, then he hauled you off to Chicontepec. Now he's forcing you to flee just like your emissary. The question is, are you going to flee or not? It doesn't matter if you do or if you just let Pizarro decide. With you Rojano always gets the last word."

Her eyes misted but didn't shed a single tear.

"I don't get it, but a few hours ago I resigned myself to fate," I went on. "I also resigned myself to this: it isn't the fate I bargained for, and I'm going to do what I can to change it. And it better not include the children."

"They're my children," Anabela said.

"It's your fight," I said. "But now I'm fighting too. I've been in this fight all along, but I never understood the rules. Now I do, but I don't like them, and I'm going to try to change them. But you're not betting the children."

"I love you, *Negro*," Anabela said.

"Not the way I'd like you to."

"I do too."

"No. But I'm getting the children out of this. This coming Monday they're going to Los Angeles."

"Yes."

"And then we're dealing with the legacy of Rojano without the children in the middle."

I checked to see what the reporter at the airport had learned about aircraft activity. There was only one flight he'd yet to verify, a non-commercial plane belonging to the Rural Credit Bank that appeared headed for Iowa, not Texas. There was no sign of Pizarro. I had the reporter book tickets for unaccompanied children on Mexicana with arrangements for them to be delivered by airline personnel directly to Mrs. Ana Rosa Guillaumín at the airport in Los Angeles. Then I had Anabela explain the situation to Alma and promised that in two weeks I'd be there myself to give her a full explanation during the Christmas holidays. Then my contact arrived. It was 11:00 at night on Friday, December 9, 1979.

Anabela received him seated on her enormous wicker throne, impassive and serene in her white caftan like the queen in a deck of cards. My contact solemnly greeted her, and we proceeded without further conversation to a tense conclave whose significance I stressed by placing on the table in the middle of the sala a box of cigars and a tray with cognac and goblets that rang like tuning forks when they brushed against one another.

My contact took a cigar and accepted a cognac. Though he was wearing a vest and a light woolen suit in the mild but constant heat of Cuernavaca, there was not so much as a bead of perspiration glistening on his brow or cheeks. The toll taken by a day's work was discernible only in the slight growth of his meticulously trimmed mustache, a bit of swelling under his reddened eyes, and a few wrinkles at the corners of his mouth. Otherwise, he was impeccable: shirt, collar, tie, and an unmistakable aroma of lotion and Mapleton tobacco. That night, for the first time, I could see that beneath the fastidious exterior was an actor at pains to preserve his image. He must have bathed two or three times a day and maintained a small portable wardrobe with private stores of toiletries as if grooming were the key to his credibility and efficiency. His persona, with its macabre combination of gloom and good manners, came across simply as the adult incarnation of a civics lesson.

("In this business your hands get dirty all the time," he once told me. "It's not all that important. You wash them in dirty water at the office, then with rosewater when you get home so they'll stay clean.")

The cigar and the cognac heightened the pink of his lips. "It's a pleasure to meet you in person," he said to Anabela. "What can I do for you?"

"You had urgent information," I said. "Can you tell us what it's about?"

"At your request we did an investigation of the Edilberto Chanes accident," my contact said. Anabela's face darkened with anger. She stared down at the floor. She looked at me, at the wall, and then back at our informant. "His trail leads all the way back to the Quinta Bermúdez in Poza Rica."

Anabela took a long drink of cognac.

"Edilberto Chanes tried to seize the Quinta Bermúdez by force last Monday," my contact went on. "He had nine people with him. Five died in the attack. The others were captured and died on the highway, including Chanes himself."

"They were executed," Anabela stated.

"There were also casualties on the other side," my contact pointed out. "Pizarro and his chief aide left the country on Tuesday to seek treatment for their wounds."

"What wounds?" Anabela asked.

"The attack nearly succeeded, ma'am," my contact said. "They got all the way to Pizarro's office, and they held him for half an hour."

Anabela took another long drink of cognac.

"That's the information I have for you," my contact said. "What do you have?"

He looked not at me but at Anabela, who stared into her cognac.

"Pizarro's leather warning pouch arrived yesterday," I said. "They had it delivered via the mayor's older child."

The news appeared to disconcert him. He asked to see the pouch, and I went to the bedroom to get it. I placed it in his hands with the motto *Whoever knows how to add*...directly in front of him. He opened and closed the dividers, running his manicured nails and his fingertips bathed in rosewater over the leather.

"Does it mean the usual?" He sounded annoyed as if his assumptions had turned out to be badly flawed. "Is it addressed specifically to you, ma'am?"

"My son brought it home from school," Anabela answered drily.

"That's not what I'm asking," my contact said. "I'm talking about the name of the addressee."

"Us," Anabela said.

"Was there anything written inside?"

"No," Anabela said. "But you know perfectly well what the message is."

"No, I don't," my contact said. "I need to know exactly what you received."

Clearly, he was confronted with a fact that went beyond his expectations. He couldn't have been more upset by the appearance of this piece on the chessboard.

"I must tell you this." My contact struggled to maintain his self-control. "Edilberto Chanes and his men almost killed Pizarro."

"Pizarro left the hospital yesterday," Anabela said.

"To go to another hospital," my contact replied.

"And on the way he sent us the pouch?" Anabela said

sarcastically.

My contact got to his feet and hastily traversed the space from his chair to the bar.

"I don't mean to offend you," he said, "but as an objective outside observer, I need to tell you some things that should help guide your decisions and let you understand what's at stake. Bear in mind that early Monday morning an attempt was made on the life of the most important mid-level leader of the most powerful labor union in the country. It was the work of a hired gun named Edilberto Chanes, who lost his life in an automobile accident while fleeing to Tulancingo. Due to the indiscretion of an accomplice," —he looked at me as if asking leave to continue— "the Mexican government is now in a position to discover that Chanes was in the pay of the widow of the former mayor of Chicontepec." He looked at Anabela as if he were now asking her leave to go on. "The widow had long attributed the lynching of her husband by the people of Chicontepec on June 9, 1978, to the machinations of the oil workers' boss. The main propagator of this tale is a well known journalist who turned out to have been the widow's lover in the year prior to the mayor's death, the very columnist who had been the mayor's friend since both were in their teens."

"I'm not putting up with this, *Negro*," Anabela said.

"This is how things stand politically." My contact brushed the protest aside, and unbuttoned his jacket. "For over a year and a half the widow and her then husband, Francisco Rojano, had been renewing their friendship with the journalist in order to convince him that the union leader had risen to power through a series of politically motivated crimes. Those crimes, disguised as accidents, were intended to facilitate the union's takeover of choice lands in the municipalities of Tuxpan and Chicontepec in the state of Veracruz. To convince the journalist they were right, the couple created false files complete with photos and coroners' reports. However, the labor leader actively promoted the political career of his accuser, Francisco Rojano, and helped him gain the coveted post of mayor of the impoverished municipality of Chicontepec, Veracruz, where Petróleos Mexicanos was expected to invest heavily in coming years. Lust for power, political carelessness, and a dissipated lifestyle led to increasing friction between the mayor and an already sullen, hostile and ignorant community. Finally, the townspeople took matters into their own hands, and in their own crude way, protested the imposition of a dissolute and disreputable outside ruler by publicly lynching him. And all because of his boundless ambition. After just a year in office, the mayor's local landholdings had grown from 300 hectares to nearly 2,000 and his wife's from less than 400 to almost 3,000 hectares of the best irrigated land in the municipality."

"You gave him all that information," Anabela said evenly. She regained her self-control by staring into her empty goblet, then holding it up to the light. She stood up, walked to where my contact was leaning on the bar, and held out her glass. "Pour me a double," she said. "Your version of what happened made my hands cold."

My contact obliged. Anabela smiled and returned to her royal seat. The minister for internal security resumed from his post by the bar. "The oil workers' union agreed to acquire the widow's holdings for the inflated sum of 32 million pesos, which came to about 1.5 million dollars in a single payment during the month of November, 1978. A year later the widow hired Edilberto Chanes to assassinate the union leader, whom she blamed for her husband's death. What else did she blame him for? For having thwarted the further expansion of the couple's domains in Chicontepec? Probably. Was the nationally known columnist in on the scheme to get even richer? Maybe he was."

"And Pizarro was the living hero of the Mexican Revolution?" Seated on her peacock throne, Anabela had fully regained her self-control

"Pizarro is a legitimate leader in the eyes of his followers," my contact said. "He's given back to the oil workers more than he's taken from them. That's the bottom line on his political balance sheet."

"Abuses and murders included?" I said.

"Yourselves included," my contact replied.

"Those are the facts as you see them?" I said. "That's what happened, according to you?"

"No," my contact said. "If that's what I thought, I wouldn't be here. I've given you the political version, the objective version. It's not the truth, but it's the reality you have to face just as if it were the truth. Objectively and without fooling yourselves."

"Your words leave me cold, counsel." Anabela was being sarcastic. "My hands are frozen. The only evidence you left out is the day Edilberto Chanes slept with the widow in Chicontepec and the recording of her saying, 'Kill him, boy'."

"I'm not making any accusations," my contact said. He took a cigarette from his spotless gold case. He'd left his cigar on the table in the middle of the room. "What I've given you is a simple reconstruction based on the facts of the case. I'm not interested in putting you on trial. That's not my job."

"Isn't justice your job?" Anabela said.

"No, ma'am. My job is keeping the peace," my contact said.

"So what are you trying to get at with all this?"

"I want to reach a negotiation."

"We already negotiated," Anabela said.

"And the terms of the agreement were blatantly violated," my contact said. "Because, among other things, you defied a power greater than yourself. You even launched an attack on the life of that power, and now your own life is in danger."

"I didn't attack a thing," Anabela shot back, rejecting the confession implicit in the way my contact framed her behavior. "For three years I've been defending myself against a nightmare named Lázaro Pizarro, your reborn hero of the Mexican Revolution, your born leader, your good warlord. Pizarro has cost me my husband, my peace of mind, my inheritance, and the chance to lead a normal life. And the safety of my children. Now, to top it off, that man's craziness has left a permanent scar on my life. What do you want me to negotiate? How to commit suicide in a way pleasing to Pizarro?"

"I'm not saying you didn't have your reasons," my contact said. "What I'm saying is you don't have the power to confront Pizarro."

"If you people cared more about justice than keeping the peace," Anabela said while getting to her feet. "We'd have had the power to contain Pizarro."

My contact inhaled and released an even stream of blue smoke from his nostrils. He seemed saddened and mildly annoyed.

"If you had chosen justice and fairness," he said, looking down at the floor, "You'd never have approached Pizarro in the first place. Pizarro would never have given you his support, and you'd never have gotten into a land dispute with him in Chicontepec. You wouldn't have needed backing from the national press, you wouldn't have broken your first agreement with Pizarro, and you wouldn't have been in such a hurry to get rich. The mayor of Chicontepec wouldn't have been lynched, Pizarro wouldn't be wounded, and we wouldn't be having this conversation."

Clearly, impersonally and mechanically, he'd played back a history of savagery regulated by a system of checks and balances beyond the understanding of its lesser actors. Its moral was competence in the service of stability and preserving the polished outer surfaces of the institutions.

"What do you propose?" I asked.

"That the lady and her children leave the country immediately, tomorrow if possible," my contact said. "Then let's try to renegotiate with Pizarro and settle the conflict. You may want to write something, get some sort of compensation from us."

"More concessions?" Anabela asked.

"Probably more concessions, ma'am."

"I'm not leaving," Anabela said haughtily.

"Let me explain something," my contact said. "You appear to have won the last battle in this war because Pizarro is never going to recover fully from his wounds. He lost three quarters of his stomach, and a bullet left him paralyzed and half blind. The paralysis is progressive. He's got about a year to live."

"In Houston?" Anabela asked.

"He was transferred to the Medical Center in Mexico City following emergency surgery in Houston. What I'm telling you comes from the Mexico City hospital report."

"And how do I know you're telling me the truth?" Anabela smiled as if the news made her feel better.

"You don't." My contact watched her, sizing her up. "You have to believe me. But I am telling you the truth. You can leave the country and wait until your enemy's corpse passes by your doorstep or you can stay here and be an easy target for Pizarro's last blow, which could be aimed at your children."

"And if I still won't go?" Anabela said. Her cheeks were red, and her eyes were on fire.

"Then you're on your own with no support from us. No guards, no protection."

"So you'd just throw us to the wolves?" Anabela stared into her backlit glass.

"A guard detail isn't going to keep Pizarro at bay," my contact said. "My job at the moment is to make you leave. It's the only way to guarantee your safety and, as a result, the only way we can do our job effectively."

"How do you know Pizarro won't come looking for me wherever I am?"

"We haven't negotiated with Pizarro yet," my contact replied. "Once the crisis passes, he's more likely to prefer concessions. Despite what your experience may suggest, Pizarro is above all a politician, not a killer."

"The latter day hero of the Mexican Revolution." Anabela shook her head, her eyes aglow, her hair floating youthfully down over her shoulders. "I need a week to get ready," she said at last.

"A week may be too long," my contact answered. "I can get you your tickets in Mexico City and take care of all the details. Visas and so forth. If you need a little money to tide you over while having your accounts transferred from here, we can also help you with that."

"Under those circumstances, we could leave Monday," Anabela said.

"Thank you for understanding," my contact said. "It's strictly temporary, an emergency measure, believe me."

"I believe you, sir, but you need to believe me about another thing in exchange."

"Whatever you wish, ma'am."

"You seem sure I sent Mr. Chanes after our benefactor in Poza Rica."

"That's the information I have direct from the source, yes," my contact said.

"The information from our journalist." Anabela pointed playfully and sarcastically at me.

"That's right," my contact said.

"What I want to tell you and him is this. I didn't send Edilberto Chanes anywhere. Chanes approached me in the street one day in Cuernavaca after I'd left the children off at school, and he told me about his designs on Pizarro. I didn't say yes or no. I just listened and kept my mouth shut. It wasn't my idea, it was his. I didn't try to stop him, but I didn't put him up to it."

"Chanes had a score to settle with Pizarro," my contact said. "I understand what you're telling me."

"Sir, I'm not asking you to understand." Her spirits had risen, and at the moment, perhaps with help from the cognac, she was radiant. "What I'm asking you to do is believe me."

"I believe you, ma'am," my contact said.

"I'm also asking you to make our journalist believe me." Looking at me, she turned the goblet around and around in her hand and smiled. She seemed inspired, even happy.

They left for Los Angeles on Monday, December 12, 1979, on Mexicana's early evening flight. That morning she'd transferred money to First National City Bank of California. It remained for me to rent The Hideaway, sell the van, and pay the monthly credit card installments. We got to the airport at 3:00 in the afternoon in two large cars with antennas and polarized windows. Traveling with us were the guard detail, Anabela's large trunk, and six more suitcases. Doña Lila held Mercedes's hand. The little girl was wearing a plaid outfit, a cap, and a scarf. Tonchis, who was nearly as tall as Anabela, joked with Comandante Cuevas. Anabela and I walked behind them in silence through the airport corridors, and behind us was the remainder of our escort.

We got through immigration and customs. At the duty-free shop Anabela spent a 1,000 dollars on a watch for her sister Alma, who was providing them a place to stay in Los Angeles. The guard detail took us all the way to the crowded waiting area. I said goodbye to Mercedes. "Call me whenever you feel like it and tell me you miss me. I'm going to visit you next week."

To Tonchis, I said, "Take care of your mom. If she tries anything crazy like taking up with a Gringo, let me know right away. I have some hired guns in Los Angeles who can make her change her mind.

"And if she takes up with a Mexican?"

"Grab him yourself and kick him out. I'm leaving you in charge. Let me know everything."

I then took Anabela to the adjacent waiting area, which was empty. She was dressed for winter in a black fur hat, high boots, a flannel skirt, and an emerald green scarf. The outfit made her seem comfortable and soft. Below the hat her eyes looked placid, and her lips and teeth were brilliant over the scarf. Diamond earrings accented her beautifully formed ears.

"It won't be for long," she said, brushing my cheek. Her hand wasn't as cold as usual.

We stood looking at each other. Her eyes were crystal clear in the intense light streaming through the huge window.

"No one knows where you're going," I said or, rather, repeated on instructions from my contact. "And nobody knows the address of the place you're going. Don't write, don't phone. Let some time pass before you go out."

"I already know that," Anabela said.

"I repeat so you won't forget," I said in a low voice.

"You're repeating so you won't have to say goodbye," Anabela said.

"That too."

"Well, you're not getting rid of me that easily, *Negro*," Anabela said, turning playful.

"Nor in any other way."

"Get yourself a boyfriend that kicks and scratches.

You're going to be alone on *Artes* the way you were when I went looking for you in '76. Remember?"

I remembered.

"I said a boyfriend because if I catch you with a little lady reporter, I'm coming down from Los Angeles to chop off your prick."

"I agree."

Comandante Cuevas stepped into the waiting room where we were and said, "They're boarding, sir."

"It's time, ma'am," I told her.

"Goodbye, *Negro*." Once again she caressed my cheek. Her hands were warm now. She looked at me a moment, then added, "I'm coming back, just like I did before."

I kissed her lightly but just firmly enough for the flavor of her lipstick to permeate my mouth.

"I'm uneasy about the children," Doña Lila said on the way back. "I get the shivers, I just don't know."

"They'll be all right," I told her.

"You'll be on the loose and surrounded by pussy, but the children... May God watch over them."

"So long as their mother watches over them," I said.

"Doña Ana has her mind on everything except her children. I can imagine the kind of protection they'll get from someone who got mixed up with you."

"Are you coming to *Artes* or shall I leave you in the market?"

"You're changing the subject, but what I said goes." Doña Lila stared out the car window. "The two of you should have let me raise them as good healthy Veracruzans in Tuxpan far from all these entanglements. Are you expecting company tonight?"

"No."

"You're at least letting a day go by?"

"At least."

"The body makes its demands just the same. I'm not going to criticize you. You'd better leave me in the market."

I let not a day but several months go by before the reporter from *El Sol* again crossed the threshold of my apartment on *Artes*. I didn't go to Los Angeles for Christmas as I'd promised, and my only communication with Anabela was two letters from Mercedes. Time passed in a sort of relaxed professional rush. I concentrated on my column. I updated and expanded my files and hired an assistant. I fell into an impersonal rhythm on the job with a full calendar, working breakfasts, lunches and dinners, and weekend excursions to different parts of the country where I'd discovered stories worth covering myself. I got results. Every day in the month of February 1980 I succeeded in offering a well documented exclusive of some sort. I was on a roll. In quick succession I disclosed ahead of any other medium PEMEX's unilateral decision to boost crude exports without bothering to consult the economic cabinet, the emergence of a new far-right group in Guadalajara named *Fuerza Nueva*, the business ties that generated million-dollar earnings for the head of the Rural Credit Bank, the name of the top CIA operative in Mexico, a summary of a confidential U.S. State Department memo in opposition to Mexico's Central American policy, the testimony of a chief of police fired for corruption, and the involvement of top Mexico City police authorities in the drug trade.

The final story of the month took up three full columns. It reported the enormous sums PEMEX was transferring to the union on the incredible pretext of granting it exclusive subcontracting rights for the company's exploration and construction projects as part of a collective bargaining agreement. The union could then outsource the work and charge finders' fees amounting—by my calculations—to between 1 and 1.5 billion dollars annually (between 25 and 35 billion pesos). The columns also described in detail the company's parallel transfers to the union of some 800 million pesos for commissions and paid leave. Most of those funds went to paying oil workers who, instead of doing their PEMEX jobs, worked for companies and businesses belonging to the union, especially the so-called "union gardens" of which "La Mesopotamia" and Pizarro's other agricultural complexes were prime examples. These net transfers of resources went a long way towards explaining the low costs and very low prices that enabled the union to boast about its efficiency to the rest of the country. It paid nothing for either skilled or unskilled labor. Its payroll was met by others.

Never did I feel so immersed in the simple task of investigating and communicating as I did in those days. Never so neutral, so remote from the political and personal implications of my column. I had no ulterior motives. I was objective and dispassionate, at absolute peace with myself.

In early March my contact sought me out. All the news I'd had from him in the intervening months was a card slipped under my door a few days after Anabela's departure. It said, "Negotiated as agreed, but vacation should continue until further notice." Was this further notice? We met on March 8, 1980, at a small restaurant in the Condesa District, the Tio Luis, which in times past had been the hangout of the bullfight crowd, on Montes de Oca and Cuautla.

"Working hard?" he said once we'd greeted each other in the protective aura of a display case where the embroidered vest of Manuel Benítez, el Cordobés, was enshrined.

"Hard and well," I said. My contact asked the waiter for mineral water only to drink, and I followed suit.

I thought back three years to Rojano and his abstemious domestic facade, his self-conscious parsimony.

"It shows day after day in your column," my contact said. "It's the best one around these days."

"Thank you."

"I've got some items for you to consider if you'll allow me."

"I'd be delighted."

"But I'd like to discuss something else with you right now."

I nodded, and he explained. "Pizarro's been declared terminally ill. He's sinking fast. At the rate he's going, the doctors say he won't last two months."

"Is that how much longer the vacation's going to last?" I said, thinking this was the news he had for me.

"The vacation doesn't have an end date yet," my contact said.

"Then why are you telling me about Pizarro?"

"I want you to go see him," my contact said.

"I'm not interested in seeing him."

"You will be," my contact said. "It's part of the negotiation about the vacationer and her future safety. Pizarro himself had me ask you."

"How crazy can you get?"

"Are you referring to me or Pizarro?"

"You and Pizarro. Why stir up that hornets' nest?"

"It's still an open file, *paisano*. I don't want to see more toads jumping out of it. Help me close it because you'll also be helping yourself. The vacationer isn't exactly the most placid woman who ever lived, *paisano*."

"That's strictly a private matter. Don't pry in my private life."

"That's all I'm trying to do," my contact said, "to keep your private life from becoming public."

"Are you handing me a bill, *paisano*?"

"I'm asking for your help in closing a file that just

happens to concern you. I've asked you before, and you've helped me through your column. For me the only difference is that this case involves you, and I admire and respect you. What's more, the interview will be of interest to the vacationer."

"Leave the vacationer out of this."

"A remarkable woman, *paisano*," my contact said. "I don't ever want to be her enemy."

"You never will be."

"There's another thing. Your recent disclosures about contracts and transfers has the union very worried," my contact said. "It's also in on this negotiation. That's why Pizarro wants to see you. It's a political matter if you know what I mean."

"I do, which is why it's not negotiable."

"Everything is negotiable, *paisano*," my contact said with a knowing smile.

I went to the restroom and returned.

"When do you want us to see Pizarro?"

He smiled once again.

Chapter 11
A TRUMPET FOR LACHO

The annual celebration of the expropriation of the oil industry took place on March 18, 1980, in Salamanca, Guanajuato. The President and his entire cabinet attended, along with an ample contingent of travel companions, speeches, and confetti. It was a time of heated debate about Mexico's possible entry into GATT—the General Agreement on Trade and Tariffs. Signatories to the pact promised to open their borders to world trade, a step which would bring an end to the long decades of industrial protectionism on which the Mexican economic "miracle" was based. The war raging among bureaucrats and the general public over the unbridled growth of PEMEX and the need to rein in its burgeoning exports had also entered a new phase.

In his keynote address that day, President López Portillo announced that Mexico would not be joining GATT and that a Mexican Nutrition System—to be known by its acronym of SAM—would be set up to mount an all-out attack on social stagnation and low productivity in the rural economy. These measures would be accompanied by a cap of 2.5 million barrels per day on crude oil production, officially laying to rest the notion that abundant oil would pay for absolutely everything including foodstuffs for the foreseeable future and whatever other imports might prove necessary.

These announcements were greeted by cheers, outpourings of emotion, and (more) confetti.

Years later we would learn that, as a practical matter, the progressive loosening of import restrictions then under way would make the question of joining or not joining GATT seem beside the point. Mexico had already opened its borders as much as it would have had to under the treaty but without the advantages to be gained by negotiating the terms for signing. With the change in presidential administrations, SAM got lost in a labyrinth of criticism and bureaucratic infighting. The token effort to put the brakes on excessive oil earnings for fear of hobbling the rest of the Mexican economy proved just as futile. Between 1978 and 1981, crude exports brought in 55 billion dollars, and by the end of 1982 the country was faced with foreign debts amounting to 80 billion dollars.

But the speech in Salamanca was the first public acknowledgment of the need to get PEMEX's runaway expansion under control. Intellectuals and journalists declared the day a turning point in the López Portillo administration. It marked the beginning of the end for PEMEX's wild growth spurt at a time when its impact on the economy as a whole and on Mexico's relations with the outside world was of increasing concern to public opinion and to the government itself.

For other observers of the president's speech, the measures announced that day had a more personal and tangible impact. First, they stifled the presidential ambitions of PEMEX director Jorge Díaz Serrano and the secretaries of the economic cabinet who had voted in favor of GATT. In other quarters the decisions of March 18 hit even harder. They curtailed PEMEX's giant investment projects, the grandest of which was the Chicontepec paleocanal and the golden city to be that drove both the ambitions of Rojano and the aspirations of Pizarro.

It was the day of my meeting with Pizarro, but I didn't see him at the ceremony. We met on the city's outskirts in a bungalow at the Club Campestre—the country club next to the Panamerican Highway where I was driven by my contact. We passed through a phalanx of guards and entered a small, dimly lit room with drawn curtains. A single lamp cast a weak yellow light from the back of the room. Pizarro was seated in a wheelchair next to the lamp, wearing glasses with pitch black lenses like a blind man's. There was a coverlet over his legs. Roibal stood behind him. He'd put on weight and was rapidly going bald. He wore a black patch over his left eye. The cord holding it in place made a line across his forehead and tied behind his neck. His face looked extraordinarily old. Little Darling sat next to Pizarro, mechanically stroking his arm.

We approached the pathetic trio, and I noticed that Pizarro's hair had gone totally gray except for a few streaks of white tinged with yellow like dirty ashes. The skin of his face sagged visibly into a wattle while the bones of his skull had grown more prominent. His nose, jaw and cheekbones seemed larger than before and his forehead wider. Something similar had happened to his sternum which thrust forward and upward under his shirt. What was most striking, though, was that Pizarro had shrunk. He was much smaller than he had been and sat in his wheelchair like a ventriloquist's dummy, unstrung, fragile, and guided solely by Little Darling's automated stroking of his arm. I watched closely as we sat down in front of him as my contact laid out the reasons for our meeting.

Pizarro listened while running his tongue back and forth over his lips as if unable to control his saliva. Now I was seeing him up close: the glasses, the yellowed streaks of white hair, the barrel chest, the doll-like arms resting on the chair, the incontinent salivation, the skull protruding towards us from beneath the skin of his face. This is what had survived the fury unleashed by Anabela, the remains of the stupid and murderous adventure that ended in the dark of night with the death of Edilberto Chanes. It was the perfect outcome for a vendetta. Pizarro wasn't dead, just inert. He'd yet to be swallowed up by the earth, eaten by worms, and forgotten. His shrunken body remained alive and aware of the satisfaction others would take in watching it turn slowly into a cadaver. He still had a ways to go before reaching the grave. This was vengeance incarnate, a gradual and irreversible death reflected day after day in the mirror of a consciousness that could feel the abysmal triviality of the oncoming silence. Each second, each hour, each day brought another measure of torture for Pizarro, forcing him to confront the unbearable certainty that his historic mission had come to a premature standstill. Imagine Napoleon before Austerlitz, or Hernán Cortés before the conquest of Mexico, or Lázaro Cárdenas before expropriating the oil industry.

"I'm out of time, my journalist friend," Pizarro said once my contact made it clear he'd be talking to me only. "My time is running down and so is my body. A day in my life is like a year in yours."

He hadn't lost his voice. It had grown deeper and richer and, in stark contrast to the body it inhabited, sounded more vigorous and powerful than ever.

"There's something I want to tell you. What's important to me is that you hear it whether you believe it or not. I'm not going after your lady. I know you had your doubts about that, and you got her out of the country. But you don't need to worry about her. That I can guarantee."

"That's not the message we got from you in December," I replied.

"I know, my journalist friend. But the message wasn't from me. The story the leather pouches tell is different. It wasn't the one you and your friends attributed to them. Not the one you published. Those were fantasies, my journalist friend, fantasies that did a lot of harm."

"Love can do terrible things," Little Darling said sadly.

"The mayor of Chicontepec is dead," I said.

"That doesn't matter any more," Pizarro said.

His lips trembled, and saliva drooled down his chin, but his voice was firm, his diction perfect. "As I once told you, people are always dying, but our people don't die in vain. They never will. Our deaths are caused by need, by history, not revenge, my journalist friend. So you don't have to worry about reprisals from us. We're not spiteful people, we're workers. As I told you, we built a river. We remove what gets in the way and put what helps in its place. That's all. Whether your lady lives or dies at this time is of no importance to our work."

He sounded like an oracle, as if someone else were speaking through him. A true, solemn, and guttural ventriloquist's dummy.

"I am asking you not to attack the union in return," Pizarro continued. "Don't meddle. The little you learned about its machinery ought to have sunk in. Don't stick your hands in the gears. Leave us to our work, don't judge us without first getting to know us. And don't try to get to know us by provoking us."

He lay his head against the back of the wheelchair. He seemed utterly overcome with fatigue. In my mind's eye I could see the immaculate corrals of "La Mesopotamia" in El Álamo, the mangroves and the stables, the parts shop and the complex at the center of it all. Once again I found myself admiring Lázaro Pizarro, the boss of Poza Rica, leader of his people, and founder of civilizations. His lips were trembling. It took enormous physical effort for the voice to maintain for even a few minutes the power and resonance required to match its owner's opinion of his role in history.

"If you'd like to ask him something, you may," Little Darling said in her dulcet voice. "We know what it's like to be hopelessly in love."

"Do today's presidential decisions mean the whole Chicontepec project is on hold?" I asked.

"It was shut down by total lack of foresight," Pizarro said, regaining his strength.

"God gave it to us, and God is taking it away," said Little Darling.

"Then it was all in vain," I said.

"Nothing's in vain, my journalist friend," Pizarro said with renewed vigor. I felt the full force of the anger driving his indomitable will, the passion smoldering in that ruined body. "Everything comes from the same source: the showers that water the land and the flood that washes away towns, lives and animals. History makes mistakes too. It gets off on the wrong track as the saying goes. Our job is to keep it on the right track, to make the corrections. And it's a high-risk undertaking, my friend, just like the oil business. You have to greet the losses with open arms. Losses, as you can easily see, are part of the game."

He thrust his head back and stared up at the ceiling, clearly exhausted. His jaw tensed. His lips had gone dry, and his hands trembled ever so slightly.

"God is taking him away from us," Little Darling said, kissing Pizarro's arm as she stroked it.

When he leaned back to rest on that same arm, the light from the lamp struck the left side of his face, exposing the moisture that came with his grief.

We started back to the hotel without speaking, but my contact made a surprise stop on the way at a small plaza with red benches and privet trees saturated with birds. He had me get out, and we stood next to a dry fountain. All around us were teenage couples, old men basking in the sun, ice cream vendors, and street sellers hawking local delicacies in the holy Mexican peace, marking the anniversary of the day the oil was nationalized.

"Now you've seen him," my contact said. He brushed

the dust out of the orifice from which one of the fountain's four frogs ought to have been spouting water. "I hope you realized his days are numbered."

"I did," I replied.

He rested his impeccable ox-blood shoe on the edge of the fountain and in his customarily deliberate fashion took the time necessary to extract and light a cigarette.

"Now it's my turn to apologize to you for what I'm about to say." He released the smoke from the first drag on his cigarette.

I began picking at a frog of my own.

"The Pizarro you were looking at in the wheelchair wasn't the work of Edilberto Chanes." My contact looked up at the sky. He furrowed his brow, trying to hold the brilliance of the open sky in his gaze. "What you saw in that motel was a man consumed by cancer, not wounds inflicted by someone else. Much less Edilberto Chanes."

"Are you telling me that Chanes never got to Pizarro?"

"I'm telling you Chanes didn't so much as launch an attack." Once again he inhaled and tried to look up into the cloudless sky. "The attack never happened."

"I got direct confirmation of Pizarro's wounds from Houston," I said drily.

"I don't know what you confirmed in Houston," my contact said. "It's true Pizarro was in Houston at the time of Chanes's death. He went to get treatment for the cancer that was eating him away and for no other reason."

I tried hard to think back. I got no information from Miller concerning the exact reason for Pizarro's admission to Methodist Hospital. She did mention they put him in the trauma unit.

"Roibal was also admitted with injuries," I pointed out.

"Roibal has been in the process of losing his left eye for a year and a half due to a car crash and an infection. That's what got him admitted. He was traveling with Pizarro and took advantage of the trip."

According to Miller, Roibal had gone in for surgery. For an eye operation? But could Pizarro's fatal or nearly fatal injuries, injuries inflicted by bullets from Chanes, have been treated in a trauma unit? No. Neither could the cancer described by my contact. Neither cancer nor bullets would have landed him in a trauma unit.

"The picture of events you painted last December was completely different." I scratched at the frog, scraping away the dirt caked in the chinks of its stone haunches.

"The picture was exactly the same," my contact said. "But at the time I had to account for another disturbing bit of information that I got from you."

"Namely?"

"That Rojano's widow had hired a professional gunman to kill Pizarro."

"Rojano's widow didn't hire anyone to kill Pizarro," I reminded him. Calling Anabela "Rojano's widow" sounded like deliberately antiseptic police jargon, and it irritated me. "She just happened to hear about Chanes's plan."

"That's right," my contact said, "but that wasn't what I heard at first. What you told me at first was the she'd hired Chanes to kill Pizarro."

"That," I suggested, "was a mistake on my part."

"Chanes actually turned out to be exactly what the widow said he was, a loose cannon, a crook on the prowl for a 'job'. Some contraband here, a hit there. It's perfectly possible he went to Cuernavaca to see if he could squeeze some money out of the widow by telling her he'd decided to 'eliminate' Pizarro. Do you know if she gave him any money?"

"So far as I know, she didn't," I said without knowing one way or the other.

"The fact is the attack never happened."

"Then how did he die?"

"That's another thing. I'll tell you if you promise not to report it."

"I can't promise that."

"I'll tell you anyway. So long as you don't print it in the next 10 days and obstruct my investigation."

"I'll go along with 10 days."

"The Chanes affair is connected to the office of our friend the chief of metropolitan police," he said. Instinctively and characteristically, he grasped his dark glasses and adjusted them on the narrow bridge of his nose.

"Would it be a connection that has to do with public safety?" I said.

He acknowledged my irony with a smile. One of his major professional difficulties lay in the lawlessness, shady dealings, and threats to public security that flowed like a river from the offices of the chief of metropolitan police.

"The Chanes affair appears to be about a settling of scores in the police department," my contact said, taking the last quick drags on his cigarette: a trace of anxiety in a haystack of self-control and restraint. "It could have been a fight over a seizure of stolen goods worth 50 million pesos. It would've taken Chanes and his pals several hauls to accumulate and warehouse merchandise worth that much, and people working for our friend would have noticed. They'd have tortured Chanes and his accomplices into confessing, then taken all the merchandise. To cover their tracks, they'd have staged the fatal road accident."

"On the very days that Pizarro's cancer took a turn for the worse and forced him to travel to Houston with Roibal?" I asked reluctantly.

"On those very days, *paisano*."

"Doesn't that strike you as too much of a coincidence?" I

shifted my gaze from the frog to him.

"Too much of a coincidence, maybe." He fidgeted with his glasses, then ran his thumb and forefinger over the corners of his mouth.

"This all happened on days when an emergency forced Pizarro to cancel at the last minute activities he was scheduled to take part in with the state security secretary for Poza Rica," I went on, bolstering my argument with objections.

"That's right, *paisano*."

"The days Chanes said he'd launch his attack on Quinta Bermúdez," I reminded him.

"Rule that out," my contact said hastily. "There was no attack. We've got that fully investigated. Never mind Chanes and the attack," he reiterated, trying once again to focus on the blue sky through the dense foliage of the privet trees.

"Which should I believe, what you say now, or what you told us in December?" I said by way of voicing my discomfort.

"You can believe one of two things," my contact said with a smile, "but only what I'm telling you now is true, *paisano*. Think about this. It's a fact that Pizarro already had cancer in December. But in December it also appeared to be a fact that Rojano's widow took a gamble on getting the cadaver killed."

"She never ordered him killed," I said, sticking to Anabela's version.

"I said *appeared, paisano*. We have nothing to go on but appearances. The widow *appeared* to have ordered the killing of Pizarro, Pizarro *appeared* to have taken out the man the widow sent to do it, and he *appeared* to have threatened the widow by sending her the leather pouch. Sheer appearances, *paisano*."

"But the pouch was delivered. Who sent it if not Pizarro? And why would Pizarro send it on the days immediately following the date when Chanes vowed to attack? And we haven't heard another word about Chanes since then. Too many coincidences once again."

"Once again coincidences," my contact said softly. "But I'm talking about facts and causes, not coincidences."

"Who sent the pouch, then?"

"I don't know. It could have been Chanes himself trying to make it easier to get money out of Rojano's widow."

"How was Chanes going to know about the pouches?"

"As I once told you, *paisano*, you have the great advantage of being a widely read columnist. Anyone who read your Chicontepec columns knew about the pouches and knows their significance according to you."

"Their significance according to Pizarro," I said.

"According to you, *paisano*, and according to your friends."

I felt him turn tough the way he had in December at the house in Cuernavaca, then he caught himself and pulled himself together. "You know where those pouches came from?" he said. "Pizarro handed them out during his campaign for reelection as president of Local 35 in 1975. The way others pass out fountain pens he gave away those pouches. Your friend Rojano made them out to be death threats to get your attention. We've already talked about that. I don't think it bears repeating."

"And by your reckoning where did Chanes get the pouch to send?"

"I didn't say Chanes sent it. I told you I don't know who sent it. One hypothesis is that Chanes did it to frighten the widow, to pressure her into giving him money."

"You didn't get that impression in December when we showed you the pouch in Cuernavaca."

"In December the situation looked to be different."

"So do I believe what you're telling me now or what you

told me in December?"

"Believe whatever you like."

He took out his lighter and a second cigarette. I understood the rhetorical usefulness of this small, becalming ritual. It slowed the pace and rhythm of any conversation, inducing cooler heads and mutual restraint, the secular muses of negotiation and harmony. He lit up and exhaled, mildly gratified. "Keep these facts in mind. Pizarro has cancer, and as you've just seen, he'll be dead in a matter of weeks. The widow's outside the country where she can't be linked to or held responsible for his death. Once Pizarro's dead, the real or imagined threat posed by the pouches is moot. Chanes was crazy, and the tangle of problems leading to his death is a whole different story that I hope to have circulating in the national press within a few days."

"With charges pending against our policeman friend?" I said, fishing for more information.

"With charges pending against our mutual friend."

"A resignation?"

"There ought to be at least one. But what I need right now is for you to understand me. In December, my only concern was to get Rojano's widow off the board."

"Just call her Anabela. It's easier."

"I use that name strictly to be precise. Don't misunderstand me."

"Don't mind me either," I said, acknowledging the senselessness of my irritation.

"If the widow made the mistake of sending someone to kill Pizarro, as you told me she did, it was in my interest to talk her out of it. With Pizarro dying of cancer, it made less sense than ever. The situation for the two of you was bad enough already, politically speaking. Too prone to scandal, too much pushing and shoving, and extraordinarily dangerous, believe me. It was dangerous for the two of you and also for the government's relations with the oil workers' union. And for me as the negotiator caught in the middle. If at the time I'd told Rojano's widow that Pizarro had cancer, she'd have simply assumed that I wanted to marginalize her. So I said her attack had succeeded."

"The widow didn't order any attack," I said, sticking with her version to the bitter end.

"Chanes's supposed attack," my contact said by way of clarification. "And that's what convinced her to leave the country for a while. I lied to her with the truth. What was true then is false now and vice versa. That's all. As for the rest..." He removed his glasses and again looked up at the sky with an expression of sadness and something like longing that disintegrated into a melancholy smile. "...let me say this. I understand you very well. The widow's an impressive woman. I still haven't figured her out, and I don't think you have either. I call her 'the widow' not to belittle her but out of respect. And also, as I might as well tell you, with a bit of envy for not having met her under more favorable circumstances. Envy of you, of the mayor, of the men who have left their scent there."

"I understand what you're saying," I said.

"I know you do, *paisano*."

He put his cigarette out on the haunch of one of the frogs, cleanly removing the ember. "Some friends are getting together in private tonight." He took his glasses off. "Do you want to come?"

I wrote up a detailed account of the interview and had an Eastern Airlines pilot take it to Los Angeles for Anabela. On April 28, I learned from the correspondent in Veracruz and confirmed with Bucareli that Pizarro was comatose. On an afternoon a week later, the newspaper got notice of his death. I happened to be in the office of the editor in chief discussing a lengthy series of interviews with labor leaders that the paper had spent a month trying to set up. The oil workers' leadership wanted me to be the interviewer, and the editor was spelling out the journalistic advantages of such an arrangement. The cable reached his desk in the hands of an aide.

"Pizarro died," it said.

My stomach did a quick somersault followed immediately by a kind of uncontrollable euphoria. "Tell them I agree to do the interviews," I told the editor, "on whatever terms you decide."

It was 3:00 in the afternoon. I left the office and called our correspondent to check on details of the death. Then, from the long distance booth at the newspaper, I called Los Angeles. Anabela herself answered the phone.

"Pizarro died at noon," I told her.

There was a long silence from the other end of the line.

"What's the date today, *Negro*?" She sounded dazed.

"Wednesday, May 4."

"Wednesday, May 4, 1980," Anabela said. "It makes me want to cry."

"Then cry."

"I don't know how to cry. Rojano was right."

"Right about what?"

"Revenge is a dish you have to eat cold," Anabela said, her voice frozen solid. "When's the burial?"

"Tomorrow in Poza Rica."

"With full honors?"

"With full union honors, yes."

"Will you be home tonight? I'd like you to talk to the children for a while. They've missed you."

"I miss them too."

"Send me a kiss. I feel a void in the pit of my stomach. It seems to me like wanting to cry."

I ate at Passy with a presidential adviser bursting with enthusiasm for the SAM project announced on March 18. I listened placidly as he went on and on in minute detail about the possibilities and resources for achieving nutritional self-sufficiency in Mexico, about the aberrant use of farmland for cattle grazing, about returning rural areas to crops strategic to the Mexican diet, about the prospect of enriching food staples in just a few years through agroindustrial processes that would add soy to tortillas and double at a single stroke the national protein intake.

After eating, for the first time since Anabela left for Los Angeles, I drank a cognac and smoked a cigar. I cancelled a commitment for a late evening meal, bought magazines from Spain at Sanborn's, and took refuge in the Cine Latino.

Back at *Artes*, I gave Doña Lila the news that the children would be calling. I took off my shoes and tie, poured myself a whiskey, and got down to reading the SAM documents I'd been given at Passy They amounted to a history of its bureaucratic gestation that began with a memo from Cassio Luiselli, who dreamed up the scheme, and culminated in ambitious agroindustrial proposals buttressed by import substitution and the adaptation of new technologies. Two whiskeys later, around 11:00 at night, I heard a knock on the door and the click of a key in the lock as she came in. She was dressed in black leather from head to toe with a red bandanna tied around her neck. She was radiant as if bathed in an aura whose power over me had been cushioned by distance and forgotten. Once again I was caught by surprise as I'd been three and a half years before. She invaded my privacy and deprived me of the means to respond to her intervention.

"I couldn't resist, *Negro*." She rolled her wheeled suitcase into the apartment as if it were a purebred dog. "I got the 6 o'clock flight out of Los Angeles. I couldn't resist."

I remained seated on the sofa where I was reading. The

sight of her maneuvering the suitcase while deploying her alibi dazzled me. In the most flattering way she could, she explained her decision to travel and come to me. She was like a model doing a turn on the runway to show off her outfit, graceful, fresh and euphoric. "Rather than cry, I decided to celebrate," she said. "But we haven't slept together. Aren't you even going to kiss me?"

I stood up and embraced her. We kissed. Then Anabela got out her cigarettes and lit one, staining it as always with her lipstick, then she sat down in one of the pigskin chairs with one leg crossed and nervously jiggling.

"Won't you at least offer me a vodka on the rocks?"

I poured her a vodka on the rocks.

"I wouldn't want to catch you off guard," Anabela said. "You need to tell me if there's someone in the bedroom."

"There isn't anybody."

"If there's someone in the bedroom I can turn my back to the hallway for about 15 minutes while you get her out of here. I promise not to look, listen or remember. Do you need 15 minutes."

"No."

"You mean she just left?"

"No."

"Then why the degenerate face of a guy who just got laid? You look like you're about to tell me you've come down with a case of Vietnamese gonorrhea. You didn't take on an admirer or a beginner without protection, then?"

"No beginners," I said

"Then veterans only? You caught the Vietnamese clap?"

"No."

"Boyfriend, sweetheart, consoler, confidant?"

"Nothing of the kind."

"So you've missed me, *Negro*."

"Lots."

"Enough to be faithful?"

"To overflowing."

"And may your cock fall off if you're lying to me?"

"May you come down with the Vietnamese clap if I'm lying to you."

She took two gulps of vodka and proceeded to the bedroom with her suitcase in tow. From the bedroom she asked for another vodka which I took to her, but by then she'd crawled under the covers and left her clothes on the floor and her earrings, watch and bracelet next to the night table.

The first encounter was quick and superficial, but half an hour later the second was prolonged and intense. I went for more whiskey and vodka. When I returned, Anabela was setting the alarm clock.

"That's it," she said. "We have to get up early tomorrow. You know why, don't you?"

She hesitated before holding my face in her cold hands, which weren't quite so cold now, and looked at me for a moment, smooth, relaxed and blindingly beautiful, before asking, "You know why I came, don't you, *Negro*?"

"For Pizarro's burial," I said.

"And to see you, *Negro*. To see you. But the burial's a one-time thing. Agreed?"

"Agreed."

"Are you coming with me?"

"I've got to improve my relations with the oil workers. I'm about to do a long series of interviews with their leadership."

"Then you're coming with me?"

"Yes."

"I bought tickets on the plane to Tampico for 7:00 tomorrow."

"I know the way," I said.

And I did.

I fell asleep thinking about the "reasons of accuracy" that invariably motivated my contact to refer to Anabela as "Rojano's widow." I was also aware of the rocky road his possession had traveled and which once again seemed to be reaching its end.

There was no need to ask the way to Pizarro's funeral in Poza Rica. All you had to do was follow the garlands and banners bidding Pizarro farewell, vowing to remember him always and to walk in his footsteps. The garlands began right at the turnoff to the cemetery on the city's outskirts and stretched all the way to its center along the major thoroughfares and down the side streets leading to the headquarters of the oil workers' union. From there the mortal remains of Lázaro Pizarro would depart on the stroke of noon. The way was even easier to follow by virtue of the crowds lined up behind an interminable string of barriers set up along the sidewalks of the route to be taken by the funeral procession. We left the car barely ten blocks from where we entered the city and set out to follow the flowers and the crowds.

During the presidential campaign, I'd seen these orderly and enthusiastic crowds hundreds of times in big cities and remote hamlets. I'd learned to look past first impressions of throngs of people taking spontaneously to the streets, and to see the efficient mechanisms of corporatist Mexico at work. I was familiar with the engineering feats that turned out masses of trade groups, clients, and sympathizers by rewarding attendance and punishing absence. The old staging skills were on display the length of the route the procession would traverse. Classes had been canceled, the city's entire school population mobilized and strategically deployed. Boys and girls from the elementary grades, adolescents, and teenagers from the high schools and trade schools were all shepherded to their appointed places by their teachers. They waved their tricolor flags and wore small black mourning bands on the sleeves of their uniforms. Members of the city's labor unions stood shoulder to shoulder behind the crowd barriers. The waitresses held red carnations in their hands. The telegraphers and postal workers carried a huge wreath woven from sticks to resemble a microwave dish with the word *adios* spelled out in purple flowers at its center. Peasants and dancers had been trucked in from the sierra, and Poza Rica's 500 taxis—lined up one after the other in the median of a major thoroughfare—were matched by a similar show of union rolling stock: tanker trucks and cement mixers, tractors and backhoes, graders and mobile cranes. Garish banners hung from the outside lighting fixtures of buildings and covered their walls, competing with one another in the expression of a single sentiment: "We won't forget you, Lacho." At street corners and intersections, barrio dwellers and office workers waved pennants promising that "Your example will guide our children" while police patrols closed streets and kept order. "The electricians of Poza Rica bid Lázaro Pizarro goodbye." Organizers of the farewell weighed down little girls and old ladies with armloads of flowers. "Healthcare workers wish Lázaro Pizarro immortal health in eternity." Cheering squads rang cowbells and blew whistles. "You are never gone and never will be gone from our memory." Prostitutes stood weeping with wilted yellow mourning flowers in their hands. With the sticks intended to hold up their signs they'd improvised a canopy that shielded them from the blazing sun. "Lázaro Pizarro, always together for the victory of the workers." The railroad workers' siren pierced the air, duly sounding the alarm that signaled disasters and emergencies. "You lost your Life, Lacho, but you made History." And at carefully staggered 100-meter intervals were the city's orchestras, marimba bands, marching bands, and other musical ensembles tuning electric guitars, rehearsing riffs on flutes and clarinets, tightening the strings of harps and violins, beating drums, and culminating in a small placard tied to a balcony. "There is only one Lacho; he is all of us" the message said.

Nearer union headquarters in the center of the city, the fiesta intensified with more banners and more slogans. I was well aware of the skeleton beneath this extravagance and excess, the administrative and orchestral clout that could energize a reception or a parade or fill a stadium with a cheering crowd. Still, I never ceased to be surprised by the sense of vivacity and strength I felt upon blending into the living stages of the pyramid, the pyramid from whose peak Pizarro ruled to the point of directing his own farewell and infusing it with the vigor of the crowds flooding the raucous streets of Poza Rica. Choked with people, the streets were more beautiful and less visible than ever before. The impenetrable tumult around the union headquarters was perfectly easy to imagine given, among other things, its visibility from blocks away where the crowd barriers yielded to a throbbing hive of vehicles and people, a giant festival closed to additional traffic. At the far side of the crowd, above the heads of the tangled mass at ground level, a bank of reflectors rained still more light on the crowd's emergent movement as a power greater than itself sliced through it. On the pulsating ribbon of the street, as if part of a mirage created by so much brilliance, the enormous bulk of two buses with their big lights ablaze revealed the spot where proceedings would begin, the offices of the union.

We pressed ahead, seeking the first vantage point that would enable us to view close-up what we'd come to witness with our own eyes. Not Pizarro's burial but the morbid details of his passing, the final chapter in the blood feud that one torch-lit night in Chicontepec sealed his fate. The block immediately in front of the union headquarters had been cordoned off by Pizarro's guards and the staff of Local 35. Behind the guards, the line of vehicles that would make up the funeral procession stretched out of view, two flatbed trucks, a union bus and the obligatory passel of motorcycles, sedans with antennas and smoked windows, SUVs, and pickups loaded with bodyguards awaiting the moment when the holy barge, in this case a white hearse, would pull out from the union headquarters and carry Pizarro on his final journey.

My press card got us through the outer guard perimeter, and we made our way down the one street to go in a tidal wave of people like us struggling to get into the union headquarters. "State government!" Anabela bellowed. She forged ahead of me waving her passport over her head, blazing a path through the tumult. "State government, ladies and gentlemen! Urgent government business, please!" Shouting and brandishing her passport, she got us to the main entrance, the one I'd first passed through four years ago, face to face with Pizarro's personal security detail.

Roibal stood in the doorway minus the eye patch he'd had in Salamanca. His left eye was clouded and unfocused as if lost in fog. He'd continued to gain weight but in an unhealthy way—from alcohol or cortisone—that made him look more swollen than bloated. His good right eye also gaped and darted aimlessly about upon catching sight of us in the doorway.

"I'm here to do interviews too," I lied.

"The national leaders are on the mezzanine," Roibal said dryly without letting us in.

As he spoke, I spotted my paper's correspondent inside and called out to him over the head of Roibal, who made a show of planting himself indifferently before the half-open door. I asked our correspondent to find someone in authority from the national leadership, and he brought the press spokesman, who doubled as public relations adviser to the maximum leader, Joaquín Hernández Galicia, *La Quina*. The adviser had negotiated the terms for my interviews of top union leaders with the paper.

The adviser spoke straight into Roibal's ear. "Joaquín says to let the journalist in."

Anabela stepped in ahead of me, and the adviser accompanied us to the vast mezzanine where Pizarro's coffin lay on an improvised bier. Gathered nearby were virtually all the top union leaders, creating a solemn atmosphere of dark glasses and tropical guayaberas. Yet another guard stood next to the open casket with his eyes glued to the men and women clustered in front of it. Behind them, a line of mourners waiting to take their place snaked down the stairs and all the way to the door where Roibal allowed small groups of people to enter as those inside filed past the casket and made their way out. I was escorted to Joaquín Hernández Galicia and introduced to him for the second time. Anabela remained standing next to the line of mourners. Hernández Galicia listed by name the four regional leaders I was to interview, and ordered his adviser to put them at my disposal.

"Will you be with us a while?" he asked afterwards.

"I just came to set the dates," I said. "I'll be back later for the interviews."

"Suit yourself," he said with a barely perceptible yet imperious glance towards Pizarro's coffin. "But it would be better if you came alone. Chicontepec is over and done with."

I looked towards the coffin. The attendants were attempting to lift it off the bier, and Anabela was preventing them from closing the lid. She looked especially formidable in her black and white outfit, transfixed and refusing to budge before the spectacle of the defunct Pizarro. I took the hint from Hernández Galicia and went to get her. In the open casket I glimpsed the lifeless face of the founder of "La Mesopotamia." His olive skin contrasted with the coffin's white lining. His body seemed shrunken, consumed by cancer or Chanes's bullets. What little remained of his hair looked burned, and his sternum protruded like a keel from the center of his chest. He seemed diminished, like the spoiled remains of a dwarf.

"It's not him!" Anabela exclaimed in my ear with a burst of whispered histeria.

"It's what's left of him after wasting away for six months," I said.

"No it isn't, *Negro!*" she murmured fiercely. Anabela rubbed her arms and began to shiver.

Wrapped in a white tunic, Little Darling approached us from the other side of the coffin. "We all lost him," she said, embracing Anabela as if she were one of the mourners. "And we must all keep him in memory. There's a party going on outside. There's no grief. It's a party in memory of Lacho, who gave us so much and now leaves us his memory."

I felt Anabela's trembling subside. Her whole body relaxed, and she clutched Little Darling's arm. She seemed to take comfort in the other woman's bereavement as if it were her own, as if she were receiving and at the same time offering consolation. The two remained inseparable for the rest of the occasion, and we found ourselves bound to an itinerary set by Little Darling. The attendants closed the coffin and lifted it off the bier. It was carried out by eight of the union's regional leaders, Hernández Galicia among them.

Anabela and Little Darling fell in behind the pallbearers, their white widows' weeds belied solely by the emerald pin on Anabela's chest. Emerging into the organized tumult of the farewell crowd, we found ourselves engulfed in the phalanx of chief mourners, surrounded by the official representative of the state government, the secretaries of state security and labor, leaders of the nation's industrial unions, municipal authorities, and Pizarro's household staff—two cooks and two teenage houseboys—that Little Darling insisted on placing in the procession's front rank. With Anabela clinging to Little Darling's arm we climbed into the SUV immediately behind the hearse. Roibal, once again wearing the patch that had covered his left eye in Salamanca, took his seat beside the driver in glum silence.

Slowly the procession got under way beneath the blazing sun of Poza Rica. We crawled through the dense crowds in the first few blocks and swam through the sea of confetti washing down from the roofs of the buildings. All at once an agglomeration of bands and ensembles broke into a single melody, *Las golondrinas—The Swallows*. The hearse inched ahead at the pace of a triumphant bullfighter while garlands and carnations plummeted down along with paper hats, handkerchiefs, the world's most forlorn old shoes, and articles of clothing as Lázaro Pizarro made his final grand exit. Little Darling was unabashed in her grief, wracked by sobbing she made no effort to contain. She half hummed, half gargled the Magnificat followed by snatches of prayers, swallowed phlegm, and Our Fathers randomly interspersed with Credos and Rosaries.

In the blocks that followed, a corps of students with drums attached itself to the hearse, and rattled out volleys of military drum rolls. Women and men alike broke through the crowd barriers in hope of a look at Pizarro. Groups with banners shouted full-throated slogans of gratitude and remembrance in unison as we passed. All the while *Las golondrinas* hovered in the background, handed off from Veracruzan harps to electric guitars, to flutes and keyboards and marimbas played by the musicians lining our way. Anabela was still holding Little Darling by the arm like a grieving sister without taking her eyes off the hearse creeping forward through the carnival bustle and the hubbub of voices rising and falling from beyond the crowd barriers. On the avenue where the taxis were parked, the music gave way to automobile horns and the shriek of ambulance sirens, driving Little Darling to bury her head in Anabela's chest, overcome by a fresh spasm of grief.

"He's going away," she sobbed. "He's leaving us behind."

"Forever," Anabela said firmly.

Roibal jerked around to glare at her and then at me with his one good eye, but its cold anger failed to conceal his grief or the sting of offense that reddened its corners and froze there.

"He's left us forever," Anabela repeated in open defiance of Roibal while she cradled Little Darling's head.

Another multitude waited at the cemetery beneath the burning afternoon sun. It was a plain cemetery, no trees, no manicured walkways, no marble mausoleums, no family crypts: a bare bones cemetery decorated with crosses, flowers, modest headstones, and nothing extra. We stepped out into the crowd and followed the coffin which the leaders of the oil workers took up once again and carried the remaining 200 meters. Little Darling grew increasingly inconsolable and distraught, and Anabela stood by her unmoved. It seemed as if the sobs and the seizures that wracked Little Darling let Anabela experience the sort of burial she wished she could have arranged. She appeared to be receiving a transfusion of raw grief that settled the scores left pending in Chicontepec.

The recently dug grave lay in the middle of a semicircle cordoned off by guards with some 4,000 sweating people clustered behind them. The guitars and mandolins of the string band of Local 35 assembled before the grave and broke the silence with one last rendition of *Las golondrinas.* Labor leaders and politicians replaced them, and the music stopped.

"He's not dead. He lives on in us," someone shouted from the crowd, filling the silence.

There was only one speech, a laconic address delivered by Hernández Galicia, the maximum leader. He declared three days of mourning by the oil worker family for its departed brother and said the region as well as the country had lost a guide. "Lázaro Pizarro isn't in that casket," he said, looking up at the crowd. "Lázaro Pizarro is here..." He placed his hand on his chest. "...in the hearts of all men of good will, of all the oil workers and the oil workers' friends. Lázaro Pizarro is in the streets we just traveled, in the head and the brain of everyone who came to wish him not 'goodbye' but 'so long.'

"Pizarro lives on in what he built and accomplished," Hernández Galicia continued, "in the achievements of Local 35, in the schools, on the job, in the stores, in the movie theaters, and union gardens. In the sad looks I see on all your faces.

"We say so long to him, to our brother, our guide, our builder. But we also welcome him to live on in what he did. Lacho Pizarro may rest in peace, but we cannot. We must honor his memory by doing more than he did. That's what he wanted when I spoke to him last. Not grief but work. And by our work we will be loyal to his memory."

Hernández Galicia grew quiet, and the crowd was silent once again. A scrawny old man with a bugle stepped forward from behind the cordon. He wiped his lips and began to play lamentably, but recognizably, *Adios muchachos, compañeros de la vida*—Goodbye my pals, my lifelong friends.

"That was also one of his last wishes," Little Darling said

to Anabela. "He wanted that played."

The bugler stood with his legs apart and his shirt open at his bony chest. The cuffs of his pants were rolled up to expose the sinewy shins that supported him firmly atop badly worn sandals. He played without rhythm, missing notes but piercing the air and the silence like a complaint, an animal lament at once metallic and electrifying as the coffin was lowered into the ground and the first shovelfuls of earth landed on top of it.

When he finished, the grave was half full, and the rest of the ceremony consisted of the rhythmic sound of falling dirt and the scrape of shovels digging and spreading it. One by one the union leaders stepped forward and dropped red carnations in the grave. Then the wreaths sent from throughout the country were stacked in a pyre nearly two meters high. People began leaving, and half an hour later Little Darling still lingered in the arms of Anabela. The two women, Roibal, and I were alone before a small mountain of funeral wreaths.

"He'll be just fine now," Little Darling said. Her voice sounded hollow, serene and exhausted. "Where he is, it isn't cold or hot. There are no rulers, no enemies, no honors or victory parades. All that remains is for me to join him."

We returned to Mexico City that evening on the 7 o'clock plane from Tampico.

"She's going to have him right there," Anabela suddenly said when were about to land.

"Have who?"

"Pizarro. Little Darling will have him right there in the cemetery for the rest of her life."

"You think there's consolation in that?"

"Consolation, no. It just occurred to me that he'd be right there where she can reach him."

The long hot day had coarsened and sharpened her features. She looked gaunt and worn out. There were small bags under her eyes, and she seemed somewhat distant and distracted. I had the impression she was still processing the transfusion from Little Darling, making sure the account left pending that night in Chicontepec was now settled.

Chapter 12
ROJANO'S WIDOW

She stayed in Mexico for two weeks. The first was celebratory and euphoric, the second bureaucratic and anomic. The first week ended with a prolonged meal at Champs Elysées inevitably accompanied by lots of Chablis and much needling of waiters.

"The only reason we're back is because we ran out of restaurants," Anabela told the maitre d'. "Don't think it's because we like French."

We ate out every night that week, then went to some show or other that didn't let out until after midnight. Inebriated, with no purpose except our own amusement, we were erotically inventive, content to let the days slip by without the shadow of Pizarro hanging over us. We awoke hungry and still excited by a lingering alcoholic buzz from the night before. By two in the afternoon we were on our way to the restaurant of the day where we ordered fresh seafood, restorative libations, and lavish meals culminating in long strolls on Reforma or through the center of the city window shopping. We browsed the exclusive stores where Anabela picked out dresses, scarves, handbags, and finally a sable coat in the hidden corner of a shop on Luis Moya.

There was in her spree an element of gloating that she never openly admitted. She simply let the evidence pile up slowly in her wake. By week's end the first signs of satiety set in, an upset stomach, a measure of erotic overload, the touch of sadness that always accompanies an excess of euphoria.

We drank the first bottle in silence on the open-air terrace at Champs. Clouds blurred the moon as it made its way through the trees on Reforma.

"There's something I didn't tell you about my last interview with Pizarro," I said to Anabela while uncorking the second bottle.

She raised the chilled wineglass to her face and began to rub it back and forth as if caressing her own cheek.

"On the way back from the interview our friend from Internal Security pulled over at a spot where we could talk in private," I said. I'd left this part out of the letter, but the omission didn't seem to bother her. She half closed her eyes and smiled, taking a first step into the soft haze brought on by the Chablis.

"He arranged the meeting," I explained. "He went with me."

"Your guardian angel," Anabela said. "What did he tell you?"

"We talked about Chanes."

"About Chanes?"

"According to our friend from Internal Security, Chanes didn't attack Quinta Bermúdez."

She smiled a gentle smile. She looked skeptical and just a bit drunk.

"Pizarro died of cancer," I went on.

"Cancer from a .38 pistol," Anabela said.

"Of terminal pancreatic cancer diagnosed a year ago."

"Diagnosed by Edilberto Chanes?"

"I'm serious." I took a quick drink. "According to our friend from Internal Security, Chanes was one of the thieves that got ripped off and killed off by the police. The story was in the papers."

"In your column yesterday?"

"It also ran yesterday in *La Prensa*, the piece about the robbers robbed by the police."

"Chanes wasn't named," Anabela said. "You didn't name him in your column."

"Neither did *La Prensa* because the names haven't been officially confirmed yet. But according to our friend in Internal Security, Chanes was involved. He had nothing to do with events at Quinta Bermúdez."

"And you believe your friend in Internal Security?" Anabela continued to rub the wineglass against her cheek before taking a drink.

"I argued with him about all the coincidences in the case."

"And what did he think about all the coincidences in the case?"

"That they were coincidences. According to him, Chanes is just what he seemed, a small-time extortionist who saw a chance to make money by promising to attack Quinta Bermúdez and get rid of Pizarro. When he saw there was no money in it for him, he dropped it. But it's possible, according to our friend in Internal Security, that he sent you the pouch in December in hope of scaring you into giving him money later on. He was biding his time on that when the Jaguar Group from the metropolitan police caught up with him and disposed of him in the Tulancingo car crash."

"More." Languidly, she held out her glass for me to fill. "What else does your friend in Internal Security have to say?"

"Nothing else. That Pizarro died of cancer, not at the hands of Chanes. That Chanes was killed not by Pizarro but by the police. And that we got our signals crossed."

"Oh, *Negro*," Anabela sighed. "There's nothing like Chablis to smooth the rough edges. This must be our eleventh bottle of Chablis in the past four days, right?" She stretched slightly. Her cheeks were red, her eyes half closed as if she were rocking herself into a daze. Then she snapped out of it, took a drink, and continued. "So you believe the version of your *paisano* on Bucareli?"

"The unanimous version in Poza Rica is that Pizarro died of pancreatic cancer. I checked that out this week."

"So you believe him?" She rubbed the full glass against her cheek, making a point of looking half asleep while at the same time mocking me. "Have you already forgotten what he told us in December?" Imitating our *paisano's* ceremonious speaking style, she said, 'You won the fight, ma'am. Pizarro will die of the wounds inflicted by your emissary.' Then in her own voice. "I didn't send any emissary." Then our *paisano's*. 'Leave Mexico, and wait for your enemy's corpse to be put to rest, ma'am. I have no interest in putting you on trial, ma'am, justice isn't my job. My job is to keep the peace.' Don't you remember that, *Negro*? What kind of big-time columnist are you turning into? Every few months they tell you another fairy tale, and you go right along with it. More."

Her manner turned sarcastic as she held out her glass and shrugged her shoulders. We had a third bottle chilled, then ordered oysters, trout almondine, and the Alaskan crab legs from the display tank in the foyer.

"Does it sound ridiculous to you?" I said, returning to the version of our *paisano* on Bucareli.

"It sounds to me like something out of a movie. Why ply me with such nonsense in December if it was all a lie?" Anabela said, again working the glass back and forth over her cheek.

"To get you out of the crossfire. To keep you from trying to find another Edilberto Chanes and insisting on getting even with a corpse."

"In order to help me, then?" Anabela said ironically.

"To help himself and keep things from getting too complicated. Suppose Pizarro gets shot. How do you explain that to public opinion? And how do you make amends with the oil workers?"

"Suppose Pizarro got exactly what Rojano got." Anabela put her glass down on the table with an air of exasperation. "What would your *paisano* on Bucareli and his bosses and accomplices in the government do then? They'd do what they did with Rojano. Try not to notice, bury the whole episode, then cover their tracks with dirt because exposing the guilty would make waves, and they don't like waves. What they want is to calm the sea. That's their job, to still the waters. Suppose there weren't any coincidences, that Pizarro was shot in the dark of night when Quinta Bermúdez was attacked. What do your *paisano* on Bucareli and his lackeys do then? They cover it up. They make up a story about cancer of the pancreas or the asshole, and, on top of that, they get you to believe it. You know why? Because you're a star witness, and part of what they have to do is discredit the witnesses. So they tell you to calm down, that nothing happened, that it was all a misunderstanding, a series of very strange coincidences. And that takes care of everything, no problems no witnesses. And don't even think about writing your memoirs some day, don't get the idea you could fight them by spilling the details about Chicontepec. You follow me? They quietly negotiate a deal with the oil workers by offering them some kind of perk in return for keeping their mouths shut and chat you up with a bedtime story that puts everyone back to sleep. They hustle off to their office and close the file once and for all. Then it's onward and upward with tales of the heroes and exploits of the Mexican miracle. The truth has nothing to do with it, and, as your *paisano* said in December, justice doesn't either. It's strictly about security and keeping the peace. He said it himself. He doesn't care about Pizarro's death, he just cares about the trouble it could stir up. And when Rojano's death had repercussions that got your *paisano's* attention, he gave us escorts, gave us tips, and, when we asked him to, he looked after us like spoiled daughters. The only reason he helped us negotiate with the union was because of what you wrote. You put it in the paper and shook them up. Otherwise, Rojano would have been just another incident—something from the police blotter, and my children and I would have joined him in his cave at the French Cemetery. Pizarro would be king of Chicontepec, and you'd have a vague memory of our time on earth. If that's not what happened, it's because we didn't let it. You, I, and Edilberto Chanes, may God bless him and keep him in gunslingers' heaven."

They brought the oysters and crab and the bottle we'd had chilled. Anabela grew calm again. She relaxed, and went to work cracking open the crab legs, but her version of events continued to float above the table like a revelation, one of the many that blossomed from my long and nearly always clueless relationship with her. She was implacable and tough, her version strictly the result of having survived. In the years since Rojano's downfall in Chicontepec, she'd never stopped assuming that she was locked in an all-or-nothing struggle, a nerve-wracking game of chance in which the only way she could assure her own safety and the safety of her children was by making Pizarro disappear. The game's favorable outcome—whether due to pancreatic cancer or the doings of Edilberto Chanes—was the reason she was sitting in front of me with her children and her inheritance safe in Los Angeles and with her nemesis buried before her eyes a week earlier. The only visible remains of her ordeal were the two small pouches under her eyes. Poorly hidden under a layer of mascara, even they were in part attributable to the alcoholic and sexual excesses of the past few days. This was her saga, her version of events. It was a triumphant and concise chronicle of revenge by survival and of plans carefully laid and carried out in order to survive. To achieve her ends she'd exploited both the press and her friends, myself included.

The Bucareli version with its long chain of coincidences, misunderstandings and myths about petty criminals seemed more like real life, full of the dramatic flaws that always appear in the loosely woven fabric of human existence. I knew certain things were true, among them the key fact of Rojano's execution in Chicontepec. But everything else vanished in a stew of self-serving fabrications, lies, false conclusions, spectacular coincidences, and the general messiness of life. By contrast, Anabela's version was of a geometrically neat struggle, a battle with sharp, cleanly drawn lines whose coincidences clearly resulted from the clash of opposing wills. Chance served only to disguise decisions and outcomes. It was the bottom line of an arithmetic that perfectly summed up Pizarro's own motto: *Whoever can add can divide.*

"So you prefer the version that gives the credit to Chanes?" I said as I finished the oysters and watched her consume her crab claws with evident gusto.

"I prefer that you take me dancing, *Negro*. And I don't have to tell you where."

The clock had yet to strike midnight when we entered La Roca on Insurgentes Sur just as we had four years before. It had been the dawn of an unforgettable anniversary of the then sexagenarian and now septuagenarian Mexican Revolution. As always there was a gaggle of whores, goons and local characters in the doorway. Inside, a rumba band alternated sets of ballads and boleros with music from the tropics. We ordered a vodka and a whiskey and were starting to drink when the band began a set of boleros and we got up to dance. Anabela was wearing a pearl gray dress with straps that left her arms and part of her back bare while fitting snugly over her legs and hips. She was, as I've not said before, only a few centimeters shorter than I, and even with very low heels she matched my height. There was also the irresistibly idiosyncratic way she went about dancing, facing me straight on and embracing me with her left hand. She made full-body contact with her first steps and by instinct settled herself into me with her firm, muscular legs intertwining with mine so that we were pressed together centimeter by centimeter in the shared rhythm of an embrace. The feel of her thighs, her sex, her stomach, her breasts, her neck, her whole body blended into a single sensation. It was as if she'd melted into me from head to toe in flawlessly perfect union.

We danced two numbers and left. Still clinging to each other, we crossed to the Hotel Beverly on New York Street. Slowly, with the lights out, next to a window that overlooked part of the city and whose chill glass made us feel as if we were outdoors, we undressed and continued on the rug the prolonged fusion begun at La Roca with hands and mouths pressed together beyond thoughts or words, in a state consisting solely of bodies and murmurs.

When I woke up at dawn, a red glow suffused the roofs of the buildings, and in the distance the early morning buses rumbled along Insurgentes. Wrapped in a hotel blanket, Anabela stared out the window from one of the sofas. Her long neck let her see over its back. She looked composed and at peace in a remote, self-sufficient world of her own. She made room for me on the sofa, and I made myself comfortable next to her under the blanket.

"I'm going to live in Los Angeles," she said. "I'm not coming back to Mexico."

"Now you can live in peace in Mexico," I said.

"I don't want that kind of peace," Anabela said. "The only thing left in Mexico that I care about is you."

She leaned back against my chest, letting her fingernails rove mechanically, reflexively over my skin. "And if you were to move to Los Angeles?"

"No," I said.

"Los Angeles has newspapers in Spanish."

"Yes."

"You could be your paper's Los Angeles correspondent."

"No."

"The children would be there. They need a man in the house. Tonchis is always asking for you. And Mercedes writes you letters every week, doesn't she?"

"Every week without fail."

"We have a good apartment, *Negro*. And in the fall we're changing to a house in the suburbs. We don't have money problems. I have an investment adviser who gets a good return on the money from Chicontepec."

"Are you offering to support me?"

Anabela smiled. "I'm offering you a rich, slightly spoiled widow," she said softly.

"Who'd be leaving an indelible stain on the state of Veracruz," I said.

"Yes." She made herself comfortable once again, shifting her position on my chest. For a moment she said nothing, then, "Come to Los Angeles, *Negro*."

"No."

"Then are you asking me to stay in Mexico?"

"I'm not asking you to stay in Mexico."

"Don't you want me in Mexico?"

"I've wanted nothing else since the 20th of November, 1976, remember?"

"I fell asleep when you thought you'd scored, right?"

"And you snored."

"You overdid the Chablis. If you get all your girlfriends that drunk, you must sleep with rag dolls who don't remember a thing in the morning."

"They all remember," I said.

"I know. And they go looking for you in the newsroom

at your paper because they want a mention in your column. A one-night stand is never enough, they're insatiable."

"And they all act insulted and leave."

"If that includes me, let me remind you I just offered you my personal fortune."

"And I'm asking you not to forget that I just declined."

"You mean you just want to get flushed down the toilet because you're a loser."

"Because I'm a shit."

"You're not up to providing long-term service?"

"Medium or long term, no"

"Neither one," Anabela said. The tone of her voice changed, and she curled herself back into a ball. "You don't have it in you."

"When are you leaving?"

"As soon as I make the arrangements."

"What arrangements?"

"I'm getting permission to take Rojano's coffin out of Mexico. I want it transferred to Los Angeles."

"You want to get Rojano's coffin out of Mexico?"

"Yes." Anabela sat up straight. "I don't want to leave Ro's body here."

"Are you serious?"

"Completely serious. I need permits from the Ministry of Health and the embassy. I already have one from the City of Los Angeles."

"You're going to bury Rojano in Los Angeles."

"I already bought a plot for him."

"So he'll be right there for you the way Pizarro is for Little Darling?"

"Yes. Why does it upset you so? Do you think it's strange?"

She supported herself on her elbow while arguing with me. Her mascara had run, and some of her eyelashes were crooked. Though disheveled and short on sleep, she looked radiant and inspired by her decision. From the depths of time, I felt the simple power that arose to confront me when trespassing on territory long since conquered and colonized by Rojano, the history that had bound Anabela to Rojano since her teens. Its bright and tender glow still showed through in her smile and restored the youth and vibrance remaining in the deepening hollows of her eyes. I pulled her to me, rearranged the blankets to cover her back, and put my arms around her.

"I asked if it seems strange to you," Anabela persisted.

"No," I told her. "With you and Rojano it seems perfectly normal."

It took another week to make all the arrangements. I called the Health Ministry myself and smoothed the way for her with the press attaché at the embassy. Shortly before the end of May, all the paperwork was in order. On May 22, Anabela flew to Los Angeles to work out the final details for the burial. To avoid issues of preservation and any other obstacles that might crop up Rojano needed to be disinterred in Mexico, taken to the plane, shipped to Los Angeles, and re-buried the same day.

I returned to my work routine and spent a week in Tampico doing the agreed upon interviews with leaders of the oil workers' union. One after the other, in each of the four interviews, I asked as if in passing about the causes of Pizarro's demise. The unhesitating answer in each instance was cancer of the pancreas. With Pizarro gone, his position as head of the union fell to Loya, the mayor of Poza Rica, and Roibal was his aide now. I interviewed him in an ice cream parlor on the plaza in front of the Hotel Inglaterra in Tampico, a few meters from where Pizarro had used the metaphor of a river to explain to me his ideas about power.

"What did Lázaro Pizarro die of?" I asked Loya half way through a dish of guanábana ice cream.

"Cancer of the pancreas," he replied mechanically and with no hesitation. Roibal sat next to him with his eye patch and a glass of milk.

"Unless you happen to know of another version," Roibal said drily, ripping a tear in the fabric of the interview. It seemed to discomfit Loya.

"There's talk about a settling of scores within the ranks of the oil workers," I said, purposely trying to annoy him.

"There's talk from where, my friend?" Loya replied haughtily. "Who says that?

"Rumors in Mexico City," I said.

"Malicious rumors, unfounded," Loya said.

"What more do the rumors say?" Roibal asked.

"That Quinta Bermúdez was attacked by gunmen in December of last year," I said, "and that Pizarro died as a result of serious injuries suffered in the encounter."

"False," Loya said. "Pure fantasy."

"And who could have carried out this attack?" Roibal said.

"I'm telling you it's false," Loya shouted. "Even talking about such a thing is offensive."

"The motherfucker capable of overrunning Quinta Bermúdez has never been born," Roibal said with somber pride.

"Edilberto Chanes?"

Roibal smiled. "That's old news."

"Lies, lies!" Loya overreacted, violently cutting off the banter for a second time. "Let's get to the point, to reality. You're a journalist not a storyteller. Stick to the facts, sir."

He was a far cry from the obsequious driver who ferried us around "La Mesopotamia" in March, 1977. Brimming with self-assurance, he had more than enough energy and vigor to cool the heated exchange Roibal was spoiling for. He brooked no interference with his lecture about union gardens and cattle ranching operations, union successes, and how the union resisted management's proclivity for handing top jobs to people from outside the oil industry. He boasted of the union's ability to censor the governor of Veracruz and dictate the contents of a message to the President of the Republic. His bizarre and disjointed ramblings were faithfully transcribed and reproduced in the series of interviews published two weeks later.

Roibal said nothing more, but he came looking for me that night in the hotel. We took our seats, and he proceeded without further ado.

"Pay no attention to those rumors," he said. "They're false. Nobody attacked anybody at Quinta Bermúdez, least of all Edilberto Chanes. He caught us off guard one night in Mexico City, that's all. Then he went around saying he'd stormed Poza Rica."

"Loya was fuming this morning," I said. "Did he order you to come and see me?"

Roibal nodded. I watched his good eye jump up and down in its socket.

"You're telling me all this on his orders?"

"It's the truth." Roibal looked away from me.

"The truth has no need for messengers," I said.

"I'm being disciplined," Roibal said glumly. "He wants to humiliate me, to make me cower and bow down before him and his henchmen. Loya's the new boss, and he's trying to break me. That's why I'm here."

"How did Pizarro die?" I said.

"Cancer of the pancreas," Roibal answered without a second's pause, but once again he looked away.

"And where did you lose your eye?"

He squirmed nervously in his chair and folded his arms as if retreating into his shell.

"On a mission," he said, "but that's none of your business."

"Defending Quinta Bermúdez?"

"No." Roibal sounded withdrawn. "I already told you. Quinta Bermúdez couldn't be overrun, not by anybody."

"But it could be attacked."

"He never saw the dawn of another day," Roibal said.

"Are you referring to Edilberto Chanes?"

"I'm referring to anyone you like," Roibal said. He got up to leave, but, adjusting the patch over his eye, he added, "I want you to know it was a good fight. Chicontepec, I mean. Even though nobody won."

"I'm asking you one last time." I got to my feet and looked him straight in his good eye. "What killed Pizarro?"

"And I'm telling you for the last time…," He smiled as if now it was his turn to mock me. "…it was his pancreas, and that's the truth. And if Loya should ask, you tell him mission accomplished."

Anabela returned to Mexico City on June 4 with the tickets and paperwork necessary to put Rojano's sealed coffin on Mexicana's noon flight to Los Angeles. At 9:00 in the morning of June 6, Anabela, Doña Lila, and I arrived at the French Cemetery with a hearse. Followed by groundskeepers, we made our way along the paths lined with willows and eucalyptus to the plot where Rojano's mortal remains lay buried. Though the spot was at the cemetery's edge four years ago, now it was well within the rows of graves creeping ever nearer the high outer wall that enclosed the place's eternal occupants. By way of preparation, the marble headstone had already been removed, exposing hard, freshly turned earth. The groundskeepers started digging, and Anabela clung to Doña Lila, who was dressed in black with a hat and a spotted veil. In short order the sweating workers reached the cement slabs separating the coffin from the surrounding earth and began hammering at the mortar that had sealed the slabs. There was a pale sun overhead, and a chill breeze blew through the trees and raised small puffs of dust on the ground.

"I want you to check the headstone," Anabela told me without loosening her grip on Doña Lila. "I want to be sure it's Rojano."

The headstone had been shoved aside face down. I turned it over and placed it where Anabela could see. It said Francisco *Rojano Gutiérrez, Mayor of Chicontepec. Remembered by his children, Francisco and Mercedes, and his widow, Anabela Guillaumín.*

"This isn't where I remember the grave," Anabela said. "It was nearer the wall."

"Others came afterwards," I said, pointing to the new rows.

"If it's not him, he's playing games with us," Doña Lila chimed in to support me. "If anyone came to give me the ride this man's getting, I'd make it a party even if there were nothing left but my bones."

It took a lot longer to break through the slabs than to remove the earth, but the final chunk was finally tossed out. We looked down into the hole and saw the black coffin covered in dirt and weeds, engraved by the vegetation that stayed stubbornly alive in spite of slabs and headstones.

"Clean it first," Anabela said. "I want to see the color."

Using masons' trowels, the groundskeepers removed the white clay and the weeds that snaked across the top of the casket like climbing plants. Little by little, its iron gray finish became visible together with its raised and totally rusted crucifix.

They cleared the remaining weeds away. Around the edges of the grave they laid out the gear normally used to lower coffins into the ground: a rectangular frame of nickel-plated iron bars attached by green strapping to a set of pulleys that would now work in reverse. The groundskeepers hooked the straps to the handles on the coffin and began to raise it. The machinery squawked and wobbled as the bands tightened, straining to hoist so much dead weight. The coffin rose a few centimeters, then dropped back into its bed.

"Something's holding it down from underneath," the lift operator said. First he dug around the base of the coffin with a trowel, then he took a crowbar to the weeds rooting it in place. He reattached the straps, and the machinery started squawking again. But this time the pulleys continued to crank unimpeded. With every turn they let out another groan as Rojano's remains arose from their eternal dwelling for the second time. When the coffin reached the surface Anabela grew pale and stepped falteringly towards it, gripping Doña Lila's arm for support.

"I want to see him." Anabela said haltingly. She lost control her voice, and it cracked as she struggled to get the words out.

"Quiet, girl," Doña Lila said with loving firmness. "You must neither offend God or desecrate the work of His hand."

The groundskeepers took the coffin by its handles and carried it to the gurney on the path nearby. Anabela put a hand on the crucifix, then removed the few sods stuck to the skirting at the coffin's base. We followed the path and one of the cemetery's inner avenues to the waiting hearse. Once the coffin was loaded, I tipped the groundskeepers, and then we were alone with the driver biding his time behind the wheel.

I took Anabela's arm, and we walked towards the exit where our car was parked next to the administration building. Anabela's pulse beat unevenly as she signed the final papers, and her normally cold hands were even colder than usual. We walked to the car with Doña Lila beside us, and I opened the front door for Anabela to get in. Several meters away, the hearse idled at the entrance to the cemetery.

"I want to go with him," Anabela said, pulling away from the car and towards the hearse.

"Doña Ana," Doña Lila said sorrowfully, "he's not there any more."

"I'm going with the coffin." Anabela corrected her coldly.

And she did. She got in the front seat next to the driver. Doña Lila and I rode in my car, making a truncated cortege en route to the airport.

"For a few minutes she brought him back to life," Doña Lila said. "You should have felt the way she trembled."

I saw her tremble one more time while signing the forms required for the hearse to gain special access to the airport. We spent the hour before boarding in the bar, silent or nearly silent in a pungent cloud of Doña Lila's perfume. At one point she excused herself and left, rooting through her handbag as she walked towards the airport's main corridor.

"You've got everything arranged?" I asked.

"Yes."

She was dressed in white with black piping just as she'd been for Pizarro's burial. Her hair was tucked beneath a cap that lengthened and enhanced her face.

"What are you going to do, *Negro*?"

"I need to write tomorrow's column," I said.

"I don't mean that. What are you going to do, generally speaking?"

"After I do tomorrow's column, I've got to do one for the day after."

She took my hand. The bags were gone from under her eyes. She looked plain and serene. She wore no jewelry and seemed unconcerned with her appearance. Part of the effect was thanks to an absence of lipstick and only the slightest touch of eyeliner highlighting the shape of her eyes.

"I ought to apologize to you," she said.

"There's something good to investigate this week," I replied. "The dope trade is on the upswing again. I got a report about it yesterday."

"Thanks, *Negro*."

"I have some letters for the children." I took them out of my coat pocket.

"Yes," Anabela said.

"And I think Doña Lila's bringing something."

What she brought was a plush doll for Mercedes and a giant puzzle that assembled into a minutely detailed representation of the Iztacíhuatl volcano for Tonchis.

"Since he likes rocks and landscapes," Doña Lila explained, "here's a picture of some very old ones that ought to interest him. And the little girl still loves stuffed dolls more than the things big girls lust after."

It was nearly two when Anabela boarded after a long embrace with Doña Lila and the few seconds when she melted into me as if we were dancing.

"If it has to be a Gringo, let it be a journalist," I said with a forlorn sense of professional loyalty.

"Thanks, *Negro*," Anabela repeated. She headed down the boarding tunnel past the scanner for hand luggage, smiling, walking erect, full of athletic freshness and her seemingly eternal youthfulness.

Doña Lila wiped some tears away. We crossed the pedestrian bridge to the parking complex without speaking, then she said, "There are lots of women and men. All that's missing are real live love affairs."

Every day I wrote my column for the following day, and

every week through the end of August I got letters from the children. Then, with my saint's day approaching, a letter from Anabela came too. The night before the ex-reporter from *El Sol* had returned to Artes. She was now editor of the entertainment page for one of the capital's major dailies, a young, even-tempered woman and a close reader of newspapers, friendly, warm-hearted, loving and inclined to domesticity. In the morning we went through the daily papers over breakfast, and I waited for her to leave before picking up the mail and getting close to Anabela again. It wasn't a long letter though Anabela's clear and expansive handwriting made it seem to be. Two pages were taken up with descriptions of greetings from the children and of the suburban house they'd moved into from their apartment. The paragraph about Rojano said the following:

"He's buried in a new cemetery with lawns and trees everywhere on a hill overlooking the city of Los Angeles. I'm still alone and happy. I don't miss corrupt journalists, but, unlike Tonchis who's just scored his first *Gringuita*, I do miss some things. Mercedes is taking modern dance at the city art school. The house has a swimming pool, and you can't imagine how calm it is. I think a lot about you and what we went through together. Sometimes I dream about it. But the nightmare always goes away in the morning. The days are so sunny. You can't imagine the peace and quiet, the way the wind blows through the trees where Rojano is now. I go every Sunday and just sit there in the wind which, as I said, is softer than you can ever imagine."

Despite what she said, I could imagine the wind perfectly well and Anabela too, secure and at peace on her Sunday visits to the new headstone on a hill looking down on Los Angeles, seated with her arms folded, gathering in the years spent preserving the memory of Rojano.

About
HÉCTOR AGUILAR CAMÍN

Héctor Aguilar Camín (born July 9, 1946 in Chetumal) is a Mexican writer, journalist and historian, and author of several novels, among them *Death in Veracruz* and *Galio's War*, of which Ariel Dorfman (*Death and the Maiden*) has exclaimed, "Without hesitation, I would call either one of these a classic of Latin American fiction." His most recent novel, *Adios to My Parents* was published in Mexico to great critical and popular acclaim in 2014. *Death in Veracruz* is the first work of his fiction to be translated into English.

Aguilar Camín graduated from the Ibero-American University with a bachelor's degree in information sciences and techniques and received a doctorate's degree in history from El Colegio de México. In 1986 he received Mexico's Cultural Journalism National Award and three years later he received a scholarship from the John Simon Guggenheim Memorial Foundation while he was working as a researcher for the National Institute of Anthropology and History.

As a journalist, he has written for *Unomásuno* and *La jornada* (both of which he also coedited), the magazine *Proceso*, and currently for *Milenio*. He founded and is nowadays the editor of *Nexos*, one of the leading cultural magazines of the country, and hosted Zona abierta, a weekly current—affairs show on national television, and has written articles for prestigious publications as *El país* and *Foreign Affairs*.

He has written a classic boook on Mexican history: *La frontera nómada. Sonora y la Revolución Mexicana*, (in translation from U of Texas Press) and numerous books and essays on contemporary Mexico. In 1998 he received the Mazatlán National Prize of Literature for his book, *A breath in the*

river. He is married to Angeles Mastretta and has three sons.
Other novels by Héctor Aguilar Camin: *El error de la luna, El resplandor de la madera, La conspiraciòn de la fortuna*, and the collection of novellas and short stories: *Pasado pendiente y otras histories conversadas*.

About
CHANDLER THOMPSON

Chandler Thompson acquired his translating chops in the 1960s as a Peace Corps Volunteer, then while writing news stories in English from raw copy in Spanish and French. He's covered Mexico as a stringer for *The Christian Science Monitor* and as reporter for *The El Paso Times*. He translated *Death in Veracruz* between hearings while working as a court interpreter.

ACKNOWLEDGMENTS

Special thanks to my daughter Elsi, the first reader in English of *Death in Veracruz*. She kept me going by always wanting to know what happened next. My partner Pauline Curry whose admiration for the work of Héctor Aguilar Camín is alway an inspiration.